Acclaim for Micah Nath

LOSING GRACELAND

"Nathan presents the reader with several fantastic characters in this rollicking, adventurous tale. Readers will pore through this fast-paced, adrenaline-filled novel and eat up the fantastic dialogue that brings Elvis back to life in a new, deliciously lascivious way." —*Booklist*

"Engaging…a blend of the slapstick and the slapdash, the ironic and the painfully sincere…a wild road trip, a yarn spiced with plenty of humor and romance…" —*The Washington Post*

"Ben has undreamed-of experiences on this strange journey… with quirky characters and homespun wisdom, this will appeal to fans of literary coming-of-age-stories." —*Library Journal*

"Thus begins the weirdest of buddy adventures, with feckless Ben playing first mate to the is-he-or-isn't-he Elvis, a superannuated hillbilly with the unearthly self-possession of a Zen master. En route to points south, the adventurers tangle with a one-eyed pimp, a trio of roadhouse sirens, a backwoods soothsayer, and other low-rent variations on a Homeric theme…[with] antic originality [and] the near-magic realism of Elvis as a geriatric Ulysses…" —*The Boston Globe*

Acclaim for Micah Nathan's

GODS OF ABERDEEN

"Soaked with gothic mood and spiked with sharp dialogue, it's *Dead Poets Society* via Stephen King."
—*The Hollywood Reporter*

"A malevolently thrilling coming-of-ager wrapped in a philosophical detective tale." —*Kirkus Reviews*

"[A] remarkable first novel...impossible to put down.... *Gods of Aberdeen* may be basically a coming-of-age story (including sexual awakenings), but it is much more than that. It also is a murder mystery and an intriguing account of a bizarre quest for the secret of eternal life. As an author, Nathan's off to a brilliant start..." —*The Tampa Tribune*

"Think Donna Tartt's *The Secret History*, with a little magic thrown in.... Nathan perfectly captures the angst and pretension of adolescents..." —*Publishers Weekly*

"Highly recommended...one of the year's best debuts."
—*Italian GQ*

"This year's strongest entry into the hallowed-halls-of-learning field...Nathan's eye for detail can be subtly spectacular, his humor eloquently wicked...Nathan [is] an extremely gifted young writer..." —*Spirit Magazine*

Micah Nathan

JACK THE BASTARD

Micah Nathan is the best-selling author of the novels *Gods of Aberdeen* and *Losing Graceland*. His award-winning essays and short stories have appeared in *Bellingham Review*, the *Gettysburg Review*, *Glimmer Train*, *Boston Globe Magazine*, *Post Road*, *Commonweal*, and other national publications. In 2010, Boston University awarded him the Saul Bellow Prize in Fiction.

MICAH NATHAN

JACK
THE
BASTARD
AND OTHER STORIES

WITH ILLUSTRATIONS BY PHIL NOTO, TRADD MOORE, RUSS NICHOLSON, AND MICHAEL ALLRED

ONE PEACE
BOOKS

Copyright © 2012 by Micah Nathan

Illustrations Copyright © 2012 by Michael Allred (pp. 32–33), Tradd Moore (p. 97, cover), Russ Nicholson (p. 126), and Phil Noto (pp. 212, 235, 330)

All rights reserved. No part of this may be reproduced or transmitted in any form or by any means, electronic or mechanical, including photocopying, recording, or by storage and retrieval system without the written permission of the publisher. For information, contact One Peace Books, Inc.

First One Peace Books, Inc. printing, July 2012

These stories appeared in the following publications: "One Act" in *The Gettysburg Review*, "As the Old Greeks Would Say" in *236*, "Five Tempered Notes" in *LEMON Magazine*, "Simulacrum" in *Diagram*, "Quarry" in *Glimmer Train*, and "The Love Life of Tigers" in *Bellingham Review*.

ISBN: 978-1-935548-22-5

Printed in Canada

Distribution by SCB Distributors
www.scbdistributors.com

www.onepeacebooks.com

She knows.

CONTENTS

One Act	11
As the Old Greeks Would Say	25
Five Tempered Notes	42
Mr. Todd and the Gibson Girl	56
Simulacrum	75
Quarry	80
The Mensch	99
The Love Life of Tigers	172
Jack the Bastard	179

ONE ACT

Ben first met Charlie Cahill on the train to New York. Charlie was reading a collection of Hemingway stories, he wore a wrinkled suit that showed too much sock, and he gorged himself on a hot dog, oblivious to the ketchup that dripped down his tie. Behind Charlie sat a young mother with her crying child; after ten minutes of wails and screeches, Charlie turned around, dangled his keys, and grinned.

"It's got a little light," he said. "See here? You can switch it off and on. Click click."

The child blinked, tears sliding over her lips. Ben thought he heard someone applaud. The mother smiled, and Charlie returned to his book.

Ben saw him again a few hours later, in the dining car. Charlie sat alone, bottle of wine on the table and the Hemingway book on its last pages. His tie was gone and he was side-lit by a small lamp. Ben gulped his beer and walked over.

"Nice work with that little girl."

Charlie looked up, squinting. Then he fumbled in his breast pocket and pulled out a pair of glasses.

"That little girl clicked the pen light off and on for thirty minutes," Charlie said. "This is why some cultures shoot annoying children."

"Interesting," Ben said. "I've never heard of any culture that shoots annoying children."

Charlie sighed. "Neither have I. But there should be."

They were the only ones in the dining car except for the elderly conductor, who sat in the back corner, cap crooked, staring out the window with his hands on his lap. Charlie motioned across the table.

"I don't want to interrupt your reading," Ben said.

"No worries." Charlie closed the Hemingway book and slid it to the side. "That is an old book, and it is a good book. It keeps me company in the way a good book should. Tomorrow I will finish that good book, and it will be no more." He grinned and refilled his wine glass.

"Hemingway," Charlie said.

"Yes, I got that."

"My pastiche. Or would it be an homage? Anyway. Are you coming from DC?"

"Frederick Park."

"Very nice. Big homes and little fences. You must be married."

"She's back home."

"Ah," Charlie said. "And first I thought you might be a fag. I don't care, you know. My father was a playwright so I grew up with fags. My first kiss was with Sergio the wispy Italian." He brushed away the memory with a wave of his hand. "Tell me what you do."

Ben sat across from him. The rhythm of the train made Charlie sway in his seat.

"I'm in advertising," Ben said.

"Selling or writing?"

"A little of both."

"Anything I would know?"

"I'm sorry?"

Charlie folded his hands across his stomach. "I love a clever ad campaign. Try me."

A decaying town swept past their window—a graffitied mill

surrounded by tall weeds, and stacks of tires and shopping carts frozen in mid-tumble down the bank of a slow river.

"We're the guys who re-branded Werther's Original caramels," Ben said.

"'Werther's.'" Charlie swept his hand across the air. "'Suck it, Grandpa.'"

"That's right."

"It's ridiculous."

"We don't mind ridiculous," Ben said.

Charlie narrowed his eyes. "What do you think I do?"

"You're a kindergarten teacher."

Charlie laughed. "I'm a playwright. Most of my work premieres in New York, off-off-off-Broadway."

"I haven't been to a play since high school," Ben said.

"Let me guess: *Bye-Bye Birdie*."

"*Barefoot in the Park*. I went with my girlfriend."

"Jesus. It's always one or the other. I bet she loved it."

"Of course. A handsome couple making their way in a Manhattan brownstone—"

"I know the plot. Neil Simon is a family friend, and he based Victor Velasco on my father. Have you ever heard of *The Comfort of Random Objects*? That was my father's show. It ran for six years at The Majestic."

Ben drank his beer and looked at Charlie's reflection in the window. He figured he'd played Ivy League football, or one of those rugged, preppy sports made for thick boys with freckles, wind-tousled hair, and cheeks red from the cold. Ben thought of his own college days: the muddy field outside his dorm, the slate skies and the forested hills.

Charlie finished his glass and wiped his mouth with his jacket sleeve. He stared at Ben.

"Any kids?"

"Two daughters," Ben said. "Neither of them annoying."

"Nice. I bet you're a popular man at work. How's your secretary?"

Ben paused.

"She's capable."

Charlie laughed. "You see? This is why I don't have any old friends. The first year I impress them with my cynicism, the second year they try to impress me, and the third year they realize I am completely full of shit. So what? Saves me the trouble of having to come up with new stories. What's your wife's name?"

"Rebecca."

"The two of you walk into a room, and the women all pat the side of their hair. Am I right?"

"I don't pay enough attention," Ben said. "But it sounds good."

"That line is from my last play. God, I am *pathetic*. What the hell, though. We're on a train." Charlie leaned forward, his mouth slightly open. "You wouldn't have a joint on you, would you?"

"Not in years," Ben said.

Charlie sighed. "Oh, well. You should come to my show tonight. It's a little one act about a dog trying to find its way back home. An Afghan hound lost in the mountains of Kabul. The story is dripping with political subtext—slave/master relations, not having a voice, et cetera. It's profound, is what I'm trying to say."

"Sounds interesting," Ben said.

"It isn't," Charlie said, grinning. "But you should come anyway."

Charlie wrote an address on his card while they stood in the middle of Penn Station.

"Show starts at nine," he said, and he stuffed the card in Ben's breast pocket. "Arrive early if you like shrimp, because that always goes first."

Ben found a cab easily. He drove through Midtown and into the Village, past brownstones and double-parked delivery trucks. A Chinese man carried a box of lettuce across the street. A young couple hugged on the corner, both of them wearing the same style jeans and hooded sweatshirt. Pigeons soared and landed on the curb. Ben leaned his head against the window and inhaled deeply.

He had the driver let him off at the Cherry Lane Theater, and walked toward Seventh Avenue. He loved autumn shadows in the city; they hide the dog shit and cigarette butts, leaving the best parts—the yellow leaves on the black street, the pale sidewalk, the chalking brick. A leggy blonde wearing stilettos clacked past and Ben nodded at her. She smiled.

He pressed the buzzer to Sarah's brownstone. She took her time answering. Ben walked slowly up the stairs, loosening his tie and unbuttoning his cuffs. He ran his hands through his hair and his tongue over his teeth.

"Hungry?"

He paused in the doorway. Sarah wore tight jeans and a little black sweater. He saw a flash of her stomach, and the half-circle of her navel. She was barefoot, with paint stains on her fingers. He smelled chicken tarragon coming from her apartment and heard talk radio playing softly.

"A little," he said, and when he picked her up, she wrapped her legs around his waist. It always happens this way, he thought. It's supposed to be spontaneous but it's the best we can do.

Sarah sat in her kitchen and smoked. She wore white cotton panties with a wrinkled T-shirt, and had one foot on Ben's seat, her other leg folded Indian-style. Ben ate chocolate-covered almonds from a bowl on the table. He found he could reduce Sarah to three parts: thin nose, high Russian forehead, and a long neck.

"If you'd like to go, then we can go," she said. She exhaled through her nose, wrist limp and cigarette dangling.

"I'm fine either way," Ben said.

"What do you want me to wear? Something nice?"

"Throw on some red heels and go as is."

She pursed her lips at him. "I'm not a fucking Natasha from the Ukraine." Her accent thickened. "*I wants to look nice for friends, yes? I wants to be…how do you say…supermodel?*"

She ashed her cigarette in his bowl of almonds, and he grabbed her foot.

"Please," she said. "I am in a terrible mood. I got nothing done today."

Ben felt his wedding ring in his pocket. He'd taken it off on the way up the stairs. It always comes off after his tie, and it sits in his pocket, patiently, warm and blind, until he's ready to return.

"Maybe you need a drink," he said.

"Of course. Natasha the shitty artist needs vodka to help forget her troubles."

"That bit is getting tired."

"So am I." She yanked her foot from his grasp. "What's our story tonight? Am I your wife, or your cousin, or—"

"We don't need to say anything. Charlie won't care. He's too busy talking about himself."

Sarah picked at the paint on her thumbnail, and Ben glanced at the easel in her living room. She'd finished the pencil sketch and had started coloring; a dark-haired figure hung from a noose in the middle of a bare room with a single window, one shoe on the floor and the other dangling from its foot. Ben hated everything about it. Aside from the technical flaws—the perspective was off, and the light falling across the floor was too narrow—he was certain she'd wanted him to see the painting and wonder if everything was okay. The manipulation made him want to put his fist through the wall, and rip the painting to stiff shreds.

"A play about a dog," Sarah said, tossing her cigarette in the sink. "God, I hate the theater."

They found the brownstone at the end of a quiet side street in SoHo. A sculpture of a lion sat on the stone railing to the left of the red front door; its eyes wept water stains and lichens stained its pitted flank a pale green.

Ben rang the doorbell and a short, older man answered. He wore a dark suit and his hair was slicked back. He carried a highball glass, half-filled. He chewed, then spit an olive pit into his hand.

"We're here for Charlie Cahill's play," Ben said.

"That's nice," the man said.

Ben led Sarah inside. They stepped into a sumptuous room, draped with tapestries and Oriental rugs. Medieval weaponry hung high on the walls; Ben saw crossed swords and polearms, axes and flails, and a matchlock mounted above the fireplace. A long table stood in the middle of the room, serving platters and tureens crowded by discarded plates filled with gnawed rib bones, wilted salads, and crumbs of cake. People wandered quietly. Charlie sat with a woman in the corner. She wore a short pink dress, like a sixties go-go dancer. Her legs were crossed, and her shoe dangled from her foot. Charlie said something and she laughed. Then he spotted Ben and waved him over.

"Just in time," Charlie said, pulling a joint from behind his ear. "Ruth, this is the man I was telling you about. He's very clever.

He did the Werther's Original ad campaign."

"Werther's Original?" Ruth said.

"It's a candy for octogenarians," Ben said, and he shook her hand. "We tried to make it hip."

"*Hip* is one of those words that's lost all meaning," Charlie said. "Like *luxury* and *genius*. Who is this clinging to your arm?"

"This is Sarah," Ben said. "We're old friends."

Charlie looked at Sarah and smiled, slowly. "Is this the girl you saw *Barefoot in the Park* with?"

"Not that old," Ben said.

"When did you see *Barefoot in the Park*?" Sarah said.

"High school," Charlie said, "so we forgive him. Please, take my hand before it grows cold."

Sarah cleared her throat and took Charlie's hand.

"This is my first time at the theater," she said. "I've never been to a play before."

"I promise I'll be gentle," Charlie said. "Would you like to see the stage? The space is remarkable. Come, before they clutter it with all my props."

Sarah glanced at Ben, who shrugged. Charlie led her away, puffing his joint.

Ben stuffed his hands into his pockets and looked up at the carved ceiling. He saw the faces of gargoyles and angels, and rows of grapevines and harvest vegetables. Ruth adjusted the strap on her loose shoe and set it down, turning it to the side.

"I was worried the straps would be too high for this dress," she said.

"It looks good," Ben said.

"I don't know. I think it's too much. This hemline is too high." She rose off her seat and tugged at it. Ben watched her thigh muscles lengthen and flex; her flip bounced along her jawline. "Charlie found this dress at a consignment shop. I don't know why I listen to him. I cut my hair yesterday and put on these ridiculous fake lashes. Really. I'm too old to play dress-up for a failed playwright. Don't you agree?"

"I don't know much about theater," Ben said, "but anyone who can put on a show in a place like this can't be a failure."

"Maybe," Ruth said. "This is Otto Anschlinger's home. Have you heard of him? Supposedly he was an SS guard at Belsen. I never read the papers but Charlie told me the *Times* ran a damning piece, a few years back. I avoid Otto whenever he's in town. What can you say to a Nazi?"

"I can think of several things," Ben said.

Ruth smiled. "Do you work in the city?"

"We have some clients in Midtown. Whenever they get nervous, I get the call."

"Because you're the charming one."

"Compared to my co-workers, yes."

Ruth touched his arm, softly, two fingers on his elbow.

"My father worked in Midtown," she said. "Sometimes he'd take me to his office, and I'd sit on the train and stare at everyone's shoes. I was too scared to look anywhere else."

"My oldest daughter does the same thing," Ben said.

Ruth smiled again. "You have to tell her she's making a mistake. She needs to remember all those unhappy, middle-aged men; how else is she going to describe them when she writes her first novel?"

A fork struck a glass, and conversation stopped. The short man who had greeted Ben and Sarah at the door stood at the far end of the room.

"Five minutes," the short man said. "Five minutes, please."

The crowd moved. Ruth opened her small purse and plucked out three red pills. She took Ben's hand and dropped a pill in his palm.

"Trust me." She took two with a swallow of white wine.

"You don't want to sit through this sober."

"Charlie told me it's only one act."

"One act divided into eight parts. And there's the prelude, and his commentary at the end…" Ruth shook her head. "Not even Charlie sits through it sober."

The theater was at the back of the house, with a black box for a stage and red velvet stadium seating. Ben spotted Sarah in the front row, sitting near Charlie, who was whispering in her ear and pointing at the set design. Sarah laughed, and Ben couldn't tell if it was sincere or polite. She played with the necklace around her long neck.

Ben sat near Ruth. He felt her thigh touch his. She stared straight ahead, fake eyelashes curled, hands folded primly on her lap. Ben felt a sudden urge to run from the room and call his wife. Rebecca was always the one who remembered these moments: the birthmark at the base of his youngest daughter's skull that faded by her first birthday, the appearance of a long-ago neighbor at his father's funeral. This was something new, and sharing it with strangers seemed a waste.

The room dimmed; onstage a blue light panned across wooden cutouts of a snow-tipped mountain range. Whispers faded. A man in a dog suit crawled from behind the curtain and sniffed the air, while a voice boomed from somewhere overhead:

"Spay called himself a vagabond in semi-ironic howls, and while he believed himself to be nothing more than sunlight shifting across the side of a great white mountain in the Khyber Pass, he also knew it didn't matter. None of it mattered."

Ruth glanced at Ben, her eyebrows raised, and Ben burst out laughing.

They found a dark room in the back of the house during intermission. Ruth leaned against the wall and let Ben fumble under her dress. His hands wouldn't move as precisely as he wanted, and he ripped her underwear. It was too violent; instinct told him she was the sort of woman who needed a soft touch. *Sorry*, he mumbled. She kissed his neck and lowered to her knees. Ben straightened his arms, pressing his palms against the wall. He focused. She was very warm. Her fake eyelashes tickled his thighs. In the dark of his closed eyes he remembered a cold autumn day, driving to see Rebecca. He'd broken his nose during a soccer game on the field outside his dorm; Rebecca had called him a war hero.

Ben wasn't sure when the other guests had left, or how long ago he'd arrived at the table in the middle of the main room, but he found himself seated between Ruth and Sarah with a wine stain on his tie. He'd been picking at a hollowed loaf of bread, filled with sweating cheese cubes and olives. Charlie sat across from them.

Charlie poured Sarah another glass of wine. "The lighting was horrific," he said. "You couldn't see his testicles, and I insisted they put testicles on the costume because the entire thrust of the play is Spay's masculinity. Why would I include testicles if they weren't important?"

"Chekhov's testicles," Ruth said.

Charlie nodded. "Exactly."

"I saw the dog's testicles," Ben said. His mouth was dry and he crunched an ice chip. "Very realistic. Were those kiwi fruits?"

Sarah giggled. Ben noticed her eyes were bloodshot.

"Spay," Charlie said. "The dog's name is Spay."

"How ironic," Ben said.

Charlie sighed. "First of all, they were tennis balls painted brown. Second, it's not *ironic*. Spay is Pashto for dog. Do you know what Pashto is?"

Sarah said something to Ruth and they both laughed. Ruth sipped her wine. Ben imagined it mixing with his sperm in her stomach.

"Let me guess," Ben said. "Pashto is what the natives speak in Afghanistan."

"Pashto is *one* of the languages spoken in Afghanistan," Charlie said. "They also speak Dari, and Turkmen, and Uzbek."

"I didn't see Spay's testicles," Sarah said. "I though the play was very sad, and a little funny. But mostly sad."

"Well, Spay had to die," Charlie said. "I was worried it might come across as heavy-handed, but those people have little regard for humans, much less pets. I remember reading about this Afghan farmer—I think it was in *National Geographic*—who talked about using stray dogs as target practice. First it was the Soviets, then it was dogs."

"But what's an Afghan farmer doing with a Luger?" Ben said.

Charlie lifted his shirt, revealing the Luger tucked into his waistline. "It's Otto Anschlinger's, and it's the only gun I could get. You can't believe how heavy it is."

Sarah slouched in her chair, tracing the edge of her wine glass with her paint-stained fingernail. "If I had children, I would bring them to see this play."

"Thank you," Charlie said.

Ben shook his head. "I didn't think the ending was right. Spay wouldn't lunge at the farmer, because that's not the type of dog Spay was."

"How do you know?" Sarah said. "It was not your play."

"He let that rabbit go," Ben said. "He was starving, and he let that rabbit escape."

Charlie sat up. "Spay is a dog, and dogs bite. Especially when they've run out of options, and they have no sense of home. Which is a long way of saying don't fuck with a cornered *dog*."

He gulped more wine and put the Luger on the table. Light reflected dull off its barrel.

"I don't know," Ben said. "I thought it was a cheat. There should have been a baby goat."

"A baby goat," Charlie said.

Ben pushed back from the table and stood in the center of an Oriental rug. "The baby goat is the property of the farmer, and Spay sees him from across the field."

Ben found himself getting down on all fours. His hands rubbed across the coarse Oriental rug, and he realized he had no idea the last time he'd felt the floor with his hands. Then he remembered: two summers ago, the living room, searching for Rebecca's contact that popped out.

"You be the goat," Ben said, pointing at Charlie. "Sarah, you be the farmer."

Charlie laughed. "You're insane."

"No, I'm Spay," Ben said, and he began to crawl. He imagined what his daughters would do if they saw him. They would cover their faces and laugh. "And I see the baby goat..."

He stared at Charlie.

"Oh, hell," Charlie said. He jogged around the table.

Charlie got down on the floor, a few paces from Ben. Ruth stood and grabbed the Luger off the table.

"That's perfect," Ben said. "The farmer sees Spay in the distance, running toward his baby goat. But Spay only wants to greet the goat, you know, touch noses—"

Ben crawled to Charlie and mimed touching his nose.

"And the farmer thinks he's going to hurt the goat."

Ruth pointed the gun at Ben. "Leave my goat alone," she said.

"Perfect," Ben said.

Sarah grabbed the gun from Ruth.

"Boom," Sarah said.

"Make sure the safety is still on," Charlie said.

Sarah frowned and Ruth leaned over. "This little switch here," Ruth said. "It should be moved to the side. Like so."

Ben felt the ring slip out of his pocket. The gun clicked. He saw the bullet shine from the barrel, cleaving the air and chewing through his heart. But there was no bullet; there was only Charlie's laughter.

AS THE OLD GREEKS WOULD SAY

I found my cousin Sarah in Delfino, a small bar at the end of Kairos Street. She wore a short white dress and was barefoot, with tawny calves and thin wrists, the sort of girl you expect to see in a vacation brochure. As far as I knew, Sarah didn't drink—maybe a sip of ouzo with her evening fish, or a dash of vodka in her morning orange juice. Still, she looked at home in that place, tucked into the far corner of the room, ashing her cigarette and waiting to be entertained. She reminded me a little of a character in one of my earliest stories: Isabella, the wife of a pipe-smoking Falangist named Esteban, the sort of young woman who refuses to see anything bad, looking into the bottom of her wine glass at the first sign of an argument. The penultimate scene with Esteban stalking his rival's retarded older brother remains one of my favorites: picture a sun-lit park, a mother pushing a carriage with squeaking wheels, the retard (hands splayed, half-smile, wearing a yellow cap) strolling past a giant mechanical gazelle, then the slow reveal of a pistol and a hollow *pop*. Half-smile still intact, yellow cap tilting insouciantly, the retard sinks to the ground, clutching his neck, believing this all to be some part of an elaborate game.

Anyway. My name is Teddy Wheeler, I'm twenty-two, and I spent last summer in Paris studying Russian literature. This was an attempt to make my writing more serious. I figured there was nothing a few plague-ridden villages and poisoned wells couldn't fix. Was I wrong. France is a terrible place to study Russian—

butter, pastry, and wine dispel the sort of chapped-skin disappointment necessary to appreciate Dostoyevsky. After Paris I returned to New York, with some paperbacks, my little notepad, and a shoulder bag full of Gogol homages. I was convinced my half-completed novel, *Of Empty Men and Cupboards*, would be pecked at and fought over by numerous agents, like sparrows darting for crumbs. Six months passed; the half-finished novel remained half-finished. I took a job as a waiter at a dusty hotel in the West Seventies. I slept with three women, two of whom I'll call attractive, and suffered one heartbreak courtesy of a Jewish girl named Rebecca. Despite everything, it was, on the whole, not a bad year.

Some history before we return to Delfino: A month after my twenty-second birthday, Aunt Jackie and Uncle William threw a party at their Westchester home. I suffered through the usual—loud jazz, guests frantically searching for drink coasters because every piece of furniture is known by its designer—until Aunt Jackie cornered me between the Rahm chair and the Hummel sofa.

She asked if I'd heard the news about Sarah, and I said I had. Then she paused, eyes reddening, hand pressed to her chest. She looked away.

"I never imagined Sarah would actually want to stay on Therios," she said, finally. "Her teachers are beside themselves. Do you realize she's missed over three months of classes?" She grabbed a glass from a passing tray. Her hair—kinky, rebellious—wavered in the air conditioning. "Your uncle and I don't even know who our daughter is these days. I never should have let her go."

Idiotically, I said, "Well, don't blame yourself."

"But I *do*." She sighed and sipped. Her lipstick left a crescent on the rim of the glass. "She was persuasive. *Very* persuasive. She takes after her father, that way. No more than three weeks, she promised. Postcards every Friday, she promised. How could I have been so gullible?" She cleared her throat. "I have such a headache, and my foot is *throbbing*. How is your mother? Is she still angry we didn't make it to your graduation? I wish we'd had the time. But William committed to that benefit dinner, and I was only eight weeks out of ankle surgery. As you may have heard, there were complications. Nothing life-threatening, though I was later told it could have swung that way. Amputation was mentioned, albeit briefly. I blame it on the stress." She grabbed my hand. "Did you get the fruit basket we sent?"

"It was wonderful."

"You always loved fruit, ever since you were a child. 'I want some dapples,' you used to say. Oh, here comes William. Very good."

He tottered over, clutching a highball, ponderous, breathing heavily, the way I imagined an old bear would move. His hand enveloped mine.

"Enjoying the party?"

"Delightful," I said.

"That's Maine shrimp." He rattled the ice in his glass. "Had it shipped this morning."

"Fresh," I said. "Very fresh."

"You working these days?" he asked.

"Uptown. I'm waiting tables."

Aunt Jackie frowned.

"It's temporary," I added. "And it's a French restaurant. They allow dogs."

She closed her eyes and rubbed her forehead. "This reminds me of the time when you and Sarah went fishing off our dock. Do you remember that summer? You had a broken wrist. Or was that Sarah?"

"I suppose Jackie told you the news," Uncle William said.

"She did," I said.

Aunt Jackie patted my hand again. "I remember—we'd bought that horrible trampoline. Six weeks it took Sarah's wrist to heal. Even now it still clicks."

"There's dozens of islands," Uncle William said, "but lucky for us Sarah picked the smallest. The police chief told me he's seen her puttering about on a blue moped. No helmet. Barefoot. Wearing a bikini top. Isn't that something? One loose patch of gravel and those pretty little legs aren't so pretty anymore."

I nodded, tried to turn it to a shrug, then gave up and tipped back my drink. Uncle William leaned in close. He smelled of cologne and scotch, sardines and sweat.

He went on. "What sort of reputation do you think a seventeen-year-old girl who rides around town barefoot, wearing a bikini top, has? Do you think she's known for her cultural acumen? For her conversational skills?"

"She's such a young seventeen," Aunt Jackie said. "Some of her opinions are so absurd."

Uncle William lowered his voice. "Between you and me, I'm not sure if she's intact. Get my point?"

"I do."

"So you appreciate the urgency of this situation."

"I'm beginning to."

"A blue moped." Aunt Jackie gulped the rest of her drink. "She could at least afford one of those tiny foreign cars. Something safer. Something…I don't know. Enclosed."

"Couldn't you cut her off?" I asked.

Aunt Jackie frowned. "Cut her off?"

"Freeze her account, I mean."

Uncle William breathed heavily. "Are you suggesting we abandon our daughter? That we sever her lifeline?"

His questions had the intended effect; I sipped my drink.

"It's bad enough we don't know the sort of medical care available in Greece," Jackie said. "Cash-in-hand is a matter of safety."

Then Uncle William said, "Jackie and I would like you to visit Therios, as a representative of the family. You're the ideal candidate: Sarah trusts you, we trust you, and you have experience living overseas. Where was that, again?"

"Paris," I said.

Aunt Jackie smiled. "Paris has the most wonderful cigarettes."

"I'd provide you with a place to stay," Uncle William continued. "And a generous per diem. You'll have plenty of time to enjoy the beach, flirt with the locals—whatever it is young folks do these days. Think of it as a vacation. When was the last time you saw Sarah?"

"Eight years. I doubt she'd even recognize me."

"Of course she would. You were always her favorite cousin." He grabbed my shoulder and squeezed.

I only knew Sarah as a little girl, a child who existed solely during the summer: blue-eyed, blonde-haired, thin as a stick with a high voice and scabby knees. I remembered she suffered from night terrors, she was afraid of dark water—anything she couldn't see the bottom of—and her tongue was perpetually stained purple and orange, from an endless supply of popsicles that Aunt Jackie kept in a huge plastic sack in the basement freezer. But as I got older Sarah became nothing more than a name from the side of the family we rarely saw, popping into existence only long enough to provide an update. *Sarah is starring as Rapunzel in her school play. Sarah broke her leg skiing. Sarah skipped two grades.*

When she was seven, teachers started labeling her an artistic prodigy. Her sculpture, *Apple Impaled on Glass*, was acquired by the Rothberg Gallery, making its debut on Sarah's tenth birthday.

The Lowe's sent us a combination birthday party/gallery opening invitation, which my newly widowed mother politely declined.

Sarah received a write-up in *The New Yorker* later that year. I stuck it to our refrigerator door, where it remains, yellowed and curling, marked with water stains and food smears:

> When Ichiro Ohi, recently visiting New York for the first public viewing of the lithograph series on Nikita Khrushchev, saw Sarah Katherine Lowe's sculpture, *Apple Impaled On Glass*, he proclaimed: "This is either the work of a genius, or a child has done this, and is putting us all on." Sarah Lowe's earliest piece, *Hunched Woman With Candle*, has been called "Rodin with a giggle." *Apple Impaled On Glass* can be seen at the Widmere Gallery…

Sarah had sent us a postcard during her junior year, from the Lowes' annual Hawaii vacation. She pasted a photo of herself over the front, lying on her back on the sand. She wore a white bikini top, her head floating in a pool of swirling blonde hair. The photographer—based on the hulking outline I guessed it was Uncle William—cast a shadow across Sarah's stomach. Later that week I caught myself staring at the photo—reading, re-reading, tapping the card's edge on the kitchen table. Sarah had written one sentence in thin black marker, not on the back of the card, but on the front, across her tanned legs:

> *Wish you were here but then it wouldn't be "here," would it?*

Two weeks after the party I quit my job, unearthed my little notepad, and took a business class flight to Athens. The half-finished novel pleaded to come along. It was a futile gesture—if cafes and long walks at dusk along the Seine hadn't worked, then greasy-haired merchants and the stink of fish would be the final thrust of the *spathē* in whatever remained of my writer's heart. Greece is not what it once was for artists—name me one author of any merit after Menander.

From Athens I took a ferry to Therios, sharing a bench at the prow of the ship with a trio of fat American men, all of them swigging beer from green bottles and spitting olive pits at the seagulls that rode the air currents. Uncle William had secured me an apartment in town, a small, white, stuccoed cube atop a grocery store, with a kitchen tiled in turquoise mosaic. I bought a bottle of ouzo and stored it in the freezer, next to a pint of strawberry ice cream. This became my breakfast: shot of ouzo, bowl of ice cream. Sometimes I wrote lousy poems while sitting on the patio. I swam in the ocean, tanned myself caramel, and flirted to no avail with the local girls.

After a week of this nonsense, I found Sarah. On a Friday afternoon, while walking through the village square, buzzed from four shots of absinthe bought for me by a loud German, I stumbled into the path of a moped. It swerved, tires squealing. I shouted a curse. Then I recognized her: the long blonde hair, the high cheekbones, the faux-naif comportment by way of wide eyes and a hair-trigger pout. She chained the blue Vespa to a lamppost near the Koriakos church and, helmet tucked into the crook of her arm, sauntered down an alley. I lost her amid the flap and whip of hanging laundry. A grotesque old Greek woman stared at me from between two shutters. I waved to the old woman. She did not wave back. I resisted the urge to pick up a stone and hit her between the eyes. I'm guessing Menander had the same urges.

Over the next few days I saw Sarah's moped everywhere: at the north beach, near the jewelry stands selling rings that flaked

"She pasted a photo of herself over the front…"

"...lying on her back on the sand."

gold when you scratched them, parked outside Delfino, and behind the cinema running an Alain Delon festival. I discovered our apartments were within looking distance—a pair of binoculars revealed Sarah's preference for vodka-spiked orange juice. I'm proud to admit I didn't scan her bedroom during evening hours, and I ignored the various men sunning themselves on her patio, their chins tipped to the morning light, cigarettes dangling from between their fingers. They were all decades older than she. This came as no surprise.

I waited and watched, finally deciding to make my move on a Wednesday night. I followed Sarah to Delfino. She sat in the back corner, by herself, smoking a thin cigarette, picking at a plate of *horta*. I simply walked to the table and sat down.

She ashed her cigarette and smiled one of those curt little lip-raises, the kind that lets you know you're only being tolerated because it's the polite thing to do.

"Nicko saw you," she said.

"Nicko?"

"He was sunning himself yesterday, and told me there was a man watching us with binoculars. You don't own the only pair of binoculars on this island, you know."

I nodded, wondering if Nicko was sitting close by. After a quick scan of the room, I asked her if she had another cigarette. She offered me the pack.

The two of us puffed away, smoke curling above our table. I said, "You can guess why I'm here."

"To bring me home."

"Honestly, I'm not sure how to go about this. Your father—"

"You mean he didn't write a speech for you?" She plucked an olive from her plate. "I'm surprised. He's very good at speeches."

I pulled a folded paper from my shirt pocket. "He instructed me to recite whatever I'd like."

"Give it to me, please."

"I don't think he necessarily wanted you reading—"

She held out her hand. "Let's have it."

I hesitated; she snatched the letter and sat back. After a few moments she sighed, crumpled the paper, and dropped it on the table.

"So I have two weeks left," she said. "Before he closes my account."

"I don't think he's bluffing."

"Maybe you could loan me some money."

"Why would I do that?"

"Because I might prostitute myself. There's no shortage of men on this island who would pay handsomely for a night with a seventeen-year-old American girl. Especially a blonde."

I laughed. "You're lying."

"Am I? Maybe. The idea has crossed my mind, though." She crushed out the cigarette and pushed her plate away. "Would you like to go for a walk?"

I took a long drag, letting the smoke leak from the corner of my mouth. That morning, binoculars lying on the small marble-top table, strawberry ice cream melting in the white sun, I'd composed a poem, admittedly too Byronic (*Oh! That we were forever keening / As lovers do at dawn / When night is surely passing / When the moon gives its last yawn*) but it brought back memories of Rebecca, the one who'd broken my heart. She had the sort of Jewish features that made her face look as though it had been frozen in mid-melt—sloping nose, sad eyes, down-turned lips—but she had a way with children, and she played the violin. I'd considered marriage. Her parents despised me.

Sarah and I walked to the ocean, picking our way down a steep bluff as cacti poked my ankles. We got to the beach and I unbuttoned my shirt, letting the wind dry my underarms. Fishing ships bobbed in a string of lights on the ocean. Sarah tried lighting another cigarette and gave up. She pushed a strand of hair off her face.

"Do you want to see the mass grave?" she said.

"The mass grave?"

We walked along the surf. "It's from the war," she said. "One hundred and thirty-seven Italian soldiers. The Greek army used machine guns and just left them to rot. They commemorate the event every year." She plucked a shell from the sand with her toes, brought it to her hand, inspected, then tossed it away. "Nicko says the place is haunted." She pointed to a promontory farther down the shore. "It's at the top of that rock. Some people bring candles."

"I've never seen a skeleton."

"They're beautiful. If you can get past the circumstances."

We walked another fifty yards, then scrambled back up the cliff. At a guardrail I offered my hand but Sarah leapt over the railing. She stumbled and sucked air between her teeth.

"Goddammit." She grabbed my shoulder. "Oh my God, that really hurts."

I knelt and held her ankle. After a few pokes and prods—I had no idea what I was doing—I looked up. "Can you move it?"

She rotated her foot. "A little."

"Should we head back?"

"No." She glanced at the ocean. "It's only a few minutes more."

We found it in the shadows of cypress trees, a dark hollow banded with moonlight. Sarah took a couple of candles from her pocket and lit them; I kicked away an old beer bottle. It was difficult to see anything—an arm, a boot, maybe a skull. I swear—

though it may have been my imagination—that a goat bleated not far from the grave.

"What do you think?" she asked.

"It's too dark. Is that a rifle? Or a ski pole?"

"Daytime is better. You can see the skull's expressions."

"I didn't realize skulls have expressions."

"Well, they do." She turned her candle upside down and watched the wax drip. "I've been painting them all month. Nicko says there's a gallery in Athens that might be interested."

"He sounds well connected."

"He knows everyone in Athens."

"So you can take of yourself."

"That's the plan."

"It's a good plan."

"You really think?" She rested her chin in her palm. "I thought you were going to tell me I'm being naïve."

I squatted at the edge of the grave. "Maybe you are. This isn't a bad place to be naïve. Better here than back in Westchester. I'm not sure what you'd do for money, though. Your father seems serious."

"I don't like my father."

"I got that."

"Do you like your father?"

"I did. He died."

"Oh." She lowered her gaze, for a moment. "I forgot. I'm sorry." She pulled a joint from her pocket. "Interested?"

I hadn't been stoned since my weekend in Lyon, when a young couple—picture a tall, rakish fellow with a Gallic nose and his equally rakish girlfriend with ample cleavage the color of skim milk—complimented my hat, as I sat, notepad in hand, in front of the Gare Saint-Paul. We'd discussed the nouveau roman, then snuck behind the public restrooms. One hour later I'd eaten too much broccoli quiche and I threw up on the corner of La rue Saint-Jean, timing it so that right before I vomited, I declared: *Voici ce que je pense d'Alain Robbe-Grillet.*

We smoked. Sarah hummed something in the minor key, candle in one hand and joint in the other. I grabbed a cypress branch and ran my fingers along its needles. A slat of moonlight finally revealed a stiff boot wrapped around a leg bone. I decided it belonged to Antonio Figarelli. From Palermo. The son of a mason, or better yet, a cobbler. On the day Antonio received his marching orders, his father—a short man, fingernails stained black from polish—made him those boots. He slaughtered a calf and tanned its hide, prayed to the patron saint of first-born Italian sons that Antonio would return home a hero, and sewed a St. Maurice medallion into the right instep. Weeks later Antonio survived a rocket barrage on the Albanian border; on a Sunday morning he killed a sniper in a mountain village. He wrote his parents that night. The letter went something like this:

Dear Pappa,

It has been a difficult month. We lost fifty-three men during two nights of sustained shelling from Greek forces. I held a friend in my arms as he died. His name was Nicko, and he was from Marsala. I admit his death filled me with rage—I became, as the old Greeks would say, 'blood-drunk.' That is, I could not wait for revenge. It came to me this morning.

We are camped in the foothills of the Pindus Mountains, under the shadow of a monastery in a farming village. Goats are everywhere. My friends use them for target practice. During breakfast someone shot and killed our second lieutenant, and we thought it was a farmer until I saw sunlight flashing at the top of the monastery. I ran to the tower and crept up the stairs. In the belfry I found him—a little man with a big rifle, kneeling at the window, cigarette in mouth. I kicked away the rifle and demanded he tell me his name. Constantine, he said. I punched him to the ground and choked him until he stopped moving. Then we barred the monastery doors and threw torches through the windows. The screams were terrible.

Also, I think a piece of shrapnel has lodged itself in my right boot. Tomorrow I'm going to cut open the instep and see if I can dig it out.

Love,
Antonio

Sarah and I met on the north beach the next morning. The sun was brilliant. She limped along, wearing canvas shoes and her white bikini. I could not believe the stares she elicited from those lecherous Greek men, as if they'd never seen a seventeen-year-old limping through the surf. There were plenty of other young women to ogle, skinny girls with thick, olive-black curly hair, lying on blankets, smoking, laughing, pinching their boyfriends. I thought of Rebecca.

Sarah squatted in the water and yanked a piece of wood from the sand. "I'm having lunch with Nicko. You can join us if you'd like."

"Maybe. My stomach has been bothering me."

"Are you calling my father today?"

"I was thinking of sending a telegram."

She turned the wood over, inspecting with one eye shut, then tossed it back. "Well, make sure you say goodbye before leaving."

"I was thinking I might stay."

This excited her. "Really? For how long?"

"I'll start with a month."

"Do you have enough money?"

"I have some savings." This was true. "I could sell a few stories. Some New York editors are interested." This was a lie—what editors? For what journals? More importantly, I hadn't finished a story in a year.

"You could give a reading at one of my art shows." She looked up at me, squinting. "I don't know if that's what writers do, but—"

"I'd be flattered," I said.

I put my hands on my hips and gazed out. Sarah stood. A wave broke against our legs.

"Have you explored the other islands?" I asked.

"Just Santorini." She hobbled in the breaking surf.

"We'll have to visit Ios," I said. "Menander vacationed there."

I agreed to meet Sarah and Nicko for lunch that afternoon, and waited for an hour on the steps of the Koriakos church before giving up. I returned to my apartment and watched a cleaning woman scour Sarah's porch. That night—full moon, warm breeze, more of the same—her apartment remained empty. I had lunch the next day at Delfino, finishing a bottle of wine and a platter of grape-leaf *dolma*, and stumbled home, imagining Rebecca with a new lover—an Italian, perhaps—the two of them riding through Rome on mopeds, scarves flapping in the wind, the whole bit. Then I imagined her on Therios, wearing a long, grey skirt, being rounded up by grim-faced Greeks, walking under the stand of cypress trees while goats bleated.

Three days later I was back in New York, asking for my old restaurant job. The boss even gave me a raise, impressed, perhaps, with my Continental tan. I unearthed the half-finished novel and wrote another five pages over the course of a month, milking the muse with a few joints bought from one of my co-workers, a middle-aged divorcé with a lisp and stained collars. I outlined a story about the Greco-Italian war, and started seeing a girl who danced for the New York Ballet.

Sarah, as far as I know, is still on Therios, though there are whispers—dark and almost gleeful—that Aunt Jackie and Uncle William haven't heard from her in months. I don't know what to believe. I do know Sarah would never succumb to that most clichéd of endings, the ingénue walking into the angry waters, awaiting a Laocoönian fate. I prefer to remember her from our last morning together. She waded deeper, arms out, tilting her head back until her hair floated like sea grass. The girls on the beach pinched their boyfriends, the old men ogled—it's irrelevant to describe anything else, though I did watch a father pulling his little girl on a raft, the girl screaming, the father determined to conceal his own joy.

FIVE TEMPERED NOTES

Max Strickland came to Tokyo in November 1997 and rented an apartment in the Setagaya neighborhood, within walking distance of Gillespie's nightclub, where he played jazz piano four nights a week. His setlist was straightforward: Evans, Brubeck, Garner, and Peterson. He saw himself as an employee rather than a musician. His boss, "Dizzy" Daigorou Shimpei—a thin, lanky fiftysomething with black hornrims and skinny ties—often pleaded with Max to accept requests. During snowy nights a few patrons would ask for Guaraldi; Sundays evoked Carmichael. Max always refused. Instead he'd just smile, launching into his rendition of Peterson's "Caravan" or Brubeck's "All the Things You Are."

His favorite part of the evening was closing time, when he'd sit at the piano and improvise pentatonic scales until Daigorou turned off the lights. The young waitress, Naoki, usually stayed with Max to the end. She'd refill his bourbon, wipe down tables, and leave with him, trading small talk as they walked up the short flight of stairs to street level. At the corner they'd separate, Naoki huddled in her fake fur coat and Max in the leather jacket bought by his wife the previous Christmas. Keeping tempo to the click of Naoki's heels on the sidewalk, he would twist the signature from 4/4 to 9/8 to 7/8 until her steps faded into street noise.

It had been four months since Max left Pittsburgh. That summer the conservatory refused to extend his teaching contract.

He'd been teaching piano for nine years. Not one student affair, not one sick day. The night after he learned his stint was ending at the end of the semester, he drank himself into a warm blur and wandered through downtown. At a bar on 8th Street he tried flirting with a trio of women celebrating a birthday. By midnight he'd spent an hour in a bathroom stall, counting the floor tiles. When he stumbled home, Ellen said nothing. She pulled off his pants and unbuttoned his shirt. Max awoke to breakfast. The bedroom smelled like someone else's cologne.

Two weeks later Max heard from a former bandmate, working as a pianist at a bar in Osaka. The pay was excellent, his friend insisted, and the hours were easy. A six-month gig in Japan was enough to save a year's worth of salary. But Ellen made a decent wage teaching high school, and their apartment was cheap, so Max took odd jobs. He tuned pianos, cleaned gutters, and ran credit reports for a landlord. Still, news from Japan found him; one morning, while standing in line for coffee, he watched a TV segment about a pregnant Sumatran tiger in the Tokyo Zoo. The experts claimed it was a minor miracle, because Sumatran tigers rarely mate in captivity.

That night, after Ellen had gone upstairs to bed, Max began sifting through old boxes of photographs from his touring days. He found Polaroids of ex-girlfriends, most better-looking than he'd remembered. Insomnia came and went. He dreamt about falling down stairwells. He started jogging at dawn. He read about the benefits of yogurt and started eating it by the pint.

On a warm autumn afternoon, while sharing a walk with Ellen in Frick Park, Max announced his plan to play jazz piano in Tokyo.

"Pete Duvall knows the owner of a club who's looking for an American pianist," he said. "It's all easy stuff—old standards, movie soundtracks. My biggest problem would be boredom.

I could bring home almost two grand a week, which means I'd only have to work for six months."

Ellen kept walking, arms folded across her chest. "I thought Tokyo is very expensive."

"I'd live cheap. No booze, no car, no sushi."

"Do you want me to come with you?"

"Well, you have school until winter break—"

"I know my schedule," Ellen said. "I'm asking if you want me to."

"If that's what you want."

Leaves scuttled across their path. Ellen said nothing. Instead she continued walking, a few feet in front of Max. He could tell she was embarrassed; to his surprise, he felt little guilt.

Daigorou let Max go home early the next night. Business was slow—a knot of executives talked quietly in the corner, two college students traded laughter at the bar—and Naoki sat at an empty table, chin in hand, half-listening to the finale of Garner's "One Note Samba." She wore her black hair in a bob, with a tight black T-shirt and three bangles around her wrist. She sipped from a bottle of beer. She waved to Max as he grabbed his coat. He nodded in return.

His apartment was tucked into the top floor of a narrow, vanilla-colored building on Senzoku Street, next to a small bookstore that specialized in American paperbacks. As he walked down the hallway to his door he thought about his apartment in Pittsburgh. It was nine a.m. there; Ellen would already be on her way to school, perhaps having shoveled a foot of snow off their car, or perhaps having someone else do the shoveling while she waited in the front seat. He could almost see her: puffy blue jacket, jeans tucked into boots, a strand of blonde hair pasted across her forehead from melting snow.

Max switched on his apartment light and hung his jacket in the closet. He grabbed a beer from the fridge, filled a saucepan with water, and set it on the stove. When he walked to the living room, he found a body lying on the carpet.

He paused, beer in hand. It was a man, mid-thirties, with short brown hair and deep-set eyes. He lay on his back, between the couch and TV, dressed in jeans and a black sweater. The man was dead; Max was certain. He saw no blood or injury, only a blank stare. The man wore Max's clothes. His wedding ring—a thin silver band—was identical to Max's. The man, as far as Max could tell, was Max himself.

Max left his apartment and spent an hour at a pachinko parlor. He finished a half pack of cigarettes and five beers, then fled into a nearby alley, where he threw up. As he braced himself against the alley wall, steam from his vomit veiled the brick, curling around an iron waste pipe. A young couple walked by the alley and stopped. To Max, they looked the same as any other young Tokyo couple—the man in fashionably thin jeans, the woman in a tight dress.

The man pointed at Max. "Isshoni odorimasenka?"

His girlfriend laughed, tottering on her heels before walking away. Snow fell. Late night revelers clotted the sidewalks. Max stood on the corner and stared up at a giant electronic billboard, his body bathed in blue light. Michael Jackson—shiny, angelic, dressed in white—held a jar of anti-aging face cream in his enormous, delicate hand. *You will become someone new,* he said, his voice lilting. *Embrace yourself—everyone and everyone.*

Max waited for Naoki outside Gillespie's, the click of her heels echoing staccato on the stairs.

"You hungry?"

She paused on the top step and smiled. "Famished."

They sat at the bar of a late-night soba café, on the corner of Komitsu and Jan-Sho. Naoki's bangles clanged softly as she slurped her soup. Two chefs stood behind the counter, in white aprons and small white caps, talking quietly while staring ahead.

"Daigorou was in a terrible mood tonight," Naoki said. "He asked me to scrub down the men's toilets. If he hadn't sent you home early, he probably would have asked you."

Max shook *shichimi togarashi* into his bowl. "I'm glad I didn't run into him."

"Don't tell me you're scared of Dizzy Daigorou."

"I'm not scared. I just don't like confrontation."

"You're a pretty meek guy."

"Pardon?"

"You jazz guys are always meek. Maybe it's because you spend most of your life having secret conversations. That's what jazz is, I think. Musicians having secret conversations with each other."

"I never saw myself as meek," he said.

"Well, you are. We've been working together for four months, and this is the most you've ever said to me, other than talking about the weather."

He shrugged.

"I'm a decent-looking woman," Naoki continued, "and I know you're married but I'm guessing your wife is back home. In America, I mean."

"She's in Pittsburgh."

"What's that like?"

"It's fine."

"You don't miss her?"

"Sometimes."

"So what happened?"

"I'm sorry?"

"Something must have happened. You're here and she's not. Also? You smell like alcohol. Like, a lot of alcohol. I never see you drink."

Max shrugged again.

"You remind me a little of that Hawthorne story," Naoki said. "You know, the one where the married man leaves home and moves across the street, without telling his wife."

"You read Hawthorne?"

She nodded. "I get my books from the American paperback store."

"I live right near there."

"I take it you don't read much. I would've seen you."

"I don't go out often."

"You should be careful. People aren't orangutans, you know."

"What does that mean?"

"It means we're not meant to live alone. Orangutans live alone. I read about it in a nature book. Once they leave their mother, that's it. Forty years of solitude. They spend their entire lives in trees, eating fruit."

"Doesn't sound too bad."

Naoki slurped her soup. "My old boyfriend tried to be like that. Of course he still managed to cheat on me. We dated for three years before I finally had the courage to walk out. He played jazz piano. Not as good as you, but he tried. My father says it's always the quiet guys you should watch out for."

Max checked his watch. Ten past one. He rubbed his face and pressed his fingers hard into his eyes.

"What I'm trying to say is, I'm not necessarily available," Naoki said. "And the last thing I need is a married man. I'm just trying to figure out why you haven't at least made an effort. Before tonight, I mean."

"So that's what you think this is about?"

"Am I wrong?"

He pushed away his bowl of soba. "Come to my apartment. There's something I need to show you."

Max knelt at his body's side. He compared the scar on his knee with that of his double, and found it an exact match. He opened its mouth and counted the fillings. All the same. It even smelled like him, that mix of bourbon and laundry detergent. Identically chewed fingernails, identically cut hair.

Naoki sat on the couch, legs folded, elbow resting on her thigh with chin in hand. "You sure you don't have a twin?"

"I'm an only child."

"A clone, then."

"A *clone*?"

"Maybe someone stole your DNA."

"They can do that?"

Naoki shrugged. "In movies."

Max walked to the window. "A clone wouldn't have the same scar as I. Or the same teeth fillings, or my clothes."

"Well, it's the strangest thing I've ever seen." Naoki pulled a cigarette from her purse and instinctively cupped the lighter flame. "But I'm a twenty-four-year-old waitress who's lived in Tokyo her whole life, so what do I know? Do you have anything to drink?"

"There's vodka in the freezer."

She stepped over the body and bent down until her face hovered just above its staring eyes. Then she walked to the kitchen, grabbed a highball glass from the cabinet, unscrewed the vodka, and poured a splash.

Max sat on the couch. He thought for a moment, hand on his forehead.

"Help me get rid of this thing," he said.

She leaned against the kitchen counter. "I don't want to do anything illegal."

"It's not illegal. It's my body."

"Sort of."

"We'll need a car."

"Daigorou has a car."

"I'd rather not involve him."

Naoki drained the glass in one gulp. "Don't worry about Daigorou."

Daigorou answered the door before Naoki had a chance to use her key. He yanked it open and squinted into the stairwell. He was barefoot, wearing a white shirt and dress pants. Behind him, in the dark club, Max saw a small table lit by a single light. A bottle of scotch stood near a stack of papers.

"We need your help," Naoki said.

Daigorou peered over her shoulder, at Max. He smiled and adjusted his black hornrims. "Let me guess. You want an advance on your next check. For the abortion. Or the wedding. Or both."

Naoki slapped his arm. Mumbling to himself, Daigorou walked away. The club was chilly; he had turned down the heat. They sat at the small table.

"It's two a.m.," Daigorou said. "This should be interesting."

"I'd like to borrow your car," Max said.

Daigorou narrowed his eyes. "Why?"

"To move something."

"What is it?"

Max glanced at Naoki. "It's personal."

"Drugs?"

"No," Max said.

"Stolen art?"

"Please."

"A body, then?"

Silence. Daigorou grabbed the bottle of scotch and sat back, his bare feet crossed. "Naoki, fetch us three glasses."

"I'm not on the clock, Daigorou-san."

"As long as you're in my club, you're on the clock. Three glasses, no ice."

Naoki muttered and walked to the bar. Daigorou remained staring at Max.

"I always insist it's the quiet ones you have to watch out for," Daigorou said. "Tell me what happened."

Max talked. Daigorou listened, sipping scotch. At the end, he took off his hornrims and polished the lenses with the hem of his shirt.

"Where are you planning to take the body?"

"Somewhere far away," Max said. "I'm going to bury it."

Daigorou shook his head. "Bodies have a way of coming back. Then what? An investigation, questions that can't be answered. It would be a mess. Might even be criminal."

"But if it's Max's body," Naoki said, "how can it be criminal?"

"Hush." Daigorou frowned. "Why even risk the possibility? Max doesn't need the hassle. Nor do I. He plays piano in my club; the press would eventually make their way here. The place would develop a bad reputation."

Daigorou sipped his scotch. Max waited. Naoki finished her drink, and shivered in the cold room.

"I have a solution," Daigorou said. "But we must act quickly."

Daigorou stood in Max's living room with his hands on his hips. "To be honest, I thought you might be putting me on."

They pulled sheets from the linen closet, spread them under the body, and rolled it up like a carpet.

"It's remarkable," Daigorou continued. "Truly remarkable. It doesn't make sense. Yet there you are. Does this building have a back stairwell?"

"It does," Max said.

"Good. You and I will carry the body down. We can't take the elevator—even at three in the morning there's always a chance we'd encounter some neurotic businessman or a drunk. Naoki, you stay one flight ahead of us. Whistle if you see any sort of trouble."

"One moment," Max said. "I'll be right back."

He shut his bedroom door and dialed the number for his wife's school. The secretary stammered when he told her it was an emergency.

He waited, staring at his white bedroom walls. An old poster hung above his bed: The Max Strickland Trio: A Night of Charlie Parker Without Strings. They'd played three hours at a small club in Harlem. A piece of skin ripped off his sax player's lip, and after every song he turned over his horn and dumped bloody spit on the stage. By the end of the show their pant cuffs were spattered red.

"Max?"

"Ellen—"

"Is something wrong? Are you okay?"

"I'm fine. Well, not really. Are you somewhere private?"

"I'm in the faculty lounge. What's going on?"

"I found a body in my apartment."

"A body."

"My body."

"Your body."

"I know it sounds impossible, but when I came home after work, I put on some water for pasta, walked into my living room, and there I was. Lying on the floor. Dead."

"So you're dead."

"No. My body is dead. My *other* body."

She dropped her voice to a harsh whisper. "What are you trying to say?"

"I'm not trying to say anything. It's the truth. There was another me, and he died."

"And now it's all clear."

"Nothing is clear. I don't understand what's going on."

"You haven't called in two weeks. Whatever it is you're trying to tell me—"

"I'm not trying to tell you anything. I found a body in my apartment, and it's me. Only it's not."

"I don't have time for this. I'm at *work*."

"But I'm telling you the truth."

"Just come out already and say it. Don't play this game."

"I'm not playing, Ellen."

"Of course you're not," she said. "And I'm not playing either."

She hung up. Max held the handset until the off-hook tone beeped. Then he ripped the cord from the wall and left, closing the door gently behind him.

"Everything okay?" Naoki said.

"Terrific," Max said.

They grabbed the rolled sheets at opposite ends; with a grunt, Max and Daigorou lifted the body.

The streets were quiet, neon blinking off the snow-covered sidewalks. Daigorou drove his tiny car. Max sat near him, with Naoki crammed into the back seat, near the wrapped body sticking out the back hatch.

Daigorou switched on the radio. He fiddled with the dial and settled on a college jazz station.

"Ah," Daigorou said. " 'Nuit sur les Champs-Élysées.'"

"I've never heard this," Naoki said.

"Miles Davis," Max said. "It's from a soundtrack."

Daigorou drummed softly on the steering wheel. "*Ascenseur pour l'échafaud*. What a film. Jeanne Moreau didn't wear any makeup. You saw her every emotion, exactly as it should be."

Max stared out the window. Daigorou kept drumming. Naoki plucked a cigarette from her purse.

"I think my wife's been having an affair for the past year," Max said.

Daigorou nodded. "These things happen."

"I don't know who he is, but I know what kind of cologne he wears. I've smelled it in our bedroom. And a few times I found bits of facial hair in the sink that weren't mine."

Daigorou glanced over. "You're certain of this."

"I am."

"And if you're mistaken?"

Max sighed. "Are you married?"

"Three times."

"Then you understand when I tell you that a husband knows."

"Ah—Chet Baker," Daigorou said, still drumming softly. "Mind if I turn this up?"

They drove on. A triptych of billboards flashed as they waited at a traffic light. An old couple carried grocery bags from a corner *konbini*, shuffling arm in arm. Max watched them. He felt he could leave at anytime, go anywhere. Prague. Barcelona. St. Louis. Pentatonic scales are universal. The Indonesian *gamelan*. The Filipino *kulintang*. The Ethiopian *krar*. As long as you balance dissonance with resolution, and don't make it obvious. The genius, Max told himself, is in the withholding.

At the sign for Ueno Park, Daigorou switched off the car lights and drove slowly down a service vehicle path. Manicured trees loomed on either side. Max saw a pavilion and a cluster of turnstiles hidden in shadow at the park's entrance.

"The loading docks are usually unguarded," Daigorou said. "You and I will carry it up the platform."

Max found the delivery gate unlocked, as he knew he would. He heaved it open; they carried the body into the dim of the food storage building. They smelled meat and kibble, ripe fruit and musky soil. At the far end of the warehouse, past pallets of watermelon, lettuce, radishes, and bananas, Daigorou unlocked the door. The chatter of animals filled the cold air.

Max had never visited the Tokyo Zoo. He heard the rumble of gorillas who stared at them from behind shock-proof glass. A leopard stalked over logs and brush. Max wondered what sort of fantasies they constructed, watching families wander down the zoo paths. Dreams of success, perhaps: a leap over the fence, a chase behind the concession stands, then blood mixing with discarded candy wrappers and paper cups.

At a large glass wall, near the quiet end of the zoo, they propped the body against a gingko tree.

"I'll carry it from here," Max said.

Daigorou bent over, hands on his knees. He looked up, through the smeared lenses of his black hornrims. Naoki lit another cigarette.

"It's okay," Max said. "I'll be fine."

The climb was steep and difficult, but by the end, Max perched atop the ginkgo tree, his wrapped body resting on a nearby limb. Low growls rose through the dark. It began to snow. He shimmied to the end of his branch. Below, he imagined the pregnant Sumatran tiger waiting in the underbrush. They were fed during the day but Naoki insisted Sumatran tigers hunted at night.

    Max pushed the body. He listened for its landing. Then a quiet pounce, the scuttle of leaves in its wake.

MR. TODD AND THE GIBSON GIRL

Seven days ago, a one-hundred-mile grin opened in the earth from Salinas to Atascadero. I have lived at the Satellite Hotel since then, one of the few buildings in downtown Los Angeles unscathed by the quake. The airports are closed and I cannot return home—Susan waits for me, sitting in our Upper West Side condo, watching news of our ruin like the old days of war, when gentry picnicked atop a hill while battles raged below.

Now I am eating dinner at Grill 7, on the top floor of the Satellite Hotel, in a large round space with 360 degrees of floor-to-ceiling windows. It's midnight and a half-Asian girl sits near me. We are the only hotel guests in the room. The décor is brushed nickel fixtures and art deco patterns—Fritz Lang by way of Martha Stewart. Flickering LED candles sit on every small table. The bartender refills my scotch, wipes the bar, then brings me dinner: chicken and asparagus.

I pluck an asparagus spear from my plate and hold it up. "I should have known."

The girl turns to me. Her lips are thin and her hair is in a ponytail. She has an angular face but her cheeks are high and full; Japanese blood softened, perhaps, by an Irish father. She sips a Gibson. The bartender and I both know she's far too young for that drink—she could be sixteen, or seventeen at the most—but we are in the middle of a small apocalypse. Conventional standards no longer apply.

"Sorry?" the girl says.

I nod at the spear. "See this line, where they cut the stalk? Asparagus should never be cut. It should be broken—the fracture point will snap where it needs to."

"Hmm," she says.

"At least the flavor is decent." I look at her martini. "You know, I can't tell you the last time I ordered a Gibson."

"They remind me of my dad," she says.

Her eyes are green. Freckles scatter across her nose. She wears black leggings and a pink sweatshirt. Her black ballet flats are scuffed.

"Is your father staying in the hotel?" I ask.

She shakes her head. "My mother and I live down the street. Well, not anymore—our building got flattened. But she doesn't care. She's been in Prague since June."

"She must be very worried."

She shrugs. "I guess. She didn't even ask about my guppies. I had a whole tank."

I sip my scotch. She bites her lower lip and plays with the stem of her drink. Then she says, "Are you scared?"

"No."

"Not even a little? The news said we should avoid tall buildings."

"There is very little chance of structural collapse. If that's what you're asking."

"That is what I'm asking," the girl says. "We're thirty stories up."

The bartender stops wiping the bar and stares at us. I take two coasters, and two cocktail onions from the condiment tray. I place the onions between the coasters and lay them on the bar.

"The foundation of this hotel is an isolated base," I say. "Imagine the bottom coaster is slightly concave, forcing the onions to pitch toward the middle. Any shock to the foundation is dispersed by the ball bearings—in this case the onions—and the design utilizes gravity to self-correct."

"How do you know all this?" she says.

"In a moment. The isolated base design does have limitations, of course." I look at the bartender. "The recent earthquake measured 6.9, correct?"

"That sounds right," he says.

"And 6.9 is more than enough to overwhelm any buffeting system. But because the severity of any quake varies according to bedrock thickness, water table proximity, et cetera, our hotel was spared serious damage."

She frowns and sips her drink. "I still think it's crazy to be up here."

"No shit," the bartender says.

"My mom got me a room," the girl says. "She insisted on a ground-level suite, near a stairwell."

"Excellent advice," I say.

The girl sets down her drink. "Okay. Your moment's up. Tell me how you know all this stuff."

"I'm an architect."

"That's cool."

"It has its moments."

"Do you work out here?"

"New York. I'm a professor."

"Ever build anything famous?"

"I am what they call a 'paper architect.' Which means my designs have never been built."

"That sucks."

"It's quite common."

She reaches over and takes an asparagus spear from my plate. "It still sucks. That's like being a writer and having a bunch of novels you've never sold."

"Well, I've sold many designs."

She bites the asparagus, then she smiles and flops one arm on the bar.

"Most architects have never had any of their designs built," I say.

She finishes the asparagus and licks her fingers. "I'm Rebecca." She smiles.

"Mr. Todd," I say, and I give her a napkin before shaking her hand.

I am lying on the couch in my hotel suite and Rebecca is sleeping in my bed. It is seven a.m.. I watch the morning news—some say the one-hundred-mile crevasse will widen all the way to Arizona; others say that seismic activity has ceased and the threat is past. *Crevasse* is not the right word, because *crevasse* only applies to rifts in glacial ice. One should use *chasm* or *cleft* to describe what has happened to Los Angeles. One could also use *clusterfuck*, and I would not argue.

Rebecca and I parted ways after her second Gibson. She asked for my cell number; I told her that would be inappropriate, and she laughed.

"Don't be ridiculous," she said. "It might be the end of the world, but that doesn't mean I'd sleep with a guy old enough to be my father."

At three a.m. I received a text.

Its Rebecca. What r u doing?

Watching a John Hughes movie.

Which?

The one where confused teens manage to come together despite their differences and gain an understanding of why adulthood is so hard.

Cool.

Ten minutes later she is at my door. Pillow clutched to her chest. Barefoot. Hair down.

"I can't sleep," she says. "Can I watch TV in your room?"

Eventually she closed her eyes, TV flickering, volume low, pillow still clutched to her chest. She looked very young in my bed. Her lips are plain and she has the hands of a child, small and pink. I watched the TV flash across her face, her eyes moving beneath closed lids. REM sleep is a luxury I have not experienced in days. I can only nap for a few minutes at a time, like a nervous cat.

After the early morning news I call the airport and a recorded voice tells me that flights to LaGuardia are still canceled. I leave a message for Susan on our home machine: *You were right. I should have stayed home. There are thousands of architects living in Los Angeles, and all of them adore the sound of their own voice. All of them can lecture on Robert Venturi and Charles Willard Moore.*

Rebecca yawns, stretching her thin arms overhead as sunrise uncovers the ruined city outside my window. Roads glitter with glass and crushed cars clot the sidewalks. Sheared buildings lean crooked, and everything they once held is vomited on to the street—papers, desks, chairs, potted plants, rugs, sheetrock, toilets, computers, coffee machines, phones, lamps, and books. Thousands of books, most of which, I imagine, are about writing screenplays. Centuries from now those books will occupy their own geological strata, like Los Angeles's version of the trilobite.

"Oh my God my breath is *terrible*." Rebecca sticks out her tongue. "I ate so many of those little onions."

"Are you hungry?"

She shrugs. "I could eat."

I order room service and give the boy a generous tip while Rebecca rinses her mouth in my bathroom and pins up her hair. We sit at a small table in the middle of my suite and share a platter of eggs and capers. After her glass of orange juice she says:

"I broke up with Brian last night." She takes another bite of eggs, lips pulled back from her teeth. I can hear the enamel clack against the tines. "I was thinking about what you told me at the bar. Remember when you said that you first have to build up a relationship before destroying it?"

"I don't remember saying that."

"Well, you did. After your third scotch."

"That's unfortunate. Too much alcohol makes me didactic."

This is where Susan would say, *Is there anything that doesn't make you didactic?* But Rebecca doesn't cut me down, because she wants to believe my ridiculous advice.

"I blamed it on the quake," she says. "I told Brian tragedy puts life into focus."

"Did I also tell you that?"

"No. My mother told me that a few years ago, right before she divorced my dad. They found a lump on her breast—it wasn't anything, but it scared the shit out of her. So she left my dad and went to Prague, with the guy who photographs her installations."

"Is your mother an artist?"

Rebecca nods. "She's famous. She did that breast cancer piece in Keuka Park."

"I'm not familiar with it."

"Cassandra Callas. That's her work name. The piece was all over the news. It was a sculpture of a giant, rotting tit with a huge scalpel stuck right in the middle. Are you sure you've never heard of it?"

I pluck a caper off the napkin in my lap and place it on the edge of my plate. "I'm certain."

"Well, Brian and I were doomed, anyway. I can't stay in any relationship for more than a few months. I already warned him, when we first started seeing each other."

"Maybe your inability to remain committed is a consequence of the divorce."

"You think? Wow. Such insight. Do you have any kids?"
"No. Everything I know about children is theory."
She smiles. "Then you probably don't know anything."
"Correct."
"So you're...a paper parent."
"Correct."

She smiles again and takes another bite of eggs. I look around my generically modern hotel room—a Barcelona chair, a trio of maple cubes, a framed print of a chaise longue near a swimming pool—and think of the chasm in the earth, fifteen miles due east.

It is afternoon and I run past destroyed juice bars with their white counters covered in ceiling tiles and dust, past tilting banks with shattered front doors and split walls, past a dozen pulverized coffee shops. They all remind me of Susan. I think about her short dark hair she always struggles with, never achieving that perfect Audrey Hepburn bob. I think about her inexplicable affinity for franchise restaurants and our disdain for anyone who mourns cultural obsolescence—turntables, bell-bottoms, Richard Marx—because they mistake nostalgia for quality. We met in a coffee shop, and we ate lunch in a coffee shop after discovering her pregnancy failed. Bookended by yoga coming into fashion, and bisphenol A going out.

I stop running at the end of a street, and bend over to catch my breath. The air smells of cement and sunlight. Construction crews pick their way through the rubble, big men in orange vests bark into cellphones and wave down bulldozers. They have erected scaffolding along the side of Richard Candee's office tower—he's been dead for six years but I know he'd feel some vindication, because his final project still stands. He named it The Valiant. No one notices me as I walk through its bent front doors.

The lobby is enormous—a marble-floored glass-and-steel cathedral soaked in light—with carpets the size of putting greens and a waterfall where children are meant to toss change into the collecting pool. The entire floor is covered in broken glass, and the furniture is enshrouded in glittering dust. The load-bearing beams that span the ceiling—imagine a dinosaur's rib cage—have buckled, but they still hold. For all of Richard's complaints about monumentalism, he went big in his old age. Male butterflies will always ignore a ready female in favor of a giant piece of colored cloth.

The Valiant won Richard the Stephen Halpern Award. I was shortlisted that year, for my design of a tubular apartment complex with a central urban farm at the base. Critics praised my marriage of brutalism and whimsy, and a New Jersey firm announced they would begin construction within the year. Funding was withdrawn six months later. These things happen all the time.

I'm wearing a white bathrobe and sitting in a black leather chair in the hotel locker room, when Rebecca calls. The news shows footage of the chasm—helicopters circle like wasps, blinking traffic cones line the edge for miles.

"What are you doing?" she says.

"Resting. I just got back from a jog."

"Did you see any bodies?"

"Of course not. They've taken them all away. Where are you?"

"On my living room floor. In the sun."

"In your apartment?"

"Yes. I lied. It's not totally ruined. There's a big crack in the dining room wall, and almost all the windows are shattered. But no one's here. It's so quiet."

"You shouldn't be there. The foundation might be compromised, and the roof could collapse."

"Okay."

"I'm serious. Get out. Now."

"*Okay*. Sheesh. I'm walking to the front door."

A pause. Then she says, "Brian called me today, but I haven't called him back."

"Maybe you should."

"Maybe you should call your wife, and tell her I slept in your bed. I wonder what she would think of that."

"Nothing. Because nothing happened."

"Thank God," she says, and I smile because she's trying too hard.

I watch the news. People hold up photos of lost loved ones. A female reporter offers her shoulder to a weeping man, and she drops her microphone as he collapses in her arms.

"Do you have a car?" Rebecca asks.

"I do."

"Would you mind picking me up?"

"Not at all, if I can navigate the streets. Are you outside yet?"

"Yes."

"Promise?"

"I said *yes*, okay? And the streets are mostly clear. We're in a rich neighborhood, so they've been working on it."

"Give me fifteen minutes."

The streets have been restricted for service vehicles only, but no one flags me down. Police talk with firemen, construction workers talk with EMTs, and the occasional L.A. beach bum—shaggy blonde hair, long shorts, muscle shirt billowing in the wind—cruises past on his bicycle, weaving around fallen traffic lights and chunks of cement spiked with rebar. A woman walks her dog. A businessman talks on his phone, briefcase in hand, forehead knit in concentration as he steps over mounds of glass and steel.

I park in front of her building. Rebecca sits on the stoop. She wears jeans and a white T-shirt, and she's tossing pieces of broken glass across the street, trying to skip them off the pavement like stones on a pond.

"I need to grab some things," she says. "Do you want to come inside?"

A dump truck rumbles past the end of the street.

"It's not safe," I say.

She rolls her eyes. "For the next ten minutes it is. Come on."

Her apartment is spacious and sunny, with polished hardwood floors and a terrace overlooking downtown. Everything is lying on the floor: the television, a clock radio, framed photographs and unframed paintings, a shattered fish tank with Day-Glo pink gravel and dried curls of guppies. Rebecca picks up a photo in the front hallway, shaking the broken glass from its frame.

"This is my mom," she says, "from a few years ago. She's in Aspen in this shot, right before she busted her leg. She had to get twelve pins."

"Your mother is very pretty."

"I know. She used to be a model. When she was my age."

Rebecca drops the picture and shrugs. "I don't have any photos of my dad here. Isn't that weird? He got all the albums. I guess I could ask for some scans."

A crack runs along the dining room wall. Plaster dust coats the floor. A breeze whispers through the apartment, and I envision the entire building folding in on itself.

"We should leave," I say. "Do you need help carrying anything?"

Rebecca shakes her head. "My mom wanted me to take some of her work. I'll just tell her I couldn't. I'll tell her it was all ruined.

We drive into the hills, where the developments are named after whatever flora and fauna builders destroyed to make room—Coyote Pass, Cedar Brook, Deer Walk. We open the windows and listen to a Top 40 station. Rebecca texts, sings along with the radio, and talks to me about the day the quake struck.

"I didn't even fall off my bike. I just felt a big *thump*, and then this really weird sound…it was like the noise a bomb makes. Not the *boom*, but everything that happens next. Glass breaking and metal breaking and car alarms going crazy, and people screaming. A lot of screaming."

"I was asleep," I say. "I woke up to watch the skyline change."

She stares out the window. "I stayed in the park, sat down near my bike, and just waited. I felt like I was the only calm person in the whole city—everybody was running. Where were they going?"

"To check on their families."

"Whatever. It's not like anybody could do anything. Whoever was in those buildings is gone. They're all…*squashed*."

We pass by gated driveways and shadow-banded privacy walls. I wonder if anyone is home, or if they have all fled.

"Why don't you have any kids?" Rebecca says.

I glance at her. "Because it didn't work out that way."

"Oh."

"We tried for years. We didn't succeed. So we moved on."

Suddenly we are on a narrow road, dappled with sun. Thin, towering trees loom on either side.

"I didn't mean to make you upset," Rebecca says.

"I'm not upset."

"Okay. Good. Can I ask you something else?"

"Sure."

"Is your wife…you know…"

"Infertile?"

She nods.

"There is nothing wrong with my wife. We started too late and ran out of time."

"What about adoption?"

"What about it."

"Well, my mom thought about adoption, because she couldn't have any kids after me. Can you imagine how many orphans are in Los Angeles now? You could probably go home with a few babies."

"It isn't that simple."

I am certain she will say something else, but instead she remains quiet. The narrow road darkens in the dense forest.

"I think we're lost," she says.

"No. We're going on a field trip, to Ken Masanobu's coffee-table house."

"What's a coffee-table house?"

"It's a house that looks like a coffee table."

She rolls her eyes.

"I've only seen it in photographs," I add. "Ken Masanobu designed six identical homes for select clients, and he lives in the prototype. The genius in Masanobu is the lack of a single passive factor in his design. Nowhere does an opening occupy the foreground; everything is determined by contrast."

"You've lost me."

"Just listen. A traditional home separates the outside from the inside, with its walls used for support. Masanobu uses walls as supporting *points*. His work is plasticism at its most pure."

"Okay."

"Do you understand?"

"Not at all."

A man runs through the trees; as we drive past I realize he's a metal sculpture. More of the same follows: the man jumping, the man landing, the man running again. The last sculpture shows the man bent over with fatigue, hands fixed to his knees, head up and mouth open.

The forest clears and Ken Masanobu's house slides into view. Small hedges clipped into tight, green cubes line the white cement path, from the circular driveway to the front door. The roof should be long and slightly upswept on one end, shades of the Katsura Imperial Villa's Shokin-tei. The front of the house should be all windows, reflecting the forest, the sky, and the surrounding hills, while making it possible to see through the house, to the backyard. The first impression should be that of a balanced relationship of unequal parts, the equality of these parts resting upon the balance of their dissimilarity, not similarity. The house should be many things, but there is a giant boulder sitting in the middle of it.

A crow lands on top of the boulder. The windows are all shattered, dark like hollow eyes. The roof—Masanobu's crowning glory—is now a jumble of scrap wood and shingles. It looks no different from any other destroyed house. Not even a hint of his aesthetic remains.

"*Squashed,*" Rebecca whispers.

A slender man kneels by one of the hedges. He wears dark herringbone pants and a thin charcoal sweater, and his black hair is cut short. His glasses rest atop his high cheekbones. His ears are set close to his skull. He is barefoot.

I park halfway up the driveway and the slender man turns to us. Rebecca finishes a text.

"Is that Ken Masanobu?" she asks.

"It is."

"He looks…*cool.*"

"Just don't tell him that," I say, as we exit the car.

Masanobu carries a small branch clipper. He stares at us.

"I'm Phineas Todd," I say. "From New York. I was lecturing on Moore and Venturi, when the quake hit."

"My city has been murdered," Masanobu says.

"Not all of it. Candee's Valiant still stands."

Masanobu takes off his glasses. "How tragic." He rubs the lenses with the bottom hem of his sweater. His eyes are small and dark. He puts his glasses on and clasps his hands behind his back.

"Your house is beautiful," Rebecca says. "I mean, the boulder obviously screwed everything up. But I can still see what it was like. It does look like a coffee table."

"I never understood that designation," Masanobu says. "Why would I want to live in a coffee table?"

Rebecca shoots me a look, and I shrug. I hear a jet cutting across the clear sky. The crow caws, then takes flight.

"My wife also thought it ridiculous," Masanobu says. "She wanted to move back to Connecticut. She said she missed her family, she hated this house, and the hills made her nervous. Because of the rock slides, you see. But they were always little rocks. Perfectly formed. I used them to build a wall in the back. There was never any danger. She refused to believe me."

He plucks something off the front of his sweater, and smoothes the wrinkle left behind. "So the coffee table is finally destroyed," he continues. "Even with all her lingering animosity, I cannot imagine my wife would take any pleasure in what has happened."

"Is your wife here?" Rebecca asks.

Masanobu frowns. "We divorced years ago. Though I wonder if she'll send a card. She was always so particular about sending the appropriate card."

"I'm staying at the Satellite," I say. "We can give you a ride, if you need—"

"There's too much to do," he says. "I must finish trimming the hedges, and my pool is covered with leaves and pine needles. They clog the filter, which strains the motor." He extends his hand. "I wish you had come a week earlier."

"These things happen," I say.

He smiles. "Do they?"

Rebecca and I drive back to the city between steep, burnt-brown hills, downtown in the distance jutting from the land like a bucket of metal and glass spikes. The sun sets, from yellow to coral to blood.

Rebecca answers her phone, rolls her eyes, and mouths *Brian* to me. She listens while picking her toenails. She tells him about Masanobu's house, how it used to look like a giant coffee table until a boulder smashed it to pieces. Then she taps my arm.

"Brian says hi."

"Hello," I say, and she laughs. She tells Brian she'll be around later, and she closes her phone.

"Let's go to the big hole," she says.

"You mean the chasm."

"Whatever. It's a big hole. Let's *go*. Seriously."

In twenty years I imagine the chasm will be lined with tourist traps: chasm-themed restaurants, casinos, museums, and gift shops.

"It's probably not safe."

"Oh, please. Don't be like that. Some of the highways are open—I saw it on the news. People go to the hole—I mean, *the chasm*—every night."

She plays the radio loud, feet up on the dash, her glossy red toenails rocking side to side with the beat. The city floats past. My first night it kept me safe and cozy with its warm glow and well-lit streets. Now it is mostly dark, lit only by emergency lights and construction crews.

She turns down the radio and rests her head against the window. Flashes of passing car headlights slip off her face.

"I lived in the Valley," I say. "A long time ago."

"Were you an architect then?"

"I was an apprentice. I also worked a few side jobs."

"I can't imagine you with a side job."

"I was a copywriter for a gourmet bottled water company."

Rebecca looks at me as though I'd suggested the moon was made of felt.

"I was quite good at it," I say. "'This water, taken from Andalusian springs, bursts with mineral citrus, balanced by notes of fresh ice, crushed pine needles, and the sensation of crisp celery at first bite.' I wrote that for a product line from Jersey."

"Sounds pretty good."

"Not good enough. The company folded after a year."

"Is that why you left?"

"I left because I was ready for something different."

"And then you met your wife."

"I met my wife here. In a coffee shop near Quarter Park. She too was ready for something different."

"How romantic," Rebecca says, without a hint of sarcasm. "I hope I meet someone I can leave with."

"You have time."

She slumps in her seat and traces her finger down the window. "I don't know. I'm very picky."

"You should be picky. You have a lot to offer."

We both say nothing for a few minutes. I exit the highway. Then she says:

"I knew the earthquake was coming."

"Are you psychic?"

She frowns. "Don't make fun of me. I'm being serious."

"So am I."

"I'm not psychic. But I knew it was coming. That's why I went for a bike ride. I figured it was safer, being outdoors. I just knew it was going to be something big. Ever since my mother got an apartment in Prague, I've had a feeling that a huge event was going to change my life."

"Well, you got it."

"Great."

"Maybe you should use this opportunity. Join your mother and leave everything behind."

She sighs. "There's nothing for me to leave behind. My friends suck. I work two days a week in the mall, at a kiosk, selling customized sweatshirts. I don't even need the money."

"I've often wondered about those mall kiosks," I say. "They seem so depressing."

"They *are* so depressing. You know the only thing that makes me happy? Getting stoned, then eating Jell-O at Jerry's Famous Deli."

"Susan and I used to eat there. They do have excellent Jell-O."

"Not anymore." She stops, turning her head away. Her shoulders hitch.

"Are you crying?" I ask.

She wipes her cheek with her sleeve. "How insightful."

I'm about to say something—some comforting advice, or maybe an anecdote about my years as an angry young man—when it appears before us. A slight rise in the road, flashing warning lights, police tape, a scattering of parked cars and trucks and empty beer cans. The yawning dark. The night sky dropped to earth. The chasm.

We park next to a Jeep with Colorado plates and walk in silence up the buckled blacktop. I'd expected a secured area in a one mile radius, packed with police cruisers and buzzing with choppers and the crackling static of walkie-talkies; instead the road simply ends, and the area is roped off, with pink spray painted symbols on the pavement—those indecipherable arrows, lines, and half-words left for utility companies —and half-crushed traffic cones with dim blinking lights. The earth has swallowed itself. Road, trees, land—it all suddenly ends in a black line beyond which lays a dark ocean. I see lights on the other side, waves of glowing dots, where I imagine people stare at our side and see the same thing. Walking to the edge of the chasm is easy; the aluminum highway railings set up all along the edge make it seem as though we're hiking on a mountaintop road.

We stop at the crest of a small hill and stand near a single tree. The air smells old, like long-buried roots and rocks. Rebecca stares at the expanse, hands on her hips.

"What do you think?" she says.

"It's dark."

"It's beautiful." She picks up a stone and throws it into the chasm. "Do you think if you fell, you would die of thirst before hitting the bottom?"

"I don't think so."

She answers her phone and walks away, staring down at her feet, kicking through dirt and pebbles. I stand near the tree, alone, watching the dark. Then I hear footsteps behind me, and I turn to see an old man walking up the small hill.

He's wearing an overcoat with plaid pajama bottoms and tan slippers. When he reaches the top of the hill, he snorts and spits. His hair is thin and uncombed.

"Drove from Encino," he says. "Had to see it."

Rebecca laughs into her phone. The old man looks at her.

"Well," he says. "There's something. She with you?"
"She is."
"Seems like a happy girl."
"She's trying."
Rebecca waves at me and I wave back.
"Anyone who can laugh in the face of this is doing all right," the old man says. "You must be proud."
"Thank you," I say. "We are."

SIMULACRUM

Henry Seton had a simulacrum of himself constructed, which he would place in his stead whenever his notoriously ill moods saw fit. Dinner, a night at the movies, a trip to see long-lost cousins—all these events Henry Seton's simulacrum enjoyed, with his wife at his side and three children in tow. The simulacrum was an artist's representation of Henry Seton, and, thus, was imperfect. Henry's sharp features were sculpted soft, his posture had been reduced to sloping shoulders and a hunched back, and his resonant voice was flattened, like a recording played in a padded room. Yet his imperfect imitation was accepted, and in time, friends and family saw Henry's simulacrum as Henry himself.

Years later, after Henry had traveled the world by ship while his simulacrum maintained a responsible domestic life, Henry found himself back home. He returned a different man: graying hair, skin roughened and tanned by sun and sea spray, a limp from a knife wound suffered in Kamchatka. Walking past the homes he'd once called neighbors, he expected things would look much different. But it was all still there—the Milligan's blue house with a picket fence in need of a paint job, the Irving's yellow house with its pulsing sprinkler—and to Henry it appeared as though time had stopped when he left, and was now slowly creaking to life with his return.

He knocked on his front door. He noted the blueberry bushes at the edge of the lawn and the towering ash tree that had tripled in size since the morning he left. His wife stood in the threshold.

She wore a green housedress and was barefoot, her feet soft and pale, the color of stripped bark. She put her hand to her chest.

Henry gazed at his wife's wrinkles with sympathy. He imagined her years had been wasted staring out the kitchen window at the ash tree, watching its branches fork and lengthen, its leaves sprout and unfurl and shudder and fade. Time was so hungry, Henry thought; it ate without pause, leaving behind hollowed bones. He felt he could see these bones scattered around his wife's feet.

I assume my simulacrum has taken good care of you, Henry said to his wife.

Your simulacrum has been gone for ten years, she said.

Henry sighed. The artist warned me it might run away. He said sometimes they become aware of what they are, and they long for other places.

Your simulacrum didn't run away, she said. It died.

Henry's wife explained how their youngest daughter had fallen into a lake while boating with friends, and the simulacrum—standing on shore, letting the sun warm its rubbery, peach-colored skin—heard her cries and ran into the water. No one had taught it how to swim; it drowned without realizing the necessity of oxygen, confused even as water filled its small lungs. The simulacrum's body was recovered later that day, caught in the reeds, its swollen face locked into an expression of wonderment.

Henry listened to his wife's other stories. They were a diary of the ordinary, filled with birthdays and graduations, career changes and surgeries, betrayals and reconciliations.

All told, his wife said, we've had a good life. Your simulacrum treated us well. We mourned its loss, not because it resembled you, but because it remained true to its creation.

Henry sat on the front step. He already missed the white scour of waves, the echo and circle of gulls, the musk of port cities. He stared across the lawn, at the ash tree with its slatted shadow thrown long over the grass. He remembered the day he left: a hurried morning, filled with visits to his banker, his financial advisor, and his insurance company. His final visit had been to the artist's home, a loft in an old mill with painted cement floors and windows running floor to ceiling. There, standing in the glare of afternoon sun, the artist told Henry that construction of his simulacrum needed more time. The simulacrum's capacity for emotion was too simplistic; in its present state it could not function as a member of the community, much less as a husband or a father.

Henry spoke to his unfinished simulacrum later that day, on their way to the harbor.

You cannot possibly understand my reasons for leaving, Henry said. Yet my family will ask you to explain, and you will feel a responsibility to answer. So tell them this: I have lived two lives as long as I have been a husband and a father. There's the wisdom of my unsatisfying life.

Henry ordered his simulacrum to help load his trunks onto the steamer vessel. Then they sat in a small pub at the end of a cluttered alley, and shared a drink and a meal while waiting for the ship's crew. People passing by their table in the darkened corner of the bar asked if they were twins, and Henry told them: Yes, we are, but I'm the handsome one. Henry remembered sharing a laugh with one such person, and the simulacrum had smiled dumbly. Not so dumbly, however. Henry recalled a tilt to its imperfect smile and a glimmer in its dull, milky eyes.

Henry stared across his lawn. He had killed a man in Bushehr, slept with the daughter of a prince in Karachi, stolen a fortune in gold in Porto Alegre. The bones of his memories were not hollow, he felt. There was no need to toss them aside. Nourishment could still be found.

His wife tapped him on the shoulder. I suppose you want to see the children.

If they will see me.

I can't guarantee anything.

He closed his eyes and listened. The chirp of sparrows sounded familiar, like the cries of a gull circling high over a ship's mast. His own breathing, rhythmic and strong, like the white scour of waves against a ship's hull. And the grass-and-sun-baked smell of the suburbs. He spoke to his wife with his eyes closed: I'll try tell you the story of my life, but I'm worried the memories will dissolve the moment I grasp for them. They will fade as if I were telling you a dream, as if I have been watching my life through a mirror, and now that I am ready to look away, I can't remember which is me and which is my reflection.

Maybe you are another simulacrum, his wife said. A better simulacrum that has made its way back here, to what was your home.

He opened his eyes. He had heard whispers of such a possibility: simulacrums made in such perfect imitation of their owners that they suffered the same longing for escape. But Henry had believed his simulacrum was unfinished. The artist warned him it could not function as a member of the community, much less as a husband or a father.

Suddenly everything was in bright focus: his wife's bare feet, the branches of the blueberry bushes, the sidewalk. Henry felt his pockets for his wallet. He looked at his shoes and tried to remember where he'd bought them. Bushehr? Karachi? Porto Alegre? Down the street?

I called out for you when you ran into the lake to save our daughter, Henry's wife said. But you didn't look back, even as you realized you were drowning. You kept going. It was your most courageous moment.

Henry stood, slowly, and limped across the lawn, toward the ash tree. He strained to hear the echo of gulls. The threshing of waves. He touched the trunk of the ash tree and tried to remember the last time he'd run his fingers across its smooth bark.

All those years on an ocean vessel, Henry said to the tree. All those years and I never learned to swim.

QUARRY

Sam saw the owl a day earlier, resting in the eaves of the barn. Their father had left for market and so Henry got the Browning and stood on a hay bale, stock set against his bony shoulder. He squeezed the trigger between breaths like his father had shown him. The owl fell in a storm of feathers and Henry set down the gun. He grabbed the bird by its tiny, curled feet.

"It didn't hurt anybody," Sam said. He stared up, at the motes swirling in stalks of morning light.

"We lost eight chickens last month," Henry said. "And it wasn't from a fox."

"How do you know?"

"Dad said a fox leaves a trail, but a bird of prey takes the whole damn thing."

"You said *damn*."

"So. You just said it too."

Henry inspected the owl. The 20-gauge had made holes in the rump and neck, but the face was unspoiled; he would clean and stuff it, and have it ready for his father.

Sam smoothed the tail feathers. They were soft as velvet and left a dusty sheen on his fingers.

"Maybe Dad will let you have it, when I'm done," Henry said.

"I'd put it over my door."

"That would look good," Henry said.

"Can I help?"

"No. There's other things that need finishing."

"But you—"

"But nothing. Fetch me the arsenic soap, if you want."

Sam crossed his arms. "Fetch it yourself."

Henry shrugged and left the barn, owl in hand, shotgun propped against his shoulder. Sam glared at his brother's back, and shivered even though he tried not to; the morning was bitter cold.

Henry set the bird on his desk. Through his bedroom window he could see the field where Sam now worked, digging out rocks from the ground softened by Indian summer and carrying them to the well near the forest's edge. The well was dry and they'd been dumping rocks in it for as long as they could remember. Years before, peering over the edge with Sam, his brother had asked him if the well had a bottom, or if it just kept going.

Henry watched Sam kneel on the dirt, and figured he was playing with the sluggish beetles he'd uncovered, using his finger to make them crawl in circles around the sockets of earth. Henry wanted to start work on the owl but it would have to wait. First a cup of coffee, and then he'd lift the heavy rocks his brother could not.

Henry frowned and set the water to boil; he sighed as he sat at the kitchen table with a steaming mug. He was fourteen and believed this ritual set him on the correct path to adulthood, because his father did the same thing every morning, preparing his coffee with great seriousness. Sometimes his father talked about common cattle diseases, sitting at the table with the mug held in both hands under his chin. Multiple abortions in the breeding herd usually meant lepto. Lameness and spongy swellings along the shoulders and hips often indicated blackleg. Henry kept quiet during his father's lectures; his sonorous voice and the thick smell of coffee were conversation enough.

Sam banged through the front door and ran into the living room, shouting Henry's name. Henry set down his mug and whistled for him.

"There's a man," Sam said, breathing hard. "In the forest. I think he's dead."

They found the man in a shallow trench along a stand of bare maples. He was missing one shoe and his toenails were dirty. Henry saw a dark hole in the man's thigh, black trails snaking down to the bottom of his blood-stiffened cuff. His brown hair was mashed to his forehead, and bits of dirt stuck to the tips of his eyelashes. His lips were almost white.

Sam picked up a stick and poked the man's shoulder. "Is he dead?"

Henry put his ear to the man's chest. "He's alive. Stop poking him."

"I'm just trying to wake him up."

"You can't. He's hurt bad. We need to bring him inside."

"Why?"

"Because he'll freeze out here. Now hold his arms, and I'll grab his feet."

"What happened to his leg?"

"Doesn't matter."

Sam sniffled. "It's from a bullet. Don't tell me it isn't."

"So what. He was hunting and had an accident."

"He doesn't look like a hunter."

"You don't know a damn thing about anything." Henry grabbed the man's ankles. "If you won't help, I'll do it myself."

The boys worked quickly and quietly. They dragged him from the forest and across the bumpy field. They rested near the broken tractor, the man lying between their feet. Henry wiped his forehead with his sleeve and spat.

"Ready?" Henry said, and Sam nodded.

By the time they'd put the man on the living room couch, Henry thought he might throw up. He ran to the bathroom and waited by the toilet. Sam knocked on the door.

"Go away," Henry said. "I'm sick."

"Is it because of the man?"

"It's because I'm sick. Hurry up and fetch a hot compress for him, and make some tea."

"Dad says that tea is for guests."

"Well, he's a guest, isn't he?"

Henry waited until he heard Sam walk into the kitchen. Then he flushed the toilet, rinsed his face, and took the necessary tools from the medicine cabinet.

Cleaning the wound wasn't as hard as he'd expected; he plucked bits of pant cloth from the clotted hole, and poured alcohol until the blood dissolved and soaked into the gauze like watered-down wine. The man moaned and shifted when Sam put the hot compress on his forehead, and Sam drew back.

"I bet you he's a criminal," Sam said.

"He might be," Henry said.

"Do you think he lost his shoe before he got shot, or after?"

"I don't know."

"If it's before he got shot, then he's just a bum," Sam said. "Walking around with one shoe. Dad won't care if we brought in a bum. Dad likes bums. Remember when we gave that smelly old man a ride to town?"

Henry probed with the tweezers; the man grunted and gripped the couch. His hands reminded Henry of his father's—large and rough, with fine black hairs.

"He looks kind of young for a bum," Henry said, and he

pointed to the man's scarred knuckles. "Those are boxer's lumps. Uncle Frank had them."

They ate an early dinner in the kitchen while the man slept. Sam drank his milk and licked froth off his upper lip, then set the glass down with a bang.

"He's probably hungry," Sam said.

Henry cut a piece of chop. "When he wakes up I'll give him some pork, if he wants. Whose turn is it to scrub?"

"Yours."

"I hate scrubbing."

"Me too."

Sam pushed his corn around on his plate, fork tines scraping.

"Henry?"

"What."

"You think we should get the doctor?"

"Not tonight," Henry said. "It's too cold, and I'm not leaving you here alone."

The man cried out, and the boys ran into the living room to find him sitting upright, glassy-eyed, the front of his shirt soaked with sweat. His hair stuck up at odd angles. He was shivering.

The man dragged his gaze across the room, and stopped at Henry.

"Did I yell something?" the man said.

Henry nodded.

"What'd I say?"

"Nothing. You just yelled."

The man coughed. "Am I in a yellow farm house?"

"You are," Henry said.

"Is your father home?"

"He's at market."

"What's he doing there?"

"Selling cattle."

Sam stood by Henry's side, holding his arm. The man smiled at Sam. His left eyetooth was missing.

"Hello. I'm Jacob."

"I'm Sam Beasley."

"You scared of me, Sam Beasley?"

"Yes, sir."

Jacob slid back down, rested his head on a bolster pillow, and held his wounded leg.

"I couldn't find the bullet," Henry said.

"You dressed it all right." Jacob closed his eyes. "Will one of you boys fetch me something I left in the woods?"

Henry and Sam looked at each other.

"I might," Henry said, but Jacob was asleep.

Cort sat in a booth, sipping coffee thick with sugar and cream. He dumped a handful of coins on the table and watched the diner's parking lot through the window. A week of Indian summer had melted all the snow; now the cold wind returned. The pavement glittered with frost, and car windows reflected the moon. Fields across the road were spiked with broken stalks.

He pondered what had gone wrong. He'd kept it simple, as always—stand in the middle of the road, wait for the bank truck, and level the sawed-off when the driver gets close. But Jacob hadn't frisked the guard properly, and the guard pulled a Chief's Special from his boot, popping off two shots before Cort leapt on him and plunged the blade into his eye. Jacob limped into the woods with the sack of money banging against his side. He moved fast despite being wounded; Cort tracked him until leaves swallowed the blood trail.

Even if the shots proved fatal, Cort figured Jacob was at least a few miles away from where they'd left the truck, and he wouldn't be dead yet. He knew if Jacob was going to come anywhere, it would be someplace like this. A friendly spot, where he could tie off his wounds and ask for a doctor. There would be questions, but Jacob wouldn't care—he was weak, and frightened, and he'd probably confess the world in exchange for a warm bed.

"More coffee?"

Cort looked away from the window. His eyes were small and dark, his black hair cut short. He had thin lips and a thin nose.

"No, ma'am," he said.

The waitress smiled. "We got some fresh pie. Apple and pumpkin."

"Apple'd be nice."

"Whip cream?"

"Yes, ma'am."

She smiled again and walked away. Cort stared at her back, wondering what she smelled like up close and in the dark. Then he returned to the window, and waited.

Jacob woke in the middle of the night. Sam was upstairs, awake in bed, but Henry sat in the living room chair. His father's shotgun lay across his thin thighs. In the dark room lit by the moon, Jacob looked like a dead man, his face drawn, eyes sunk behind large black circles. He moved his hand to the wet, sticky gauze laid over his wound.

"You been sitting here all night?" Jacob said.

"I have."

Jacob grinned. "Watching over me."

"Just watching," Henry said.

"You're being smart. You'd be even smarter if you got my bag from the woods. It's near that old well."

Henry nodded at the bloodied sack sitting on the floor. "I got it."

"Finders keepers," Jacob said.

"I don't want it."

"Your father might."

"He won't."

"We'll see about that."

"We will. He comes back Friday."

"Friday?" Jacob winced and drew in a deep breath. "You don't have that long."

"There's a doctor ten miles south," Henry said. "Our tractor's broke, but I can send Sam first thing. The doctor is good. He fixed my arm a few years back."

"Do you have a phone?"

Henry shook his head. "The lines haven't made it out here, yet. They were supposed to have them done by last year."

"Goddamnit." Jacob rested his arm over his eyes and sighed.

Henry waited. He heard the kitchen faucet dripping into the sink.

"I'm sorry," Jacob said.

"For what?"

"For not dying in a ditch, far from this place."

Henry gripped the butt of the shotgun.

"You know, I killed a woman in Litchfield," Jacob said. "Six months ago. She was young. Younger than me."

Henry imagined his father driving back home, through the night, gripping the steering wheel and staring ahead. *It's just a feeling I got*, his father would say. *My boys are in trouble. I couldn't sleep. Saw their doom in a nightmare.*

That's not how life works, Henry told himself. Stop thinking like a child all the time.

"Funny thing about that woman," Jacob continued. "Wasn't what I expected. You ever watch *Death Valley Days*?"

"We don't have a television."

"Well, that's good. Nothing about it is real. Makes everything look clean. I shot that woman in the throat, and she flopped around for a full minute. The worst thing I ever saw, swear to God. She made these *noises*." Jacob paused. Then he uncovered his eyes and looked straight at Henry. "Take your brother and leave."

"Why?"

"You have to. He's coming."

"Who is?"

"He's looking for his money."

"Who?"

"Goddamnit," Jacob said, and that's all he would say, no matter how many times Henry asked.

Ed's Bar was dim and quiet, the sort of bar Cort preferred because it reminded him of his youth, when he'd sit at a corner booth with a pint of cheap beer, and watch the crowds until closing. Now a small scattering of men sat along the bar, and at tables pushed against the rough plank walls. Cort ordered a beer and took a seat in the back. He sipped and waited.

After an hour, Cort approached a man seated in the far corner.

"You ever make it down to New Haven?" Cort said.

The man glanced up. He wore a baseball cap pulled low, and a felted sweater. Years of farm sun had creased his face. His nose looked like it had been broken several times.

"I'm certain I've seen you there," Cort said. "At Charlie's Tavern. Am I right?"

"Never been to Charlie's," the man said. "Nor New Haven."

"My mistake."

"No harm." The man tipped back his beer and smacked his lips. Cort sat down and rested his elbows on the table. "I'm just passing through. Selling watches, if you can believe that."

"You should keep passing. Nothing here except dogs and ditches. Couple of farms still trying to make it, but give them time. They'll suffer, just like the rest."

"Does that include you?"

"It does."

Cort grinned. "I wonder what our wives would think of us, now. Wasting our days."

The man held up his left hand. Cort held up his own ringless hand.

"Only way to go," the man said.

"You know it."

"I got close, once."

"I didn't," Cort said.

The man looked at Cort.

"What was it you came over here for?"

"A ride," Cort said. "My transmission dropped."

"I thought you were selling watches."

"I am. Selling other things, too."

"What sort of things?"

"That all depends on what you need."

The man paused, glass held in mid-air. "I might help you, provided one of them watches looks good enough."

Cort grinned. "It all looks good."

The man finished his beer, and wiped his mouth with the back of his hand. He looked over his shoulder, at the shadowed room. Everyone sat with their heads down.

Cort followed him to the parking lot. He retrieved his shotgun from a stand of weeds, tucking it under his coat. The man drove a blue Chevy sedan, rust spots over the wheel wells and a long crack across the windshield. They pulled onto the main road and Cort rested his head against the window. He stared at the pale morning sky.

After a few miles Cort said, "I have to piss. You mind pulling off somewhere?"

The man slowed near an elm with a scarred trunk, and killed the engine. He looked in the rearview, at the empty road.

"Bit public, for my tastes," the man said. He dropped his hand to his crotch and left it there.

"I'll be careful," Cort said. He reached into his boot and withdrew a short blade. He turned and thrust it into the man's throat. The man grabbed Cort's arm. He kicked and gurgled as blood streamed down the front of his shirt. Cort pulled out the blade, watched the pump of blood slow to a trickle, then hauled him across the seat and switched places.

After he'd dumped the man by the side of a pond and covered him in a loose scab of leaves and twigs, he rinsed his hands in the icy water and looked to the cloud-covered sun. He walked back to the blue Chevy, drove to the main road, and found the first farm within minutes.

Two men worked in front of a red house; a dog loped across the yard. Cort crept through the bare woods, shotgun low and ready, white breath rising above his head. He didn't mind if the dog smelled him—he figured he could shoot the thing and get back to his car before the owners knew what had happened. Cort sat on a crumbling stone wall and watched the men work, one pushing a wheelbarrow and the other walking in and out of the barn. The scene was perfectly normal, he decided, so he got back in the Chevy.

Before dawn Henry felt better, but Jacob's breathing had turned ragged. Sam stood at the end of the couch and pressed a cool cloth to Jacob's forehead. Henry left the shotgun on the floor and waited by the window, for what, he didn't know—he just felt like staring at the frost-covered fields still lit by the moon.

"I shouldn't have fought with you," Sam said to Henry. "I should have hurried up and helped you carry him."

"You did."

"But I didn't want to."

"It doesn't matter, Sam."

"It does. He's real sick. Is he dying?"

"I think so."

"We should go for the doctor."

"Not until the sun's up. It's too cold."

"But he's dying."

"I know."

"Don't you care?"

"I do." Henry continued staring out the window. "We'll leave at sunrise. I promise."

Sam eyed the bloody bag, sitting on the floor. "What's in the bag?"

"Money," Henry said. "Don't touch it."

"I shouldn't have poked him with that stick."

"It wasn't your stick that hurt him. He was *shot*."

Sam started to cry. Henry stared at the floor. He heard the rattle in Jacob's lungs, and remembered the same sound at his mother's side, when Sam was a baby sleeping in the other room.

"Minute the sun comes up," Henry said, "we'll head out."

"Promise?"

"I promise. And after doc fixes him, we'll finish hauling those rocks. Everything will work out just right. Now go on and take a bath. Make the water good and hot. We got a long walk ahead of us."

Sam glanced at Jacob.

"He'll be okay," Henry continued. "I'll change his bandage

and make more tea."

Sam frowned. "Are you just saying this to make me feel better?"

"No."

"Swear?"

"I swear."

Sam inhaled deeply and scratched his head. "You call me back in if anything happens?"

"I will."

Sam wiped his cheeks and ran upstairs.

This is how it should be, Henry thought, and he picked up the compress. This is what men do for each other.

He wrung the compress into a bowl and re-soaked it. He laid it on Jacob's forehead; the man groaned and opened his eyes.

"Told you to leave," Jacob said. He started to say something else but his voice caught; he coughed and whooped. He inhaled once more and fell slack, mouth open, hands twitching. Henry scrambled back and tripped over the bowl of cold water. He crashed on the floor. The room smelled of shit and sour sweat.

"Pardon me?"

"I said I'm looking for a man. Brown hair, big eyes, young face. Might have a limp."

The woman with her hair in a tight, gray bun looked past Cort's shoulder, to the blue Chevy parked in front of her porch. She drew in her robe and shivered. The living room felt warm at her back, but far away.

"Well, I haven't seen anyone fits that description," she said.

"You sure, ma'am?"

"Of course I'm sure. What kind of silly question is that?"

"It's not silly if you're standing where I'm standing."

Cort narrowed his eyes toward the living room, the warm house, the sound of children playing upstairs. The porch felt small and confining.

"Where's your husband at?"

"He's on a job," she said.

"What's he do?"

"That's none of your business."

"I'm just curious. This is a fine home. Looks like a man of great care lives here."

"He's a carpenter."

"Like Jesus."

"If that's how you want to put it."

"That is how I'm putting it. You checked your barn this morning?"

"Every morning," she said. "Now if you'll excuse me—"

Cort stepped forward, boot toe knocking against the threshold. He stared at a strand of gray hair that had fallen across her forehead. It waved in the cold wind, inquisitive-like.

"Something about my car interests you," Cort said.

"No, sir." Her voice quivered.

"Go on. Tell me."

"I'd rather not."

"Rather doesn't enter into it. Tell me."

The woman drew in a sharp breath. Her daughter squealed upstairs.

"That's Ed Dobber's Chevy," she said.

It was late afternoon and the boys had cleared the rest of the rocks, letting Jacob cool in the living room because they didn't know what else to do with him. For a few hours Henry almost forgot what was waiting for them, back in the house. When they'd dumped the last of the stones, Henry squatted on his heels and looked up at the sky. Sam stood near him, breathing hard in the cold.

"Tomorrow we'll dig a grave with Dad," Sam said, and he sniffed, and put his hands on his hips.

They walked back to the house. Sam fetched the good sheets from the linen closet while Henry stripped Jacob to his underwear and sponged his legs clean. He bundled the soiled jeans into a paper bag and set them by the front door. Sam combed Jacob's hair, slicking it back with some of their father's pomade. Then he wiped Jacob's ears with a washcloth, and folded his arms across his chest. They finished covering Jacob with a sheet when Henry spotted someone walking up the driveway.

The man stopped in front of their house. He wore a long black coat and narrow boots. His eyes were small and dark, like doll's eyes.

"Get upstairs," Henry said to Sam. "Wait in my room, and don't come down until I call for you. No arguing this time. Just *go*."

Sam ran up the stairs as Henry picked the sack off the floor. He spotted the Browning, leaning against the old china cabinet. The man knocked, sharp and loud.

Henry opened the door. Cort stood on the porch, hands in his pockets, eyes narrowed.

"Your father home?"

"No, sir. He's out back."

Cort glanced at the driveway, at the rusted tractor sitting in the field. A cluster of sparrows sat huddled on its hood, chests puffed against the wind.

"Maybe you could go get him for me," Cort said.

"He's working. I'm not supposed to bother him when he's working."

Henry saw a fine spray of dried blood on Cort's neck, and a

spot of blood in his ear.

"I'm looking for someone," Cort said. "Might have come this way."

"I haven't seen anyone."

"Let me finish. He's about yea tall, may have a limp."

"No, sir. It's been me and my brother all day."

"And your father."

Henry nodded. "That's right."

Cort looked back at the driveway. Henry wondered if the man could hear his heart pounding. It was the loudest thing he'd ever heard. It drowned out the wind and everything else. Just his heart, running fast and hard.

"I did find this, though," Henry said, and he grabbed the sack from behind the door and held it out for Cort.

Cort smiled slightly, and opened the sack while Henry held it. Then he took the bag and pulled the sawed-off from underneath his coat. He leveled it at Henry, tilting his head to one side.

Henry stood, frozen.

"You had me fooled," Cort said.

"Take the money."

"Oh, I will."

"Just remember I didn't have to give it to you."

"Yes, you did." Cort rubbed his forefinger against the double triggers. "Where's Jacob?"

"He's dead. We found him in the woods."

"And your brother?"

"In the house."

"Call him."

"I will not."

Cort smiled again. "Call him, son."

Henry tightened his lips.

"You know when I was your age, this was something I wondered about every day," Cort said. "How often you get a chance to see the end before it comes. You ever wonder about that?"

"Sometimes."

"Now that's a shame."

Cort settled back on his heels and lowered the shotgun level with Henry's chest. Something flashed and boomed behind Henry; his right arm stung like hornets and he cried out. Cort stumbled sideways. He squeezed both triggers of the sawed-off. A chunk of the porch exploded. Splinters peppered Henry's legs. The air smelled like firecrackers.

When Henry looked up from his bleeding arm he saw Sam standing on the porch, holding the Browning, smoke curling from the mouth of the barrel. Cort had fallen onto the front gravel path; he lay there, coat shredded and blood blooming across his white T-shirt. Henry knelt by Cort's side and inspected his face. His breathing was shallow. A few pellets were embedded in his cheek.

"You got him," Henry said.

Sam dropped the shotgun, and ran to his brother. Henry let him hug as he gazed across the field, toward the edge of the woods. His arm throbbed and he didn't know how he felt. Sick, or sad, or maybe even excited. Maybe all three.

"Fetch the wheelbarrow," Henry said.

Sam stared down at Cort.

"*Sam.*"

Sam blinked.

"Go on and fetch the wheelbarrow," Henry said.

"But he's still breathing."

"Don't you worry about that."

"They waited a long time."

They pulled Cort out of the wheelbarrow. Henry grabbed him by his belt with his good arm, and hauled him over the lip of the well, as Cort groaned and his eyes fluttered beneath his lids. Sam dropped the sack of money into the yawning hole, watching the white disappear.

"On my count," Henry said.

Sam pressed his hands against Cort's warm side.

"One. Two. Three."

Cort fell. The two boys peered over the edge, staring into the dark, waiting to hear the sound of his body. They waited a long time.

THE MENSCH

"I just knew it." Roman Roth leaned back and drummed his fingers on the armrests. His glass of tonic sat untouched, lemon disc floating among ice slivers, the ceiling fan reflected on its surface. He grinned. The chair creaked. "Minute I finished your story, I told myself: Here's a writer who can take an ordinary situation—say, the two of us, sitting here, in my office—and extract a drama. Is that the correct word?"

Max sat in a small folding chair on the other side of Roman's desk. He looked at the single window, the stuffed bobcat mounted on a log in the corner, the walls covered in movie posters—a bikini-clad blonde holding a flamethrower, a werewolf in a tuxedo under a chuppah.

"You're asking me if extract is the correct word?" Max said.

"I am."

"Extract is good. Though—"

"Can I get you something to drink? An ice water?"

"No, thanks. And *extrude* might be more accurate."

Max watched the drumming fingers—stubby and thick, with square nails cut straight across.

"Extrude," Roman said.

"It's the process of shaping something." Max shifted in his seat. He wore a shirt and tie, collar stiff, his feet sweating in wool socks. Chicago had been cold, but April in New York was hotter than he'd expected; it was sweltering. He hoped his room had decent AC. "The way it works is, I take an idea—"

"A scene."

"A scene, an idea. Anyway, I take—"

"You're sweating like a fat guy, and this is coming from a fat guy." Roman buzzed the intercom. "Julie, please bring Mr. Beeber some water. Lots of ice." He raised an eyebrow at Max. "Lemon?"

"Okay."

"With a lemon slice, Julie. The good lemons." Another raised eyebrow. "We just got a fruit basket from a Florida investor. Ever had a Meyer lemon? *Amazing*. You can suck them like an orange. Julie?"

"Yes?" the intercom said.

"Bring an orange as well." He leaned back, fingers drumming again. His jowls quivered; Max watched a single bead of water run down his thick neck and slip under his collar. "Point is, Beeber, I need your talents. Any other film, ask me if I give a shit. You know my highest grossing title?"

"I don't pay much attention to—"

"*Death Pool*. Did a hundred million worldwide. A psycho makes each victim choose the next by throwing darts at a phone book. Now tell me something, and be honest: Do I look like the sort of man—"

The door opened and Julie walked in, carrying a fruit basket and a glass of ice water with a lemon slice. Max folded his arms across his chest, hoping to cover the half-moons spreading from his armpits.

"Thank you." Max sipped the water and nodded. "It's the perfect amount of ice."

Julie teased a strand of dark hair from her temple and inserted it into the corner of her mouth. Her lips were cherry-soda red, teeth white as a nurse's uniform. She wore heels and a knee-length skirt. "How long are you in town, Mr. Beeber?"

Max looked at Roman.

"As long as it takes," Roman said. "But no more than one week."

"One *week*?" Max said.

"Two months we've been waiting on rewrites. Writers come, writers go—can I skip the hand-holding? Your kind is *soft*. No one can do their goddamn job. This is a page one, but still—we're not extruding the whole goddamn story. Julie, leave the boy alone. He's already nervous. Have you ever seen someone sweat so much?"

"I just wanted to recommend a good dry cleaner," she said. "Your collar, Mr. Beeber. It's icky."

Roman grabbed an orange from the basket and ripped off a curl of skin. Julie walked out. Max rubbed the back of his neck, took another sip, then set the glass on the floor.

Roman paused, peel in hand. "Where was I?"

"You were asking me if you were the sort of man—"

"That's right." He held an orange wedge across the desk. "Suck your slice, then try this."

"My slice?"

"Your lemon slice. Suck on it, then try this."

Max did as he was told. He dumped both rinds in the trashcan.

"Well?" Roman popped a chunk into his mouth.

"The lemon was definitely more sour—"

"It's a goddamn lemon. And these are Valencia oranges, so let's not get too literal. But you get my point. Sweetest lemon you ever tried, am I right?"

"Absolutely. Mr. Roth—"

"Roman, please."

"Roman, I just want to say—"

Roman held up his hand as juice dribbled down his chin. Max watched it patter onto the desk. "Fifty years, Roman Pictures has gotten by on guns and tits," Roman said. "Page one, tits. Page six, guns. Arousal and catharsis. You know all this—you're a writer. But I want this project to be *art*. Thus you, thus this meeting, thus your four, maybe five days fixing what my incompetent schmuck of a director has done. He took my idea—can I call it my life's dream? He took my life's dream, dropped his pants, and shit all over it. You remember what you told me last week?"

"Of course. It was only last week."

"Well?"

Max cleared his throat. "I said I could make your script sing."

"*Sing*." He slapped the desk. "Skinny guy like you, barely thirty years old, with one story in a fancy journal—what was it called?"

" 'Butterflies at Moonlight.' "

"Skinny guy like you writes some story about love and despair in small town America—stop the fucking presses—and suddenly you're telling me you can make my script *sing*. You haven't even read the goddamn pages and you can make it *sing*." He patted his bulging stomach. "But I trust my gut."

"Mr. Roth, to be perfectly honest—"

"Never be perfectly honest. Go on."

"I just want to write a good movie."

"Of course you do. And I want you to write a good movie. And my partners want you to write a good movie." Roman stood, grunting, fists atop the armrests. "I don't care which coast you're on. You won't find another producer that respects writers the way I respect writers, because I appreciate how you extrude—great word—how you *extrude* a compelling scene out of the everyday, and that's the stuff of *art*. Now—" He clapped his hands and kept them together. "I gave you my notes. I gave you the script. Keep it between you and me, understand? Good. Julie will call you a car. It's—" He glanced at his watch. "Almost two, so you're probably eager to get started. Tomorrow morning, then. Let's meet for brunch, say eleven. At The Swan. We'll nosh, have a few drinks, and you can show me your pages."

"Tomorrow morning?" Max said.

Roman nodded.

"Tomorrow morning." Max stood, slinging his shoulder bag. "Eleven. The Swan. Yes. Okay."

Julie sat at her desk, book in hand. A classic cars calendar hung on the wall, every square empty except for one, marked with a heart sticker. Max stared at it a moment, then rubbed the back of his neck and cleared his throat.

"Mr. Roth said you could call me a car."

She turned a page. "I'd rather call you Max."

"What? Oh. Good one."

"You're staying with Mrs. Barclay?"

"Uh-huh."

She glanced up. "What do you think of Shane's script?"

"It's a good start."

"You haven't read it yet."

"I've read the outline. I know it's about redemption."

Julie held up her finger and grabbed the phone. A brief conversation—*yes, he's going to Flatbush, yes, charge it to the Roman Pictures account*—and she hung up.

"Could you give me the name of that dry cleaner?" Max said.

"Excuse me?"

"The dry cleaner. For my icky collar."

"Jimmy Chang's. Right down the street. If you drop off your shirt now, they'll have it done by five."

"But I'm staying in Flatbush tonight."

"Cab it."

"For a shirt? I have other shirts."

"Of course you have other shirts. Do you understand what *all expenses covered* means?"

"I just don't want to be excessive."

"It's a shirt. We're not talking Caligula here." She sighed, sitting back, legs crossed. Her red pump dangled off her heel. "I read your story by the way. A little internal for my tastes, but Mr. Roth fell in love. Obviously. Did your agent submit it?"

"I didn't have an agent. I just sent it in."

"Wow. How lucky is that?"

"Well, I'd like to think talent may have—"

A knock on the door—Max saw an outline through the frosted glass—and Julie buzzed the lock. In walked a wiry man wearing a black T-shirt over jeans. He had thin lips, a narrow face, and dark hair slicked back so tightly it seemed to raise his eyebrows. Max couldn't place his age. He was built like a lightweight boxer, or an outdoor cat.

Julie smiled. "Good afternoon, Mr. Martin."

He brushed past Max and entered Roman's office. The door slammed.

"Teddy Martin," Julie said.

"Seems intense."

"That's one word for it. Teddy's got a thing about people staring at him. If you ever meet, avoid eye contact."

"Who is he?"

"A producer." She lowered her voice. "He moved from London a few years ago. Supposedly he was a rabbi."

"Was?"

She shrugged. "That's the rumor. Anyway. We were talking about your story."

"I'd rather not."

"Okay."

"No, it's—I just don't like talking about my work. People go on and on about how much they loved—"

"I hated it."

"Ah."

"A tortured soul allegedly falls in love with another tortured soul, and through a series of allegedly dramatic events they both allegedly learn something. How original."

Max paused. "Are you a writer?"

"I took some classes at Smith. Is this your first time in New York?"

"I came here once with my father, when I was a boy. We had lunch on the roof of the Empire State Building."

"My God, that's so...sweet."

"I know. I don't travel much. I always thought I'd be the type of writer who travels, but the truth is—"

The intercom buzzed. "Julie?"

"Yes, Mr. Roth?"

"Did you leave a message for Shane?"

"Twice this morning."

"Leave two more. And keep leaving them every hour until that prick calls. *Every* hour."

The intercom clicked off. She smiled. "You should head down to the lobby. If you want to catch your car."

Max re-slung his bag. "Did you really hate my story?"

"I'm a d-girl. I hate everything."

He extended his hand. "Maybe I'll see you tomorrow."

She took his hand slowly, barely letting her fingers touch his. "Only if I'm lucky, Mr. Beeber."

Max walked up the brick pathway to Mrs. Barclay's house, a white mansion with Greek columns along the front and a stable in the back, hidden by fruit trees and a willow. He rang the doorbell. Across the street a boy chased another boy with a squirt gun, both of them screaming. Max watched.

The door opened and he turned. A little girl—pigtails, red

shorts—stood in the threshold. She clutched a sandwich.

"Hello. I'm Max Beeber."

She stared. "I'm not supposed to answer the door."

"Are your parents home?"

"My mom is sleeping."

"Could you tell her that Max—"

"But I'm not supposed to answer the door."

"Well, maybe you could wake your mom, for me."

She took a bite of her sandwich.

"That's a good-looking sandwich," Max said. "What is that? Turkey?"

She nodded.

"Turkey is my favorite," he said.

"You can't have it."

A scream. He glanced over his shoulder. The taller boy had the other cornered and was squirting him in the face, laughing.

Max turned back. "If you could just tell your mom that Max Beeber is here, I'd really appreciate it."

"You can't have my sandwich."

"I don't want it."

"But you said turkey is your favorite."

"It is, but that doesn't mean—"

"You can't have my sandwich."

"I don't want your stupid sandwich."

"It's not stupid. You're stupid."

He rubbed his forehead. "Why don't you close the door, I'll ring again, and this time let your mom answer."

"She's—"

"Sleeping, yes, I know." He stepped back and shouted at the second floor windows. "Mrs. Barclay!"

The little girl took another bite. "Our last name is Swanson. Mrs. Barclay lives in the small house." Then she closed the door.

He continued down the driveway, toward a carriage house with overgrown hedges lining the front. He knocked. Several footsteps later the door yanked open.

A tall, thin man appeared, dressed in shorts and a faded Yakov Smirnoff T-shirt. His black hair was cut close. He was barefoot, with stubble shading his jaw.

Max smiled. "Hi, I'm—"

"I know who you are. Do you swim?"

"Pardon?"

The man put his hands on his hips. "*Swim*. Splash splash. I'm just cleaning the pool. The pH is fine, the chlorine is perfect."

"I didn't bring a suit. It's cold in Chicago."

"We're in Brooklyn."

"I know. I'm *from* Chicago—"

The man grabbed Max's luggage and walked inside. Max followed. The living room was small and dark, tapestries on the walls and the windows covered in thick curtains. A grandfather clock stood in the corner, behind an umbrella stand with dozens of umbrellas, their handles linked by cobwebs.

"You can borrow my shorts." He looked Max up and down. "Or swim naked. My mother doesn't care. She's almost blind."

An old woman's voice echoed from the back. "Thomas? Is our guest here?"

The man shouted, "Yes!"

Mrs. Barclay emerged from the dark, hunched and shuffling, holding a triple-pronged cane. She wore baggy black capris and a turquoise Chinese blouse, her hair trimmed skull-close. "Thomas," she said. "Can you bring a pitcher of lemonade?"

She waited until he pushed through the kitchen door, then she turned to Max and said, "Is Peter autobiographical?"

"Peter?"

"From your story. Peter. Maddy's beau."

Max felt himself blush. "Oh, no. I'm not rich. Or handsome. I mean, I don't think I'm terrible-looking—"

"You're a bit long in the nose." She moved toward him, eyes narrowed. Her hand shook atop the cane handle. "Easily fixed, if that's what you want. Talent alone is nice, but Sylvia Plath showed what one can do with sad songs and cheekbones. What do you think of Shane's script?"

"It's a good start."

"It's an awful start. All directors think they can write. He ruined my story."

"Your story?"

"Isabella Pranikoff is based on me."

"You were in Dachau?"

She nodded. "The character of Bruno Asher is my first husband, Heinrich Holzer. And Heinrich most definitely did *not* listen to Wagner. Shane couldn't even get that right."

Max put his hand to his forehead. "You were in *Dachau*?"

"Yad Vashem won't touch it. But we don't need those bastards." She shuffled past, cane stabbing the floor. "How are Roman's notes?"

"He says the movie is about redemption."

"I like that word. It says so much without meaning anything." She walked to the doorway and peered out. "Look at those dreadful children. All they ever do is run around." She slammed the door. "Do you have any unusual appetites, Mr. Beeber?"

"Well, I'm not a vegetarian, if—"

"You'll find Thomas very helpful. And discrete. Berkley Hammond stayed here in 1967. He was partial to Quaaludes and eighteen-year-old girls. I believe they were called *mandies* at the time. The pills. Not the girls."

"I'm just a food and water guy."

"How clever." She smiled. "Thomas will show you to your

room. Leave whenever you'd like and don't worry about saying good-bye or hello. I can't be bothered."

Thomas returned with a pitcher of lemonade sitting atop a dented silver tray. He handed a glass to Max.

"Tomorrow it rains," Thomas said. "If you want to swim, do it soon."

```
FADE IN

EXT.   EARLY MORNING — DACHAU

BRUNO ASHER, a tall, tight-lipped SS
guard, strides across the grounds,
sweeping his gaze left to right. He's
unmoved by the horrors--children with
their ribs showing, men digging ditches-
-until he sees a beautiful young woman
standing at the bread table. This is
ISABELLA PRANIKOFF. She wears a schmata on
her head. She serves crusts of bread to
the hungry workers.

          ISABELLA
     It tastes better because of the
     spices I added.
```

Max sat at a small desk in the corner of his room, staring at his laptop, chin resting in palm. He'd changed into a wrinkled T-shirt and his socks lay on the windowsill. The room had no air conditioning; instead, a rotating fan stood on the dresser. He closed his eyes, exhaled, then rolled his fingers along the keyboard. After a few more breaths, he typed:

> HUNGRY WORKER
> Spices? What is this spices?

> ISABELLA
> Hush now, Moishe. We don't want
> the guards to hear.

Bruno approaches one of his guards.

> BRUNO
> That woman there...with the
> cloth on her head...

> GUARD
> It is called a schmata. In their
> tongue. Yiddish, yes? They have
> taken our language and poisoned
> it.

> BRUNO
> Who is she?

> GUARD
> (smiles knowingly)
> Isabella Pranikoff.

He picked up his cell phone and dialed, leaning on one elbow, hand over his eyes.

"Paul. It's Max. Listen—what? I'm fine. The room is fine. I'm hot. I didn't pack appropriately. Listen. I've rewritten the first scene and my changes are…honestly, they're terrible. I feel like I'm—no, they *hate* his script. All of it. They want something more audience—what? I'll tell you." He shuffled through Roman's notes. "It says 'skewed female, eighteen to thirty-four, amp the romance.' Less *Holocausty*. That's Roman's word. And more food. A strong push on the food themes. Well, it's about redemption." He scanned the notes again. "They insist I mention Isabella's bread recipe on page one. People are being marched to the gas chamber and we're supposed to care about a bread recipe?" He paused. "You have a Jewish woman falling in love with a Nazi, he discovers her talent for baking, they escape—just hear me out. They escape and open a Jewish bakery in the Bronx. It's inherently—" Another pause. "I understand, Paul. It was a lot of money. But he wants the pages by Friday. That's five days—"

Max listened. He looked down at the desk, at graffiti carved in black ink: *It is hard for thee to kick against the pricks.*

"I understand," Max said. "A lot of money. Paul, can I—can I ask you something and not have you freak out? What are the chances of us re-negotiating with Roman? Okay. That's what I thought."

Max closed his phone and leaned back. Between the curtains he watched Thomas doing laps in the small inground pool, only three strokes long. Mrs. Barclay sat on the deck, asleep in a lounge chair, mouth open, cane standing at attention.

Thomas brought an egg salad sandwich and a gin and tonic for dinner. Max rewrote the first page a dozen times. As the sun set the room grew hotter, air thick with the smell of old wood, baby powder, and mothballs. Max heard scratching in the walls; an inspection of the floor revealed mouse droppings. He found a box of half-eaten rat poison in the closet, next to a wire hanger and a dust-covered earplug. He drank a second gin and tonic, then rested his head on the desk. The laptop fan whirred.

It is hard for thee to kick against the pricks. Below the carved words, he found two more: *Bill Faulkner*.

A knock. Max sat up. Teddy Martin walked in. He looked around the room, eyes narrowed.

"Hot as a cunt in here." Teddy sniffed. "Don't know how you do it. Writing like this. Fat kike should've put you up someplace nice. Waldorf. Four Seasons."

Max closed his laptop. "I don't think we've met."

"Teddy Martin." He walked to the bed and pressed down on the mattress. "You smoke?"

"No. But feel free—"

"Right." He sat on the bed, pulled a handrolled cigarette from his shirt pocket, and wheeled a black Zippo. "Mrs. Barclay treat you well?"

"Yes."

"And that poofty son of hers. What's his name—"

"Thomas."

"He's not giving you the squint, is he?"

"No."

"Good for him. Boy's learned something past few years. Work going all right?"

"A bit slow. But steady."

"Steady Betty. Crack that window. Hot as a cunt." He ashed on the floor. "Look, mate. I'll be honest. Isn't my style beating around. I don't know you. Don't read the mags, fancy journals. Don't give a fuck about agents, critics, whatever. *Story*. That's my Jane. You sure you don't want a smoke?"

"No thanks."

"It's just you're staring at me. Like I got something you want."

Max cleared his throat. "I'm just…listening."

A quick drag. Teddy shot twin streams from his nose. "Only reason me and that fat bastard get along is on account of our shared interest: Story. Got to be compelling. Got to say something. You understand? Course you do. You're a writer. Eleventh writer we've had. Know how many times I've given this speech before?"

"It sounds well-practiced."

"What's that? You think I sit in my car and plan this all out?"

"Mr. Martin—"

"Teddy. I'm not a fucking bank manager. *Teddy*. The Mensch, if you'd like. Mensch is Yiddish. Means an iron man. Crack that window, mate. Don't want to ask again."

Max yanked on the sill. It opened with a screech.

"Eleventh writer," Teddy continued. "I have my way, you're the last one. What do you think of Shane's script?"

Max folded his hands on his lap. "It's interesting."

"Interesting?"

"There are some structural issues."

Teddy flicked the cigarette across the room. "What did Roman say?"

"He said the film is about redemption."

"Fuck all that. What did he say about Shane's script?"

Max grabbed the first page off his desk.

"Verbatim," Teddy said.

"Okay. Here we are." He cleared his throat. " 'A mess. Dull and weepy.' "

"Go on."

" 'Slow-paced, overwritten…' " Max scanned. "And he says more of the same. Teddy, all I'm getting at—"

He held up his hand and cocked his head. "You hear that?" He stood. "Something in the walls?"

"It's mice. I found drop—"

"Shut up." Teddy walked to the middle of the room. After a few moments he squatted at the far corner, ear pressed to the wallpaper. He stood, waited, then wound up and kicked a hole just above the baseboard. Max jumped. Teddy kicked again. Plaster dust plumed. He knelt and thrust his hand into the hole.

"My London flat was infested. I'm like a rat-assassin, all the killing I've done." He pulled out a limp rat by the tail. "The window, mate."

Max watched the swinging rat—black eyes, blood dewed on the whiskers—as Teddy stalked toward the desk. A flick of the wrist, and the little brown body sailed. Max heard a small splash.

"Now." Teddy wiped his hands on his jeans. "You were saying something about Shane's script being interesting. What are you staring at?"

"There's a giant hole in the wall."

"Cause I fucking kicked it in. You were saying."

"I was just saying there are structural issues."

"And you can fix it."

"Absolutely."

"Good. I paid you fair ackers to do this job. You need something—anything—just ask me. That's my job. You stay focused. *Focused.*" He pulled a card from his pocket and handed it to Max:

Teddy Martin
Muse

"Cheers," Teddy said. He clapped Max on the shoulder, turned, and walked out.

Max sat at the desk, card in hand. The dresser fan rotated. The room smelled of smoke.

———

He dreamt of Roman Roth sitting at his desk, eating a giant platter of turkey sandwiches. Behind him Teddy measured the single window. *What are you measuring it for?* Max asked, and Roman smiled, turkey juice dripping down his chin. Teddy rolled the yellow tape. *Seeing if you fit,* Teddy said. *How about a sandwich before going out?*

Then someone shouted his name. He awoke to a dark room. The mattress sagged. The laptop fan whirred. He heard scratching behind the walls.

An old woman's voice: "Mr. Beeber!"

Max stood and walked into the hallway. Light spilled from under a door. Someone groaned.

"Mrs. Barclay?"

"My bag." Her voice was tired. "I can't—"

"Are you okay?"

"Just come in."

She sat on the closed toilet. Her nightshirt was lifted, triple-pronged cane lying on the floor and a rubber pouch taped to her ribs, with a tube running around her stomach. "My bag is full. I need it emptied."

"Is that a colostomy bag?"

"I won't sugarcoat it, Mr. Beeber. It's disgusting. But that Chinese food went right through me, and I have no idea where Thomas is."

Max rubbed his eyes with one hand. "No problem."

"You'll need gloves." She pointed to the sink cabinet. "Do you have a latex allergy?"

"I don't think so." He rolled his pant cuffs.

"Why are you rolling your pants?"

"In case."

"We won't flood. I can assure you of that."

"Still, I'd rather—"

"Fine. Just get on with it. The bags are by the toilet brush. It's a very simple process. You'll need to clean it, though. That's the most unpleasant part. What did Teddy have to say?"

Max ripped a bag from the roll. "He offered words of encouragement."

"In the usual Teddy fashion, I'm sure. Money never trusts talent. Now make sure to pinch the tube when you disconnect. And don't mind the gas."

Max worked. She said, "Your room must be—yes, just pour it right in—it must be so uncomfortable. Someone stole our air conditioners last summer. They just plucked them from our windows. If you need another fan—oh, that must be the Kung Pao; never sits well with me—if you need another fan there's one in Thomas' room. The alcohol is near the gloves. Give it a quick rinse, if you don't mind."

He finished. A gag rose but he choked it back.

Mrs. Barclay sighed, hands in her lap, as Max reconnected the tube. "I did love him," she said.

"Who?"

"Heinrich." She adjusted the bag. "He risked everything. His life, his home, his future. Even now I shudder at what would have happened if they'd captured us." She paused. "There was this doctor in the camp. Reinagel. A small, bald man, with eyes like little black buttons."

"Page sixty. The lab scene."

She nodded. "He did experiments. Vivisections without anesthesia. Hanging children upside down until death. I asked him once: 'Why would you do this? How can you do this?' He told me a story about his first love. She wasn't much of a beauty, he said, but it didn't matter because she still made him hard. The war, he said, was like that first love. It made him hard."

"That scene should be in the script, Mrs. Barclay."

"I'm not the writer. Do what you must."

"But Roman's notes want the baking montage. Reinagel's lab, when Isabella sneaks in and uses the incinerator for her sourdough—"

"That happened, too. The truth isn't always tragic."

"I don't understand how you can have both."

She shrugged. "You're the writer. You'll figure it out."

The Swan was exactly the sort of New York joint Max figured he needed—Midtown, a single room filled with leather and dark wood, conversation, the clink of silverware, and the foamy shush of tap guns behind the bar. He'd stayed awake after helping Mrs. Barclay to bed; five hours yielded two pages. His cellphone alarm went off at nine thirty and he almost stomped on it. Max wished he'd napped during the ride back to the city, but maybe, he thought, The Swan would inspire him to work harder. This is what screenwriters did, he told himself. They got it done despite all obstacles, eating and drinking on someone else's dime, fumbling through pages, typing until dawn.

Roman and Julie sat at a high-backed booth in the corner. She wore jeans and ballet flats. Roman wore the same suit. He waved at Max, who walked over, squeezing between tables and avoiding waiters.

"There he is." Roman grinned, menu in hand. "Sit. Relax. I recommend the mushroom omelet. They sprinkle it with—what's that spice, Julie?"

"Fennel," she said.

Roman nodded. "It tastes like black licorice, only better. Did you take a dip in the pool?"

"I worked," Max said. "Maybe tonight."

"And Mrs. Barclay?"

"She's very nice."

"I understand Teddy paid a visit."

"He did. He killed a rat."

"A rat?"

"In the wall. She's got rats in the walls."

"That poor woman. Years ago she sold the big house on account of bad investments, and now, the way she lives…with her shit bag or whatever it's called…" He shook his head. "Anyway, some nouveau riche family moved in; you think they ever speak to her, say a simple hello? Tell me about the writing."

"You know, I'd like to get something to drink first—"

Roman held up his hand. "Say no more." He waved to the waiter. "Bloody Mary for my writer—Tabasco okay, Beeber? Good. Bloody Mary, double the vodka. Another tonic for me." The waiter left and Roman leaned forward on his forearms, grinning at Max. "So this gentile walks into a clothing store. He sees a jacket he likes, he tells the salesman, 'What a fine jacket. How much is this jacket?' Salesman says, 'Five hundred dollars.' Gentile says, 'Great, I'll take it.'"

Max stared. "I don't get it."

"Well, I tried. Anyway—I have to piss. Julie, when Mr. Slowpoke comes back with our drinks, tell him I'm having the eggs Benedict, extra Benedict, hold the hash browns."

Roman lumbered away, the crowd parting before him.

"This is a nice place," Max said.

Julie put down her glass. "It's a museum. What do you think of Shane's script?"

"I think it's unfixable."

She paused. A slow smile.

"I don't know where to start," Max said. "You have a Holocaust movie that's not really about the Holocaust. It's a love story. Between a Jewish girl and a Nazi guard. The whole thing is clichéd."

"Clichéd?"

"Stockholm syndrome. Only it's worse, because of the whole bakery storyline. I mean, we're supposed to accept that this guard—this terrible man—is so in love with Isabella—" He looked away for a moment. "Heinrich was a *Nazi*. What audience is going to fall for him?"

"She did."

Max rubbed the back of his neck. "Act two ends with this tunnel scene, when the Polish boy gives Isabella a bag of caraway seeds. For her rye bread. Julie, I'm dying here."

"What about Roman's notes?"

"They're worse. *Worse*." He pulled a folded paper from his pocket. "I worked for five hours last night. This is all I have."

Julie scanned the page. The waiter brought their drinks and they ordered.

"I've never drunk this much in my life." Max wiped his mouth. "I don't even like tomato juice. It always tastes like I just bit my lip."

"Just write the script," Julie said. "It doesn't have to be good. It has to be finished."

"I can't."

"Then you'll be in breach, and he'll ask for his money back." She grabbed Max's glass and gulped it dry. "Problem solved."

"The money's gone."

"Gone?"

"You know, writers don't have a lot—"

"I know how much writers make. Are you a gambler?"

"What? No. I'm—it's been a very difficult few years. I had to borrow a bunch of money from my friends." He looked into his empty glass. "I really need this job."

Roman returned. "I just ran into Chester Lapidus. Looks pretty good, considering." He lowered himself into the booth, hands on the table, glasses rattling. "The poor guy had a stroke two months ago that paralyzed the lower half of his face. Now he drools like he's at the dentist. I didn't even know that was possible. I thought the brain worked in—you know, side to side, not up and down. Anyway." He nodded at Julie. "He sends his best. Says congratulations, et cetera. Beeber, you made quick work of that Bloody Mary."

"It was delicious."

"Good. How's the writing?"

"Fine. Great. I'm restructuring, adding more beats—"

"Second act is a mess, right? That tunnel, with the Polack kid and whatever it is he gives her—"

"Caraway seeds," Julie said.

"*Caraway.*" Roman shook his head. "You know how to fix it?"

"Scrap the whole scene," Max said.

"What?" Roman frowned. "That's the heart of the movie. Remember this: It should be a handful of raisins. Close-up of his grubby little hand, seven, maybe eight shriveled raisins in his palm. What do you think?"

Max cleared his throat. "I think we can work that in."

"Of course, her prize bread then becomes raisin, not rye. Minor detail. Anyway. Let's have a look."

"I'm sorry?"

"The pages. Let's have a look."

"I didn't bring them."

Roman stared.

"I'm superstitious," Max said. "Never bring pages to brunch."

"Who said that?"

"Wilder."

"Gene?"

"Billy."

"No shit Billy." Roman frowned. "I'm fucking with you. Are you holding out on me?"

"I wouldn't do that."

"Uh-huh. This brunch superstition of yours—does it include breakfast?"

"No."

"Then bring them tomorrow morning."

"How many pages do you want?"

"How many do you have?"

"How many do you think I should have?"

Roman looked at Julie, then back at Max. "How the hell should I know? You tell me how many you have, I'll tell you how many I think you should have."

"Fifty."

"That's good." Roman nodded. "I should've put you on salary." He laughed.

"It's a rough fifty," Max said. "Unedited, almost skeletal at times—"

"The next writer will polish. I'm just fucking with you. Don't start sweating again. Tomorrow morning, my office. Nine a.m. Julie, have Swarinski's drop off a lox plate. Beeber, we need to get you another drink. Where the hell is Mr. Slowpoke?"

Max walked after brunch, heading in the direction of the Empire State Building. He thought about the trip he'd made as a boy: the smell of the hot sidewalk, the swooping pigeons, men in suits riding bicycles, and the feel of his father's rough palm. His father had worked in a Chicago printing factory changing plates; sometimes he brought home discarded letter blocks. Max remembered making sentences on his bedroom rug. *Nixon is a bastard; I love pickles; My stomach hurts.*

The New York City weekend was the only trip he'd ever made with his father. His mother preferred to stay home, often in her room. He had no siblings, no pets. Once he caught a praying mantis, named it Rashi, and kept it in a jar. Throughout high school, mystery stories were Max's thing—Chandler knockoffs with slow-eyed cynics and vampy dames. Teachers hated them; his parents made photocopies and passed them out to their friends.

Max bought a bottle of water from a corner deli and sat on a bus stop bench. The sun was relentless. A mounted policeman clopped past. Pigeons swooped overhead.

Max's cell buzzed. He answered.

"It's Julie. Are you in Flatbush?"

"I'm still in the city."

"You sound drunk."

"I'm very drunk. And nauseous. I can't go back to Mrs. Barclay's like this. It's so hot in there. It's like Miami. What am I talking about? I've never been to Miami. How can a writer *write* anything if he hasn't seen—"

"Shane left me a message. He wants to meet with you."

Max closed his eyes. "Oh, God."

"Don't worry. He loves your work."

"He read 'Butterflies at Moonlight'? Can I be honest? It's a con. I can't believe anyone would fall—"

"Where are you?"

"I'm not sure. I can see the Empire State Building."

"How helpful. Do you have plans tonight?"

"I'm writing."

"Well, after you meet with Shane, I was thinking we could go to this great Vietnamese place on Lex and Ninety-Fifth—"

"God, the thought of food is—"

"But their egg drop soup—"

"Hold on." He put his head between his legs and vomited. He rinsed his mouth and vomited again. Then he sat up, phone still to his ear, eyes closed.

"All I can taste, and smell, is tomato juice," he said.

"Did you just puke?"

"I did."

"Drink some water. Shane is staying at the Algonquin, under *Rick James*."

"Of course he is.

"Bye, Max."

"Bye, Julie."

Max hung up. He opened one eye and saw a little boy with his father, standing at the corner, waiting to cross the street. The little boy waved. Max waved back.

Max sat cross-legged on the floor, back against the couch. The hotel suite was modern, everything in shades of gray and taupe. He heard the shower turn off, Shane whistling to himself, then the buzz of an electric toothbrush. Molly—on her stomach, feet up, soles clapping together—bit her lower lip and stared at her cards.

"Seven of clubs," Max said.

"Go fish."

"Come on. Seriously?"

Molly nodded, giggling. Her freckles and short, rust-colored hair reminded Max of Peppermint Patty. He plucked a card from the pile.

"You have a lot of cards, Mr. Beeber," she said.

"I told your dad I'm no good at this game," Max said.

Shane walked from the bathroom, toweling his hair. He wore boxers and slippers. He grabbed a bottle of Jameson from the kitchen bar.

"Molly," he said, "go watch some TV."

"But I'm winning—"

"TV. *Now*. No arguments. And no movies."

She sighed, dropped her cards, and walked away, looking back at Max, who crossed his eyes and stuck out his tongue. Molly laughed.

Shane poured himself a glass. He sat at the end of the couch, towel across his lap, wet hair stuck to his forehead. "So, Max. You were saying."

"Can I show you the first page?"

A sip. Shane shook his head. "Unless you've changed it to *Death Pool 2*, I don't need to see anything. The script is fucked. Everyone knows it. Except Roman, but he doesn't count."

"Then say something to him. You're the director."

Shane's cell—sitting on the coffee table—chirped, and he grabbed it, read for a moment, and started typing. "My last film was *Baby Spies*," he said, still typing. "Did you see it?"

"Is that the one with—"

Shane looked up from his phone. "Yes. The baby spies." He closed his phone. "I can't write for shit. I hate writing. I really do. I don't think in words. Only images."

"Everyone thinks in images."

"Really?" Shane shrugged and took another sip. "Well, my images are fucking vivid. Example: You're a woman and I'm your boyfriend, husband, whatever. We're sitting here, eating dinner—candles, open bottle of wine, et cetera—when BOOM—a guy busts in through the door. He's swearing, screaming for help, he's covered in blood. I mean, *dripping*. You start screaming, I start shouting, our glasses of wine spill, there's red stuff everywhere. Then? *Another* guy comes in behind him, only this guy is wielding one of those linoleum knives. You know what I'm talking about? The ones with the small, curved blade? Anyway, he plunges the knife into the screaming guy's throat. Now you're still screaming,

I'm screaming, the guy is dying—he's choking on his blood, gurgling and shit—and his killer jumps out the *fucking window*, lands on the awning, fucking *bounces off*, and hits the sidewalk like a cat. You with me?"

"He hits the sidewalk like a cat," Max said.

"Exactly. Then? We cut to an apartment down the hall, where two bodies—let's say a hot blonde and her jock boyfriend—are lying in the bathtub, sliced to fucking *ribbons*. I'm talking serious gore—it glistens. It makes squishy sounds. We cut to *another* apartment, across town, where the rotting *corpse* of a woman sits at her kitchen table. We hear the buzz of flies, maybe some maggots drop from her mouth. So now we know we're dealing with a superhuman serial killer. His weapon of choice? A linoleum knife. His powers? Unbreakable bones, super agility, maybe super strength. And there isn't a line of dialogue in that whole sequence. What do you think?"

"It's fucking vivid."

"I wrote a couple of scenes for *Death Pool 2* on spec." Shane lowered his eyes to half-lid and slumped back in the couch. "We were thinking about Ashton Kutcher as the alcoholic cop, but whatever. There were funding issues."

Max grinned. "'Don't serial kill me, dude!'"

Shane stared a moment. "Anyway. Julie told me about that story you had published."

"She said you loved it."

"I didn't read it."

"Oh."

"I never read," Shane said. "I mean, I read scripts. But that's not *reading* reading. The last book I read was…I don't know." He bit his lower lip and gazed upwards. "Something about a boy escaping with a slave, and there was a river—"

"*Huck Finn?*"

"We cut to another apartment, across town, where the rotting corpse of a woman sits at her kitchen table."

"No. Well, maybe. Did someone get cancer?"

"I don't think so."

"Marissa would know. She's totally into books. Full disclosure: Julie hated your story. I told her she was jealous. She called me an asshole." Shane sipped. "But it's hard to stay mad at that girl. Her smile keeps getting in the way."

Max tossed a card. Shane's cell chirped again.

"Roman's going to say I'm in breach," Max said. "When I show up tomorrow—"

"Don't show up," Shane said, looking at his phone. "Stay here."

"I can't do that."

"Sure you can. I haven't spoken to Roman in over a month. As long as you finish—and you'll finish—everything will be—" He paused, head raised, listening. "Molly Michaels? Are you watching a movie?"

No response. Then, from the bedroom: "I'm watching a show!"

"What show?"

"I don't know."

"Who's in it?"

"I don't know."

"Press *info* on the remote. Tell me who's in it."

"Richard Greico."

"Turn it off. *Now.*" Shane closed his phone, finished his drink, and looked at Max. "Listen, I know this movie seems like the most important thing in the world, but you're overthinking. Just get the pages written."

"But I want to write a good movie."

"This isn't that movie. It's a Holocaust rom com."

"The truth isn't always tragic," Max said.

"What does that mean?"

"Mrs. Barclay." Max tossed another card. "She told me a story about Doctor Reinagel."

"The lab scene? With the sourdough? That was Roman's idea."

"No, this was serious. Reinagel did experiments on people, and she said that if they'd caught her and Heinrich, they would have—"

Someone knocked on the door.

"Hold that thought," Shane said. He jogged across the room and flung open the door, revealing a tall, raven-haired woman, dressed in a long coat and a short black dress. She sighed, arms folded across her chest, then said:

"How's the sit-in?"

Shane smiled. "Day thirty-two and counting."

She looked over his shoulder, at Max. "Who's that? The delivery boy?"

"That's our new writer." Shane pointed at him. "Max Beeber. He's very talented. Max, this is Marissa."

Max waved. Marissa flashed a smile and dropped it.

"Molly awake?"

"She's in my room," Shane said. "She and Max were playing cards."

"How sweet," Marissa said. "I don't feel like coming in, so if you don't mind."

"I wasn't going to invite you in," Shane said. "We're very busy."

She looked at his slippers, at the bottle of Jameson on the kitchen bar, and at Max, who sat on the carpet, a pile of cards at his side. "Clearly," she said, then she cleared her throat and shouted, "Molly Michaels!"

The thumping of feet, the click of a door, and Molly ran across the room. She collapsed against her mother's legs and looked up, head thrown back, mouth open.

"It took you *forever*," Molly said. Marissa gently pushed a strand of hair off her daughter's forehead. "But now I'm here."

"I was playing with Max," Molly said. "He's *really* bad at cards."

"I'm sure he was going easy on you."

Molly frowned. "He was not."

"I wasn't," Max said. "She's a shark."

Shane smiled. "Well," he said, "this is almost domestic."

"We're much better in small doses," Marissa said. "Tuesday?"

"Tuesday," Shane said.

Marissa flashed another smile at Max and took Molly's hand. Max waved good-bye. Molly giggled. They left, leaving Shane at the door. He paused, then closed it.

"She's beautiful," Max said.

"Yeah," Shane said. "I really fucked that one in the ass." He grabbed his drink and returned to the kitchen bar. "Not literally, of course. Marissa's not into the anal thing." He refilled his glass. "Eight years." He picked up the glass. "Yeah." He gulped, slammed the glass down, and exhaled sharply through his teeth.

Max started to say something but Shane's cell chirped. He opened it, nodded, then jogged down the hallway to the back of the suite.

"We're having some guests," Shane yelled. "You need a different shirt?"

"What?"

"Your shirt, man. It's pretty stiff."

Max looked down at his shirt.

"Last week I had lunch with Ben Kingsley," Shane continued. "Sorry, *Sir* Ben Kingsley—and he gave me some leftover swag from an awards show. He said he was too fucking old to wear anything with a mime on it, but I told him he's nuts. He's Sir Ben Kingsley. He can wear whatever he wants."

Shane reappeared, dressed in jeans and a buttondown. He tossed Max a T-shirt.

"Anyway, he didn't agree. So there you go. The Sir Ben Kingsley special. Give it a whirl."

Max held up the shirt. There was a mime on the front, swinging from the gallows, with jagged red text beneath reading: DIE MIME.

"You like this?" Max said.

Shane nodded. "Totally. Shot of Jameson?"

"Thanks, but I have to get back. I have so much writing—"

"Come on. *Relax*. We have plenty of time. And put that shirt on." Shane jogged to the kitchen, plucked two shot glasses from the cupboard, and filled them both. "Post up, Beeber."

Max switched shirts on his way to the kitchen. "It looks kind of—"

"Awesome. Now *drink*."

They drank; Shane refilled. "I've been going *crazy* in this place," Shane said, puffing out his cheeks. "I'm so glad you stopped by. We're going to make a good fucking movie. You realize that, right? This is how it starts, man. Get yourself attached to some big names, wear Ben Kingsley's shirts…you'll be set."

Max sat at the bar. "I've been broke for so long that I don't know what it would be like to actually plan anything. I mean, saving for a vacation or buying a car has always been a concept."

"Not anymore. Holocaust flicks…people love them. Seriously."

"I hate them."

"Because you have taste."

"Because I had family that died, and I—" Max paused. "I just don't want to be reminded all the time. It's like Jew overload, or—"

Shane downed another shot. "Big-time Jew overload. You know, I'm like a quarter Jewish. My great-aunt married a Jew."

"She converted?"

"I don't think so."

"Well, technically it's passed down from the mother's side, so unless she—"

"Passed down?"

"It's a rule," Max said. "You have to be born of a Jewish mother."
"Ah. Of course. That's why Jews all look alike."
"We don't *all* look alike."
"Sure you do."
"What do we look like?"
Shane shrugged. "You, man."
Someone pounded on the door. Shane held up his finger. "Hold that outrage," he said, jogging around the bar. He opened the door with a flourish and three blondes strode in, followed by a short, bald, portly man wearing a Hawaiian shirt and sandals. Hugs, kisses, and the portly man clapped Shane on the back as the three blondes kicked off their shoes and headed for the kitchen.

The first blonde smiled at Max. "Hi."
"Hi," Max said.
She took his shot and emptied it. "Ooh. That's smoky." Her lipstick left a crescent on the glass rim. "Are you a friend of Shane's?"
Shane shouted over, "That's Max. He's writing my movie."
"Bully for you," the first blonde said. Her two friends pulled bottles from the cupboard and lined them up on the bar.
"So, Mack," the second blonde said, "where are you from?"
"It's Max," Max said.
"Who?" the second blonde said.
"*Max*. My name is Max."
The third blonde hit the second on the shoulder. "Mack!" she said, laughing. "Like that guy we—"
The second blonde guffawed. "Oh my God, I totally forgot about—"
A hand landed on Max's shoulder. He turned; the short, portly man stood behind him, mouth open, wide smile, appearing to Max like some sort of giant, shaved infant. He held a highball

filled with ice and booze.

"Burt Phillips," the man said, then he waited, eyes wide, still grinning.

"Should I know you?" Max said.

Burt sighed. "Ten years ago I had scores of young men who would do anything to write for one of my shows. We're talking rug burns on the knees, you get me?" He tongued a piece of ice into his mouth and crunched. "Ever hear of *Sea Wolf*?"

"Sunday nights, nine p.m.," Max said. "My friends and I never missed an episode."

"That second season time slot was the best." Burt belched. "Goddamn dating show took it from us. That co-host, with the monstrous tits—*she* was a good one. Didn't mind losing out to her. But her faggy sidekick? Troy what's-his-name? Borderline retarded. Seriously. He was illiterate. His agent read all his contracts for him."

"I loved *Sea Wolf*," Max said. "I had the biggest crush on Dr. Knox."

"We had an affair for three years," Burt said. "She had unbelievable tits." The first blonde rolled her eyes. Burt pouted at her. "You have unbelievable tits, too," he said, then he raised an eyebrow at Max. "Am I right?"

"Yes," Max said. "They're very skillful."

They stared at him. Shane answered the door and another group of blondes entered. Someone turned on the stereo, switching songs to a chorus of *boos* until something by Serge Gainsbourg stuck and everyone cheered.

The third blonde tapped the first on her shoulder, nodding toward the living room.

"Bo Bailey," the third blonde said in an awed whisper. Max watched a strikingly handsome young man promenade through the crowd. His hair was short and spiky, his jeans were rolled at the bottom, and he wore a thick leather cuff around his wrist.

"What's he doing in New York?" the second blonde said.

"*Today Show*," the third blonde said. "He's doing a promo for that vampire flick."

Burt handed his drink to Max. "Don't go anywhere," he said, and he walked away, arms outstretched, grinning maniacally at Bo.

Max's cell buzzed and he looked down. It was Roman. He put it into his pocket and sipped his drink. Shane eyed him from across the room, making his fingers into the shape of a gun, taking aim at Max, and firing in slow motion. Max mimed catching the bullet in his hand. He noticed the suite was suddenly packed—music thumping, bottles being passed around, the smell of weed growing exponentially.

"What's up with your shirt?" the first blonde said. Max didn't realize she was talking to him until she touched his hand.

"It was Ben Kingsley's," Max said. "It's supposed to make me look cool."

"Does anyone use that word anymore?"

"Cool?" Max said. "I use cool. I hear people using it all the time."

She leaned in closer. He could smell her breath, a tart blend of alcohol, strawberry gum, and menthol cigarettes.

"Yeah," she said, "but are they *cool*?"

"So you and Burt," Max said, as she sipped his drink. "Are the two of you…"

"We fuck. Sometimes. I don't know if I can call it fucking. The bed squeaks. He sweats. I inspect my cuticles. Here—don't say I never gave you anything."

She handed him a small white pill.

"Designer," she said, with a wink.

Shane stumbled into Max, spilling bourbon onto the carpet. He righted himself and yelled in Max's ear.

"That fucking shirt is *awesome*. I'd kill a fucking mime, you know. Seriously—if no one could ever find out? Fucking perfect murder, too. Just pretend I got a knife, make stabbing motions, and if he's a good mime he'll go down. If he's dedicated to his *craft*." He narrowed his eyes at the first blonde. "You taking care of my boy Maxie? He's a little uptight. He could use some fun, *capisce*?"

"She's trying," Max said.

"Oh, well, she's *trying*." Shane tottered a moment before grabbing Max for balance. "Sounds like she has an excellent work ethic. Oh—what's this?" He plucked the pill and held it up.

"It's for Max," the first blonde said.

Shane washed it down with his drink, then cleared his throat and stared at Max, their faces inches apart. "Listen, Maxie. What do you think about Bo Bailey?"

"Bo Bailey is a child," the first blonde said.

"But a talented child," Shane said. "And I'm talking business with Maxie, so please shut the fuck up. Now, Maxie, what do you think about Bo Bailey playing Bruno?"

"Bruno Asher?" Max said. "An SS officer? The *Schutzhaftlagerführer* of Dachau?"

"The kid has range. Don't let his baby face fool you."

"But Bruno is in his forties—"

"Just think about it, okay? Bo is very popular with the tweens, and those little shits flock to the theaters. You know the only reason I'm on this movie? Because they all saw *Baby Spies*."

"Oh my God," the first blonde said. "That was *you*?"

"Careful," Shane said.

"I wept," she said. "Seriously."

A voice called out behind Max: "Max Beeber?"

Max turned. Bo stood there, holding an open bottle of champagne, looking even younger close-up—Max pegged him at eighteen, at most. He extended his hand; it was the softest hand Max believed he'd ever held.

"I loved your story," Bo said. "I read it twice."

"Really?" Max caught himself—he didn't want to appear fawning, but Bo was so…well, *pretty*, he realized, that he elicited the urge to schoolgirl giggle, or blush.

"I'm a writer." Bo smiled sheepishly and looked away. "I mean, not as good as you, but I'm learning. Are you a Cheever fan?"

"You're asking me if I'm a John Cheever fan? As in *The Swimmer*?"

"Great movie," Shane said. "Burt Lancaster was fucking iconic. '*You loved it. You loved it! We both loved it. You loved it!*'"

"I'm partial to 'Goodbye, My Brother,'" Bo said. "It's not as pat, you know? Maybe pat isn't the correct word."

Max nodded. "I understand. And you're right—'Goodbye' is the better story."

"Shane said you were working on his next film. It takes place in the Holocaust, right?"

"*In* the Holocaust?" Max said.

"Yeah." Bo swigged his champagne. "Sounds very serious. Like all genocide movies. They're entertaining, but they also teach. The first movie I ever saw was *Amistad*. I was six. I cried."

Shane's head appeared over Bo's shoulder. "Maxie, is this a brainstorm?"

"We're just spitballing," Bo said.

"Fuck you, *spitballing*. Max can write anything. We were just talking about you playing one of the guards. The *head* Nazi guard."

"Really?" Bo made as if to run his hand through his hair but grazed just over the top. "Oh, that would be incredible. I mean, I'd have to work on my accent. It would have to be perfect. People take the Nazi thing seriously, you know?"

"Yes," Max said. "I do know." The music got louder. Shane

and Bo wandered off into the crowd. Max watched Burt start dancing, arms akimbo, pelvis gyrating. Max's cell buzzed and he took it out of his pocket; it was Roman. Someone grabbed his arm. He looked up.

"Hey, you," the first blonde said. She reached into her clutch, pulled out another white pill, put it on the tip of her tongue, and kissed Max deeply. The pill transferred. Max swallowed. Then she pulled him away, letting her hand glide down his arm. She led him into the living room, past a gyrating Burt, a break-dancing Bo, and a convulsing Shane.

Max looked out the row of windows and realized it was still daylight. The first blonde flicked his ear with her tongue.

"Do you feel it?" she whispered.

"Feel what?" Max whispered back. She laughed, mouth wide, pulling him along by his hand, toward the back. She shoved a bedroom door open and hauled Max inside. He felt the music vibrating his feet and he tottered on the edge of the bed before falling, arms out.

She took off her shirt and bra.

"Well?" she said.

Max golf-clapped. "Spectacular."

Then she giggled and stripped off her jeans, balancing on one leg. Her eyes widened and she stumbled. Something hit the edge of the bed with a loud knock and she yelped.

Max scrambled. "Are you—"

She popped up, holding her nose, eyes beginning to tear.

"Let me see it," Max said.

She looked up at him, still holding her nose, shaking her head.

"Come on," Max said. "It'll be fine."

She dropped her hand. A trickle of blood peeked out from one nostril.

"See?" Max smiled. "It's just a little blood. You want me to get you a tissue?"

She sniffled. "Am I still sexy?"

"You are."

"Tell me again."

"You're very, very—"

She jumped onto the bed, shoved him down, and clawed at his belt. "Tell me how sexy I am," she said, but before he could answer, she thrust her finger against his lips. "But say it smart. Like I'm worth the effort."

"Like Arthur Miller would say to Marilyn?"

"Oh, *yes*. Just like that."

She mounted him, legs astride, and began to play with her breasts. Blood trickled down her lips, over her chin, pattering onto her breasts. Max fumbled with his belt.

"You're a sexy kitten," Max said.

She closed her eyes. "That sounds stupid. Come on—"

"You're sexy like a first kiss. Like the whisper of a bra off a virgin's shoulder."

"Better." Her hands smeared blood over her breasts; she let her head fall back, mouth open. "Keep going."

"Can you just…lift up your right leg—no, your other right—"

Max glanced up and saw blood streaming from her nose, running over her chest, and splitting into twin streams as it flowed down her stomach. She kept her eyes closed, tugging on her nipples, still rocking and grinding.

"We might need a towel," Max said. "Uh—"

He saw something move in the hall; there was Burt, standing, staring, hand near his crotch. He raised his eyebrows at Max and leered.

"Burt?" Max said.

She paused. "He's watching?"

"Yes. He's…I think he's playing with himself."

"That's his thing."

"Well, it's not my—"

She opened her eyes and looked down at Max.

"Just ignore him. Burt is—*oh my God.*" She saw it then: bloody smears over her breasts, her hands red and sticky, blood on the sheets, on Max. She screamed, hands pressed on either side of her face as Max squirmed and leapt off the bed, pulling up his pants. He careened into the hall, shoving past Burt, and into the crowd. The music blared. Max felt something in his brain shift. Sounds distorted. The room tilted. Bo grabbed his shoulders.

"*Mein Fuhrer*!" Bo shouted. "I got the accent, man. *Mein Fuhrer!*"

Max pushed him away and stumbled to the front door. Bodies pressed in; he pushed back.

Shane appeared, beaming, eyes unfocused. He shouted over the music: "Don't overthink! Just get it written! Nobody gives a shit about this fucking movie!"

Max yanked the door open and birthed into the hall. The door slammed shut. He heard the faint pulse of music. He breathed deeply and began his journey toward the elevator, letting his fingers bump over the wallpaper while the floor wobbled.

The cab pulled away as Max walked past the mansion. The little girl with pigtails sat on the porch, leaning against a pillar. She ate a sandwich and stared. Max waved. A large man—sweatshirt, blond hair buzzed close—banged through the screen door and clomped down the steps.

"Excuse me," the man said.

Max stopped.

"You're staying with Mrs. Barclay?"

"That's right," Max said.

"Are you a nephew or something? One of Thomas' friends?"

"I'm a screenwriter."

The man walked closer. "Word of advice—don't talk to my daughter again."

"I'm sorry?"

"You called her stupid. What kind of man calls an eight-year-old girl *stupid*?"

"I didn't call her stupid. I lost my temper and called her sandwich stupid."

"Her sandwich?"

Max put his hand to his forehead. "It was a mistake. I was hot, I was tired—"

He poked Max in the chest with a thick finger. "Just stay away from my daughter. Are we clear?"

Max nodded. The man walked back inside. The little girl stared, chewing.

The house was empty. Max's laptop sat patiently. The day passed. His phone rang but he turned it off. He made a gin and tonic; the last lime was shriveled but he squeezed what he could. Roman's notes lay scattered on the bed. The screen stared back at him:

```
INT.   TUNNELS UNDER DACHAU - NIGHT

Black and white, dramatic Jewish-type
music, etc. Isabella, Bruno, and a Jewish
boy named JOSEF are running.

                 JOSEF
      I am too tired. I cannot go on.
```

                    ISABELLA
          You must!

Josef stops. He coughs, gives Isabella a
handful of raisins. One by one they drop
from his hand to hers.

                    ISABELLA
          But without these raisins you
          will starve.

Josef closes Isabella's hands around the
raisins. Shouts in German echo down the
tunnel. Bruno grabs Isabella's arm.

                    BRUNO
          Schnell, mein frau. The guards
          are gaining.

                    ISABELLA
                (to Josef)
          Please keep one. Just one. Give
          it to your father.

                    JOSEF
          It is too late for him.

                    BRUNO
          Isabella, we must--

Josef smiles and touches Isabella's face.

```
            JOSEF
    When you make the bread--


          ISABELLA
    I will name it for your father.
    I will call it Izaak's loaf.
```

A final glance, then Isabella and Bruno flee down the tunnel. Josef waves. Close shot of his face—a tear cuts the dirt on his cheek.

Max leaned back, eyes closed, hands on the keyboard. He heard the little girl singing. The doorbell rang. It rang again, so he closed his laptop and left the room.

Julie waited outside the door, holding a plastic bag. Behind her, the little girl jumped rope as the sun set.

"I brought Chinese." Julie smiled. "You hungry?"

Max sat at his desk and Julie propped herself up with pillows on his bed, a carton of fried rice in her lap. She was barefoot; her thin ankles, red toenails, and graceful arch convinced Max she'd been a dancer.

"I can't believe you didn't at least try the Kung Pao." She fished out a cube of pork.

"I had a big lunch."

"You hardly ate. Are you hungover? Did Shane make you drink? No wonder you're cranky. There's a Dutch film playing at Le Strad. Something about a Moroccan restaurant and a wedding. It might inspire you."

"I don't need inspiration. I just need focus. I can't—" He

rubbed his forehead. "Mrs. Barclay told me this film is based on her life."

Julie plucked another cube of pork. She started to say something, but stopped.

"What?" Max said.

"It's bullshit."

"What's bullshit?"

Julie sighed. "Mrs. Barclay grew up in Passaic. Her father owned a plumbing supply company, or something like that. I shouldn't be telling you this. Writers love to think that the truth is somehow more authentic. But if Roman wasn't—"

"*Passaic?*"

"So the facts aren't entirely accurate. So what? You didn't grow up in some Waspy Connecticut community, but your story takes place there."

"I never said it was *real*."

"But you wish it was real. You wish you were like Peter, because he's everything you aren't. He's tall, he's rich, he has a beautiful, aloof girlfriend—"

"I don't like aloof women."

"My point is, we don't know everything that's happened to Mrs. Barclay, and it isn't our place to assume." She set the carton on the floor and clapped her hands clean. "Maybe she had a sister who fled a concentration camp. Maybe it was her mom. Who knows? You're overthinking."

Max began to pace. "Stop saying that. Everyone keeps saying that. What does that even mean? Writing *is* overthinking. People think. Writers *over*think." He stopped. "I can't do this. If she's lying, I can't do this."

"Max, truth can't be a contingency for art."

"That's good." He laughed to himself. "Did you learn that at Smith?"

"It's a line from your story."

"I thought you didn't like it."

She shrugged. " 'Butterflies at Moonlight' is an awful title, but who cares. It broke my heart a little."

He stared at her. A car pulled down the driveway, headlights sweeping across the pool. Mrs. Barclay's voice, Thomas protesting, then the front door creaked open.

"I just want to write a good movie," Max said.

Julie patted the bed. "I know you do. Now come here."

Max awoke in the middle of the night. Julie lay at his side, her head tucked into the crook of his elbow. She snored. A screensaver floated across the laptop screen. Something scratched in the wall behind his head, followed by a squeak. He slid his arm free and sat up. The carton of fried rice had spilled and a trail led across the room to the dresser.

Julie yawned. He turned around and whispered, "I have to write. Go back to sleep."

"Sleep," she murmured, then her eyes snapped open. "What time is it?"

"I don't know. Midnight or—"

She scrambled for her purse, whipped out her phone, and looked at Max. "Call me a car."

"Just crash here. I'm sure Mrs. Barclay doesn't—"

"I was supposed to meet Richard for drinks. *Shit.*" She hooked her bra. "Didn't you feel my cell vibrate? It was right near your head. Richard texted like eight times."

"Richard."

"My fiancé. Call me a car *now*. I have to fix my hair."

She pushed past him and left the room, purse in hand. He heard her padding down the hall, then the click of the bathroom door. Max waited a moment before following.

The bathroom light glared; he squinted as Julie tousled her hair in the mirror, turning side to side, eyes narrowed. "Did you call that car?" She wiped her lips with a tissue. "Jesus, it smells like a bag of shit in here."

"Because there's a bag of shit in here."

She looked at him in the mirror and Max pointed to a full colostomy bag lying in the bathtub. "I guess Thomas didn't feel like cleaning it," he said. "She must have a spare."

"*Gross*. Why didn't Roman put you in a hotel? Call that car. *Please*."

"How long have you and Richard—"

"Long enough. And don't act like you didn't have fun."

"I did have fun. It was awesome. That thing you did with your finger—but that's not my point—"

"Do you have a girlfriend?"

"How is that relevant?"

"So that's a *yes*."

"I don't know anymore. She's going through some sort of 're-awakening' or whatever—"

"Do you love her?"

"Do you love Richard?"

She pulled lipstick from her purse. "I love him very much."

"Then what are you doing?"

"I had a moment of weakness. I was wooed by your talent." She blotted her lips on a tissue. "And I get one freebie before marriage."

"When are you getting married?"

"Three weeks."

Max groaned. "The heart sticker on your calendar. The congratulations from that stroke guy—"

"Chester Lapidus." She checked her teeth and capped the tube.

"He always had a thing for me."

"I'm such an idiot. I actually liked you. I mean, I thought there was—"

"You're not an idiot. I don't fuck idiots. Are the pillow lines noticeable?"

"No."

"Good. *Jesus*, that bag reeks. Seriously, Max. I don't know how you get anything—"

A knock on the bathroom door. Max felt a flash of terror. He and Julie exchanged glances. The door opened and Thomas stood in the hall, hands on his hips, wearing Bert and Ernie pajamas.

"Can you guys keep it down to a low roar, for Christ's—"

Julie held up her hand. "Thomas, I need a ride to the city."

Thomas paused. "Now?"

"Richard was expecting me for drinks at ten."

Thomas looked at Max, then back at Julie. "Of course. I'll just throw on a jacket." He nodded. "Max."

Max nodded. "Thomas."

Thomas walked away. Julie followed, stopping for a moment to grab Max's shoulder. "Nine a.m.," she said. "Don't be late."

She hurried down the hall. Max heard the jangle of car keys. Into the dark, he shouted, "Doesn't anyone around here care about the truth?"

He woke up at his desk, a puddle of drool by his mouth. Thomas was swimming; Stan Getz played on a radio by the pool. Max closed the blinds and crossed the room, stepping on the trail of fried rice. He paused by the door and squinted in the light. Wednesday morning. The laptop clock read ten-thirty. He grabbed his phone and turned it on.

Five voicemails, four from Julie—*Where the hell are you? Are you being weird because of last night? We need your pages and Roman is freaking out*—and one from Paul. He erased it before listening, then changed his clothes, did a yoga stretch he'd learned a few month earlier, and sat at the desk. The graffiti stared. *It is hard for thee to kick against the pricks.*

His phone buzzed but he ignored it. He thought if there'd been a bottle of bourbon within reach he'd drink the whole thing, and not because he liked drinking; because they'd driven him to this. Maybe, he realized, this is what they wanted. The artist self-destructs, and from the ashes—Max pictured a phoenix—arises the work. Or something like that. Maybe a crucible is a better image, he wondered. Of course both are clichéd, he thought.

The room grew hot. He wrote pages and erased them, arranged the scenes on index cards, and paced, hand to his forehead, bare feet mashing the rice into tiny white discs. The phone continued buzzing. A knock on the door; Thomas poked his head in.

"I'm sorry to bother you, but you have a visitor."

"Tell them to go away," Max said.

"I can't."

The phone buzzed again. Max leaned back in the chair.

"It's Teddy," Thomas continued. "He's waiting in his car. Out front."

"What does he want?"

"You. He said he's been calling all morning."

"How does he seem?"

"Seem?"

"His mood. Is he—"

"It's Teddy. He's always the same—like he just swallowed a hornet."

Max covered his eyes briefly. When he opened them, he closed the laptop. "I need you to be honest."

Thomas stepped into the room. He wore jean shorts and a

Burt Reynolds T-shirt.

"Did your mother grow up in New Jersey?"

Thomas looked down. "I don't know."

"You have to know. It's a simple question."

"I don't care. It's her story."

The cell buzzed. Max glanced at it.

Thomas started to leave but looked back. "If you've ever tried her bread, you wouldn't even be asking me that question."

"Sheepshead Bay." Teddy flicked his cigarette out the window and cranked the AC to high. They whipped down Ocean Avenue in his black Porsche, Max strapped in to the passenger seat. He tried to ignore how fast Teddy was driving but the blaring horns made it impossible. "You ever been?" Teddy continued. "Nice place. Boardwalks. Piers. Character, like everywhere in Brooklyn. *Character*. Not a block without it. You think London's got the market cornered on personality, but mate, let me tell you: fucking Pakis changed all that. Shadows of a mosque on every fucking corner." He offered Max a cigarette. "You all right?"

"I'm good. Where are we going?"

"House call. Now you got women in head scarves, men with camel-fucking beards—you know what I'm talking about. Long and trimmed. Like a Hittite. Hittites is what they were. Before we wiped them out. Sent them back to their caves. Tell me one thing those people invented since the curved sword. Go on. I'll give you this fucking car if you can tell me."

"Astronomy."

"What?" Teddy lit another cigarette. "Fuck off. They didn't invent astronomy. I don't know who did, but I can bloody well guarantee you, wasn't some bloke with a turban. Here we are."

Teddy skidded onto a side street. In front of a modest brick two-story, he slammed the brakes and parked at the curb. He kept one hand on the steering wheel.

"How's work?"

"Good," Max said.

"What's that mean?"

"I'm making progress." Max checked his cell. Another voicemail from Julie. He sighed. "I was supposed to meet Roman this morning. I just stayed in my room and wrote."

"Not a confessional, mate. Whatever works."

"Have you read the script?"

Teddy shook his head. He blinked slowly, gazing out the windshield. "Not my thing. Don't care, really. Movies are books for stupid people."

"Then what was all that stuff about story—"

"*Motivation*. I'm bleeding money. Got that useless fucking director on wage, and he's gone all Lindbergh's baby." He turned to Max. "You have any idea where he's at?"

"The director?"

"That's right." He pulled deep on the cigarette and let the smoke crawl up his face. "Shane Michaels. The director."

"Can't say I do."

Teddy returned his gaze to the windshield. "Got to be perfect, really. Subject matter might ruffle a few feathers, fucking Nazi doing what he did. Got to be careful. *Sensitive*. Got to be *authentic*. Most of all, got to get this cunt of a script finished." He turned to Max again. "This is where you say: 'Don't worry, Teddy. It's under control.'"

"Well, it is. Under control, I mean."

Teddy puffed. "It's time."

They walked to the front door—Teddy smoothing back his hair, Max re-tucking his shirt—and Teddy knocked twice, hard.

"So are we here on a social visit," Max said, "or—"

A short, middle-aged man opened the door. He wore a brown bathrobe and loafers with tassels, his thinning hair cut short. He looked as though he hadn't shaved in a few days. He held a magazine in one hand.

"Teddy?"

"David. Bad time?"

"Uh…no. Were you in the area or something?"

"This is Max. He's our new screenwriter. Max, this is David."

David cleared his throat and smiled.

Teddy dropped his cigarette. "Aren't you going to invite us in for a cuppa?"

"Of course. Please." He stepped aside and Teddy marched past, Max close behind.

The living room curtains were closed. The room smelled of old fabric and coffee. Max saw a portrait of a glaring, bearded man over the mantel and a pencil sketch of Jerusalem hanging on the wall behind the couch. The rug was gold shag. On the mantel sat a photo of David and a woman with curly black hair pinned high atop her head.

"I'll put on some water," David said.

Teddy walked over to the photo and picked it up. "How's the old gal?"

"Cheryl? She's sleeping. You want me to—"

"No need." He put the photo back. "You just tell her old Teddy sends his best."

"She'd love to see you, I'm sure. It's been a long time."

"How long, you figure?"

"A year. At least." David looked to Max, as if searching for verification. "Definitely no less than a year."

"How about that tea?" Teddy said.

David paused, hand in mid-air, as if about to make a point, then he dropped his hand and pushed through the swinging kitchen door.

Teddy narrowed his eyes at the portrait. "I met David at Yeshiva. Little nippers, the two of us."

"So it's true," Max said.

"What's true?"

"You being a rabbi."

"Course we took different routes. I got into the film business, David did whatever the fuck he did. Shuffling numbers from one interested party to the next. Never could keep track of it, tell you the truth." Teddy slipped a hand into his pocket and looked at Max. "Things going all right at Barclay's?"

"Yes, Teddy. You already asked me that."

"Okay, okay—no need to get snippy. Thomas all right?"

"Nothing but helpful. I wanted to ask you something about Mrs. Barclay. Did you—"

David pushed through the kitchen door. He stood with his hands on his hips. "Water's on," he said, "and I woke up Cheryl. She's so excited to—"

"Wish you hadn't done that, mate," Teddy said. He clubbed David across the face with a black sap. David dropped. He screamed and Teddy hit him again. Blood spattered on the shag rug. Teddy swung. It sounded to Max like something heavy dropped on wet cardboard.

Max shouted and grabbed Teddy's arm. Teddy stood, breathing hard, red sprayed across his hand. He spit. "Fucking *khazer*," he said. "Look at him." David whimpered, clutching at his face. His lip was flayed open; blood streamed and Max couldn't make out his nose. He saw a tooth fragment stuck to his chin. "All *ungabluzum*," Teddy continued. "Can't take his beating like a man."

Max pulled on Teddy's arm. "That's enough."

The kitchen door swung open. Cheryl—black hair pinned high, fresh lipstick on her wide mouth—screamed, hands on her cheeks.

Teddy wiped his mouth with the back of his bloodied hand. "Oi, there she is. You have a nice nap?"

She wailed. "What are you *doing*—"

"Shut up. Not a word. Not a fucking *word*. Letting this man stay in your home, in your bed, dipping his little prick in your twat whenever the fuck he pleases? Used to be a nice girl, Cheryl. Respectable. Used to be marriage material, if you want the truth." Teddy kicked David in the ribs; Max heard a deep crack. "You're pathetic," Teddy said to Cheryl. "You bottomed out. Not the girl I knew."

Max stepped in front of Teddy. He felt David grab at his ankle. "Whatever you're trying to do—"

"Not your call, mate. Step away."

"Teddy—"

"I'll take your fucking eye, you don't step away. This CUNT TOOK MILLIONS. Bloody MILLIONS. Mrs. Barclay lost her house on account of him." He pointed at Cheryl. "That's right—your boyfriend cheated a little old lady. A Holocaust survivor. That's not all. College funds. Shoah foundations. Cunt did them all in." He returned to Max. "Now you don't back off—"

"I won't."

Teddy paused. He looked at Cheryl, who was sobbing, mascara running down her cheeks, hand on her forehead.

"Right." Teddy slipped the sap into his back pocket and smoothed his hair. He lit a cigarette. "My guess is the ten writers before you didn't know the first thing about pain. Need to dip in the muck sometimes. Get dirty." He slapped the back of his hand against Max's cheek and pulled it across, leaving a red smear. "Kill bulls. Fight men. Fuck biffers. The stuff of life. Makes the work authentic." He knelt and took two quick puffs, gently brushing matted hair off David's forehead. David shivered, trying to talk, but Teddy shushed him. "Now, Max. Take what you seen here, and use it. Maybe this script, maybe the next. I've given you something."

"You're goddamn crazy," Max said, backing away.

Teddy sighed and stood. He looked at Cheryl. "Once those tears dry, you'd do best kicking him out. I'm just saying."

Teddy left through the front door. Max closed his eyes. Cheryl sobbed.

Max paced on the lawn in front of Cheryl's house, cell to his ear. "A nightmare, Paul. It was *horrible*. I don't care about the money, or the—no, I don't care. Then we leave it on the table. That's right. Because he would've killed him. I'm serious. The guy is psychotic—wait, I'm getting another call." He clicked over.

"Is this Max Beeber?"

"Who's this?"

"Richard. Julie's fiancé."

Max waited.

"She told me," Richard said.

"Told you what?"

"Max. Let's not pretend. She told me everything. Julie and I value the truth; our relationship depends upon absolute—"

"Can you just hold—"

"Don't run from this. I'm taking the high road—"

Max clicked over. "Paul? Listen. I want you to call Roman and—well, fine, then I'll be in breach. Can you just let me finish? It's not always about the money. I'm in serious—*Jesus*, hold on." He clicked over.

Julie cried on the other end. "I'm such a mess."

"Julie—"

"I'm a trainwreck. I fuck all the writers. Well, not all of them, but it was *different* this time. I just felt so guilty because you were talking about your girlfriend—"

"Richard called me."

"I'm sorry. I didn't want him to."

"Is Richard a big guy? I mean, should I be worried?" He paced faster. "You can't just go around sleeping with whoever you want and then telling—"

Another sob. "Maybe it's because I'm nervous about marriage. I don't even know. But I love him. You have to believe me. He's so patient, and strong. He's such a mensch. Oh, and Roman is furious. He's been calling your agent—"

"Julie, hold on. Can you hold on?" Max clicked over. "Paul?"

"WHERE THE FUCK IS MY SCRIPT?"

"Roman?"

"Goddamn right, you little shit. I've been calling you for DAYS—"

Max clicked over. "Paul?"

"It's Richard."

"Okay—"

"I'm taking the high road, Max. Do you understand what that means?"

"I do, and I appreciate—"

"I'm not looking for appreciation. In fact, you're in no position—"

He clicked over. "Julie?"

She sniffled.

"Tell me what to say," Max said. "I don't want to ruin your marriage."

"Richard likes to talk. So let him talk."

"Okay. Hold on." He clicked over. "Richard, before you start, let me apologize. I don't know exactly what Julie told you, but whatever may have happened between us was quick, meaningless, and normal—by *normal* I mean ordinary, nothing experimental.

Boring, really. And I was very drunk. *Very* drunk. Not to say being drunk is an excuse, but I've been under enormous pressure."

Silence. Max said, "Hello?"

Laughter on the other end, then Shane's voice: "Welcome to the club, man."

"Shane?"

"You dog," Shane said. "You dirty dog. Richard *called* you? What a tool. Hey, I've got Bo on the line—"

"Hey, man," Bo said. "What's up?"

"We were just talking about grabbing some lunch in the Village," Shane said.

"Vicarro's," Bo said. "My buddy's the head chef. Amazing manicotti. They use buffalo mozzarella."

"This isn't a good time," Max said.

"Then dinner?" Shane said. "Tonight?"

"My manager has a penthouse on East Fifty-Seventh," Bo said. "We could get a case of champagne—"

"Not tonight," Max said. "Or tomorrow. I'm HAVING A HARD FUCKING TIME HERE DO YOU UNDERSTAND?" Silence. He looked at the phone. The screen was black. He held the power button and waited. He shook the phone. He punched it. The front door of the brick house swung open and David stepped onto the lawn, ice pack pressed to his face. The front of his robe was stained dark. One loafer was missing.

Max stared, phone in hand, as David walked across the grass. He nodded at Max. Both eyes swelled. His nose was crooked and mashed, upper lip split, revealing purple flesh.

"You should…" Max paused. "Probably get to the hospital."

A sigh. Then a distorted voice: "I called a car."

Max pointed to his own chin. "You have a bit of tooth, or something."

David brushed it off. "Thank you."

They stood on the lawn, side by side. Max glanced at his phone again.

"Do you live in Brooklyn?" Max said.

"Manhattan. Upper East."

"Nice area."

"It's pleasant."

"Well, if you have to live in New York." Max cleared his throat. "I'm staying in Flatbush. Working on a script."

"Sounds fun."

"You'd think. They advanced me fifteen grand. Plus another fifteen when I finish. Problem is, I *can't* finish. The script is awful. It's unfixable. And I need this job. I have debts. Not illegal debts, of course, but I've been living off credit for the past year, and my girlfriend—ex-girlfriend, I guess—is moving out."

David coughed and spit blood. Max continued.

"Anyway, here's the kicker—the script is supposed to be based on a true story but it's not. Are you sure you don't need an ambulance?"

"It hurts when I talk, so if you don't mind, please stop asking me questions."

"Of course." Max shook his phone and tried to turn it on. He looked at David. "Sorry. My battery died. Could I share your car? I'll pay extra."

"No problem."

"Great. Thank you."

Max stood on the lawn, hands in his pockets.

```
INT.   ISABELLA AND BRUNO'S NEW YORK APT. -
NIGHT

Isabella and Bruno lie in bed, in each
```

other's arms. The room is small and dark, sirens wail in the distance, pigeons coo outside their windows. A couple argues in the room next door--typical Italian New York accents. Close push to Isabella's face. Shadows run across her eyes.

                    ISABELLA
          I have such guilt.

                    BRUNO
          I know, my love. But you need
          your sleep. Put it out of your
          mind.

                    ISABELLA
          I cannot.

Bruno sighs. He lights a cigarette.

                    BRUNO
          Tomorrow Izaak's loaf will
          become famous. That is how we
          will honor him.

                    ISABELLA
          She is only a food critic. What
          can she do?

                    BRUNO
          Her words have the power to turn
          our little bakery into something

         special. Izaak would have wanted
         this.

                    ISABELLA
              (taking Bruno's cigarette)
         Izaak would have wanted to live.

Silence. Bruno kisses her on the cheek.
She smokes, staring at the ceiling.

Max pushed away from the desk and grabbed the bottle of gin. His bag lay in the corner, clothes spilled. He'd packed after sharing a ride with the bleeding man, stuffing his clothes as Thomas and four shirtless men prowled on the deck, splashed in the pool, and tanned on lounge chairs, while smoke from the grill seeped in the windows of Max's room, swirling in the fan's currents.

A gin and tonic for the road, Max had promised himself, but there were no limes so he drank straight from the bottle until he didn't feel like leaving anymore, then threw his bag against the wall. He wrote. Thomas and his friends laughed outside. The fan rotated, creaking, pushing hot air. A helicopter whupped over the house; Max saw flames leap from the grill. His cell phone sat on the bed, recharging. Four new voicemails waited. He texted Julie: *Flatbush. I'm still only in Flatbush.* Then he danced across the room, smoke stinging his eyes, bottle in hand.

Max squatted near the dresser and pressed his ear to the wall. He listened, then stood and kicked. He kicked again and cried out. Sitting on the floor, he grabbed his foot and sucked air between his teeth. The big toe was bent at a horrible angle. A rat scrambled from behind the dresser. Max brought the bottle on its body, shattering the glass and spilling gin. The rat squeaked.

It lurched forward and shuddered to a stop. Blood dewed on its whiskers.

The door opened. Thomas held a paper plate, hot dog in the middle with a heaping of potato salad.

"Is this a bad time?" Thomas said.

Max looked up. "What does *khazer* mean?"

"Pig." Thomas kept one hand on the door and reached to the bed, where he left the plate.

When Max awakened at the desk, the laptop was running a virus scan. It was dark outside; the room smelled of charred meat. He traced the graffiti with his finger. He limped to the bed, flopped on his back, fished Teddy's card from his pocket, and dialed. Voicemail answered. He closed his eyes.

"Get up, you cunt."

Max opened one eye. Daytime. A bar of sun fell across the rat on the floor. Broken glass glittered. Outside, a radio played Gloria Estefan.

Teddy sat at the desk. He wore a shirt and tie over dark jeans. A cigarette dangled from the corner of his mouth. "Got your message."

Max sat up. The room spun. "I finished the script."

"Fucking disgrace, it is."

"Now, just *hold on*—"

"Bigger fucking disgrace is you trying to blame it on the poor old woman. Fucking New Jersey. Fucking *Passaic*. Who do you think I am?"

"Teddy—"

"Not some plump dumb cunt, I can tell you that. This is

sensitive subject matter, mate. You're telling me the old lady is pulling my leg?" He jabbed his finger at the laptop, still staring at Max. "That's your excuse for this garbage?"

Gloria Estefan played louder; Teddy started tapping his foot impatiently.

"I had to follow Roman's notes," Max said. "They had to win first prize in that baking contest—"

"Shut up."

Gloria Estefan played louder.

"I didn't want to write it that way," Max said. "You have to believe—"

"*Christ* that music's got me in a right piss." Teddy stalked to the window and threw it open. "Oi! Put a cork in that radio you Brighton Rock-swallowing spunk—"

Someone shouted, "Fuck off!"

Laughter. Gloria Estefan played louder. Teddy sucked his cigarette, dropped it, and stormed from the room. Max limped after him. He caught a glimpse of Mrs. Barclay sleeping on her bed, Thomas by her side, tube in hand. They exchanged glances.

The little girl jumped rope on the driveway. A tall, bronzed man stood on the deck, skimming the pool. Another man lay on a towel. Two others floated in the water. Teddy marched to the deck, grabbed the radio, and whipped it at the side of the house where it exploded into shards.

The tall man dropped the skimmer. "What the hell?"

Teddy narrowed his eyes. "Say it, mate. Go on."

"Just ignore him," said one of the men in the pool. He wore sunglasses and a wide grin. "That's one of Thomas' exes. He told me all about—"

Teddy picked up the skimmer pole and brought it down on the grinning man's head. The metal clanged. The tall man lunged for Teddy, who chopped him in the throat and kneed his face as he pitched forward. The man on the towel scrambled to his feet as Teddy pulled the sap from his back pocket. He struck the tall man. Someone screamed. Teddy struck him again.

Max limped back to the house just as a car pulled down the driveway and a large, broad-shouldered man got out. His hair was perfect—blonde and parted at the side. He wore a high-collared white polo.

"Max Beeber?"

"Not now—"

"I'm Richard. We need to talk."

Max held up his hand. "Not *now*."

The little girl stared as Teddy battled against a skimmer-wielding man.

"Tell your daddy to call the police," Max said.

The little girl looked at Richard, then the pool, then at Max. "I'm not supposed to talk to—"

"Just tell your daddy to call the goddamn *police*!"

The little girl burst into tears, and Max limped into the house. "Thomas!" he shouted, shuffling to the back, where Thomas scrubbed his hands in the bathroom. A full bag—filled with thick, brown liquid—lay in the bathtub.

"Teddy's lost it." Max put his hand to his forehead. "You have to get your mom out there. She's the only—"

"I slipped thirty milligrams of Valium into her orange juice." He rinsed. "Otherwise I could never have my friends over. She doesn't approve. God, I *hate* cleaning this shit. Seriously, if I ever lose my colon just give me a bottle of Quaaludes and a pint of—"

"He's going to kill them."

"Who?"

"Teddy. He's going to kill your friends."

Thomas dried his hands on a towel. "My friends can take care of themselves. The thing about Teddy is—"

A gunshot. Max and Thomas looked at each other.

Richard stood by his car, frozen. The little girl's father stood in front of his daughter, arms out. Teddy paced along the deck, sweeping his gun in a semi-circle. His forehead trickled blood into his eyes, and he wiped it away with the back of his hand. The tall man lay on his side. He moaned. His three friends backed away.

"Teddy." Thomas walked slowly toward the pool, Max close behind. "Just stay calm."

"It was a fucking mistake," Teddy said. "Tell them that night didn't mean anything. Could've happened to anyone. I'm no queer. Not by a half."

"They know," Thomas said. "One night didn't mean any—"

"Wasn't in my right mind. Doesn't make me a queer. I love women. Fucking love them. Dated Cheryl Rabinowitz. You know her—nice little Doris, lives in Sheepshead Bay. Broke my heart."

"I know," Thomas said.

"Bum-fucking's not my Jane." Teddy looked over his shoulder and smiled. "I asked Max if you'd given him the squint. Like I'm jealous and all. How funny is that?"

One of Thomas' friends stepped forward and Teddy aimed the gun at him. "You're the bloke split my forehead. I think I'll shoot you in the face."

Thomas ran forward; Max noticed the bag in his hand. He brought it down on Teddy's head and the bag burst, spilling liquid shit. Teddy dropped the gun and Thomas kicked it toward the pool, where it dropped into the water. Teddy stumbled back, hands to his eyes, spitting and gagging.

Everyone watched as Teddy lurched toward the pool. The little girl screamed and her father vomited. Teddy roared, tore at his shirt, and fell back. The water turned brown. After a few seconds a hand slapped on the edge of the deck, then another, and Teddy pulled himself up. He rolled onto his back.

"Like Chinese." He spit. "Smells like fucking Chinese food."

"Kung Pao," Mrs. Barclay said, and she shuffled past Max, triple-pronged cane stabbing the ground. She stopped on the deck. "It never agrees with me."

Teddy got to his knees. He looked up at Mrs. Barclay. Brown water dripped from his hair. "Were you in Dachau?"

"Mom—" Thomas began, but she held up her finger.

"It's my story," she said.

Teddy looked at Max. "Get your laptop." He stood, slicked back his hair, re-tucked his shirt, and nodded at Richard. "Oi— Mr. Collar. Where'd you come from?"

"Pardon?"

"Where are you coming from? Queens? Long Island?"

"Lower West."

"Traffic on the bridge all right?"

"Uh, yeah. It was fine."

"Good. Max, I'll be in the car. Bring some towels. Air freshener, if they have it."

Max limped past Richard and patted him on the shoulder.

"Julie loves you," Max said. "It was my fault. I got her drunk and took advantage."

Richard stared, frowning.

"You have a good woman who loves you," Max said. "My girlfriend hates me. I know the difference."

Max entered the front office, laptop in hand. Teddy followed, shirtless, brown stains along his neck and shoulders. Julie put down her book.

"Morning, Jules." Teddy kicked Roman's door and the frame

splintered. "Roman in?" He kicked again; the door banged open.

Roman sat at his desk, peeling a lemon. Shane sat across from him, also peeling a lemon.

Roman leaned back. "Teddy—"

"Shut up. You read Max's script?"

"Max? As in Mr.-Won't-Call-Me-Back Max? As in the little shit standing behind you?"

"Fucking *rom com*?" Teddy shook his head. "Who writes a Holocaust rom com? I read your notes. *Disgusting*." He looked at Shane. "And your draft was worse than disgusting. We need a new fucking word for your fucking talentless, fuck-all fuckery."

"Teddy—" Shane began.

"It just needs a quick polish," Roman said. "Nothing that can't be fixed. The important thing is we've balanced the comedy with the pathos." He drummed his fingers on the armrest. "It's a good combination."

"It's a terrible combination," Max said.

Roman held up his hand. "Now, just wait a second. We can't go full Holocaust. The genre is dead. What, another film with some Jews trying to escape another concentration camp? Or with a father trying to protect his son from the reality of their fate? Or with yet another handsome SS guard—"

"Well, we did want Bruno to be attractive," Shane said.

"Of course." Roman chewed a wedge of lemon. "In that buttoned-up Nazi kind of way. But my point is, we need to do something—*God*, what smells like shit?"

"Shit." Teddy pulled a wet cigarette from his pocket. "Go on."

"My point is, we need to do something special. Shane and I were discussing bringing on a different writer. Obviously, Max can't give us what we need. For Christ's sake, he pitched Shane the idea of Bo Bailey as Bruno Asher."

"Who the fuck is Bo Bailey?" Teddy asked.

"A teen pop star," Julie shouted from her desk. "He sucks."

"He doesn't have the gravitas," Shane said.

"Teddy, just listen for a second," Roman began, juice dribbling down his chin, "I found this new kid—he worked on Eddie Shiner's flick last summer. The one with the pimp who becomes a cripple? The kid's a genius."

"I followed your notes," Max said. "To the letter. And Mrs. Barclay was never in Dachau—"

Roman slapped his desk. "You didn't return my calls, you didn't show up with the pages you promised, and now you're trying to blame *me*? Did your agent tell you I'm suing for two hundred grand? No? Good. I wanted to give you the news myself. I'm suing you for two hundred grand."

Max stepped forward. "On what grounds?"

"I don't need grounds. I just need a lawyer. But since you asked: failure to fulfill the terms of your contract, and directly contributing to production delays, which, if we factor in Shane's salary, and the time I'm spending on this project, when I could be—"

"I'll tell everyone the script isn't real."

"Go ahead. It doesn't matter. Nobody gives a shit. I always thought you were naïve, but I didn't realize—"

"Treblinka," Teddy said, quietly.

Roman frowned. "Well, I don't see the problem with Dachau, but if you want it changed to Treblinka—"

"Historically, Treblinka might be a smaller death camp," Shane said, "which could cut down on design costs. Julie? Could you Google *Treblinka*?"

"My grandfather, Morris Garber, died in Treblinka." Teddy pulled the sap from his back pocket.

"Such a tragedy," Roman said. "We all lost someone."

"Along with his daughter, Amy." Teddy blinked. "His son, Samuel."

Roman nodded. "I lost a second or third cousin."

"My great-uncle, Israel. And his son, Eli. And his wife, Rachel, and their daughters, Rebecca and Sarah. Rebecca was pregnant. I got one of Sarah's teeth. Little gold cap. Don't know if it's hers, but it's *someone's*. It's bloody *someone's*."

Teddy brought the sap down on the lemon, spraying juice and pulp.

"Whoa," Roman said, dropping his lemon.

"They made Rebecca give birth on a cement floor. Left the baby there. To see how long it lived, how long it cried, before it gave up. Alone on that floor. Covered in filth. Mucus drying on its little face. Cousin Muriel told me it fought for days. Nothing she could do to save it. Now, Muriel's the only one who survived. Everyone else—my family, my blood—is gone."

Roman swallowed. Max watched a bead of sweat trickle down his neck and slip under his collar. Roman licked his lips. "Max," he said, "did Julie send you page ten?"

"Page ten?"

"My notes. Shane and I had some other ideas. In case—you know, Mrs. Barclay's story didn't hold water."

"I don't have it."

"That's what I thought." Roman buzzed Julie. "Julie?"

The door was still open; Max could see her at her desk. She was writing on a piece of paper. She shouted back, "Yes, Mr. Roth?"

"Could you give Max a copy of my page ten notes?"

"Of course." She stood, straightened her shirt, and walked into the office. Her skirt fell to calf-length, her blouse buttoned high. "Mr. Beeber." She handed him the paper.

Max looked at it. A single sentence in the middle of the page:

Make something up.

They all stared at Max.

"Tonight," Max said. "I'll have it fixed by tonight."

Teddy glanced over. "You can do that?"

"He's a damn good writer," Roman said. "He can extrude anything."

"Burt Phillips wants him to work on a *Sea Wolf* reboot," Shane said.

Teddy narrowed his eyes at Max. "I read your little story. One with that handsome bloke and his moody girl. Bit tough to swallow, all that crying on the beach, arguing on the yacht. But I liked it." He clapped Max's shoulder. "Tomorrow morning. Ten a.m. We'll get lox from Swarinski's. You stay focused, mate. *Focused*."

"I will. Goodbye, Teddy."

Teddy squeezed, briefly, allowing himself a little smile. Then he walked out.

Roman exhaled and Shane slumped back in his chair. A pause, then Roman looked at Max's shirt.

"What the hell is that supposed to be?"

"It was Ben Kingsley's," Max said.

Roman nodded, impressed. Shane pointed at Max, fingers in the shape of a gun.

"I have such canker sores." Roman winced. "All these goddamn lemons."

Max folded his shirt and zipped the bag. The room was finally cool, afternoon rain clouds hanging low, a gentle patter outside the window, dotting the pool and plinking along the gutters.

His laptop fan whirred. On the screen, the last page he'd written:

INT.   ISABELLA AND BRUNO'S KITCHEN - NIGHT

Isabella and Bruno stand in their kitchen, bottle of champagne on the counter. Jazz plays on the radio. A half-eaten loaf of bread sits on a cutting board. Bruno gets two glasses from the cupboard. He flicks the rim and listens, smiling, as the crystal vibrates.

>BRUNO
>Did I not tell you? The judges were astounded.

>ISABELLA
>I've made better. In the camp, with fewer ingredients--

>BRUNO
>(tearing foil off the champagne bottle)
>You are always so hard on yourself. Izaak's loaf was perfect. And with the article in today's paper, and the bank's loan--my little Bella, we will be a success.

Isabella nods. Bruno slips the bottle between his thighs and strains with the cork.

                    BRUNO
          Mein Gott, this seems to be
          stuck. Can you fetch me a knife?

She pulls a knife from the drawer and
approaches Bruno.

                    BRUNO
          Sometimes a piece of wire gets
          lodged--

                    ISABELLA
          Let me.

He hands her the bottle. She places
it on the counter. She stares at the
bottle label. It's a sparkling wine from
Rheingau.

                    BRUNO
          Our success will honor
          him. Izaak's name will be
          immortalized.

                    ISABELLA
              (still staring at the wine)
          And his son? Josef?

                    BRUNO
              (beat)
          He expressed no interest, but we
          can certainly--

                        ISABELLA
            His wife? Rose?

                        BRUNO
            Of course.
                    (beat)
            Bella? Is something--

She turns and thrusts the knife into
his stomach. He gasps and she pushes it
deeper, driving him back until he presses
against the refrigerator.

Close zoom to her face. Her lower lip
trembles. Bruno's breathing is ragged. He
struggles to speak.

                        ISABELLA
            Does it hurt, my love? This is a
            taste. Only a taste of what my
            people suffered.

A wet ripping sound as she twists the
blade and pulls it up. Camera stays on her
face.

                        ISABELLA
                    (continued)
            I hope you die. But if you do
            not, I have severed your lower
            intestine. And this--

>   (Another twist; Bruno cries out and his
>   hand clutches at Isabella's cheek. The
>   hand slowly slides off, smearing blood)
>   This is your stomach. Every time
>   you shit into a bag you will
>   think of my eyes, staring at you
>   without a hint of mercy.
>
>   She pulls out the knife. Bruno slumps
>   to the ground, holding his stomach.
>   Blood covers his hands. Isabella kneels,
>   and tenderly brushes his hair from his
>   forehead.
>
>   ISABELLA
>   (continued)
>   Farewell, khazer.
>
>   Cue klezmer music. Slow zoom to the loaf
>   of bread on the cutting board. We hear
>   Bruno gasping and crying in pain, the
>   clatter of the knife on the floor. Then
>   footsteps, the front door opening, and
>   slamming shut.
>
>   FADE OUT.

A knock. Max closed the laptop. "Come in."

Thomas entered, holding a thick mailer. He wore a Judy Tenuta T-shirt. "You never got in that swim."

"I'm not really a pool guy."

"Yes, well, we're having it drained, for obvious reasons. You know they found a rat stuck in the filter? Anyway, this is for you." He handed the mailer to Max. "Some guy dropped this off. He looked bad. Like he'd been hit by a truck. In the face. Anyway, I figured you didn't want to be bothered."

"How's your mom?"

"She's good. No more Kung Pao. I'm putting my foot down."

Max slipped the laptop into his shoulder bag. "Is your friend okay?"

"A busted nose, but he's tough. How's Teddy?"

"I don't know. I'm FedExing my pages and heading straight to the airport."

"Probably a good idea. Knowing Teddy."

"Probably."

"So. Max."

"Thomas."

They shook hands. Thomas left. Max sat on the bed and ripped open the mailer. Inside, another envelope, and inside that, thick rolls of hundreds, wrapped with rubber bands. He dumped the money on the bed and counted fifteen thousand dollars. Tucked into the bottom of the mailer he found a single page, handwriting at the top:

From a khazer to a mensch.

Max paused. Rain continued to fall. He gathered the money into a small pile on the pillow and left it there. Then he placed the note on the desk, slung his shoulder bag, and limped out.

THE LOVE LIFE OF TIGERS

Henry told the girl with short brown hair that he was sorry he couldn't join her for lunch even though he found her very pretty, and under different circumstances maybe they would have shared a bottle of wine and talked until dusk. But he was late and he was lost, and his wife was expecting him, and somewhere along his travels he'd misplaced his luggage. Now all he had was a frayed green duffel bag. Impossible, Henry thought, that he should go on a trip without something more. But it was all he had, so he stepped off the train at an unknown station, and gazed at the surrounding trees while the girl with the short brown hair stared at him through the window and waved a small good-bye. She might have been politely covering a yawn.

Henry watched the train shrink down the tracks and disappear around a bend in the woods, then he looked into the forest beyond. Soft tall trees on a late summer day; pools of light and dappled gold soaking into the quiet forest floor. No underbrush or fallen limbs. He walked up a gentle rise and stood atop an outcropping of boulders blanketed in moss and leaves. He hiked his duffel bag over his shoulder and picked his way over the rocks, canvas rasping against his expensive suit, twigs crackling beneath his polished shoes. Strange, he thought, this green duffel bag. Like something a boy returning from the army would carry. But he'd never been in the army, never owned a green duffel bag. His wife would know where he got the bag. Women, Henry thought, remember those sorts of things.

The forest ended at a lush green lawn, a hill with a white-pillared mansion at the top, and a gravel driveway that snaked down from the mansion to a high stone wall and a wrought-iron gate. He heard music somewhere, piped-in orchestral strings and piano. He made his way across the grass, mindful of his frayed bag, and his expensive wrinkled suit, and his polished shoes now flecked with forest dirt and bits of leaves. He set the bag down and wiped his shoes with the inside arm of his suit jacket. Then he heard something that sounded like the creak of a door, a low and guttering staccato.

Across the lawn, past the winding gravel driveway, there prowled a tiger. Broad, muscled shoulders, whiskers like cactus spines, yellow fur striped with rust. Its footfalls whispered in the grass. It raised its black snout to the fading warmth and sat on its thick haunches as its rumbling purr sifted the dirt below.

Henry saw other animals. A trio of peacocks, feathers shimmering emerald and cerulean, with quills the color of chalk. They preened past a row of hedges trimmed square and sharp as cubes. From the hedges leapt a raccoon. It scampered up the driveway and gave the tiger wide berth, continuing toward the white pillared mansion. Beyond the hedges Henry saw a bear on a platform surrounded by iron stakes. The bear pawed and growled. It paced and swept its head from side to side. It bellowed. It harrumphed and pushed against an iron stake, claws scraping on the metal.

Henry walked to a cluster of lounge chairs where two women lay. A black bikini and a white bikini. They wore sunglasses and their toenails were painted red. They sipped from margarita glasses frosted with sugar, filled with liquor the color of jade.

You're in my sun, the white bikini said to Henry. Her hair was black and long.

It's not him it's the trees, the black bikini said.

Is it really that late? the white bikini said.

It is, the black bikini said.

We've been out here all day.

We have. Are you tired?

A bit, the white bikini said. It's the alcohol, you know. I would never get tired if it wasn't for the alcohol.

The black bikini looked at Henry over the top of her sunglasses. You can take off your jacket, if you'd like.

I'm okay, Henry said.

Suit yourself, the black bikini said, and the white bikini laughed.

There's a tiger, Henry said.

Of course there is, the black bikini said. It's no bother.

What if it's hungry?

They keep it well fed, the white bikini said.

But tigers kill for sport.

Do they? the black bikini said. We're keeping our distance.

Tigers run, Henry said.

Well, so do we, the white bikini said, and she ran her fingers over her smooth thighs. See these legs? These are runner's legs.

Henry looked up and saw a man in a black suit carrying a silver tray with cocktail glasses. The man stalked across the lawn, tray still aloft.

The man stopped, out of breath. He stared at the green duffel bag.

Excuse me, sir. Are you a guest?

Phillip leave him alone, the white bikini said. He's not bothering us.

I'm lost, Henry said. I got off at the wrong station. None of this looks familiar.

This is a private place, Phillip said. And if you are not a guest, or the family of a guest, I'm afraid—

You know I could sure use a drink, Henry said.

Phillip frowned. These drinks are for guests, sir.

Oh Phillip, just give him a damn drink, the black bikini said.

Ma'am if it were up to me—

It is up to you, the black bikini said.

Phillip frowned again. Then he plucked a glass from the silver tray.

Be quick about it. No sipping.

Sipping is for guests, Henry said.

Correct, sir.

Henry finished the drink and set the glass back on the silver tray, and Phillip led him down the hill. They walked past the tiger which sat with its eyes closed. Late sun melted over the green, gnats hovering in slants of light, bouncing among translucent tips of grass. At the high stone wall Phillip set down his silver tray and unhitched the iron gate.

There is a bus station in town, Phillip said.

Where do the buses go?

I don't know, sir. I don't take the bus.

Then Phillip picked up his silver tray and rearranged the cocktail glasses, his lips pursed, empty glass pushed to the edge. He snapped a curt bow and closed the gate with a sharp click.

A row of cars sat against the curb, engines running. Henry smelled exhaust and hints of autumn. The fatigue of leaves and flowers. He walked down the line of cars. Young men in vests and dress shirts jangled keys and shouted numbers and drove away. At the end of the line a woman with thick blonde hair sat in a black convertible, two children fussing in the back seat. She leaned over the seatback and hushed them.

Beautiful car, Henry said. Is this a—

Unlikely, she said, still glaring at her children. The children quieted and shrank into the soft leather.

Well whatever it is, it's beautiful.

Thank you, she said, glancing at his wrinkled suit. His frayed green duffel bag.

Beautiful, Henry said once more, and he walked across the street. There, on the sidewalk, he watched a young man in a vest and white shirt take the blonde woman's keys. She hurried away, long, pale fingers clutching her children's hands, black heels clicking against the sidewalk.

Henry watched and wondered where his children were. He ran his hand across his green duffel. Perhaps he'd taken someone else's bag by mistake and left a soft leather case on the train. Stuffed with baubles for his children and jewels for his wife. A set of keys for his house on the hill where he could stand in the living room and gaze out the windows at the valley. His wife would call him for dinner. He could hear the footsteps of his children. Their giggles. Their sing-song laughter. He couldn't remember their names. Colin and Isabelle. Jack and Ashley. Named for his father and mother, perhaps. Or his wife's grandparents. She would remember; he never could.

The young man jangled the blonde woman's keys and looked at Henry. You waiting for one of us?

No, Henry said.

You a guest?

I'm afraid not.

Well, that's all right. The sidewalk is free.

Henry looked down the street. A flashing red light, a pile of windswept leaves crowded against the curb. He heard the tiger's roar.

The young man jangled the blonde woman's keys again. Say, you need a ride somewhere? To town, maybe?

Henry thought for a moment. The bus station, he said.

Bus station it is, the young man said.

Henry crossed the street and stopped at the stone wall, listening. Faint screams. He ran down the sidewalk, green duffel bag slapping against his side, and looked through the wrought-iron gate, up the lawn where late sun melted across the green, and saw the tiger crouched atop a lounge chair. Yellow fur flecked with red, white whiskers dark. A woman lay on the grass. Jumble of naked limbs, long black hair like spilled ink. Sunglasses hooked over one ear. The tiger pawed at her gently. She shifted limp under its claws.

The crack of a rifle; the tiger leapt. It bounded over the lawn, low and long, eyes narrowed, curved claws digging into the grass. It skidded at the edge of the forest and lifted its black snout. The bear pushed on its cage. Phillip stalked across the gravel driveway, rifle held in both hands. He raised it to his shoulder and fired again, and the tiger slipped between the trees, leaves whispering. Henry and the young man watched Phillip kneel by the broken woman.

Sometimes they catch them, the young man said. The guests, I mean. Sometimes the tigers catch them.

I warned her, Henry said. She said she was a runner.

Well, it's done now, the young man said. You still want that ride?

What about that tiger?

They'll find it. Come on.

Henry sat in the black convertible. Its soft leather seat was warm. Much more comfortable than the train, he thought.

I don't want you to get in trouble, Henry said.

No trouble, the young man said. The bus station is too far to walk. That tiger might get you on the way. You never know.

Henry sat with his bag in his lap, fingernail scratching against the canvas. He stared out the window at the brown blur of the stone wall. It would be dusk soon, he thought. The end of their bottle of wine, had he chosen that way. The pretty girl with the short brown hair. They would have had lunch, at a restaurant with thick white linens and quiet waiters. The menu printed on a single page, bits of multi-colored food stacked high in the middle of white plates. The food would have been good but not excellent, just disappointing enough to give Henry something to make fun of, and he would say something witty and maybe she would laugh, dizzy with wine, and her long pale fingers would brush against his and he would think back to the train stop in the middle of the forest. An outcropping of boulders for someone else to climb upon. Someone else's wrinkled suit and polished shoes. Someone else to hear the scrape of black claws on iron stakes and see white whiskers stained dark. Someone else entirely, with a wife who remembered those sorts of things.

JACK THE BASTARD

Now, gods, stand up for bastards!
—*King Lear* Act 1, Scene 2

KILLING TIME

Jack rumbled through southern Texas in a pale white El Dorado, mesquite trees coiling from the plains and barbed wire zipping past in a ragged line. Carcasses of armadillos and belly-swollen coons lay bloated along the side of the road, straddled by vultures. Jack saw silos and windmills, slanted barns with sun-grayed boards, water towers with faded town names painted across their sides: El Ray, Bass Drop, Temple-On-The-Hill.

The El Dorado's AC was useless so he drove with the windows down, the hot wind ruffling his hair and rippling his T-shirt. He'd never been to Texas before and found it just like in the movies; hard plains surrounded by mountain ranges, and except for the occasional rest stop—gas stations where attendants reclined on porch chairs, bottle of Fizzer cola propped in their lap—Jack felt as though he'd stepped back in time. He would not have been surprised if a cavalry rumbled past, swords and badges gleaming. Then the El Dorado's wheels locked.

Jack felt the engine hitch and grind. He slammed on the brakes and the Caddy skidded along the shoulder, spraying dust, gravel clanging off its underbelly, slowing to a stop with its tail sticking out in the road. He stared out the window a moment. He cut the engine, listened to the metal tick, laughed to himself, and popped the hood.

It was an hour before another car passed. A black pickup slowed to a stop on the shoulder, in front of the El Dorado. A mounted shotgun flashed in the cab's rear window. A dwarf stepped out of the truck. The dwarf wore a child's baseball cap and cowboy boots with steel-tipped toes. His hands were small and tight-skinned, his eyes shadowed in deep sockets.

Jack got out of his car.

"Overheat?" the dwarf said.

"I think it's the transmission."

"You check the fluids?"

Jack nodded and the dwarf looked under the hood. He squatted down, hung onto the fender, and pulled himself under the car. After a few moments he said:

"You got a cracked boot. It looks like it's been cracked for a while, so your drive train could be shot." He pulled himself back out and stood up. "Course it could be the transmission. But it could also be the engine. Look here—you can see where someone repaired the gasket. Sloppy work." The dwarf dusted off his jeans and T-shirt.

"Are you a mechanic?" Jack said.

The dwarf shook his head. "I'm a cook. My dad was the mechanic." He put his hands on his hips and shot the car a final disapproving look. "How much did you pay for this thing?"

"Five hundred."

"Where'd you get it?"

"Dallas."

"Is that where you live?"

"I'm from Detroit."

"I figured."

"Accent?"

The dwarf pointed to Jack's shoes. "Sneakers. Where you headed?"

"Humble."

"*Humble*?"

"That's right."

The dwarf stuck out his hand. "Foxhall Gantry. I'm from Humble. You want a ride?"

Jack leaned his head against the cool window of Fox's pickup truck and stared at the sky. Banded clouds stretched in rows. Far off, on a ridge dotted with green juniper bushes, he saw a stand of cattle. He shifted in his seat and winced at the flare of pain in his leg.

"You were limping back there," Fox said.

"I was."

"What happened?"

"When?"

"Whenever you got that limp."

"I had an accident."

"What kind of accident?"

"A bad one."

"Oh." Fox drummed on the steering wheel. "Those are the worst kind. You a tourist?"

"I'm looking for Owen Cahill."

Fox stopped drumming. "I knew Owen. He's gone. Moved away."

Jack knocked his head against the window. He fingered the watch in his pocket.

"He left last year," Fox continued. "I can't blame him. Who the hell would stay in Humble?"

"Not Owen."

"Are you his friend?"

"I couldn't call myself that."

"Well, I've lived in Humble my whole adult life. My folks were from Fuller. You know that town? Stone's throw from Humble if you got a decent arm. There used to be a cable factory but the county ended its contract and Fuller dried up and blew away. Some of that dust landed in Humble."

Fox kept one hand on the steering wheel and fished a joint out of his T-shirt pocket. Jack noticed he was sitting on a telephone book, a wooden block strapped to the bottom of his right foot.

"Mind if I light up?"

"Not at all."

Fox lit the joint and snapped the match out his window. "My dad worked at the cable factory. One year left before my dad could retire and the whole place burned down. He had a full pension and all that. The fire took him. My mom had a heart attack six months later. *Poof.* All gone. Up in smoke, as they say. The factory didn't rebuild and the town sued. Lawyers wrangled for ten years before we got a settlement. My cut was two grand. I told Sheriff Wade: 'You think two grand replaces my parents?' Nothing he could do, but what the hell. Two grand and my folks are still dead, and Fuller still has no factory. No factory meant no jobs, and no jobs..." He spit a fleck of weed. "Most everyone with enough money and ambition got out. The losers moved to Humble. How far do you think I'm going to get with two grand? Maybe to Coldspring, and I wouldn't live there. So I took that two grand and had a week in Tejon, and those little brown women laid the grief right out of my soul."

Fox snorted smoke from his nose.

"I'll tell you the worst thing about Humble, though. Standing at the end of Main Street and staring straight ahead, toward Yell Lake. I can take it all in, in about ten seconds, and know that's all I'm ever going to see. The rest of my life. The lake and the dust. I may as well be blind. Nothing new under the sun." Fox paused. "You want me to shut up?"

"I'm just listening."

"Because I have a tendency to ramble. I talk to myself all the time. I figure if I talk fast enough I can't tell what I'm going to say next, so it's a surprise even to me. Of course that doesn't make much sense but it sounds good." He held out the joint and Jack shook his head. Fox took another hit, his hand perched on top of the steering wheel. Ash floated in the AC stream.

He glanced at Jack. "What do you do in Detroit?"

"I paint houses."

"Do you like it?"

"I don't hate it."

"Pays the bills, in other words."

"That's right."

"Married?"

"Nope."

"Girlfriend?"

"Yep."

Fox nodded. "I had a girl in San Antonio, years back. Met her in college—well, community college. She was a little crazy. Not dangerous crazy. Just…she had these *moods*. And she talked to herself a lot. Especially when she was doing dishes. She'd argue with herself but I couldn't hear what she was saying because the water was too loud. I think she wanted it that way. Anyhow. We rented a tiny apartment, overlooking the river." He drew slowly, letting the smoke glide up his face and curl around the edges of his nose. "Then my dad died, and she wouldn't come to Humble with me. I understood. I mean, I was pissed but I understood. You know anything about Buddhism?"

"A little."

"If I could be anything, I'd be Buddhist. It makes the most sense. You have your four essential truths. First says: 'Life is suffering.' They just come out and say it: 'Life is suffering.' The righteous don't get their way and bad things happens to decent folk. All those Buddhist monks walking around their temple practicing kung fu—" Fox clenched his fist and punched in the air. "They grab hot coals with their bare hands and run up and down the mountainside, in the middle of winter, wearing nothing but a loincloth. Know why?"

"Pain tempers the soul," Jack said.

Fox nodded. "Life is suffering so you better get used to it." He took another hit and flicked the joint out the window.

"What about the other three?" Jack said.

"The other three what?"

"The other three truths."

"I don't know. I only went to the first class."

Jack looked back at the shotgun hanging in the cab's rear window. "Is that your gun?"

Fox shook his head. "That's Roy's gun. This is Roy's truck."

Jack nodded. Collecting names—Foxhall, Roy, Sheriff Wade. He'd ask them about Owen. Someone would know where he went. He figured everyone knows everything in a small town.

The green sign for Humble popped into view on the horizon, and as they drew closer Jack could read it:

> Welcome To Humble
> Pop. 38
> The Lord Will Bless What He Loves

There was Humble suddenly, sitting on the plain, a cluster of brown cubes, flashes of sun glinting off the windows of its low-lying buildings. They passed by tin shacks with corrugated roofs, and a yellow trailer standing in the middle of a dirt field, a wooden cabin attached to the side, covered by a tattered awning. Jack saw a dog bolt from the side of the cabin, barking and scrambling after the pickup until the chain ran out and the dog snapped back on its hind legs.

They drove into town, past a lone willow oak. The interstate blacktop crumbled into a dust road, and Jack saw boarded storefronts and sagging brick buildings with their windows punched out. He saw a Laundromat—Buck-A-Wash—with washing machines on one side and shelves of rental movies on the other. He saw a clothing shop—Chayban Denim—and a convenience mart with an old, cracked plastic sign that read Yellow Goose. A knot of teenagers sat on the curb in front of the mart, staring at Jack as he rolled past. Past the mart stood a church—Emmanuel First Baptist—painted white with a tall steeple stark against the sky. A police car waited in front of Chayban Denim.

Fox stopped at a crossroads and pointed down a smaller street lined with big homes.

"That's Sage Street," he said. "Where Owen lived." He pointed ahead. "And that's where I work."

Fox pulled into the front parking lot of the Busy Bee Diner. It looked like every small-town diner Jack had ever seen, from its big front window to its blue buzzing neon sign that commanded EAT. The front door was papered in faded fliers, advertising events long since past: spaghetti dinners at the church, fundraisers for the now-defunct fire department, coupons for free vaccinations at the old veterinary clinic. Across the street from the diner was a cemetery, treeless and dotted with jumbled rows of crooked tombstones.

Jack got out of the truck. He heard the wind. No planes or helicopters. No car horns or people yelling from their apartment windows. Nothing on the street except a paper cup blowing and skipping through the dust.

Fox unstrapped the wooden block from his foot. He opened the door, eyes narrowed against a swirl of grit. "Lunch is on me."

Jack limped into the Busy Bee Diner. He felt the stares as he sat at the counter. A ceiling fan paddled quietly. A cooler stood in the far corner, and its compressor shuddered to life. Booths ran the length of the front window. The floor was old, yellowed tiles of linoleum, curled at the seams where it met the counter and cracked at the holes where the booths and tables were bolted to the floor. An old man sat a few stools down from Jack, methodically eating a steak, pushing buttered grits onto his fork with the edge of a knife, sipping his sweating bottle of Fizzer Cola. The old man wore a baseball cap, pulled low. His hair was white, cut close, and his skin was tanned the color of clay, cracked with wrinkles. He turned and regarded Jack with a nod, then went back to his steak.

Jack could hear the old man chewing. He heard whispering behind his back, and the rustle of Fox's apron as he slipped it over his head. He glanced over his shoulder. Two people sat in a booth; a son and his father, Jack guessed. They both had short, black hair. A bar of sunlight fell over their plates stacked with flapjacks, sausages, and cupped strips of fat-sparkled bacon. The young boy munched a piece of bacon with both hands, staring wide-eyed at Jack like a squirrel caught in mid-nut. The father drank his coffee, cowboy boots scuffed with dust, hands corded with veins. His arms were long and tanned muscle. Jack saw a faded tattoo on the bicep: a boot crushing a snake, the snake sinking its teeth into the heel.

"Anything on the menu," Fox said. "Except the Angus burger. We're out."

"I'll have a BLT," Jack said.

Bacon sizzled on the flat iron. Jack wiped his forehead with a napkin. Fox slid him a glass of ice water. The old man moaned as he ate.

The father looked up. His eyes were small and dark. "Hey Fox.

You get that valve all right?"

"Got two," Fox said. "In case one's defective I didn't feel like making the drive again."

"How about my wonton?" the father asked.

"Shanghai Charlie's was closed."

"Closed? For lunch on a Tuesday?"

"I guess they had a plumbing problem."

"I was looking forward to that wonton. How come you can't cook up something like that?"

"Because I'm not Chinese."

The father plucked a bacon strip from his plate. "Neither is Shanghai Charlie. His ass is Vietnamese." He munched slowly, eyeing Jack. "What's this you picked up?"

Jack kept his back to their table. He sipped his water, took an ice chip in his mouth and cracked it in half with the point of his canine tooth.

"Roy, this is Jack," Fox said to the father. "I found him on 95, at the 609 junction. His car—"

"The tranny dropped," Jack said.

"Anyway," Fox continued, "I was thinking if Willie can't give him a tow, maybe I could borrow your truck. It wouldn't take but an hour—"

"No." Roy rested both hands flat on the table. "I got business. Wait on Willie."

The old man belched. "You wait for that old nigger, you'll be waiting until the end of days." He pushed his empty plate forward. "Might still find him at the church, though. Reverend said carpets needed cleaning."

"I'm in no rush," Jack said.

Fox sliced a tomato. Red juice spurted off the blade, dotting the cutting board. The cooler's compressor shuddered to a stop and Fox slid Jack his BLT.

The diner door jangled and a young man walked in. His head was shaved and a pink scar ran from under his left ear to the nape of his neck. His arms were thin and hard, with sun-reddened knobby shoulders.

"Morning, Curtis," said Roy.

"Morning, Roy," said Curtis. "Hey Eli."

The old man nodded. Curtis took a seat near Jack and eyed his sandwich.

"I'll have one of those," Curtis said. Then he looked over his shoulder at Roy, and nodded his head in Jack's direction. Roy shrugged.

"Jack here is a friend of Owen Cahill," Fox said.

Curtis scratched his shoulder. The edges of a fresh tattoo peeked out from his T-shirt sleeve—an eagle's claw, clutching an x-shaped bunch of arrows.

"I think he went to Laredo," Curtis said. "You must not be that good of a friend, seeing as how he moved away without telling you."

"We haven't talked in years," said Jack. "I called him a few weeks ago but his number was disconnected."

"You came all the way to Humble to see a friend you haven't talked to in years?" Curtis grinned. "Where you from?"

"Detroit."

"Must be one lonely sonofabitch, coming all the way here for a friend who didn't bother telling you he left."

"I have my moments," Jack said.

Curtis rubbed his shaved head. "Tell me about it. Already made my way through every good piece in this town. Nothing left to stroke, you get what I'm saying?"

"You can't find something to stroke," Jack said.

Fox laughed.

"Hell you laughing at?" Curtis said.

"Nothing," Fox said.

Jack took a deep breath and rolled his head to one side.

Fox quickly finished making Curtis' sandwich and slid it to him with a slice of pie, then wiped his hands on his apron and hopped up on his stool.

"I saw Willie at the church," Eli said. "Maybe half hour ago? Wasn't doing nothing. Just sitting there. Carpets didn't look no cleaner."

Roy walked to the counter, boots clomping, thumbs hooked into his belt loops. Jack looked over his shoulder. They really walk like that down here, he thought. He saw the caption on Roy's snake tattoo: *Don't Tread on Me*.

"Feels like the AC isn't doing its job," Roy said to Fox. "Just so you know."

"Tell it to Willie," Fox said. "He hasn't cleaned the filter in a while."

Roy swept his finger along the edge of the counter. "Looks like nobody's cleaned anything, in a while."

"Maybe we're all depressed," Fox said. "It's been going around."

Roy left a folded bill on the counter. "Curtis. Eli. Be seeing you tonight." He nodded at Jack. "Stranger."

"It's Jack," Jack said.

"I prefer stranger," Roy said, and he walked back to his table, gathered up his boy, and left the diner.

Curtis finished his pie in two bites and slid off the stool, sandwich in hand. He brushed against Jack and banged through the diner door like it had stepped in his way.

Eli sucked his teeth. Fox sighed and cut into his fried egg.

"We should probably go find Willie," Fox said to Jack. "If you ever want to get out of here."

Jack walked from the diner to Sage Street, dust and gravel rasping under his sneakers. Sage Street was two hundred yards of suburbia dropped into a Texas cauldron. Drought-stunted mesquite and prickly Osage orange lined either side, dwarfed by sagging mansions. Juniper and prickly pear ran wild across the front lawns, where Jack imagined the owners had watered their manicured grass every day, and the smooth blacktop driveways—where he imagined children played four-square, hopscotched, and drew dinosaurs with fat tubes of chalk—now slowly cracked under the sun.

He found Owen's home as he figured he would. The curbside mailbox had CAHILL stamped along its side. It seemed Owen had been one of the last to leave—his white Victorian still had some patches of unpeeled paint. Jack limped to the front door and knocked. He looked up and saw a bird's nest tucked in between the slatted porch ceiling and the top of the door frame. There was a feather stuck in the wiry ball of twigs, barbs vibrating in the hot breeze.

He tried the door and it opened, and he stopped on the threshold. A grand staircase stood in front of him, between a living room and a dining room. The air smelled of wood. He called out *Owen* even though he knew no one would answer.

He limped into the living room, where he found furniture: a red velvet couch, matching chairs, a faded Oriental rug. There was a fireplace with a scrolled marble mantel, and a framed picture above of what looked like Venice—tall, askew buildings, lining a canal with water painted Mediterranean blue, and a gondola tied to a boardwalk.

Jack walked to the couch and saw a cup sitting on a glass coffee table. The cup still had a spoon sticking out of it, and a shriveled tea bag sat at the bottom, its string pasted to the side. A pad of paper lay nearby with a poem scribbled on top:

The dud-blimmed ride is juiced, and everywhere
The incense of matrimony is frowned.
Which explains why I cannot get laid
I cannot get laid.
I cannot get laid.

The kitchen was empty—white tiled floor, bare table, bare counters, and bare cupboards. Jack went upstairs. It was hotter on the second floor. He walked from bedroom to bedroom, throwing closet doors open until he found one with something in it other than wire hangers and balled-up socks.

A black T-shirt lying in the corner. The front read TITTY KAT KLUB. A shoebox sat on the closet shelf. Jack pulled it down. Stuffed inside were dozens of letters with gutted envelopes. He picked one.

O,

Not that I'm surprised you refuse to send even a postcard, but some sort of communication would be better than what we have now. What we have now is a Cold War, and despite me accepting full blame and spending gallons of ink apologizing, you continue to hold your grudge like it's worth something. You should know how sorry I am because I'm not one to bitch and moan about anything. If mom were alive she'd do all your hating for you, so why don't you pretend she's already called and told me how wrong I was.

Love,
Jack

In the bathroom Jack found a toothbrush in a plastic cup on the sink's edge. He picked up the toothbrush and ran his fingers along the bristles. He opened the medicine cabinet and there was a nail clipper, a crinkled tube of hydrocortisone, and a half-empty bottle of Valium.

"Sir?"

He spun around. A chubby young man, wearing a cowboy hat and a police uniform, stood just outside the bathroom. His gun sat on the front of his hip, holster hanging off his thick black belt.

"Deputy Bob Garrett, Humble Police Department," the young man said. His face was pink from the heat and he blotted sweat off his upper lip with a handkerchief. One hand remained at his belt, within reach of his gun. Jack guessed he'd never drawn the thing.

"I didn't hear you come in," Jack said.

"I'm a light walker. Can I ask what you're doing here?"

"Looking for Owen Cahill."

"Identification, please."

He took out his wallet and handed over his license.

"Are you a relative of Mr. Cahill?" Bob glanced at Jack's license, then at Jack, then back to his license. "I guess you are. When was the last time you spoke to Mr. Cahill?"

"Years ago."

"How many years?"

"Five."

"Well, he's gone since then."

"Did he say where he was going?"

Bob shook his head and looked at the license once more. He pulled the handkerchief from his pocket and dabbed his upper lip. "You're not supposed to be in here."

"I didn't see any trespassing signs."

"There's no signs because the whole street's condemned. We had a kid fall through a staircase just last year." Bob looked around. "I'll have to bring you to the station, Mr. Cahill."

"Call me Jack."

"I prefer Mr. Cahill, if you don't mind."

Jack shrugged. "It's better than stranger."

Police headquarters were behind a makeshift wall in the back of Chayban Denim, with a door and a window, and the words HUMBLE POLICE SHERIFF WADE GARRETT DEPUTY BOB GARRETT stenciled across the door. The front of Chayban Denim had a rack of jeans and denim shirts. Jack didn't see anyone working behind the register.

He sat on a metal office chair while Bob sifted through some papers, took notes on a yellow pad, and made a copy of Jack's license. With his hat off Jack noticed his little-boy buzz cut and his sunburned ears.

Jack rubbed his eyes. He wanted to find Willie, retrieve his car, and figure out where the hell Owen was. Forget seeing Austin, he thought. I should get back home while there's still time to patch things up with Sarah.

They'd broken up countless times before, always the same routine: A cross word or tone leading to accusations of indifference and criticisms of their respective families, followed by failed make-up sex, a spectacular blowout, and radio silence for a week. Then she'd show up at his door on something like a Wednesday, and they'd fuck, still angry and sad, until everything had been pushed down far enough to pretend it never existed. He knew one day their drama would run out. He figured she'd meet someone, get married within six months, get pregnant six months later, and she wouldn't damn herself for having wasted so much time on Jack because she wouldn't remember who he was. *He was always so sad,* she'd tell her husband. *After all our time together, that's all I can tell you about poor Jack.*

An older man walked in. Papa Wade, Jack thought. Wade Garrett shared the small blue eyes of his son, but where his son was pudgy and soft, Wade was lanky and tall, hard edges and sharp points, his face scoured like a weathered fence post, hands mottled from the sun, with long fingers, knobby knuckles, and thick-corded veins. He held his cowboy hat, swept back his longish gray hair behind his ears, and looked at the paperwork on Bob's desk with the narrowed stare of a man long accustomed to sniffing out trouble.

"My son says he found you trespassing in the former Cahill residence. Says you were looking for Mr. Cahill." Wade picked up the copy of Jack's license. "How come your brother didn't tell you he was moving?"

"We haven't talked in a while."

Wade drummed his fingers on his gun's grip. "You just decided to pop in for a visit, that right?"

"That's right."

"All the way from Detroit." Sheriff Wade shook his head. "Hell of a trip for a pop-in. You just finding out about your mother?"

"I know she died," Jack said. "I've been trying to call but Owen's number is disconnected."

"Sounds to me like he didn't want to talk."

"That's why I'm here."

"To patch things up."

"If I can, yes."

Wade stared at Jack a moment longer, then handed him his license. "That'll be a two-hundred-dollar fine, for trespassing. We'll take cash. And I am sorry about your mother. She was a good woman. Bit on the private side, but she never complained."

Jack pulled the money from his wallet and held it out for Bob. Wade took it instead. Jack stood and shook out his leg.

"Fall off a ladder?" Wade asked.

"War wound," Jack said, and he limped out of the office.

Fifteen years ago Jack spent most of his days killing time in a small apartment in the village of San Benedicto, at the top of a steep, winding road cobbled with brick and patches of dirt. San Benedicto was built into the side of the smallest mountain in Honduras, a scattering of whitewashed buildings like dice on a green board. Shops and bars were tucked into shadow-speckled alleys, the mountain air kept the streets cool until the afternoon, and every morning Jack walked down to the grocery store and bought a glass of orange juice that a shirtless boy squeezed by hand while Jack waited. Then he'd sit on the curb, watching women with their children, watching stray dogs pick scraps from garbage bags and lap water from the gutters that ran along the sidewalk. He drank his juice and pretended no one knew who he was. Like all the American agents pretended, all day every day, while they ate in *palapas*, drank *guaro*, and ignored the stares.

Later that day Jack met a company man named Judge at Mayorga's, the bar of choice for homesick soldiers, where Carlos the owner wore an I LOVE NY T-shirt and the TV behind the bar showed dubbed reruns of *Welcome Back, Kotter*.

What's the word? Jack asked.

Just killing time, Judge said. He was a hulking man, forever dabbing the sweat from his forehead with a red handkerchief. His eyes were lost amid swollen, capillary-strewn cheeks and dark sockets, his thick lips were perpetually sunburned, and he breathed with great effort every time he moved. To Jack he looked like a slowly melting glacier, plucked by the gods and dropped into the tropics, dissolving, dripping, leaving behind a detritus of empty pop cans and cigar stubs.

One year earlier, six nuns had been shot dead and found in the alley behind the Santa Rosa Church. There had been whispers of a connection with the Hidalgo cartel—local Marxists partnering with Mexican drug money to buy arms for the always-rumored insurgency—but Jack hadn't heard anything definitive, so Judge was his man. He was everyone's man; the "white elephant" they called him, lumbering through the streets, feeding stray dogs, flipping quarters to children.

I've heard some things, Judge said. He leaned back and folded his hands across his large stomach. His pop can waited patiently. *Innuendo, at this point. Nothing I'd hang my hat on.*

Then why call me here? Jack asked. His morning buzz was gone; he itched for its return.

I'm lonely, Judge said. *Don't you ever get lonely?*

Sometimes.

Judge sipped from the can. *There's this doctor I've been following for the past year. A gynecologist. He owns a bakery in Puerto Cortes. At night the bakery becomes an abortion clinic. On weekends the bakery shuts down, and this doctor goes to work for his employers, the Hidalgo cartel. Last year one of our guys got his cover blown, and the cartel handed him over to the doctor. He tortured the guy for a month. Cut off all his limbs, kept him alive with blood transfusions and antibiotics. When we finally found him he was just a stump with a head. The doctor had taken it all off. Anything that stuck out—his nose, his ears, his dick. Poof. Gone. Before the informant died he told us the doctor cauterized the wounds with a blowtorch.*

Judge shook his head.

That doctor kept that poor sonofabitch alive until the Hidalgo cartel extracted every ounce of pain they could. And then they left him on our front step wrapped in a blanket, like a baby in a basket. Now I'm thinking: *what has to happen to someone to make them that evil? You can't tell me it's just crossed wires or the wrong chemicals squirting out of the wrong glands at the wrong time. I think there's something else at work here. Someone evil enough to chop off a man's arms and legs, then his nose, ears, and worst of all his johnson...that's someone with the devil in their heart.*

The devil's an excuse, Jack said.

Judge shook his head again. *I call it the devil but you might have a different name for it. Doesn't matter—we're talking about the same thing. It's like an infection, you know? You're around it all the time, and it gets into you.*

I know, Jack said. *So I prefer not to think about it.*

Judge stared at him. *You have to remind yourself that what you see isn't normal, because your definition of normal changes. I've watched it happen—company men who've been doing what I do for a long time. The devil wears them down...makes them believe they can only fight evil with evil. You know what we're going to do once we haul in that doctor? Torture him, then bring him to trial. If he survives. Maybe he strokes out on the table. Maybe, when we're shoving glass shards under his fingernails, he blows a gasket. Who knows? Who cares?*

Not I, Jack said. *You need a hand, give me a call.*

Judge dabbed the sweat from his forehead, mouth set tight. *All I know is, I don't want to become another company man.*

You'll always be different, Jack said. *You're on the right team.*

They ate lunch, ceviche and guaro, watched two episodes of *Kotter*, and when the check came, Judge took out a thick fold of bills.

11:30 tonight, Judge said to Jack. He dabbed his forehead once more. The front of his shirt was soaked through with sweat. *Avenue Rialdo, number 10. Something might happen.*

Like what?

Judge put on his sunglasses. *Like something. Get there early and introduce yourself. HFA doesn't like surprises.* Then he lumbered away, pushing through the crowded street.

HFA, Jack thought. Honduran Freedom Alliance. American bad boys too stupid to make it into the officer's club, too loyal to cut off, and always expendable. Jack's superiors operated from on high, but the HFA were rogue. No paperwork. No accountability. No killing time.

That night Jack drank mango juice and vodka while watching *Hollywood Squares*. At 11:15 he put on a baseball cap and left the apartment. He walked down an alley, plastered walls and shuttered windows on both sides. A dog loped ahead, stopping to drink from a puddle underneath a line of laundry.

Jack found them waiting on the corner of Rialdo and Espenza: three HFA bad boys, dressed in black. He flashed a card and the tallest of the men flashed his standard issue 9mm.

You new? the tall man asked. *You look new.*

Jack shook his head.

How long you been in town?

A year next month, Jack said.

Seen any action?

Fits and starts.

The tall man grinned. He had a missing canine tooth. *So you got something official for us?*

Jack looked at the three men. *I'm ready for whatever.*

Whatever with your whatever, the tall man said. *You got something official?*

Judge sent me.

That's all the permission I need, the tall man said.

The tall man kicked down the door and they rushed in, guns

drawn, yelling in Spanish. Jack hung back in the doorway, clutching his gun, scanning the street. They'd told him a major dealer lived at this address, that this dealer personally knew one of the men who killed the six nuns.

They shot the husband in the head while he sat on the couch with his wife, watching TV, then dragged her into the bedroom as she screamed and kicked. Jack saw something move in the far corner of the room; he raised his gun.

Pare! he shouted. *No se mueva!*

An outstretched arm, the outline of a head. Jack squeezed off three shots; the body dropped. He moved quickly and silently across the living room, gun still aimed. He knew what it was before his eyes recovered from the muzzle flash. It was their son, of course, or maybe a nephew, a boy of twelve or thirteen. Jack switched on his Maglite. No weapon in the boy's hand. Short brown hair, staring eyes, red blooming across the front of his yellow T-shirt. He was still breathing, shallow and quick, then he stopped.

Jack stared for a moment. He searched for guilt but found little. This wasn't the first kid he'd killed during his eighteen months. Duty could get sloppy—after a while, he couldn't even remember their faces.

THE EDUCATION OF SOLEDAD SANTANILLO

It was on Luisa Santanillo's deathbed that she finally told her daughter the true fate of her father, Rafael Santanillo. The previous story had been that of a car accident on a rainy night, and in her childhood nightmares Soledad heard the squeal of rubber and saw her father swerve and crash into a tree. Sometimes he'd crawl from the twisted wreck, bloodied fingers and ripped clothes; sometimes the car would explode like cars always did in the movies. But every time he'd be calling her name, *Soledad*, and every time she'd look for him, suddenly in an empty field by the highway, with glittering cubes of windshield falling all around, the smell of burning plastic and smoking metal rising in the cold night air. Of course she could never find him, and she'd run through the field, his cries behind a tree, at the bottom of a footprint, under the skeleton of a rabbit that she remembered had been devoured by a wolf in an earlier dream.

Su padre no murió en un accidente, Luisa Santanillo confessed while machines clicked and tubes dangled from her arms. *First things first. You were not born in Buffalo, nor were you an only child. You have a sister, Paloma, and you were both born in Texas, in the town of Fuller, which is a very small town, pale like a half-buried bone. I brought you to Buffalo because I was afraid my past would one day return, and I did not want you around when that happened. Also, Buffalo had cheap housing and Aunt Ruth promised me a job. I know how you feel about your aunt, but, remember, she wasn't always so bitter. Buffalo does that to people. It's the snow, I think. And the unhealthy food.*

Your father was head librarian at the Fuller Library. He was a terrible husband, a wonderful father, and an insatiable reader—he cursed at his books and threw them against the walls, he praised them and drew obscene pictures in the margins. I remember your father's voice in the morning, rising from the end of our bed, as he sat hunched over with his glasses balanced on the tip of his nose and a book held like a baby in his small hands. It didn't matter to him what he read: the back of a bathroom cleaner spray can, the list of ingredients on a cereal box, the directions on a chopstick sheath. The morning of his death he read to me from Don Quixote. *The significance of that will be made clear soon enough.*

Luisa clicked the morphine button. Soledad waited, paper cup of water clutched between her hands. Outside the hospital room door a nurse walked past, sneakers squeaking.

On a Wednesday afternoon at the Fuller Library, on a rainy day when the leak in the ceiling of the children's books section plinked in the green bucket sitting on the floor—I don't remember if it was green, actually, but it's such a vivid image —a man brought Don Quixote *to the counter and asked to borrow it, even though he had no library card. Your father had read* Don Quixote *332 times. He loved that book as much as he loved anything. I remember one afternoon, when I returned early from the dentist, and found your father lying on the kitchen floor, pants down, book in hand—*

You were talking about the library, Soledad said.

Yes. Of course. So your father refused the man because he had no card. The man asked again, and again your father refused. Your father suggested the man apply for a card, and as it was told to me, the man slapped your father in the face.

'You are not worthy of Cervantes,' said your father. 'Go find something by Thomas Wolfe or James Patterson.' Then the man drew his sword and cut off your father's head with a single blow.

I am told your father simply sat back down on his chair even as his head rolled off the counter, and he died with Quixote *in his lap. Were that the end of this sad tale, the tragedy would be enough. But there is more.*

I knew the man who murdered your father. He had demanded my affections the day before his fateful library visit, and I refused. Not because I was a chaste woman—your father's bibliophilia left me very lonely, at times—but that man wasn't my type. That is, he had a cruel way about him. I have always preferred nervous men, the sort who avoid conflict and turn their rage inward. But the devil will not be denied. After murdering your father the man came to my home. On my living room floor he crushed me beneath his bare chest while he grunted and his toes curled. When he finished he cut me—here, on my forehead, where I told you windshield glass had sliced deep—and because you were watching from your crib, the man cut you as well.

(When my story is done I want you to take your compact, go into the bathroom, and look under your chin; you will find a small crescent moon.)

Your sister was asleep in her room at the time. Thank God she did not witness the horrors that unfolded upon my living room floor—the groans, the grunts, the sweats, the gasps, my hands clutching his strong shoulders and clawing his back, the way he cruelly pinched my nipples, the way he bit my delicate neck—but I am certain subsequent horrors have been visited upon her thousandfold, for the devil then stole her from me. She did not cry as he carried her out. She only stared at me. My night terrors? My pills? My drinking? My gambling? My age-inappropriate clothes? My shoplifting? My forays into various cults? My fad diets? My felonious boyfriends? I blame him. Not an hour has gone by over the past twenty-four years that I don't think of Paloma.

I swore I would find her and bring her back, but I lacked the courage. I was only a poor housewife, you see, widowed, with one remaining child. I couldn't leave you. My only revenge was to raise a good daughter. Of course there are worse methods of vengeance, but now I only tell you the truth because my guilty heart has hardened and cupped like a scrap of leather.

Luisa paused. Then:

The man who killed your father and stole your sister is Esteban Gallegos. Hear his name, my beloved daughter, and despair.

Soledad buried her mother the following week. After the caterers left and the sympathy cards slowed to a trickle, after she stopped crying herself to sleep and the oddest things no longer made her sob—the scent of Ivory soap, department store Muzak, certain bird songs—she took inventory of her life. She was twenty-six and single. Men were plentiful and predictable; they were suckers for her child-like eyes, thick dark hair always in a ponytail, lips looking as though she'd just applied red and licked them. She worked as a manager at a clothing store in the mall, underpaid, of course, but mollified with employee-discounted designer labels. Her friends were succumbing to the ticking of their sociological clocks, already obsessing about wedding plans, broken alliances among co-workers, and perceived slights from former college roommates. A Friday night spent at the local bar suddenly seemed absurd. *These are the best times of our life,* one of Sol's friends said to her, without a trace of irony, and Sol wanted to punch her in the face, right there, at TGIF's.

It had been three months since her mother's death. Now, whenever the phone rang, her stomach leapt. The far-off wail of sirens brought attacks of diarrhea, as did thunder, firecrackers, and loud music in restaurants.

She stopped dating. Old boyfriends sent emails asking if she'd gotten engaged. Her childhood nightmares returned, only this time she was in a field with her sister, both of them searching for their father. Soledad had one photo of Paloma, taken when she was two years old and Paloma was ten. It was a photo she'd seen many times, but her mother had always told her the girl with the blue shorts and pigtails sitting next to her on the porch steps was the child of a family friend. Now the photo became something else. She read an entry in her long-ago abandoned journal (a small leather-bound book found at the bottom of a shoebox):

What did I do this summer? I listened to Pink Floyd in the backyard and enjoyed the smell of cocoa butter on my skin. I smoked a pack of Black Cat cigarettes every week, those long blue menthols that Ray the cashier sells me at Red Barn because he likes my ass. I dated a boy from Rochester who I met at a poetry reading at The Locust, and even though he was a dweeb I let him take my virginity one month before school started. It didn't hurt and it didn't frighten me because I think he was a virgin too, and all that bullshit about saving yourself for marriage is so terrible because I can't imagine not hating the boy who took your virginity. You hate him and it isn't fair but it doesn't matter. He takes the girl out of you. It needs to be done. Though sometimes I fantasize about cutting his throat. Just watching it drip-drip onto the floor.

Sol posted an online ad one Monday evening, after a Sunday brunch with the girls was interrupted by stomach cramping and a subsequent sprint to the restroom, the result of the restaurant jazz band striking up "Days of Wine and Roses":

SWF seeks swordmaster/gun specialist. Serious inquiries only. No fetishists, please.

Two weeks later she found a teacher one mile from home, in a town called Lackawanna, where abandoned steel factories loom like iron mountains and chain-link fences stand guard over empty parking lots festered with weeds. Her teacher was a small elderly woman named Mariko Murimoto, who lived in a brown house with a crooked roof like a half-raised eyebrow.

Every morning Mariko taught Sol *iaido*—the art of drawing

the sword—and in the afternoons she taught her the Tokugawa school of swordsmanship.

The Tokugawa school ultimately concerns itself with only three cuts, Mariko explained. *The first is* itto ryodan, *or 'splitting the opponent with a single stroke.' The second is* zantei setsutetsu, *or 'cutting through nails, severing steel.' With the first cut, there is no swordsman alive who can withstand its fury. With the second, even God himself would take pause.*

And the third? Sol asked.

Shinmyoken, said Mariko. *'Divine sword.' Were one to master this stroke, one would find oneself capable of destroying the universe with a single blow.*

When do we get to the guns?

Mariko smiled. *Shooting is easy. Swords first.*

Soledad ran at dawn, every day, five miles along the shores of Lake Erie, under the shadows of grain elevators and brick mills. After her morning exercise, Mariko would place her in front of the mirror leaning against the basement wall. First, she taught her how to stand with a sword. Then, she taught her how to move with a sword, having her cut the air three thousand times until her arms trembled and her muscles leaked acid, while Mariko struck her feet with the end of a PVC pipe if she stayed in one position too long, struck her arms if they wandered too high or too low, struck her knees if they weren't bent enough. Mariko stressed *sanguku*: posture, arms, legs, and sword. *Sanguku.* Always sanguku, always sanguku, over and over until Sol dreamt the word and it stuck in her head like a song that wouldn't leave.

Sol tried sleeping with her *katana* lying next to her, as Mariko had suggested, but she found it too ridiculous. She barely tolerated the ice-cold showers, standing with her arms wrapped around her chest, teeth clattering, concentrating on keeping her breathing measured while she meditated upon her death:

Every day, without fail, one should consider one's self as dead. I will die on a mission of revenge, or waiting in my car at a traffic light. I will die in the midst of a great battle, or in my bathtub. The elders say: Step from under the eaves and you're a dead man. Leave the gate, and your enemy awaits.

Peter, a manager at the local sporting goods store, had been after her for months; she finally relented and they went for drinks. Peter was funny in a self-deprecating way, with soft deep-set eyes and Kurt Cobain–style hair that he often pushed behind his ears. Sol drank two beers, refusing his offer to pay. They played pool. A hard-looking man placed his quarters on the side rail but Peter didn't notice, and he racked the balls for another game.

My turn, the hard-looking man said.

Peter paused, triangle in hand. *I'm sorry?*

Take a seat. We got next.

But we're not finished.

The man sniffed. *You are now. Those are my quarters.*

Yes, but we're not finished.

The man put down his bottle and took a step forward. Peter raised his hands, palms out. Sol grabbed her cue and struck the man across the face; when he stumbled she thumped the butt end against the point of his knee. He fell. She jabbed the tip into his throat, standing over him, her face calm, her breathing measured.

Everyone stared. Peter dropped the triangle. The man coughed and clutched until Sol dropped the cue.

I'm sorry, she said.

Ten minutes later Sol sat in Peter's car, in front of her apartment.

Do you want to come in? she said.

Peter rested his elbow against the inside of the door, fingers massaging his temple. *I don't know*, he said. *I really like you, but*

you seem to have a serious anger problem.
I've been in a rough patch.
Clearly.
Six months ago I discovered I have a sister who was kidnapped—
Whoa.
By the man who murdered my dad and raped my mom.
But you told me your dad had a stroke.
His head was cut off. With a sword.
Jesus.
So I've been training.
Yeah, that pool cue thing was ridiculous.
Ridiculous in a bad way?
Sort of. You looked crazy.
I'm going to get my sister, and I'm going to kill the bastard who took her.
Okay. Good luck, I guess—
We don't have to make this into a big deal, you know. We can just fuck.
Are you kidding?
Are you?

He started the car and stared out the windshield.

The next morning, Sol told Mariko she was leaving for Texas.

The old man crossed his sun-wrinkled arms, worked his chew, eyed the empty Coke can sitting atop the Blue Bonnet Inn's guest ledger, and decided not to spit just yet.

"You could take Route 17 and cut through Pandora," he said. "But police are buzzing all over the scanner. Seems a trailer overturned. Traffic is backed up for miles."

"I didn't think you had traffic here," Soledad said.

"We do now. And Route 17 is the only way out."

"There's no other way?"

"Nope."

"My map says there's another way."

"Well, ma'am, your map's wrong. Look here. Your map shows 195 running over Mt. Davis. What it doesn't show is what happens to Mt. Davis when the rain hits. Storm like this and you may as well hitch a ride with Noah and his ark because I wouldn't send a fish over Mt. Davis on a day like today."

"Then what do you suggest?"

The old man spit. "We got plenty of rooms. Take a shower, relax, wait out the storm."

Soledad leaned back against the counter. She'd been on the road for a week, spent the night before in Marshall, and had driven the seven hours to Bug Tussle before the sky split.

"I'll take a top-floor room," she said, "and send up a bottle of Scotch."

The old man sniffed. "You need a drink, there's the Turnaround Bar, just down the street."

Her room was nicer than she expected—small and tidy, with a firm bed and floral wallpaper that had some color despite years of sun. A schoolroom desk sat in the corner, near the window, an old stationery pad atop it next to a yellowed copy of *Field and Stream*. The magazine cover showed a man standing in a boat, holding up a salmon, with a coffee ring slicing his face in half.

Sol flopped back onto the bed and put her arm over her eyes. In the dark she saw the road, the sun vibrating on the baby blue hood of her station wagon. She'd taken two weeks to drive from Buffalo to Texas, stopping at small towns and interstate motels, letting the highway ground her former life to dust, letting the wind and sun scour whatever remained of her soft past.

She'd never traveled outside of Buffalo, yet she found most places looked alike—clusters of nuclear-glow franchise restaurants, neon towers sprouting from the same spots her mother had driven past twenty-four years ago. She liked walking the malls in every city she drove through, browsing stores that sold candles shaped like wizards and puppies. Food courts felt like home—all those slack-jawed teenagers selling teriyaki chicken chunks and Bourbon Street barbecue riblets. Department stores with high-haired women dressed in lab coats sprayed her with perfume and gave away coupons for lipstick, eye shadow, and exfoliating scrub. Daily meditations upon death had given Sol a newfound appreciation for the banal. Thus explained her favorite koan:

> How will the universe end?
> Clean the drain and rinse your sponge.

Bug Tussle's reputation had mellowed to the point of kitsch; the Blue Bonnet gift shop sold hand-painted bobblehead dolls of its most notorious citizens—Two-Gun Lyle, Earl "Midnight" Dobber, and Henry "Widowmaker" Winslow, among others—and fifty-cent guidebooks detailing Bug Tussle's gruesome murders, the most infamous being the Turnaround Bar massacre. Fifty-five years earlier, twenty-eight-year-old Esteban Gallegos had tracked one of his father's killers, and there, in the alley behind the bar, Esteban slaughtered thirteen men and dragged their heads on a rope through town.

    Sol sat at a table in the corner of the Turnaround Bar, sipping her beer while rain pattered on the roof. A broken mechanical bull served as a coat rack. The walls were paneled in rough-split pine and dotted with old business cards: AJ's Siding and Roofing; Stephanie Wheeler, Real Estate Agent; The Hot Poke Tattoo Parlor. Jacob the bartender stood at the end of the bar, arms crossed, white cloth slung over his shoulder.

An old man shuffled from the bar to Sol's table. He set down a bottle of Scotch and sat across from her. He wore a stiff denim shirt and snakeskin boots. His dentures were ill-fitting and made his upper lip stick out. His thin white hair was combed straight back. He had the face of a once-handsome man before age grew his ears and nose and his smooth features sank into deep wrinkles. His eyes were all he had left—a clear and piercing blue; glacial ice at dusk—but even they had sunk, Arctic glimmer lost in the shadow of bone and mottled skin.

"In town for a while?" the old man asked.

"Just waiting out the storm," Sol said.

"Road trip?"

"Something like that."

"Where you from, missy?"

"Missy?"

"Too young for ma'am. That a Midwestern accent?"

"It is."

"You married?"

"Nope. But I had a grandpa, once."

The old man chuckled and pinned his dentures to his gums with his tongue. The other old men, sitting at the bar, turned and stared.

"You know where you are?" the old man said.

"Bug Tussle," Sol said.

"You know what Bug Tussle is?"

"I know what it was. I visited the gift shop."

He grinned. "Maybe you think those days are long past."

"I'm just drinking my beer," Sol said.

"That so? Pretty lady sitting alone in my bar, just drinking her beer. You know—" The old man sat back and put his boots up on the table, bottle in one hand. He took a swig and bared his

"His eyes were all he had left—a clear and piercing blue; glacial ice at dusk..."

teeth. "Twenty years ago I'd finish this bottle, then fuck you 'til I sweated sober. And if you screamed for God's mercy, I'd tear off one of your fine tits and stuff it in your smart mouth. Now what do you think about that, missy?"

The four old men at the bar laughed. Sol thought for a moment. "I think you're bored," she said.

He watched Sol finish her beer, then took another swallow of Scotch. "You know who I am?"

Sol shook her head. She glanced at her watch.

The old man unholstered his gun—a Schofield revolver, mother-of-pearl handle, etched curlicues along the barrel—and opened the chamber. He dropped a bullet into his palm. Sol saw ED carved into the casing.

"Earl Dobber," the old man said.

"I read about you in a guidebook," Sol said. "It said you were a cold-blooded killer."

The old man smiled. "That was a long time ago."

The bar door swung open and in walked a tall, middle-aged man dressed in a wrinkled suit with dust staining the back and elbows. He wore a white shirt with no tie. Sol saw an edge of blood hidden behind the black silk lapels of his suit jacket. His face was tan and stubbled, his Rolex held together with a safety pin. He sat at the bar and ordered a highball of whiskey and water, then ran his hands through his hair, patting down strays.

Earl turned slowly and eyed the tall man at the bar. Sol listened to the rain rattling down the gutters. The bartender polished a shot glass.

She set down her beer and made as if to go.

"You best stay put," Earl said to her. His hand had slipped back down to his waist. He kept his eyes on the tall man. "It'll be over in a minute."

Earl stood, Schofield held low, while one of the old men at

the bar reached over to the tall man and pulled a garrote tight around his neck. The tall man jerked back and squeezed his highball until it exploded. He stumbled off his bar stool, clutching at his neck with one hand. His other hand fumbled inside his suit jacket; a small silver pistol clattered to the floor.

Earl walked to him, raised his gun, and stuck the long barrel in the tall man's ear. The Schofield roared. A clot of blood spurted from the tall man's eye. He tottered for a moment, as if deciding where to fall, then his legs buckled and he collapsed like an empty sack.

Sol whispered around the table and stopped in the middle of the room. Earl looked over his shoulder. The old men stood slowly, bar stools squonking across the floor.

"I'm looking for Esteban Gallegos," Sol said. "I don't have a problem with anyone else, and I'd like to keep it that way."

Jacob the bartender grabbed his sawed-off shotgun and aimed it at Sol.

"Esteban Gallegos hasn't been in this bar in fifty-five years," Earl said.

Sol paused. "You know him?"

"I might," said Earl. "Why do you ask?"

Sol paused again. "It's complicated."

Earl tapped the grip of his gun and grinned. "We need to talk, missy. Soon as Jacob cleans up the mess I made."

Earl Dobber waited downstairs while Sol knelt by the toilet and stared at the black-and-white-tile bathroom floor of her room. The remnants of her beer swirled in the coiling water. She rinsed her face and looked in the mirror. It was the face of someone who'd witnessed murder, now. No different than before. She tried to stand, then returned to the toilet once more.

They met in the back room of the Blue Bonnet Inn, a small office with calendars tacked to the wall and a shotgun leaning in the corner. Sol sat at the table with packed bag and katana by her side. Earl Dobber sat across from her. Next to Earl sat the caretaker of the Blue Bonnet, the nice old man who Sol soon discovered was Henry "Widowmaker" Winslow. Jacob the bartender served them all coffee.

Sol told them the story of her father's murder, the rape of her mother, and the kidnap of her sister. She showed them the scar under her chin and the photo of Paloma sitting on the porch steps. The old men simply listened and nodded. They were no strangers to revenge tales. Injustice had never been scarce in their line of work, but even they admitted this was a particularly heinous offense. That it came at the hands of the infamous Esteban Gallegos—the six-gun samurai, the scourge of the Texas plains—was no surprise.

"The murder I can understand," Earl said, then quickly added: "The scarring of an infant and the kidnapping of a child, however…" He shook his head. "Esteban roared across these parts for thirty years. Didn't spare child, woman, or beast. Like the god of the Old Testament, he was."

Henry grunted in agreement and spit into his empty Coke can.

Earl took out his map and laid it on the table, tracing a line along the Texas border, east from Bug Tussle, past Coldspring and Fuller, to the border town of Tejon.

"According to what I heard—and there's no reason to believe otherwise—Esteban still lives in Tejon, same place he's been since I was a kid. If your sister is still with him—mind you, that's a big *if*—then most likely she's either retired from whoring or she's servicing deviants who prefer older women. Esteban's ancient but I gather he's no less dangerous. So if you march into Tejon with that pig-poker and your cute little ponytail, you'll be cut down before you can scratch an elbow. You any good with a rifle?"

"I'm decent."

"Then how come you're using a sword?"

She shrugged. "It seems appropriate."

Henry nodded and spit. Earl stared at Sol.

"What are you proposing?" she asked.

"A partnership," Earl said.

"You and your gun. Me and my pig-poker. And cute little ponytail."

"Henry, too."

She sat back, arms crossed.

Earl pulled a steel flask from his pocket. "Don't have much to look forward to, these days." He took a sip and smacked his lips. "There's serious history between Esteban and I."

"Is this a redemption thing?"

"Don't believe in redemption. Wouldn't want it anyway."

"This is my mission," she said.

"Course it is."

"I say what's what and what isn't."

"Course you do."

"Okay."

Earl narrowed his eyes. "Okay as in you'll think about it, or okay—"

"Okay as in I could use your help."

Earl slapped the table. "Sweetheart, you've made my day. Now do you really know how to use that sword?"

"Of course."

"Well, that's good," Earl said. "I hate an unfair fight."

A grin, a sharp breath. Sol grabbed for her sword. Henry had switched her katana with a broom handle, and as she leapt from her chair she brought it down on Jacob's right hand. His sawed-off shotgun fell to the floor. She broke the handle across the side of his head.

Jacob fell onto his ass. Henry sat back in his chair, the katana lying across his lap. Sol jumped over the table, holding the splintered broom handle like a dagger, legs tucked, ponytail streaming behind like a vapor trail. Then the world exploded and she dropped.

Jacob slowly got to his feet, smoke rising from the business ends of his shotgun. He unhinged the breech and let the two spent shells bounce off the floor. Sol coughed. She clutched her side and cried out.

Earl sipped from his flask. "It's just rock salt. Painful, sure. But not fatal—at least, not where Jacob aimed."

Henry spit into his empty Coke can. He looked down, grinning. "Thought you were dead, didn't you?"

She ran her trembling hands over her bloodied legs. The jeans were pocked with holes.

"You're running with killers, now." Henry spit again, and Earl laughed. "Yes, you are, missy."

While you're healing up I want you to ponder this: Against a man like Esteban Gallegos, two old-timers and a desperate suburbanite aren't going to do much in the way of revenge. In my estimation we are outnumbered by more than twenty to one, and we need reinforcements. Henry and I know some people in the town of Curacon, and we also know these people are the sworn enemies of Esteban Gallegos. If you think Texans hold a grudge, you've never seen a pissed-off Mexican. I suggest on the way to Tejon we make a detour south of the border, stock up on some of Curacon's finest soldiers, then head for Tejon.

What do you think?

I think I'd be crazy to listen to the man who okayed me getting blindsided with two shells of rock salt.

In the old days we would have taken your left tit.

Thanks. That makes me feel much better.

The village of Curacon lay fifty miles past the Mexican border, tucked into the side of a green mountain and surrounded by the most beautiful vistas Earl said he'd ever seen. Earl told Sol he'd lived in Curacon for a year, in his youth, recovering from injuries he said were well-deserved, and while there he fell for a young girl named Epiphany.

"She wasn't particularly beautiful," he said, "or particularly smart. But one morning I walked down to the river and saw her bathing in a sparkling pool, and the sight of her bare brown body almost made me give up my murderous ways. Almost."

Earl sat in the backseat of Sol's wagon, next to Henry, and the two old men slept. The station wagon rumbled across the plains, bouncing along dirt roads littered with fist-sized rocks. Soon the air thinned and sweetened as the land shifted. Sol drove up the mountain and looked out over a valley where tumbling green folds bathed in shadow, and red poincianas and jacaranda trees with purple flowers spread their arms to the orange sky. A flock of birds flew past, gliding from sun shaft to sun shaft, bright against the clouds like swatches of yellow silk.

The trees suddenly parted and the road widened; before them lay Curacon. A high cement barrier, with broken beer bottles sunk into the top, surrounded the village. The gate had fallen from its hinges. An oak tree stood just outside the wall. From its thickest limb hung the bodies of three skinned men, dangling from ropes like long, dried fish.

Sol rolled into town. A peccary bolted in front of the station wagon and snorted its way into the forest. The sounds of a radio lifted in the hot wind. Sol heard music. Bluegrass, she soon realized. She stopped the wagon and walked with Earl and Henry down the center of the road.

Two men sat on a bench under a drooping thatch roof. One man wore sunglasses and smoked a pipe. His companion sat with his arms crossed, a .22 lying on his lap.

"We're looking for Vargas," Earl said.

"Judge hung him," the smoking man said. He lowered his sunglasses and stared at Sol. "That a sword on your back?"

Sol walked on. Earl nodded at Henry, and Henry stayed put, double-barrel Winchester propped over his shoulder.

They passed by a man butchering a strung-up peccary. The man split the bristled meat with long strokes of his machete. Past the butcher they found a Mexican woman sitting on a rocking chair, drinking wine from a jug. A tattered blanket covered her legs. Flies swarmed.

"Something smells nasty," Earl said, and he snatched the blanket off the woman's legs.

When the flies cleared Sol looked down; the woman's calves were eaten almost to the bone, the maggots having worked their way up, past her knees. The woman groaned and reached out for her blanket. Flies crawled over her hair, perched on the tip of her eyelashes and hid in the hollows of her ears.

Earl unholstered his gun. "I'd be doing her a favor."

A giant man stumbled out of the forest, barefoot and stripped to the waist, sweat glistening on his broad, hairless chest like seawater on a whale hump. His head was huge and shaven, and his left ear was gone. A brown man lay slung over his shoulder. The giant grunted and dropped the man, then squatted next to him.

Sol saw a necklace dangling across the giant's chest, dried ears strung on a nylon cord. The giant set his pistol on the ground and pulled a Bowie knife from his leg sheath. He whistled as he cut a slit in the dead man's stomach and pried the flesh apart. Blood spilled and ran in a black stream, picking up clots of dust and flecks of plant before slowing to a stop at a stand of wire grass. Sol held her hand to her mouth.

"What manner of hell is this," Earl said.

The giant worked his hands through the tangle of intestines, plucked a small pink lump from the glistening mass, and held it up.

"Does this look like a baggie to you?" he asked.

"I'd say that's a kidney," said Earl.

He frowned and reached back into the gore. "They usually swallow the evidence, if they have the time." He worked his hands. "Judge likes to see the evidence."

He made one final sweep, then shook his huge head and walked to a watering hole. He rinsed his hands and wiped them dry on his pants. He stared down at the body, twirled his knife, fingered the ears on his necklace, and looked at Sol.

"Are you a half-breed?" he asked.

Sol stared back at him, gripping her sword hilt.

He sighed. "*Habla Espan*—"

"I speak English," she said.

He grabbed the dead man by the hair and dragged him to the forest's edge. "I'm Hector. You any good with that sword?"

"Good enough," she said.

He tossed the body into the woods. The woman on the rocking chair groaned, and Hector looked at her and laughed. Then he turned back to Sol. "Judge'll want to see you two."

The giant led them to a sagging Victorian house on the edge of town. Judge reclined on his chair in the living room with his feet elevated. He dabbed his forehead with a red handkerchief. His mouth hung open and his forehead was a series of canals and creekbeds dug deep from constant worry. He worried about the encroaching forest and the dwindling morale of his men, he worried about the seemingly endless stream of cocaine being transported across his mountain, he worried about his quotas and the fickleness of his suppliers, who expected results while refusing to grant his monthly requests for more weapons and manpower.

Give me what I need and I'll wipe out every single drug runner within a one-hundred-mile radius, he'd told them ten years earlier.

What do you need?

Aside from a priest, which I've requested hundreds of times, I need M2HB machine guns and L224 mortars. Plus dynamite, blasting caps, and a few big screen televisions with every Lee Marvin film you can get ahold of. I find Marvin is good for morale.

I'll submit a request for those televisions. And would you settle for James Coburn, instead?

Instead, they sent more pistols and antibiotics, and Judge soon realized his presence was a security blanket for the agency. As long as a white killer was on the mountain, they didn't care if he pulled a Kurtz and set himself up as a minor deity with half-naked savages worshipping at his feet. After fifteen years of loyal service, Judge decided to keep the confiscated cocaine for barter—there was no shortage of hungry mercs willing to sell their lives for a kilo or two of uncut coke—and FedExed his superiors the head of his most recent catch. The next month, he mailed them the man's feet, then his hands, then his heart wrapped in wax paper, sealed with a Mr. Yuck sticker. The phone calls stopped but the supplies didn't; for the first time ever they came with a handwritten note:

Keep up the good work.

Sol and Earl stood in Judge's living room where sunlight cut through the filmy windows. Across the room a man slept on a couch, his arm covering his eyes and a semiautomatic pistol resting on his rising and falling stomach. The room smelled of heat, foot powder, and sweat.

Judge pointed at Sol with his glass of water. "I dreamt of you," he said. "A Mexican woman would come to my village, and she would ask why I destroy her people. I told her in my dream, and I'll say the same to you: sometimes at night I set out food and I sit on my porch and I wait, and they come from the forest like little brown rabbits. Little brown rabbits stealing from my garden. I shoot them dead. Do I regret it?"

He took a gulp of water and shook his head. "This is neutral territory, the universe's virgin soil. This mountain is where Armageddon starts. Not in the streets of our great cities but here, hidden in the forest. This house, this town, this sun-cracked mountain. *Curacon*. This is where it all starts."

Hector had taken Earl's Schofield and Sol's katana, and now sat at the dining room table, digging dried blood from under his fingernails with the tip of his knife.

"I found this place two years ago," Judge continued. "I was living on the other side of the mountain, in the village of Zaragoza. Curacon's whereabouts came to me in a dream. It cost me twelve good men and two long weeks but eventually I arrested Gilberto Vargas and kept him locked in the root cellar for six months. Then I hung him and fed his body to the peccaries. My men tell me you came here looking for Vargas. Were you his friend?"

"He did me a favor, many years ago," Earl said.

Judge nodded. "Then you must have been aware of his involvement in a major Mexican drug cartel, which he operated out of this town, in this house we now stand in." He wrung the sweat from his red handkerchief into a bucket and dabbed his forehead. "So I have to make some calls. Important calls to unimportant people. Sometimes they answer right away, sometimes it takes them months. Until they do, the two of you must remain in Curacon. I'll have Hector clear the rooms upstairs."

The front door creaked open and the old rifleman strode in. He ducked under the chandelier in the foyer. In his right hand he carried Henry's Winchester. In his left he carried Henry's head.

"Did you get a name?" Judge asked.

The rifleman set the head on the floor and took an AARP card from his pocket. "This says he was Henry Winslow."

"Good," said Judge. "Pack the card with the head and load it on the truck."

The rifleman brought Sol a yellow dress. She sat in the corner of her room, back against the wall, barefoot, listening to the moans of the rotting woman in the rocking chair. The sun cast long shadows across the floor.

"Dinner in an hour," the rifleman said, then he walked out.

Sol stood and looked out the window. Men patrolled the grounds, stopping to chat, light a cigarette, uncap a bottle of Fizzer. She picked the dress off the bed and held it up. Calf-length, a low neckline, some label she'd never heard of. She untied her ponytail and shimmied out of her jeans.

They sat at a long table in the dining room, Judge at one end and Sol at the other, with Earl, the rifleman, and Hector seated in between. An old man in a tattered white suit brought a tureen of soup, a monkey on his shoulder carrying a loaf of bread that it ripped off pieces from and handed to each guest.

Judge dabbed his forehead. "The caldo de pollo is excellent. Luis' specialty." He smiled at Sol. "Tell me what you think."

She sipped. "Very good."

The old man in the white suit bowed slightly. His monkey threw a piece of bread at Hector, who caught it. Earl slurped.

"I apologize for the heat," Judge said. "The air conditioning unit broke last month, and getting parts has been slow. Everything is turning to mold—my rugs, my linens, even the bread—"

"This bread is fresh," the old man said, frowning.

"Not *your* bread, Luis." Judge dabbed his upper lip and sipped his water. "Your bread is excellent. But tomorrow morning, whatever remains will be covered in mold. *Mold*. I'm allergic to the stuff. Terribly allergic. The heat has made sleeping very difficult." He shook his head at Sol. "Do you ever suffer from insomnia?"

"Sometimes," Sol said.

"And you?" Judge looked at Earl.

Earl shrugged. "I sleep like a baby."

Judge sighed. "I've been suffering for months. I've tried everything: pills, acupuncture, colon cleansing, hypnosis. Every morning I wake up at 3:32 and perform the same routine—sit on my porch, in my robe and slippers, and wait for the sunrise. Sometimes I spy a line of ants in search of food; I hear them crawling through the dirt and scaling blades of grass. When I had your friend Vargas in my custody, I would allow him to sit by my side. Together we would watch the ants. One morning he tried to escape. I had his left foot crushed with a sledgehammer."

Luis cleared the soup bowls. A platter with a roasted peccary replaced the tureen. Hector carved the meat, smooth and efficient, spearing slabs with the tip of his knife.

"Vargas wasn't a friend," Earl said.

Judge chewed as juice dribbled down his chin. "No?"

"I knew him from years back. We came here looking to hire

some of his men."

"Hire?" Judge chewed again. "What for?"

"Help," Sol said.

"*Help*," Judge repeated. "How wonderfully vague."

"Like a mercenary," Earl said.

Judge paused, fork in mid-air. "Go on."

Sol and Earl glanced at each other. Luis' monkey leapt off his shoulder and landed on the table. It snatched a shred of meat.

"I'm going after someone." Sol swallowed with a wince. "Earl thought Vargas might be able to help."

Judge nodded. "Who are you going after?"

The monkey sprung from the table, landing atop a china cabinet. "Esteban Gallegos," Sol said.

Judge thought for a moment. "The name is unfamiliar. Are you an assassin?"

"Not officially," Sol said.

"Have you ever killed someone?"

"No."

"How do you think it will feel?"

Sol shrugged.

Judge steepled his hands. "It's much like everything else; it happens, and little changes. Of course *you* change, but the world does not. With blood on your hands you still need to buy groceries, pay the bills, go to the dentist. I have been trapped on this mountain for fifteen years. Countless men have died under my orders. Yet, I still have responsibilities. The air conditioning must get fixed. My men must eat. Mold must be eradicated."

Hector sliced another piece of meat.

"Yesterday morning," Judge continued, "I was sitting in my usual place, on the porch, when I saw a man emerge from the forest. He was my exact replica, wearing my robe and slippers, standing at the forest's edge. I wanted to leave the porch and walk to him, but I knew something very bad would happen if I did, like the beginning of a nightmare, that feeling of dread when you realize your dream is about to darken and twist. So I just sat there, on my porch, staring at myself. He turned his head to me, we looked at each other, and I believe I saw what it was. My dream had fallen asleep and begun its own dreaming. As though my insomnia—"

The monkey landed in front of Sol and motioned to take a piece of food from her plate. It blinked at her, tiny paw outstretched; she smiled; it plucked a morsel and dashed off.

"As though my insomnia were a birthing process." Judge dabbed his forehead. "A sort of *pregnancy* for my unconscious. So I ask myself: Is this the solution I've been searching for? The escape I've been unable to make? Maybe my sleeping self has found a way to live apart. Free to wander, to switch, to disappear and reappear. Maybe it's formed its own memories, its own reality. What would happen if it left? Where would it go?"

A pause. Earl looked up from his plate. Hector gulped his wine. Sol sat as demurely as she could, chin lowered, eyes wide.

"One memory tells me I returned to bed," Judge continued, "where I fell asleep, and awakened when I heard news of your arrival. Another memory tells me I walked into the forest and switched places with my other. Yet another memory tells me I shot myself. One clean hit—" He put his finger to the middle of his forehead. "Then a peccary ate my body. This same peccary we are now eating. Are you ready for dessert? Luis makes an excellent flan."

After dinner Judge dismissed them with a wave of his hand. Tomorrow, he said, he would place those phone calls. Until then he expected them to remain in their rooms. Standing in the upstairs hall, Sol asked Earl if he thought Judge would ever let them leave.

"Not a chance," Earl said.

All night the rotting woman in the rocking chair wept. Sol heard Hector laughing somewhere in the house, then the chatter of the television and the clink of glasses. Men no longer patrolled the grounds. She had slipped off her dress and left it folded on the bed.

She climbed out the window and shimmied down a trellis knotted with rose vines and wasp paper. A sprint across the front lawn—she watched for shadows in the windows—then she leapt over the fieldstone wall, stopping at the woman in the rocking chair.

"He has sent you to kill me?" the woman asked.

"I'm looking for my car. It's a white—"

"You will get me a gun, then. Please." The woman clutched Sol's arm. "I will do it myself. The pain. It is so *terrible*. It *burns*—"

"We can take you away from here, and bring you to a hospital. But I need a car."

"Hospital?" The woman smiled. "The things he has done to me, I do not want to live even if I could. He has eaten my flesh. Do you understand? The giant sliced off pieces of my legs and brought them to *him*. Brought them to me. For *me* to eat." She put her hand to her forehead. "He keeps a boy in his house. In one of the rooms on the top floor, where I can see his shape in the window. I used to hear the boy crying but he doesn't make a sound anymore. The boy is my nephew. His name is Mincho. You must take—"

The woman moaned and Sol heard laughter. Hector slipped off the top of the fieldstone wall.

"Beautiful night for a walk," he said. He was naked except for his necklace.

Sol snapped two spindles from the rocking chair. Hector hefted a sledgehammer.

The iron head whistled past Sol's face. She bent her knees and thrust at his stomach. The first spindle sunk deep into his side and the second impaled his left palm. When Hector sensed the broken tip had passed into the bones of his hand, he clenched his fist and jerked the spindle from her grip.

He swung his hammer again and missed. Then he kicked Sol in the stomach; she tried to turn but stumbled, feeling his boot thud into her gut, pushing out all the air, a moment of nothing then a rush of twisting, pulsing pain. She fell back. He charged, grabbing her hair and yanking her forward, into the point of his knee. He pulled her head back by her hair, pausing to grin before butting his forehead against hers. For a moment the world tilted. Hector's laughter was a faint peal. She stabbed his shoulder with the remaining spindle and ripped down, hearing herself scream as if from far away. She stabbed into his armpit, his flank, his groin, until his sledgehammer lay in the dirt and the spindle was a wet stub in her hand. Blood ran into her eyes from her forehead. Her stomach hurt when she breathed.

Hector sank to his knees. Sol dropped the spindle.

"It worked," she said. Then she heaved the sledgehammer and caved in his skull.

She found her katana and Earl's Schofield where Hector left them—on the kitchen counter next to the coffeemaker. The living room was empty, though the television still chattered and flashed. Judge's sweat bucket sat by his chair. The monkey watched her from its perch atop the china cabinet. Sol held her finger to her lip. The monkey returned the gesture. Sol tucked the Schofield into the waistband of her pants and crept upstairs, back sliding against the wall, sword held close.

She found Earl lying in bed, in the dark, hands behind his head, his boots still on. She gave him his Schofield and they crept down the darkened hall. Light shone from under Judge's door. Earl stood with his Schofield aimed into the dark. He nodded at Sol and she kicked in the door.

Judge stood, naked, over a bare-chested boy, flabby arms akimbo, penis erect. The boy's arms were mottled with bruises and his left eye was blacked. Judge looked at Sol. "My little brown rabbit," he said, grinning. "Was it what you expected?"

Her blade severed Judge crosswise at the chest. Blood sprayed Mincho while Judge's lower half spasmed and his upper half toppled. Earl fired at the rifleman running up the stairs. Two bullets for the man's knees and one for his chest; Earl shot the next man through the throat. He gurgled and spat blood onto the wall. He fell back down the stairs, wide-eyed, as though finally solving a question that had plagued him for years. Earl strode forward and took Henry's Winchester from the rifleman's hand. He checked the breech and snapped it shut.

Mincho hugged the woman in the rocking chair. She whispered she was sorry she couldn't have killed Judge herself, then she touched his face and he stepped away. Earl did what they had all agreed to. He fired a single shot between her eyes. She took a short, sharp breath, and slumped.

Mincho sat with Earl and Sol on halved logs by the edge of the watering hole. He was pigeon-toed and tall for his age, with deep-set eyes and an uneven haircut. Until a year ago, he said, he'd lived in Santa Rosa, before Judge took them to Curacon.

"We'll drive you to Santa Rosa," Sol said. Her katana was strapped across her back and she'd cut her hair short with kitchen shears rather than scrub off all of Judge's blood.

"Santa Rosa is gone," Mincho said. "My aunt and I were the only ones left."

"How old are you?" Sol asked.

"Eleven."

She nodded, staring at Hector's body, lying in the dirt by the fieldstone wall. The boy munched on a cracker and Earl passed him a wedge of cheese.

A LONG WALK DOWN A SHORT DIRT ROAD

Jack and Willie stood in Willie Manford's Auto Shop, a cinderblock box attached to a garage, at the end of Main Street past the Busy Bee. The shop was filled with old parts, gears, hoses, and belts stacked floor to ceiling. Hubcaps hung on the walls, their spokes draped with cobwebs, next to calendars of bikini models looking out over empty coffee cups, plastic lids, balled-up sandwich wrappings, and cigarette butts scattered across the floor. From the garage windows Jack could see the junkyard. It stretched for a half-mile back, cicadas buzzing in the hollows of car doors, mice nesting in exhaust pipes. A faded yellow school bus with clear plastic garbage bags for windows sat on blocks. Its hood was propped open, a stepladder leaning against the grill.

Willie put his hands on his hips and shook his head at Jack's El Dorado. "It ain't worth fixing." He coughed and spit into a handkerchief.

"Fox thought it might be the engine," Jack said. "He also said something about a cracked boot."

Willie smiled. "That small fool wouldn't know shit if he had a mouth full of it. I'll tell you what I know and you can decide. This car ain't worth fixing, and even if it was, I don't have the parts. Now, I got an old Pacer out back. You can have her for five hundred. She looks like hell, but she's sound."

Jack pulled a fifty from his wallet. "This is all I got. You take credit cards?"

"No."

"Consider this a down payment. I'll send the rest when I get out of here. I'll even throw in an extra two hundred—"

"I need the cash up front. All of it."

"Mr. Manford—"

Willie held up his hand. "I don't know a thing about you. How can I trust someone I don't know?"

"I'm not asking to marry your daughter. I'm asking you to front me some cash for a used Pacer."

"And I'm telling you it costs five hundred."

Jack sat on the front bumper of his El Dorado and rubbed his eyes. He kept them closed, listened to the old man breathing and the buzz of cicadas.

"Maybe you can help me with something else," Jack said.

Willie eyed him.

"I'm looking for Owen Cahill."

Willie spit a ropy thread into the dirt and ground it dry with his shoe. He slammed the hood shut and wiped his hands on his overalls. "What you want Owen for?"

"I have something for him."

"Well, you're a day late and four hundred fifty dollars short."

"Maybe I should check Tejon," Jack said. "See if anyone there knows where he is."

Willie stopped and turned around. "Son, you ever been to Tejon?"

Jack shook his head.

"If you had, and if you knew Owen, you'd know that was a stupid question. Come back when you have enough money for that Pacer. Otherwise, stop wasting my time."

It was a little past three. Jack thought about swallowing his pride and calling Sarah for some money—he needed a payphone because his cell was useless; he hadn't seen a single bar since arriving in town—but then he realized there probably wasn't a place to wire it to.

He walked back down Main Street. In front of the cemetery a gaggle of young girls stopped and stared. One of them called out.

"Are you that strange man Jeremiah Beasley told me about?"

"Who's Jeremiah Beasley?" Jack said.

"Skinny kid, black hair," the girl said. She rubbed her freckled nose. "Looks like a squirrel."

"Is his father named Roy?" Jack said.

The girls nodded.

"Then I'm that man," said Jack, and he continued on into the diner.

Fox sat at the counter, staring off into space. Eli sat in a booth, reading a newspaper, eating another steak. Jack cleared his throat, and Fox turned to him.

"Hey," Fox said, blinking like he'd just awakened. "Heard you met the Garretts."

"Word travels fast," Jack said.

"Word doesn't have anywhere else to go. Can I get you something?"

Jack sat at the counter. "A car. Some cell service. Maybe a bus back to Detroit."

"You talk to Willie?"

"Five hundred bucks for a Pacer. I don't have the cash."

Fox reached into his pocket and pulled out a large roll of bills.

"No thanks," Jack said.

"It's not a big deal." Fox smiled, showing the gap in his front teeth. "It's the town money. Next month I'll buy a new shirt, and Bob Garrett will come in for lunch and give me some of that money back, and I'll pay Willie for a new filter for my AC. You're just buying Willie's car with Willie's money."

Jack looked at the roll. Fox pushed the money into Jack's hand, then walked behind the counter and grabbed his apron from a hook.

"You want something to eat?"

"Anything cold," Jack said.

The diner door swung open and in walked the gaggle of young girls. Two of them sat at a booth. The third walked to the counter.

"Hey Fox," she said.

"Hey Pepper."

"Can I get a cherry Fizzer?" she said.

Fox walked to the cooler. "You meet Jack?"

"We talked," Pepper said. "But we haven't met."

She sat near Jack and pulled her hair into a ponytail. Her nose was freckled and her hair was dark as the core of an old tree stump, with eyes to match. She wore a white blouse unbuttoned to the edge of her collarbone, the sleeves rolled to her elbows. She wore white Prada sneakers. Her gray skirt fell to mid-thigh.

"How old are you?" she said.

"Forty-one," Jack said.

"I'm seventeen."

Fox returned with the Fizzer. He popped the cap and dropped in a straw.

"Do you dye your hair?" Pepper asked.

"What?"

"My dad dyes his hair." She crossed her legs, elbows on the counter with the Fizzer bottle between them. "He's forty-two."

"Jack is from Detroit," Fox said.

Pepper's eyes widened. "Really? What are you doing here?" One of the girls at the booth called Pepper's name, and she turned around and whispered, "*Hush!*"

Jack chewed a piece of pecan pie. "I'm looking for an old friend."

"Owen," Fox said.

"I knew Owen," Pepper said.

Jack put his fork down.

"He was a nice man but his mom was a total bitch," Pepper said. "They lived on Sage Street. I heard he was sick for a while and then he left for Dallas...or somewhere like that. I don't know."

Jack stabbed another forkful of pie. Eli ruffled his newspaper.

"*She wore white Prada sneakers. Her gray skirt fell to mid-thigh.*"

Jack banged on the front door of Willie's shop and shouted his name, then went around back, picking his way through half-buried scraps of metal and tires. He tried the garage door, but it wouldn't budge. Pepper strolled past. She stopped, chewed her thumbnail for a moment, and jogged over.

She was barefoot, her blouse replaced with a thin white T-shirt, dots of sweat along the stomach and between her small breasts. She wore a fresh coat of lipstick.

"Hey," she said.

He smiled, quick and curt, then started walking back to Main Street. "Shouldn't you be in school?"

Pepper followed him. "It's summer."

He knew what he would see—the Busy Bee with its papered front door; the Yellow Goose convenience mart; Wade Garrett sitting in his cruiser parked near Chayban Denim, rolling a cigarette or cooking a pot of beans or doing whatever cowboys do in their spare time. Jack knew he'd see the small hill past the end of town, beyond the trailer with the tattered canvas awning and the angry dog. *A one-look town,* Fox had said. The sameness was obscene, he thought. No human should have to live like this.

Roy Beasley walked out of the Yellow Goose, carrying a six-pack of beer. He got into his pickup and drove to the first house in town, then disappeared into the driveway, hidden by the house next door.

"Fox told me your car broke down," Pepper said.

Jack stopped in the middle of the street.

"Something wrong?" Pepper pinched the front of her shirt and pulled it in and out, fanning herself.

"How well did you know Owen?"

She stuck her foot forward and turned the sneaker from side

to side. "I liked him. A lot. And I think he liked me. He got these at a Prada discount store in New York—I almost died. A *Prada* discount store. How cool is that?"

"Very cool," Jack said.

"He was different than everybody else. Honestly? I don't know what he was doing here."

"Taking care of mom."

Pepper paused. "So he's your—"

"Brother."

She punched her fist into her hand. "I *knew* it. You're not like any of Owen's friends I ever met. Most of them were from Coldspring. My best friend Charlene Roker moved to Coldspring. She told me they have a museum and a Chinese restaurant. I've never had Chinese food but one time Owen made me and Charlene a cheese soufflé. He said he got the recipe from a New York chef. Owen used to work as a waiter in New York. Well, you probably knew that—"

"We haven't spoken in a long time."

"Did you grow up here?"

Jack shook his head. "Our mother was born a few towns over. She moved back after father died, and when she got sick, Owen took care of her. I stayed in Detroit."

"She died, you know."

"Yes. I know."

Pepper toed the ground. "That was a stupid thing for me to say. Obviously she died. I mean, she'd still be here if she didn't." She shook her head, muttering to herself.

Jack reached into his pocket and pulled out the watch. It had a dull gold casing and a cracked face. "This was our grandfather's." He handed it to Pepper. "Owen always carried it around when we were kids. Pretended he was a private detective. Like Marlowe."

"Who?"

"Never mind."

She ran her fingers over the face.

"I'm giving it back to him," Jack continued. "He always asked for it, and I always had an excuse."

"Why?"

"Stubbornness. Pride. I don't know."

"Sounds like you do."

Jack smiled.

"What if you never find him?"

"I will."

"But it's just a *watch*." She handed it back. "Can't you call him or something?"

"I don't know where he is."

"Wow. He must hate you."

Jack nodded. "He sort of does." He looked away. "You know where I might find Willie?"

"My school. Maybe. He sleeps in the basement. I'll take you, but I have to get a soda first."

Jack followed her into the Yellow Goose. Pepper grabbed a bottle of Fizzer from the floor cooler and dropped a handful of nickels and dimes on the counter. The self-serve Slush Puppie machine was long broken, its giant cup frozen in mid-twirl. Eli sat behind the counter, working on a crossword with a chewed pencil nub. A rotating fan swept back and forth.

The door jangled and Curtis walked in with his friend Ike. Ike had the same look as Curtis—small black eyes; thin, veiny arms. Curtis grabbed a bag of chips from a wire rack, then came up behind Pepper and squeezed her sides.

She elbowed him away. "Quit it."

Curtis dropped the bag of chips on the counter. He plucked a few sticks of jerky from a plastic tub, then slowly turned to Jack.

"Thought you'd be in Dallas, by now." Curtis ripped off a piece of jerky. "You still looking for your long-lost friend?"

"Still looking," Jack said.

"You still waiting on that old nigger to fix your car?"

"You mean Willie."

"I mean that old nigger."

Jack said nothing.

Curtis snorted. "I'll fix your car for half as much as that nigger charges. Throw in your new girlfriend and I'll do the job for free."

Ike looked up from a women's magazine and laughed.

"Don't be *stupid*," Pepper said.

Curtis tore off another piece of jerky. "You ain't his girlfriend?"

"I'm nobody's girlfriend," Pepper said.

"Then how about a kiss," Curtis said.

"Gross," Pepper said.

"Yeah?" Curtis squeezed her sides again; she shoved him away, but he held on.

"Stop," she said. "Curtis, quit it. You're hurting—"

Curtis grinned, squeezing as Pepper tried to twist free. "Come on. You know how—"

Jack grabbed Curtis' arm. He twisted his arm at the elbow and pushed forward. Curtis stumbled back, catching himself on the counter's edge. He straightened up. Ike dropped the magazine. Eli fumbled his pencil nub.

Curtis slipped his hand into the waist of his jeans. "Let's try that again."

Jack allowed himself a little smile. He saw the tip of a black handle hidden in Curtis' palm. Switchblade or lockback, he figured. Curtis would keep the blade close. Use his other hand as a distraction. Maybe Ike had his own knife, he thought. Not enough space in the mart for both of them to attack. Still, it was lousy odds. He'd get cut, or worse.

Curtis stepped forward. Jack heard a sharp *click* and saw the blade peek out from Curtis' hand. Jack looked at Pepper, who stared wide-eyed, bottle held close to her chest. Then he held the door open, motioned for her to leave, and followed.

They crossed Main Street. She whipped out a cigarette from the waistband of her skirt. Jack looked back, at the Yellow Goose. Curtis stood in the entrance, hands resting on the doorway, grinning. He waved good-bye.

"Curtis is such a pig," she said. "I don't know what he's trying to prove."

"Everything," Jack said.

"Do you have a light?"

"No."

She sighed and slipped the cigarette back into her skirt. "Are you a black belt?"

"No."

"Well, you looked like one. Were you going to fight Curtis?"

"No."

"Why not?"

"Because I hate fighting. No more questions."

They stopped in front of the Emmanuel Baptist Church. Manicured bushes lined the front. The front door was huge, carved with acorns and fruits around its edges.

"So this is my school," Pepper said. "We used to be in a real school, but there's only fourteen of us and Sheriff said it was too expensive to air-condition the whole building."

They walked into the church and through its main room, a high arched ceiling with beams and stained glass on either side. Jack remembered the last time he'd been in a church. A day after his discharge from the Honduran hospital. His leg was still raw from where they'd cut out the bullet. He felt he'd never seen something so beautiful as the traffic-packed street outside the hospital's front doors. He bought fresh-squeezed OJ from a street vendor and ducked into the first church he saw.

Forgive me, Father, for I have sinned, Jack said, sitting in the warm wooden dark of a confessional booth. *This is my first time in a confessional because I was raised Lutheran. But I've always thought the confessional was a good idea.*

What are your sins?

I've killed a lot of people.

Oh dear.

Many of them deserved it.

Retribution is the Lord's role. You must ask the Lord to forgive you.

Lord, forgive me.

It's not that simple.

Well, I'm trying.

How many have you killed?

I don't know. Twenty, thirty—does it matter? At this point it seems academic.

Of course it matters.

Then let's say twenty-six. Mostly bastards who had it coming. A few women. And children.

You aren't the first American to sit in my confessional, you realize. Or the first American to confess your aim has been…less than true.

That's putting it nicely.

How else can I put it?

Of course it's a goddamn cliché—

Please. Not in here.

Sorry. It's a cliché, but you know I see their faces every night? The kids. They give them guns. At least we suspect they do. You spot something in the dark, there's no time to shine a light. But still—

You must turn away from this sinful life.

Six months left. Once I earn pension, then I'll turn away.

Jack and Pepper sat in a pew.

"You know this whole town could burn down and no one

would notice?" she said.

"You could say that about a lot of places. Spend some time in Detroit."

She sighed. "I feel like I live on the moon. Like all this stuff is going on everywhere else, and I'm stuck here."

"It isn't all bad. There's a stark beauty to it."

"Are you serious?"

"Not really."

She sighed again, then said: "So you and Owen don't talk much."

"Nope."

"Why not?"

"I said some bad things."

"Did you ever apologize?"

"I tried."

"But not in person."

"Not in person. And not for a long time."

"You sound stubborn."

Jack laughed a little. "My girlfriend says the same thing."

She looked up, toward the stained-glass windows. "Seriously, if I had a brother, and if he said the kind of things you said—like, bad enough to make us not talk for years—I don't think a pocket watch would make any difference. But I like holding grudges."

"So do I," Jack said. "That's what got me into this mess."

Roy Beasley stood by the sheriff's office window, beer in hand. He stood for a long time, drinking, as Wade sifted through paperwork. He watched Jack leave the church with Pepper at his side. He watched the houses lining Main Street, their shades drawn.

"Curtis told me the new guy is causing problems," Roy said.

Wade crumpled a sheet of paper. "Curtis would know."

"Maybe I should have the boys crowd him a little," Roy said. "See if he's got any iron in his blood."

"Better watch your dogs. You might not be able to call them off."

"They'll back off. They always do."

"Not always."

Roy tapped his bottle against the window. "I doubt your brother appreciates that gimpy stranger spending time with his daughter. You've seen how Pep looks at him."

Wade crumpled another sheet.

"And Esteban doesn't want anyone causing a stir," Roy said. "Too many questions make people nervous."

"Esteban doesn't run this town," Wade said.

Roy tapped his bottle against the window again and watched Pepper walk across the street. Cute little ass twitching. Skinny legs smooth and tan.

Wade sat back, hands on his stomach, boots on the desk. "Lean on him and see if he knows anything. If nothing comes up, just leave it."

Roy turned around. "And if he knows something?"

The shadow of the church steeple fell across the street. The air conditioner rattled.

"There's plenty more hills around here," Wade said. "Plenty of shovels, too."

Roy Beasley stepped out of Chayban Denim. He set his bottle of beer on the sidewalk, took off his cowboy hat, and wiped his forehead with his arm. Jack walked past the Buck-A-Wash.

"Something I can help you with?" Roy said.

Jack stopped. "I'm looking for Willie."

"He probably made a quick run over to Tejon, to appreciate the ladies. What about you? You appreciate the ladies?"

"Depends on the lady. If you see him, tell him I got the cash."

"And then you'll be heading on out."

"I might. Or I might stay a while. I'm beginning to enjoy it here. Everyone's been so nice."

"We're just a bit skittish, is all. Humble likes its privacy. Your mother liked her privacy. I don't believe she said good morning to me once in fifteen years."

"She was a difficult woman."

Roy grinned. "Reverend gave a decent eulogy, though. Called her 'stalwart.' I liked that. Must've been hard, missing her funeral."

"I didn't know she'd died until the paperwork came."

"You were in the service, right?"

"You could call it that."

Roy craned his neck, revealing a scar stretched across his Adam's apple. "Machete attack. Priest gave me last rites. Six months later I was back in the jungle, hauling thirty pounds on my back, laying waste like nothing you ever seen."

"Impressive," Jack said.

"Goddamn right. Where'd you serve?"

"Far from here."

"Clever answer. How about you get serious for a moment."

"I'd rather not."

"You one of those flashback types? Talking about it makes you shake and sweat?"

"It's just not worth talking about."

"Then we'll talk about other things. Like you spending time with Pepper. She's pretty as a tulip, wouldn't you agree?"

"If I was sixteen."

Roy frowned. "Sixteen or not, any man can see the beauty in that girl."

"She's helping me."

"With what?"

"With finding Owen."

Roy put his hat back on. "I already told you. Owen's long gone. You're wasting your time."

"I won't argue with that."

"You would. If you had any friends here in Humble, I reckon you would. But you don't. You're all alone. And you aren't acting in your best interest, understand?"

"You don't know my best interest, Roy."

Roy's expression darkened. "Now listen here: Sheriff knows what happened between you and Curtis, and he's willing to let it slide. But next time you threaten one of our townsfolk, I'll haul you in myself."

"Curtis has lousy manners."

"Keep being clever. I ain't messing around."

"I believe you."

Roy paused a moment, head cocked to the side, eyes narrowed. Then he picked up his beer and walked back down the street, thumbs hooked into his belt loops. Jack watched him a long time.

The sky sank and put its full red weight on Jack as he wandered to Sage Street. He found Fox stocking cans in the back of the Busy Bee and asked if there was any place to stay in town, and Fox gave him a room above the diner. "Twenty bucks a night," Fox said, then added with a half-smile: "Just tack it on to what you already owe me."

The room was small with a four-poster bed, a desk, and a window overlooking the graveyard. The bathroom had an old-fashioned pedestal sink and a tiny bar of wrapped soap. He showered, shaved, and lay down on the bed, staring at the ceiling until the shadows grew long.

He walked down the street turned molten yellow from the sunset, the western side of Humble's buildings painted orange, brick and shingle sucking in the last of the day's heat. Wade Garrett sat in the front seat of his cruiser, watching, parked at his usual spot in front of Chayban Denim. Other eyes watched as well, peeking like prairie dogs from the windows of their homes.

Jack found Willie in the garage. He was rooting around a box of nuts and bolts, plucking them out and holding them between his grease-slicked fingers up to the strip of fluorescent lights.

"Is that Pacer still for sale?" Jack said.

Willie stood slowly, hands sliding down the front of his overalls until he propped himself straight. "Sold it this afternoon."

"*What?*"

Willie coughed into his handkerchief. "Sheriff Wade came by and said he needed a backup. I told him the Pacer was in decent enough shape—not gonna chase down any crooks, but I figure he'll want me to install a light bar and juice up the engine. Ever seen a turbocharger on a Pacer? Me neither. I will, soon as I get to it. I got Roy comin' in for new headers tomorrow, so I told Sheriff Wade I won't—"

"Where's my El Dorado?"

"Stripped."

"Who gave you permission to strip my car?"

"You did. I told you it ain't worth fixing, and that was that." He handed Jack fifty bucks. "Got two tires and a fuel pump out of it."

Jack took Fox's money from his wallet and the fifty dollars from Willie, and stuffed the wad into the front pocket of Willie's overalls. "Find me something in your junkyard by tomorrow morning. I don't care what it looks like. I don't care if it has a radio, or air conditioning, or even a windshield. Just get me something with four wheels and an engine."

Willie pulled the money from his front pocket and started to count the wrinkled bills. "You should head on over to Tejon, get yourself something to relax. Tell Esteban, Willie sent you. He'll treat you right."

Jack stormed back onto the street. He stared in the direction of the single hill outside of town, a crooked tree at the top, behind it a blazing half-circle swallowed by a line of mountains.

I can take it all in, in about ten seconds, and know that's all I'm ever going to see. The rest of my life. The lake and the dust. I may as well be blind. Nothing new under the sun.

He walked until it got dark and soon found himself on the shores of Yell Lake, staring over its black water. The lake was bigger than he imagined, a giant oval carved out of the plains, with a dock jutting out over its waters. A tethered rowboat knocked gently against the pilings. Across the lake he saw the lights of Tejon.

He thought of summers at his uncle's house, he and Owen paddling across the lake in a pea-green canoe. Sometimes they fished; Jack never wanted to actually catch anything, and when he did, he insisted that Owen do the gutting. They didn't talk much, even then. Owen was ten years older—Jack felt they only had a hatred of their family in common, inmates pacing in the same cell, marking days on the calendar until parole. Their mother hid herself away and their father's rage was a blade, blunting itself on Owen first, so summers became the only respite. The two brothers exhausted themselves in a frenzy of What Normal Kids Do: swimming, canoeing, hiking, and just lying on the beach, arms behind their heads, gazing at the cloud-speckled sky.

Jack heard the crackle of tires on grit. He turned and saw a pickup truck skidding to a stop. The headlights popped off, the driver's side door opened, and Pepper slid out. She wore jeans and a pink tank. Her sneakers gleamed in the dark.

She walked up to Jack, hands in her pockets. "I saw you walking," she said. "Guess you didn't get your car."

He stared over the lake.

"Are you going to church tonight?"

"I wasn't invited."

Pepper toed the dirt, eyes lowered. "Well, I'm going. I have to." She picked up a rock and whipped it into the water. "Also? Fox wanted me to ask you over for dinner."

"At his house?"

"Yeah. Church doesn't start for another few hours, so if you—"

"Okay."

She burst into a smile and did a little shuffle, but then stopped. She looked at Jack suspiciously. "Are you being sarcastic?"

"No."

"I was sure you'd say something sarcastic."

"I know. I can be a real bastard sometimes."

Fox lived in a small house, behind the diner, with a front porch, empty plastic flowerpots hanging from the porch beams, and a swinging bench with one snapped chain. An abandoned vegetable garden sat to the side of the house. A watering can lay on its side, near a coil of hose.

Pepper walked with Jack past the dumpsters behind the diner, then broke into a run and banged on Fox's front screen door.

Fox jumped up from his couch. The TV was on and a bag of corn chips sat on his coffee table.

"Jack's coming for dinner," Pepper said. "I told him it was your idea. Don't say anything, okay?"

"Pep, I—"

"I can grab something from the diner if you want. Just don't tell him this was my idea. Promise you won't."

Fox scratched his head and looked around. He brushed the crumbs off his undershirt.

"He's coming," Pepper said. "Promise you won't say anything?"

Jack limped to the porch and looked at Fox over Pepper's shoulder.

"Hey, Fox."

"Hey, Jack. Thanks for accepting my invitation." He swung the screen door open. "Sorry for the mess. I wasn't expecting you so soon."

"I bet you weren't," Jack said.

Fox made sloppy joes and grits and served the last of the slaw. They sat in the corner of his living room at a small round table with a plastic veneer top.

"You know," Jack said, pushing the last of the grits onto his fork, "this is the first time I've ever had grits."

"You ever been down south before?" Fox asked.

"Nope. Unless you count Florida."

"What was in Florida?" Fox said.

Jack sipped his bourbon. "Army base."

"Were you in a war?" Pepper said.

He thought for a moment, then pushed away from the table, lifted his bad leg onto the side of Pepper's chair, and pulled up the cuff. A long scar revealed itself, running from his ankle, coiling up his calf to his knee.

"That's *nasty*," Pepper said.

Jack pushed his pant leg back down. "Infection from a bullet wound."

"Who shot you?" Pepper asked.

"*Pep*," Fox said.

"A woman shot me," Jack said.

Pepper's mouth dropped open. "A *woman*?"

Jack nodded, taking another sip.

"Was she a soldier?"

"No."

"Was it an accident?"

"No."

"Then why?"

"You don't have to answer," Fox said.

"I killed her husband. She was in the bathroom, with a shotgun."

"Where did this happen?" Fox asked.

"Honduras. '87."

"We were at war with Honduras in '87?"

"Not officially."

Fox cleared his throat and refilled his glass. Pepper poured herself a splash of bourbon.

"Pep—" Fox began, but she shushed him.

"Please," she said, rolling her eyes. "Like I've never had alcohol before. Just don't say nothing to my dad. *Anyway*." She gulped, sucked air between her teeth, and looked at Jack. "Tell me about that husband you killed."

"What do you want to know?"

"How did he die?"

"I shot him."

"Like, in front of his family?"

"He was alone. In the kitchen. Eating cereal."

She looked at Fox and mouthed *Wow*. Then, to Jack: "Was he a bad guy?"

Jack thought for a moment. "Define bad guy."

"An enemy," Fox said.

"He was a compromising figure. That's the term we used."

Pepper took another gulp. "How many compromising figures

did you kill?"

"Plenty."

Silence. Fox and Pepper looked at each other.

"Anyone for ice cream?" Fox asked.

After dinner they sat on Fox's porch, and Fox rolled a joint. Pepper had fallen asleep on the broken bench, curled into a ball, her head on one of the couch pillows.

Jack took the joint from Fox. This was how he originally envisioned his trip: a quiet night, the Texas plains, a full moon, Owen and he sitting together, making things right.

"Humble isn't all bad," Fox said.

Jack glanced over. "What's that?"

"I said it isn't all bad. This place."

"There's a stark beauty to it."

"*Stark beauty.*" Fox smiled. "I got a rowboat, you know. You can borrow it anytime. A night like this, head out for the middle of the lake, maybe bring a joint or one of Esteban's girls. I'm telling you, it's not bad." He took the joint from Jack. "Point is, you can have a decent time here, provided you understand where you are."

"And where is that?"

"A small town holding on for dear life."

"I know a drop station when I see it."

Fox looked at him.

"This morning, when you picked me up," Jack said, "where were you coming from?"

"Coldspring."

"For a valve."

"That's right."

"What kind of valve?"

"The important kind."

Jack nodded. "You don't need to worry. I'm not interested in your business. I'm just interested in finding Owen."

"We already told you—"

"He moved. Yeah, I got that."

Fox exhaled a white plume. "When you said you were looking for Owen, I thought maybe you were...you know."

"Maybe I am."

"I don't mind if you are. I just didn't want to come out and say it. Of course, Owen was as discreet as he could be, but like I said, word travels fast."

Pepper sat up. Her hair fell over her face. Fox hid the joint behind his back.

"Oh, *please*." She rubbed her temples. "I know what weed smells like. My dad smokes all the time."

Jack stood suddenly. "Pep, would you mind if I borrowed your truck?"

"It's my dad's," she said.

"I'll have it back tonight. I only need it for a couple hours."

Pepper frowned. "Are you going to Tejon?"

Jack nodded.

"I *knew* it," she said, with drunken sadness. She lay back down, curling up with the pillow held to her chest. "Every guy goes there. And they always say the same thing: 'Those little brown ladies screwed my brains out.'"

QUARRY

Earl told Soledad about the death of his father. He'd been thirteen, two years older than the pigeon-toed boy they found in Curacon. His father was Harold Dobber, a man who'd outlived four wives and had Earl when he was fifty. Harold Dobber owned El Ray, parted the streets like Moses, brought down the thunder and lightning. Then Esteban Gallegos came to town.

It had only taken a rumor, a whisper in an alley; one of Harold's men had been part of the gang that killed Esteban's father. No one knew the truth, least of all Esteban, but it didn't matter. Revenge, Earl said, has its reasons that reason knows nothing of.

Earl's father fought two of Esteban's men—gouged out their eyes with his thumbs and ripped open their throats with his teeth—while Earl huddled in the corner of the living room and Esteban sat on a chair, smoking his brown cigarette. Harold lifted his head from the throat of one of the fallen men, blood and spittle dripping down his chin. Then, as Earl told it, Esteban smiled at Harold, raised a steady hand, and shot him between the eyes.

"Sounds like Esteban killed a lot of fathers," said Sol.

"We ask around long enough," Earl said, "and we'll have ourselves an army."

They drove on, past the dark serpent of the Rio Grande. Earl fell asleep with his head bobbing against the window and drool trickling down his chin. Mincho awoke but pretended he was asleep until the sun's rays blistered across the plains. He sat up and looked around. Sol's sheathed katana lay near him, on the floor, next to the Winchester.

"Where are we?"

"We just crossed into Texas," Sol said. "Earl said close to here there's a town called Bass Drop. We'll stop for breakfast."

"I'm not hungry," Mincho said.
"You should eat," Sol said.
"But I'm not hungry."
"Fine. You can sit and watch."

Mincho rubbed his eyes and curled himself up against the door.

They rolled into Bass Drop and stopped at Pritchard's Place, a small diner with stools at the counter and booths along the front window. Earl unfolded the road map across their table and pointed with a nicotine-stained finger.

"It's another five hours until Coldspring," he said. "We can get a good night's sleep there, then it's another three hours to Fuller." He traced a line. "Tejon's a few miles from Fuller."

"We'll drop off Mincho in Coldspring," Sol said.

Mincho sat back. "No way."

"You can't come with us," Sol said.

"I can do whatever I want. I'm an orphan."

Sol looked at Earl, who shrugged. Sol mouthed *Thanks*.

"And if you leave me in Coldspring," Mincho said, "I'll walk to Tejon."

Sol looked around. They were the only customers in the restaurant. She let her head fall back and stared at the stuccoed ceiling. She knew if she closed her eyes she'd fall asleep, right there in the booth.

Instead she took out her photo of Paloma in the blue shorts and pigtails. She glanced at Earl, who sat tonguing his dentures, staring into space. She wondered what men like him think about in their quiet moments. Maybe they remember their victims, or what they ate for dinner the night before, or maybe they think of nothing. Maybe they just exist, half-awake, like an old, sleepy dog.

She remembered how easily Earl killed that man in the Turnaround Bar, how he'd shot the woman in the rocking chair with the same stoic expression, and how she'd felt, right before slamming that sledgehammer into Hector's head. She needed Earl, but believed there wasn't much difference between Earl and Esteban Gallegos. Maybe there wasn't much difference between her and Esteban. She wondered how she'd look to her former co-workers at the mall. Would they see the old Sol, or the new? Were the two that much different? Had she been serious when she fantasized about killing that boy who'd taken her virginity? When she aimed the broken pool cue at that roughneck's throat?

"How are you doing for money?" Earl asked.

Sol awoke from her daze. "I have a couple hundred bucks left."

A year ago at this time, she thought, she'd been enrolled in an oil painting class. There'd been a cute guy who kept looking at her; by the last class he had her laughing. Then her mom got sick, and something switched off. She remembered feeling like everyone—her co-workers, her friends—talked in code, never really saying what they meant.

"You two wait in the car." Earl stood and twisted his back until he felt it pop. "I'll take the check."

He watched Sol and Mincho shuffle out of the diner, her thin brown arm resting tentatively across the boy's shoulders, then he slipped the Schofield from his waistband and walked to the register. A heavy black man stood to the side of it, filling in a crossword puzzle, double chin planted in the pink palm of his hand.

Earl raised the revolver. "Empty the register."

The black man frowned. He held his pen to the newspaper. He was bald, his left eyelid drooping like a broken window shade.

"I'm the owner."

"Then be a smart owner and do what I say."

"I can't do that."

Earl narrowed his eyes. "Excuse me?"

The owner set down his pen and straightened up. "My father

opened this business fifty years ago. He never gave his hard-earned money to any thief, and I'm not about to break tradition. So you may as well walk on out."

"Hard-earned, my ass," Earl said. "No refills on our coffee, and we haven't seen our waitress in twenty minutes."

He paused. "Twenty minutes? And no refills on your coffee?"

Earl nodded.

The owner turned and shouted, "*Nadine!*" Seconds later their waitress pushed through the swinging kitchen doors. She wore a white denim miniskirt and white Keds. Her hair was pulled back in a high ponytail, kept in place with a plastic clip. When she saw Earl with his revolver leveled at her boss, she screamed.

The owner folded his thick arms across his chest. "This gentleman tells me you didn't refill his coffee."

"I was scared," Nadine said.

"Of what?"

She shook her head. "Well, you're kind of looking at it right now."

"Did you know the customer had a sidearm?"

"No. But the woman he was with? Her neck was covered in dried blood."

The owner held out his hand. Nadine stared at it a moment, then pulled the check out of her apron pocket and placed it in his palm. He ripped up the check and turned to Earl.

"I hired her last week. First time waitressing."

Earl pulled back the hammer of his Schofield. "I still need what's in the register. Along with the safe in the back."

"I already told you—"

Earl stuck the mouth of the barrel in the center of his sweating forehead.

"Jesus *Christ*," Nadine said. "Just give him the fucking money."

"Nadine, shut up." The owner set his large hands on the counter.

"Five seconds," Earl said. "Open the register."

"You could give me a hundred years, and it wouldn't make a difference."

"Four—"

"There's only seventy bucks in the register, so if you shoot me—"

"Three—"

"You'll be killing a man for seventy bucks."

"Two—"

"Which in my book is bush league. Despite appearances—"

"One—"

"I don't think you're bush league."

Nadine screamed and bolted, banging through the swinging kitchen doors. The owner pressed a button under the counter's overhang. A thick steel spike shot out from the counter, sinking into Earl's thigh.

Earl grunted and stared at his impaled leg. He touched the spike with his gun hand. Blood blossomed into his pant leg. He continued to stare at his leg even as he raised his arm and shot the owner above the right eye.

Earl yanked his thigh off the spike and limped behind the counter. He took money from the register, then pushed through the kitchen doors. Blood soaked the cuff of his jeans, dripping onto the red-and-white-checkered floor.

The kitchen had a small stove with pans hanging from hooks in the ceiling. The door to the owner's office was open. The walls were white and a fluorescent panel buzzed overhead. Neat stacks of papers covered his desk. A filing cabinet stood in the corner. A small boxing trophy sat on the edge of the desk. *Darius Pritchard. Welterweight Golden Gloves.*

Earl found Nadine at the back door. She pushed and clawed at the boxes of papers Darius had stacked in front of the door to be taken out to trash. She saw Earl and she screamed. Her plastic clip dangled from a twist of long hair. Earl aimed. Blood streamed down his leg.

"I won't say anything I promise swear to God won't say anything please don't please don't—"

Earl pulled the trigger; the world suddenly tumbled and darkened. He heard himself curse as the blast echoed in his ears, and he knew even as the floor smacked him in the face that he'd missed the bitch because he still heard her screaming.

They covered fifty miles in a half hour, the engine straining while Sol white-knuckled the steering wheel and kept one eye on the rearview. Earl bled in the backseat. His blood filled the seat seams and spilled onto the floor. It covered Mincho's hands, smearing his cheeks, soaking through the blanket he'd tightened around Earl's thigh.

There was nothing between Bass Drop and Coldspring—just fence posts, jackrabbit holes, and hills that rise and fall like the waves of a dry ocean. Cattle bones lay tangled in a knot of wire by the side of the road. A shuttered farmhouse dissolved into the ground. Earl stared out the window. As far as last looks go, he thought, you could do worse.

"You pissed at me?" Earl said.

Sol glared in the rearview.

"That nigger spiked my goddamn thigh. If he'd just kept his wits—"

"*I don't murder innocent people,*" she shouted, turning her head around so fast the car swerved onto the shoulder. Gravel spit up onto the windows. She jerked back onto the road. "This is my show, Earl. *That was the agreement*—"

"We needed money."

"Then take out your own fucking money."

"I'm on a fixed income. I was trying to help. If my services aren't appreciated—"

"Appreciated?" She punched the dashboard; the car swerved again. "We're going to have the Texas police—"

"Rangers." Earl tightened the blanket around his leg. "They're called rangers." He looked at Mincho. "There's money in my pocket. Take it out."

Mincho retrieved the blood-soaked bills and squeezed them dry. "Count it."

He thumbed the wet strips. "Seventy-six bucks."

Sol looked in the rearview again. "You killed that man for *seventy-six* dollars?"

Earl took a deep breath and closed his eyes. He slumped against the back door. Mincho put his head to Earl's chest.

"He's still alive," he said.

"Too bad," Sol said, and she floored the gas pedal.

Dr. Harry Bedlam lived at the top of Coldspring's only hill, in a jumbled, sprawling mansion with a hedge maze in the backyard. Peach trees shadowed the front lawn. A large fountain stood at the foot of the driveway, filled with green water.

Soledad sat in the parlor and leafed through a *People* magazine. Mincho wandered the living room, stopping at a row of jars sitting on a shelf next to the couch. The jars held deformed infants—two-faced, no-faced, some with no hands and feet, and others with hands for feet and feet for hands. A preserved whale penis floated in a six-foot glass tube. Shrunken heads dangled on a frayed rope. In the corner stood a dark wooden cabinet, doors secured with a padlock.

Dr. Bedlam walked down the stairs, pulling off bloodied latex gloves. "Your father is resting comfortably," he said to Sol.

"He's not my father. But thank you."

He blushed, scratching his head. With his white wispy hair and bushy eyebrows, Sol thought he looked like a mad scientist. "He's a lucky man," the doctor continued. "A quarter inch to the left, and we're not having this conversation."

Sol smiled politely. "How much do I owe you?"

"Five hundred should do it."

"I don't have five hundred."

Dr. Bedlam stuffed the bloody gloves into his pocket. "I only take cash." He scratched his head again. "Don't have any dishes that need washing, either." He laughed loudly, then stopped. "I suppose I could bill the hospital for sending you here—"

"They didn't." Sol put down her magazine. "We can't go to a hospital. We just asked some kids on the street if they knew any doctors in town."

He narrowed his eyes. "Uh-huh. And why can't you—"

"I'd rather not answer any questions, if that's all right by you."

"Well, it's not entirely all right. But…" he looked at the boy, then at Sol. "Pay me whatever you can afford."

"Seventy-six dollars," she said.

"What's in the box?" Mincho asked.

"Which box?" Dr. Bedlam walked into the living room and stood next to the dark wooden cabinet. "This box?"

"Let's see it," Mincho said.

Dr. Bedlam clasped his hands behind his back. "Seventy-six dollars. That's all you can afford."

"Money's tight," Sol said.

"I usually charge for the show."

"Maybe you can make an exception."

Dr. Bedlam smiled, cleared his throat, and spoke:

"*'My sword was not to be compared with thine Phoebus of Spain, marvel of courtesy, Nor with thy famous arm this hand of mine That smote from east to west as lightnings fly.*' The words of Señor Don Quixote, as written by Miguel de Cervantes. Cervantes was buried in a Trinitarian monastery in Madrid on April 23, 1616, the same day, incidentally, as William Shakespeare was buried in England. Fifty-four years later, the grave of Cervantes was found unearthed, and his head—to the horror of the Franciscan monks who maintained his gravesite—was missing. For centuries the head of Miguel de Cervantes was sought after, until 1901, when the famous German explorer Rudolph Hesch claimed the head of Cervantes was kept in a guarded shrine in a remote mountain village in the Pyrenees, by a group of men who believed Don Quixote to be the messiah. After an epic battle, Herr Hesch liberated the head and burned the village to the ground. He then returned the head to its rightful place—atop Señor Cervantes neck—but refused any reward, claiming that responsibility for his eternal peace was reward enough.

"The truth, however, is that Rudolph Hesch did not find the head of Cervantes, but rather the head of Efrain Sandovar, a failed actor and struggling writer who met his demise during a poker game with Basque merchants, and whose only achievement of note was the accidental invention of the French tickler, which he originally conceived as revenge against his wife whom he believed to be an adulterer. The real head of Miguel Cervantes had been sold to the poet William Fricke, who thought of it as his muse in the most literal sense—he claimed the head dictated poems throughout the night, and William Fricke presented these poems to the public as the genuine product of Miguel de Cervantes. 'For he is the poet and I am his living pen,' claimed William Fricke, though the public agreed if Cervantes was the poet behind Fricke's creations, death had given him a serious case of writer's block. Destitute and a morphine addict, Fricke eventually sold the head to Dr. Henry Tanner, a Mississippi physician, who kept it in his office closet for fifty years, until selling the head to yours truly."

Dr. Bedlam dabbed sweat from his brow. Mincho sat on the floor at his feet, staring up.

"Henceforth, it is my honor, and my pleasure, to present to you the authentic head of Miguel de Cervantes, truly one of the greatest writers the world has ever known, and, as you will soon see, not a bad-looking man, considering his preserved head is over four hundred years old."

He unlatched the cabinet and opened the small doors. The head floated in tea-colored liquid. One eye was open, a shred of skin clinging to the tip of its eyelash, wavering in the formaldehyde. The hair on the head was surprisingly thick and black, though some of it had sunk to the bottom of the jar. Sol clasped her hand over her mouth.

It was her father, Rafael Santanillo, and when his other eye, shut for twenty-four years, fluttered open, she screamed.

She took her father's head to Earl's room and placed it on the dresser. Then she took the boy for a walk while Earl slept off the painkillers. They went into town, down the hill, and past the leaning water tower, along the train tracks that had since been unbolted and stacked in rows. Mincho told her about his home back in Santa Rosa, about the parrots that imitated ringing phones and the spider monkeys that made off with his father's laptop, and how he'd climb trees all day, racing friends to the top and winning every time. Sol told him about her old job in the mall, happy hours at the local TGIF's, and training with swords in Mariko's basement.

At the bottom of the hill they stopped at Kane's Pharmacy and sat on the curb in front. Sol gave Mincho some blood-soaked bills. He returned with fireballs, licorice twists, peanut butter–filled pretzels, Skittles, Pixy Stix, Doritos, and a twelve-pack of assorted Fizzer cola. They ate in silence, enjoying the sun on their faces. Then Mincho said:

"My uncle was in a movie."

"No kidding," Sol said.

"*Supervivientes de los Andes.* Ever hear of it?"

"No, but that doesn't mean anything. Was it famous?"

Mincho shrugged. "It's about these people that crash into a mountain and only a few of them survive, and because they're starving they have to eat the dead people. My uncle's the first person they eat."

Sol crunched a fireball. "That's cool."

"His character is cut in half by the crash, so the audience only sees his legs and a little bit of his chest. He gave me a poster signed by the director."

"Might be worth something."

"It burned up. Along with my house."

"I'm sorry."

"It was a stupid movie anyway."

"Doesn't sound stupid."

"Well, it was."

Sol rubbed her palms on the warm curb. Mincho popped the rest of the fireballs into his mouth and stared at her. He grinned, his teeth red, cheeks lumpy. She laughed.

"I'm sorry about your dad," he said, cracking a fireball.

"Me too."

"It was weird, how his eye opened."

She leaned back, fingers pressed to her temples. "This has been the weirdest year of my life."

"Want some Doritos? Try them with the candy—it's really good."

"Uh, sure."

"It's good, right?"

"Not bad. I used to work with this girl who only ate Doritos. An entire bag for lunch, every day. She was fairly disgusting."

"Where did you work?"

"The mall."

He laughed. "What did you sell?"

"I didn't sell anything. I just sort of…wandered around, folding clothes, flirting with the shoe guys."

"Do you have a boyfriend?"

"Not since my mom died."

"I bet you get asked out a lot."

"I used to."

They crunched Doritos for a few minutes. Then, Sol said: "You ever been on a plane?"

"No. My uncle's movie scared me."

"I called some friends back home. They're sending money for your ticket."

"Did you tell them where you were?"

She shook her head. "I told them I was in India, on a spiritual journey."

"India?"

"That's what American women do. So listen: I have cousins in Buffalo who could take care of you. They're very nice, and they live in a big house—"

"No thanks."

"Mincho, this isn't going to end well. Do you understand what I'm saying?"

He licked his fingers. "You're going to die."

She paused.

"The old man you're going to kill," he continued. "He might kill you first, or his friends will do it. Earl told me it was a…" Mincho closed his eyes for a moment. "A suicide pact."

"It's not suicide."

"But you'll still die."

"I hope not. I'd like to go back home."

"Well, I'm an orphan, and I can do whatever I want." He ripped open the bag of Skittles. "And I'm staying with you."

Sol tipped her head to the sun while Mincho chewed and chomped.

THE LITTLE BROWN LADIES OF TEJON

Jack parked Marty Garrett's pickup on the edge of Tejon and limped into town. Dark shops lined Avenue de Quere, injection-molded statues of Mayan gods scowling from their perches atop shelves, holding plastic purses and hand-braided belts and tourist T-shirts of tequila-swigging iguanas. He peered into the shops and saw the shop owners, sitting behind their counters, watching the flicker of televisions. At first he didn't notice the women but as he walked farther down Avenue de Quere he saw them all. Slinking down stairways and slipping their thin legs from hammocks, draping over bar stools, sidling along the sidewalks like a prowl of cats.

Jack stopped at a line of chairs sitting in the middle of the street, blocking off what looked like an outdoor party, where men danced cheek to cheek with little brown women. A radio played Mexican wedding music—violins and *jarana*—and Christmas lights hung everywhere.

A young woman walked up to Jack. She wore a little red dress, pleats whispering around the tops of her thighs. Her small breasts were pushed together with a black lace bra. Bare feet, dusty toenails painted red. A yellow scorpion with a missing claw crept along her shoulder, hidden in her thick black hair, and an ashen scar ran across her cheek, from ear to nose. She flashed a well-practiced smile, then took Jack's hand and placed it on her chest.

"No thanks," Jack said. As soon as his words fell away another woman slithered into view. This one was taller, with long legs the color of almond skin. Her eye shadow was baby blue, sparkles glittering under the streetlights. Her face was angelic, Jack thought, smooth skin and full lips, a child's nose, and wide, green eyes. But her neck was horribly burnt—a mat of pink, scarred flesh crawled across the front of her throat.

Jack pulled Owen's photo from his back pocket. He held it out for the tall woman. "I'm looking for this man. Owen Cahill. From Humble."

The woman looked at the photo.

"Do you speak English?" Jack said.

She rolled her eyes and walked away, disappearing into the throng of slow dancers under the Christmas lights.

He walked on, past short women in mini-skirts, fat women in tight shorts, older women with hennaed hair, women who looked too young, with nubs for breasts and their doll faces painted in makeup. The women paced on porches and slinked in the shadows, they gave head in alleys while squatting in their high heels and fucked in dirty rooms on sweat-sodden mattresses. Jack could smell them all. The singularity of Tejon struck him, as though it were this throbbing thing in the middle of the desert.

He ducked into the last cantina on Avenue de Quere and ordered a whiskey. The room had a low ceiling, lit dimly. A buzzing neon sign, hanging from the mirror behind the bar, read Pistolero Tequila.

A young man sat near Jack. Jack waited a few minutes before looking over.

"No girls tonight?" the young man asked. He was Mexican, his hair cut close. He wore a thick leather belt that creaked when he moved, and its brass buckle was the head of a tiger. There's a blade in there, Jack thought. He could see where a hand would fit atop the tiger's head, between its ears.

"Not tonight," Jack said. He swished the remaining whiskey around in his glass and laid the photo on the bar.

"Are you from Humble?" the young man asked.

"Just visiting. I came to see an old friend. Owen Cahill. Someone told me he might live here." He tapped the photo.

The young man shook his head. Then he smiled, flashing a gold incisor. "That would be very unlikely without Señor Gallegos' permission." He drummed his fingers on the tiger head. "I could get you whatever you like. Dark, light, fat, skinny, old, young. There's a man from Humble, close to your age. He prefers the young ones. He tells me they smell sweeter." He laughed. "His favorite is Mariana. She's very good. Tonight I'll let you try her for a special."

"I appreciate the offer," Jack said. "But no thanks."

The young man held up his hands. "Okay, okay. Drink your whiskey. But don't bother the women with questions."

"I'll try my best," Jack said.

The young man rested both hands on his belt buckle. His face hardened. A melodic, resonant voice rose from the back of the room.

"*Octavio…venido aqui.*"

"Mire éste," the young man said to the bartender, and he walked to a corner table, where an older gentleman dressed in a white linen suit sat alone, with a single candle and a glass of rum, reading a book.

Jack finished his whiskey. He wiped a trickle of sweat from his forehead and stared at Owen's photo.

"Amigo."

Jack turned. The kid with the tiger head buckle stood with his hands resting on his belt.

"Señor Gallegos would like you to join him."

Jack turned away. "Some other time."

The kid grabbed Jack's arm. Jack looked down at his hand.

"*Octavio!*" the older gentleman at the back of the room shouted. Octavio withdrew his hand, letting it rest again on his belt. He drummed his fingers.

"Please," the older gentleman called out. "One drink."

Jack left a five on the bar and limped to the back of the room, standing under a moth-eaten steer head and a cloud of cigarette smoke. Esteban Gallegos looked up and tapped ash onto the floor. A scar ran from beneath his left eye down to his jaw. His hair was white and worn short. He had small, straight teeth, yellowed with tobacco. He closed his book, poured Jack a splash of rum from a small ceramic pot, and motioned for him to sit.

"I have heard about you," Esteban said.

"You're Esteban."

"And you are Jack."

Jack dropped Owen's photo on the table.

Esteban sipped his rum and took several slow puffs on his brown cigarette. He mumbled something to himself in Spanish, gazing at the photo. "Roy told me you were looking for your brother. This is him?"

Jack nodded.

"I had a brother. Alejandro." Esteban pulled a sword from behind the table and laid it between him and Jack. "A Cazoleta rapier. It was my father's sword, and when Alejandro died, it passed to me." He ran his index finger along the blade. The cuphilt gleamed gold. "Forged by Guillermo Espoza, tempered in the blood of his first born—at least, that is what the story says. You know how stories are." He grinned. "There are many stories about me. For example, there was a newspaper article some years ago, claiming I distribute a certain product. Not my women, mind you—" He held a hand to his chest. "I would never refer to my beautiful ladies as a *product*. No, this product was something else."

Jack drained the rum in a single gulp.

"With one story," Esteban said, licking his lips, "this reporter made my life very difficult. He made my friends in Humble very nervous, which in turn made me very nervous. Fortunately, I discovered a solution."

He picked up a red leather-bound book from his lap and slipped on a pair of gold-rimmed glasses. Opening the book, he read:

"*'What led me into it was a certain thirst for vengeance, which is strong enough to disturb the quietest hearts. I am by nature tender-hearted and kindly, but, as I said, the desire to revenge myself for a wrong that was done me so overturns all my better impulses.'*"

Esteban put down the book and slid Owen's photo across the table. "I had the reporter dissolved in acid. Dangled from a rope, lowered feet first. He screamed himself bloody. Literally, you understand. There was blood spilling from his mouth. I have never seen that before."

"Learn something new every day," Jack said.

Esteban grinned. "So. Are you here searching for your brother, or for something else?"

"I'm here for Owen. Your business is your business."

Esteban tapped the photo. "Then perhaps I was mistaken. Perhaps I have seen your brother with another man, here, in this bar. They shared a girl. Mariana. Very beautiful. Very smart. I cut her…" Esteban traced a line down the middle of his forehead and shook his head sadly. "Beauty is a terrible burden. I take that burden from them. It is my gift. To the ones I love."

Jack met Mariana in the upstairs room of the building next to Esteban's bar. The room was dark and hot, walls slashed with light from the shuttered windows. A mattress with a burlap sack pillow lay under a row of hat pegs. Mariana sat on the mattress and slowly undressed, pulling her skirt over her head.

When she finished undressing, she lay back and waited with

her legs spread, small, delicate hands resting on her hip bones, stomach flat and dotted with sweat. Jack stood on the other side of the room, against the wall.

"I am ready," she said.

Jack limped to the window. He drank from a bottle of whiskey.

"Have you seen the man in that photo?" he said.

"Last year. I remember him because he only watched. His friend worked and he watched. He did not seem to like watching. I think he may have fallen asleep. They came to me many times, and always the same one worked, and the same one watched."

"Who was his friend?"

"An angry man."

"Do you remember his name?"

"Yes."

"Will you tell me?"

Mariana stared at the ceiling. She traced the line down the middle of her forehead. Esteban had worked coarse salt into the wound after he'd cut her, to deepen the scar. "Harley Pike," she said. "He lives in a trailer outside of Humble."

Jack knelt by the mattress, pain sizzling up his leg. He guzzled the whiskey and thought of Sarah. A million miles away. She would be watching a movie. Or taking a bath. Maybe thinking of him.

He dressed quietly and paid meticulous attention to the details of his dressing like men do after visiting whores—he tucked in his shirt, brushed dust off his shoes—then staggered down the stairwell and back onto Avenue de Quere. The dancers were gone; in their place lay dead locusts and cigarette butts. Christmas lights swung in the breeze, flashing blue, yellow, and red across the sidewalk.

"Amigo."

Jack stopped. Octavio stepped out from an alley, hands resting on his belt. Behind him a tight mob of men, faces hidden in shadow.

"Maybe we'll see you again, amigo," Octavio said to Jack. "Maybe next time you have a drink with my friends."

Jack said nothing. He limped down Avenue de Quere. Octavio and his friends laughed, their laughter lost in the swirl and whip of the wind.

Jack parked Marty Garrett's pickup truck where Pepper told him: in the parking lot of Yellow Goose. As he'd rumbled through the hills and rocked over bumps and ditches, he'd hit a goat, a huge, shaggy beast with foam bubbling from its mouth, lying in the yellow of the truck headlights. The poor thing kicked and bleated until Jack found a large rock and put an end to its misery, then he dragged it off the road and buried it under a ridge.

There was no moon, no stars. Far off he could see the faintest of lights on the horizon, other towns calling to him like voices from outside a dream. He thought he might walk to them. Instead he found the Saint Emmanuel Baptist Church.

Reverend Fowler's service had just ended, and Jack sat in the corner of the church basement, on a child's chair, holding a brownie in one hand, a napkin in the other. He saw Pepper across the room, at the punch bowl. She gave him a small wave, then wrapped her arms around her father and listened to him talk with his nephew, Deputy Bob. Jack saw Willie talking to Eli, both of them on folding chairs, eating slices of pie off paper plates. Reverend Fowler held court in the far corner, surrounded by schoolgirls and their parents.

Fox cut through the crowd and sat on the floor near Jack. He rested his head against the wall. "How was Tejon?"

"Educational," Jack said.

Fox grinned. "I take it you met Lucia."

"Mariana."

Fox sat up. "*Mariana?* Mariana is Esteban's girl."

"She wasn't his girl tonight. She knew who Owen was. Said he was friends with Harley Pike."

"Harley doesn't have any friends."

Jack stood and leaned his shoulder against the wall for support. He pushed through the throng and up the stairs. He limped down the aisle, head swimming from the whiskey, and pushed through the church door. The street was empty. Buildings loomed on either side.

I'm doomed to wander this single street for eternity, he thought.

Curtis sat by himself on the curb, under the shadow of the steeple.

"Fee-fi-fo-fum," Curtis said. He dropped the roach pinched between his fingers and let it smoke on the dirt like a spent shell.

Jack turned.

"Missed a good one tonight." Curtis stood, brushing dust off his jeans. His shaved head gleamed like a bullet. "One of Reverend's better sermons. Usually it's a load of shit, but tonight it was all about sacrifice." He rubbed his eyes hard. "I realized my whole life has been a sacrifice. Living *here* has been a sacrifice. How fucked up is that?"

"Depends."

"On what?"

"On what your plans were."

He grinned. "I just take every day as it comes. I watch TV. I work out. I read. I never been anywhere except this street. What do you think about me?"

"I don't."

Curtis strode forward, chin lowered. "I think you're lying. I think you had me pegged the first time you saw me at the Bee."

"Curtis—"

He ran up to Jack and shoved him. Jack sprawled and skidded across the pavement. Skin ripped from his palms and chin. Gravel bit and stung. If I were sober, he thought, I could have fended him off. Talked things over. Bought the angry young man a drink.

"You better stay down." Curtis stepped forward. "I'll drop you again, you don't stay down."

Jack began his slow ascent, leg crackling, head pounding.

"I told you to stay down," Curtis said.

The flash of a blade; a quick scuffle. Curtis collapsed and his knife clattered across the street. Jack twisted Curtis' arm across his back, knee pressed into his side. Blood trickled from Curtis's nose. He struggled but Jack held him firm. Jack twisted harder. Curtis cried out, eyes shut.

"Next time you pull a knife," Jack said, "make sure it gets used."

He waited a moment, then released the arm. He picked up the knife and dropped it into his pocket, where it clanged against the watch.

Fox pushed through the church door. Curtis sat up, holding his shoulder, as Jack limped down Main Street. Fox ran after him.

"I need a gun," Jack said.

"Jack, listen—" Fox grabbed his arm. "People are talking. You're making everyone—"

Jack pulled away. He walked with Fox to the edge of town, past the old post office and the willow oak. The plains glowed blue.

Harley stood in his kitchen while rain drummed on the trailer roof. He uncapped a bottle of aspirin and filled a glass of water.

A voice from his bed: *I can make breakfast.*

Harley swallowed a handful of pills. *Not hungry.*

How about some toast? the voice asked.

No toast. Nothing.

A rustle of sheets, and Owen slithered off the bed and walked into the kitchen. He wrapped his arms around Harley, who put both hands on the counter, head lowered. Pillow lines creased his face. His hair was flattened on one side.

Owen slipped his hand down to Harley's bare stomach. Never as flat as he'd imagined—soft, cold, and covered in coarse hair. Harley looked better in his black T-shirts, tucked in snug. Not a fag or a queer but a tough guy. A rattlesnake. A wolf. No one dared throw a mean glance his way. Not Curtis, not Wade, not even Roy.

Harley walked into the TV room. Owen put on a record and got dressed. Harley grabbed a pair of balled-up jeans from the floor, and pulled a crumpled pack of smokes from the pocket. He slipped on a black shirt that read TITTY KAT KLUB on the front, and SECURITY on the back.

We should go to Coldspring, Owen said. He dropped bread into the toaster. *I'm in the mood for Chinese.*

Not today, Harley said.

I thought you got the weekend off.

He lit his cigarette. *I have to make a delivery.*

Oh, come on. Tell Roy to ask someone else—

There's no one else.

What about Curtis?

Roy trusts me.

You mean Esteban trusts you.

Whatever. I'm going.

Then you should have said something earlier. Pepper wanted to go shopping in Macon, but I said I couldn't because I thought we—

Well, now you can go. Harley took a long pull off his cigarette. *Have a fucking blast.*

A fucking blast?

You know what I mean.

Yes, I do. You're in one of your moods—

I've been hearing things, Harley said.

Always with the melodrama.

I'm serious. People are talking. You know who I mean.

Let them talk, Owen said. *They have to talk to let everyone know they disapprove. That's how it works.*

The toaster popped and they both jumped. Owen laughed but Harley shook his head.

It's different this time, Harley said. *You don't understand Humble.*

Owen plucked the cigarette from Harley's mouth and took a drag. The rain stopped. They could hear it dripping off the roof's edge, plinking into the puddles that dotted the plains.

Just tell Roy you're not feeling well, Owen said. *What's he going to do?*

Harley stared at the opposite wall. *I don't know. That's what I'm worried about.*

Harley's dog bolted from its spot near the trailer door, chain slithering behind, like a snake, until it snapped taut. The dog stood on its rear legs, barking, snarling, spitting ropy froth. Jack reached out and patted the dog's head. He felt the contours of skull and veins beneath the fur. He unbuckled its collar and the dog trotted off, snout held to the ground.

"Harley's never home," Fox said. "You're wasting your time."

Jack tried the door. The thin metal screen swung in easily.

"You can't go in there," Fox pleaded.

"You smell that?"

"Jack, listen to me. If Sheriff Wade finds out you broke into Harley's trailer he'll string you up. Jack—"

Jack fumbled in the dark, left hand passing over a TV and a crate filled with albums. His right hand found a pull-string.

The single bulb showed enough: Harley Pike lay on the linoleum floor, on the edge of the brown shag carpeting, back slumped against the wall, arms at his side and palms up, as though he were weighing the options before pulling the trigger of the shotgun that lay across his knees. The back of his head was spread across the wall, blood and hair plugging pellet holes. One eye was open. His tongue was black. Jack shouted for Fox, and the dwarf reluctantly stepped inside.

BEDLAM

Sheriff James T. Baird slipped past the fountain and signaled for his men to take their positions in the row of hedges along Dr. Bedlam's driveway. All of Redden County had heard the reports on the scanner: An old man, a woman, and a boy. The old man killed some poor nigger in Bass Drop and tried to kill a waitress. The waitress was pretty sure they were driving a white station wagon with a Six Flags bumper sticker.

Frank Kane, smelling like a bar floor, had stumbled into the Coldspring police station and told them how a Mexican boy he's never seen before paid for a whole bunch of candy with blood-soaked bills. *I followed him and his pretty lady*, Frank said. *They're staying at Doc's house.*

The white station wagon with a faded Six Flags bumper sticker was parked in the driveway. Officer Rawlins ran the plate—it came back *Soledad Santanillo, Shoshone Street, Buffalo, New York*. No priors, not even a speeding ticket. Rawlins said she looked like a girl accustomed to being chased by men. Sheriff Baird commented on the irony; within thirty minutes every cop in Coldspring was hidden in the shadows outside Dr. Bedlam's home.

The door exploded off its hinges; by the time Officer Rawlins stumbled into the living room, shoulder throbbing, Sol had grabbed the boy and dashed for the stairs. She didn't think they'd shoot but she knew only what she'd seen in the movies—cops bursting into a room with a hail of bullets and smoke—and she made sure Mincho had the inside line up the stairs in case they fired.

Sol ran into Earl's room. Earl shot up from his bed, I.V. tubes dangling from his arms, his thigh wrapped in gauze.

"Police," Sol said.

Earl ripped the tubes from his arms and grabbed his Schofield.

Sol opened the window and looked out over the back lawn, then gently took her father's head from the dresser and set it on the nightstand. She pushed the dresser in front of the door. Police clomped down the hall, kicking open doors. Earl unlatched the muzzle and loaded his gun.

"No killing," Sol said.

The door banged against the dresser. Mincho lowered his shoulder and pushed back.

Earl raised his Schofield and Sol hit his arm just as he fired. The bullet chunked into the door frame. She grabbed Earl by his shoulders and pulled him across the room, both of them struggling, and shoved him through the window. Shattering glass, a tumble, weightlessness, silence, then he slammed into the soft grass.

She whipped around and looked at Mincho. "If he's alive, take him to the car."

"Are you coming?"

The door banged again and the dresser legs squawked across the floor. A tangle of arms slipped between the door and the jamb.

"Wait for me in town," Sol said.

"*Where?*"

"Behind the pharmacy."

Half of Sheriff Baird's body was squeezed in. He craned his head and glared at Sol. "Get on the floor with your hands—"

Sol kissed Mincho on the forehead and he climbed out the window, sliding slowly down the roof, cutting his palms on the broken glass. When he made it to the gutter he grabbed tight and let his body hang, then let go.

She kicked the dresser against the door. Sheriff Baird screamed in pain. She kicked again and he fell back into the hall. Officer Rawlins peeped in. Sol kicked once more. The frame bounced off his head and he yelped and disappeared.

More clomping boots; Sol heard Dr. Bedlam shouting. She looked out the window and saw the glitter of glass and a strip of gauze lying on the lawn. She looked at her father's head, floating in its jar.

The door burst open and the dresser toppled just as she leapt out the window. Her socks slipped on the slate. She dug her fingers into the cracks and grabbed a lightning rod and pulled herself up. When she reached the top, she crawled along the peak to the front of the house, keeping herself low. The station wagon squealed out of the driveway.

Sol heard the click of a revolver. She turned. Officer Rawlins stood on the roof, with an odd half-smile, gun held at his waist. He fired. She rolled, falling to the roofline below. Rawlins walked to the edge and Sol looked up at him, then he holstered his gun and ripped the lightning rod from the slate.

He jumped, landing next to her and bringing the black iron rod down on her back. She screamed. The metal thrummed. He struck her in the head and she stopped moving. He stared for a moment. He traced a line across her cheek with the end of the lightning rod, pushing the tip into the side of her neck, slowly, carefully. He took out his cuffs and knelt.

Sol seized Rawlins by the hair, yanked his head down, and plunged a spike of cracked slate into his throat. He roared blood and kicked and scuttled back, clutching at his neck. He coughed and spit and drew in giant, whooping breaths. Sol sat up. Her head rang. Officer Rawlins stared at her, gurgling, blood pumping from between his fingers. He kicked one final time, then stopped.

She heard shouts and the static crackle of walkie-talkies. She dragged herself to the roof's edge, wrapped her legs around a pillar, and slid down.

Sol found Earl and Mincho sitting on milk crates behind the pharmacy. Her wagon idled with its headlights off. Earl sipped a can of Fizzer, holding his side.

"Temple-on-the-Hill ain't far," Earl said. "We can gas up there and head out for Fuller first thing. I got a detour mapped, 'cause I figure they'll have roadblocks set up." He swallowed with a wince. "You broke a few of my ribs, you know."

She stopped and bent over. Her head throbbed. She thought she might throw up. After a few deep breaths she turned to Mincho.

"Did you kill anyone?" he asked.

"Get in the car."

Mincho said nothing. Instead, he opened another bag of Doritos.

STRAY DOGS

Sarah wiped her hands on the dishtowel and picked up the phone.

"Sarah?" Jack's voice was hollow on the other end. "Sarah, it's me."

She paused.

"Sarah? Hello?"

"Yes." She propped her elbow on the kitchen counter and rested her chin in her palm. A strand of blonde hair fell across her forehead. "I'm here."

"I'm in trouble," Jack said.

"Where are you?"

"Texas."

"Funny. I stopped by your apartment, the other day. I thought I saw your shadow in the window."

Jack rested his head against the cool metal of the pay phone.

"Are you really in Texas?"

Jack peered over his shoulder. The Busy Bee was empty. Fox was somewhere in the back, unloading boxes and smoking a joint. No Eli, no Roy. He hadn't seen Pepper. He hadn't seen anyone since leaving the police station.

"I'm a murder suspect," Jack said.

Sarah straightened up. Her thumb trickled blood, from the wine glass she'd just cracked.

"I found a body last night—"

"Wait," Sarah said. "You're a *murder* suspect? In *Texas*?"

Jack swallowed back a spurt of bile. He'd spent the afternoon in bed, drinking a six-pack of beer he'd bought at The Yellow Goose. Last night he'd staggered back to his room after finding Harley's body. Fox was useless, babbling about Sheriff Wade and Curtis. Then morning crashed through his window, Sheriff Wade was pounding on his door, and they dragged him to the police station. The sun was high and strong, blinding no matter how hard he squeezed his eyes shut. They hauled him across the street—folks staring, whispering—and gave him four hours at the police station, sitting him in an uncomfortable chair with squeaky wheels.

You're wasting my time, Jack had told Sheriff Wade. *He's been dead for a week, at least.*

Last I checked you weren't a forensics expert.

Doesn't take a forensics expert to smell rot.

So you've seen plenty of rotting bodies in your day.

I have.

"Are you calling me from jail?" Sarah asked.

"No…not yet," Jack said. "I don't know. I'm—"

"Drunk."

"Very. And I need money. There's no ATM here."

"No ATM?"

"That's what I said. It's a shithole. I can't even buy a used Pacer."

"You're not making any sense. Just slow down—"

Sheriff Wade had leaned in close enough for Jack to smell his cologne and sweat. *I'll tell you what I think. You've been acting wrong the minute you stepped foot in my town. Asking too many questions, bothering the good folk who mind their own business. Who the hell do you think you are? You want a bullet in your head?*

Are you threatening me?

I was waiting for you to catch on.

"Isn't there a Western Union or something?" Sarah said.

"Are you kidding?"

"Then how am I supposed to send you money?"

"I don't know. I haven't thought that far ahead. I've been borrowing money from this guy named Foxhall. He's nice. He's a dwarf."

"Of course he is."

"He takes it in stride. He knows life is suffering."

"You need to get sober."

"This is payback, Sarah. It's been due for a long time. This town—"

"Whose body did you find?"

"Some redneck in his trailer."

"What were you doing in his trailer?"

"Long story."

"Jack, listen to me. The first thing you need to do is get a lawyer."

"I don't know if there's one in town. And if there is, it's probably the sheriff."

"Then go back to your room, lock your door, and don't talk to anyone until we figure something out. What are you doing in Texas? Is this about Owen?"

"I've been a miserable bastard," Jack said. "You've been nothing but good to me—"

"Is Owen there? Did you actually hear from him? I can't believe this. Tell me where you are. I'll buy a ticket tonight."

Jack stared at his warped reflection in the pay phone's speckled faceplate. The door jangled and a group of men walked into the Bee, led by Curtis and Ike. Jack ignored them. He could still smell Harley. In his hair, on his clothes, under his fingernails.

I want you out of my town by tomorrow morning. We can do this one of two ways: either you walk out, or we carry you out in a zippered bag. I don't care which, but some folk here would rather you pick choice number two.

Tell me where Owen is and I'm gone. You'll never see me again.

You stupid sonofabitch. You just won't quit.

Jack heard Sarah calling out to him from the handset. "Jack? Are you there? *Hello?*"

He hung up.

He walked back to the counter, where Reverend Fowler sat on a stool, eating a slice of pie. His collar was open and his hair was freshly oiled. He smiled.

"Are you having dinner?" the reverend asked.

"I'm not hungry."

"Water, then."

"Only if you're buying."

The reverend grinned. He rang the counter bell, and Fox walked out from the kitchen. "Water for this fine gentleman," the reverend said, then he turned to Jack. "I'm Reverend Fowler."

"I'm Jack."

"I know." His face was clean and clear, not a hint of stubble or wrinkle. His teeth gleamed. "I spoke with Sheriff Wade. He told me what happened last night, about that nasty scene you and Foxhall stumbled upon. I assured Sheriff Wade you were in the wrong place at the wrong time."

"Thank you."

"I trust my instincts. You're a good man."

"But you don't know me."

"God knows you."

"Ah."

"And God told me you're righteous."

Jack sipped his water. "I doubt that."

"Just let the sheriff do what he has to do. He's playing his role."

"What role are you playing?"

"Keeper of the peace."

"You can start with that table in the back." Jack nodded toward Curtis and Ike, sitting at a booth, menus closed.

"I'll have a word with them. But my concern is you. I know you've been asking about Owen—"

"I'm surprised you knew him. My brother wasn't the church-going type."

The reverend cleared his throat. "May I ask you something?"

"Shoot."

"Don't you think if your brother left without telling you where, that it might be best to let it go?"

"I've been letting it go for ten years."

"Your mother forgave you."

"Pardon?"

"We spoke at length. She was a private woman, but in her final weeks she found her voice. She forgave you. You should forgive yourself."

"My mother was a cruel bitch." Jack stared ahead. "Her forgiveness doesn't mean anything."

"Well, I promised her I would convey the message."

"Consider your promise kept. Thanks for the water."

Jack left through the front door. It didn't take long for Pepper to find him. She ran across the street, loosely tied sneakers clopping against her heels.

"I heard about Harley," she said. "Are you okay?"

The group of men left the Bee and spilled out onto the street, Curtis in front, Ike in the back. Jack reached into his pocket and felt for the knife.

"Tell Fox I'm at the church," he said to Pepper.

She looked back at the six men standing across the street. They began to walk slowly, staring, silent.

Pepper stood on her tiptoes and pecked Jack on the lips before he could do anything. "They never lock the front door," she said, then she ran.

Jack ran too, limping across the Yellow Goose parking lot. He heard whispers of pursuit, a pack of wolves behind him, the rasp of their shoes on the street and the huff and puff of their breath. He clenched his teeth, pumped his arms, and galloped over the front lawn of the church. He burst through the doors, slammed them shut, and grabbed the coat rack, lodging it between knob and carpet, jamming his foot against the bottom of the rack.

A voice outside the door, quiet and teasing:

"Jackie boy. Open up, Jackie boy."

Jack took out the knife.

"You hear me, Jackie boy? Come on out. Be a hero."

Doesn't do anything for me? How many times do I have to tell you? How many times are you going to ask—

Hush. I got your point.

No, Harley. I don't think you do. Because if you did, you'd stop.

This was the last time. I promise.

Owen stumbled over a half-buried rock. The moon slipped behind a veil of clouds.

Don't feed me any more of your bullshit, Owen said. *We—you—stayed because you like fucking Mariana. And I know what you sound like when you're having a good fuck—*

Shut up with that.

With what?

With that. We don't need to talk about it all the time.

Owen stumbled again and Harley grabbed his arm. They came up on the Busy Bee. Owen stopped in the middle of Main Street.

You can fuck a man in the dark, Owen said. *But when you fuck Mariana you want the lights on, nice and bright.*

Keep your voice down, for Christ's sake. I told you it was the last time.

Owen waved him away. *Please. I put up with that self-denying bullshit back in college. It didn't work for me then, and it doesn't work for me—*

Just keep your voice down.

But last time I checked, wasn't me who forced you to suck my cock. Wasn't me who forced—

Curtis stepped out from the shadows of the Yellow Goose parking lot. Ike was with him, trailing behind.

Owen looked at Curtis, then at Harley.

Harley felt his breath stagger. His head pulsed hot and sharp. *I warned you, O. Swear to God I warned you—*

Fee-fi-fo-fum, Curtis said. He hefted a piece of rusted rebar over his shoulder.

Faces peered from darkened homes. The Yellow Goose sign buzzed and flickered. Owen stared at Harley, and his face fell into shadow as the moon slipped behind the clouds again.

"It's Fox. Let me in."

"You alone?"

"Yes."

The door opened and Fox walked into the church. Jack shut the door and pushed back the tables he'd carried up from the basement. He sat on one of the tables, knife in hand.

Fox held out a sword. Its blade was bent and rusted, snips of steel missing from the edge. "It's the best I could do. My father's old hunting rifle is all gunked up."

Jack took the sword, turning it from side to side.

"I saw Curtis yelling at the reverend," Fox continued, "and Roy yelling at the reverend, and Sheriff yelling at all of them. Even Bob got into it."

Jack looked down the length of the blade. "Where'd you get this thing?"

"My garage. I think it's an antique."

"You think?" Jack tossed the sword aside and pressed his temples between his hands. "I need a gun."

Fox thought for a moment. "I got an oar. From my rowboat."

"An oar."

Fox shrugged. "I'm just spitballing, here."

The stained-glass windows glowed softly from the moon. Fox took out a joint and sparked his lighter. He sat on the table, near Jack.

"I don't know what to do anymore," Fox said.

"Take me to Owen."

Fox stared at Jack. His eyes rimmed red with tears.

The moon had risen by the time Jack and Fox got to Two Tree Hill. The hill was naked and wrinkled, its single tree a stunted oak, stooped like an old man.

Fox sat against the oak and rested his elbows on his knees. "When I was a kid I used to come up here all the time. I'd climb this tree and look out over the plains and pretend there was something out there worth looking at."

Jack took the watch from his pocket and hefted it in his palm. He stared down at Fox.

"Nobody planned it," Fox said. "What I mean is, it just sort of happened. You have to believe me. I even tried to warn Owen, but he—"

Jack saw his shadow flanked by two other shadows. He turned; something heavy struck him across the chest. He dropped to all fours. A boot thudded into his ribs. The rebar struck his back, his legs, his arm. He didn't remember rolling over but suddenly there he was, staring at the night sky while two men towered over him. Curtis held the piece of rebar. Ike had a .38, business end pointed at Jack.

"Told you to stay down last time," Curtis said.

Ike aimed the .38 at Fox. "Get out of here."

"Sheriff said nothing rough." Fox scrambled to his feet. "Sheriff said he was going to cuff him and—"

"Sheriff had his chance," Curtis said. "I'm here on Roy's word."

Ike cocked back the hammer.

"Never again," Fox said. "That's what we all promised."

"Shut up," said Curtis. "You just better shut up, or I'll crack your little fucking head."

Ike looked down the site of his .38, black tip between Fox's eyes.

"Don't worry about me," Jack said. "I'll be at the Bee in time for dinner." He tried to stand, but Curtis hit him again, across the shoulder blades, and he fell, coughing, trying to catch his breath.

Fox agonized a moment longer, then walked past, pushing Ike aside. Jack watched the top of Fox's head disappear behind the ridge. He heard his feet scrabble down the gravelly hillside. He looked up at Curtis and Ike.

"I always knew it was coming," Jack said, closing his eyes. "I've done a lot of bad shit in my life."

Curtis tightened his grip. "That makes two of us."

When they finished, they yanked Jack to his feet. Ike pistol-whipped Jack in the back of the head; Curtis pushed him up against the tree and had Ike hold him there while he kneecapped Jack with the rebar.

Curtis took off his belt and Ike did the same.

"Roy didn't want me to kill you." Curtis pulled Jack's arms behind him, around the oak, and tightened the belt around his wrists. "Lucky for you but too bad for me, cause I would've fucked your mouth with this rebar. I'll tell you that right now. Fucked. That. *Mouth*."

Ike pulled his belt around Jack's neck. He pulled the strap until he heard the leather creak. Jack gasped for air and kicked one heel against the oak's trunk.

"Struggling only makes it worse," Curtis said.

"Christ," Ike said. "I think he just smiled."

Curtis worked his chew and spit. "He's delirious, is all. Lack of oxygen."

Ike put his face close to Jack's. "You smiling at me? You don't know how much I'd like to plug you with all six shots." He whooped and spun and shot at a rock sticking out of the ridge. "What are we supposed to do with him?"

"Roy didn't say," said Curtis. "The tree was my idea. Saw it in a Schwarzenegger movie." He twirled the rebar and swung at a rock on the ground. "Roy wants him, he can cut him down."

Curtis jogged down the hillside. At the bottom he dug his heels into the dirt and took a deep breath.

Ike paused at the ridge and aimed his .38.

"Do it," said Jack, but his voice was lost in a clot of blood.

Ike shot at the ground near Jack's feet, let out another whoop, and ran down the hill.

Reverend Fowler left his car parked behind the church, keys in the ignition. In a pew he found the crinkled Polaroid of Owen, and he stuffed it into his pocket and paced in the attic of the church, bathed in sunlight, waiting for an answer.

"I did my part," he said. "I told him to leave. I kept Curtis and his friends at the table as long as I could."

He heard Jesus say: *There is much sickness, here.*

"Yes. I've known this for a long time."

Yet you do nothing.

Reverend Fowler fell to his knees and stripped to the waist.

He stared up at the attic window, awash in purple from the stained glass pierced with high noon.

"I do what I can. I stand above judgment." Reverend Fowler pressed his palms to his ears and touched his forehead to the floor. "Forgive me. Please." He began to cry.

You know where he is. They are both there. Go to them.

Fowler stood, slowly, and wiped the snot dribbling from his nose. He walked to his office, took the thick leather strop from its hook on the wall, and fell again to his knees. "I am undeserving of mercy," he said. He whipped his back, relishing the *thwack* of the leather against his skin.

"I am undeserving of forgiveness.

I am undeserving of salvation."

He whipped thirty-three times, until his flesh numbed and blood ran. He stood, legs shaking, and left the church. The sun dried his flayed skin, sitting like a hot pan on his flesh.

Fox sat in a booth in his diner and waited, staring out the window. His oar lay behind the counter. Roy Beasley and his sons sat in the booth behind him, eating breakfast. Jeremiah Beasley soaked a corner of his toast in bacon fat, and his older brother finished his bottle of Fizzer. Eli sat at the counter and sucked a rye seed from his molar.

Reverend Fowler walked down Main Street. Sheriff Wade and Deputy Bob stepped out of Chayban Denim.

"Where you headed, Reverend?"

He turned to the sheriff. "A pilgrimage."

Wade tipped back his hat. "Then you're headed the wrong way." He grinned. "Tejon is behind you."

The reverend walked on.

"Hey, Rev!" Bob shouted. "What happened to your back?"

"Son, let him be," Sheriff Wade said.

"What's wrong with him?"

"Just mind your business," Wade said. "Reverend has a special relationship with God. If he's walking into the desert with his back looking like he took a cheese grater to it, then that's between him and the Lord."

Bob stared at the reverend as he walked out of town. He looked at his father, at his gun belt with his Smith & Wesson hanging lazily against his thigh, his wide-brimmed hat, his white ironed shirt.

Wade pushed his longish gray hair behind his ears and squinted at the sky. "Not that God listens anymore." He paused. "Reckon he's got better things to do."

Reverend Fowler found Jack pinned and peeling against the oak. A horned lizard lapped at the blood on his sneakers. Vultures had lit upon his shoulders and roosted on his head; Reverend Fowler screamed and they flapped their massive, black wings and hissed back. The reverend cut the belts with his boot knife and carried Jack down the hill, to Fuller, through its ghost streets and past the crumbled mounds of burnt wood, over rabbit holes, half-buried Gatorade bottles, and faded Slim Jim wrappers. The church was in ruins—only a half steeple and a jaw of charred brick wall remained. Revered Fowler picked his way over the skeletal black pews. He laid Jack down on the remains of the altar, the back wall standing tall enough to throw shadow.

The reverend tore off the leg of his pants and soaked the cloth in his bottle of water. When he'd cleaned off most of the blood and dust from Jack's face, he wrung the cloth clean and wet it again. He put it on Jack's lips.

Jack awoke into darkness. He felt someone near him. He felt for his face, and his fingers came up against a bandage. A hand grabbed his wrist.

"Leave it," a voice said. "They're as clean as I could make them."

Jack grabbed a corner of the cloth and ripped it off. "I can't see anything."

Silence.

"I can't see anything," he repeated.

"Just keep still," the voice said. "He's here. Don't be afraid. He's with you now."

No dreams. Then:

The sun on my face. There's no light, but the sun is on my face.

"Hello? Are you still there?"

Jack heard the scrape of grit on rock.

"I'm still here, Jack. How do you feel?"

Reverend Fowler, thought Jack.

He sat up, slowly. He felt the ground—sharp stone, dust, the chalkiness of wood. He touched his face and felt peeling skin. His lips burned. His nose was crooked and swollen. His eyebrows were caked with blood. All was dark.

"Where am I?"

"In a church."

"Your church?"

"The old church in Fuller."

"I thought Fuller was abandoned."

"It is," the reverend said. "It's safe."

Jack reached for his eyes. The bandages were back in place.

"You may lift them up," the reverend said. "But please don't take them off. You don't want an infection."

"Bring me into the sun," Jack said.

"You're badly burnt."

"I don't care. Bring me into the sun."

The reverend put his hand on Jack's shoulder, and Jack crawled.

"Here," the reverend said.

Jack felt the sun on his face, a scorching beam that singed his lips and made his skin throb. He lifted the bandage and waited. He ripped them away. He dug his fingers into his eyes but felt only a moist hole, and when his fingers scraped against the sides the bone ached like a bad tooth.

"Oh God—"

"Black vultures," the reverend said. "They eat the eyes of newborn sheep. Come back into the shade."

Jack crawled. When he'd returned to the spot still warm from his body, he collapsed onto his stomach. He dug his fingers into the dirt.

Never realized dirt looked like this, he thought. He saw his apartment. The brown couch. The blue rug. Sarah. Sarah.

Curtis was a giant vulture with a shaved head and a tattoo of an eagle on his scaled ankle. He straddled Jack and flapped his wings. Dust devils spiraled off across the plains.

Roy didn't say anything about eating. Too bad for you, Jackie boy.

The giant vulture craned his serpentine neck and plucked out Jack's eyes, and he screamed.

He awoke. "Reverend?"

The reverend slept. Jack heard his breathing.

He struggled to his knees. His hands found the crumbled brick wall. He dug his fingers into the cracks and pulled himself to his feet. His knees throbbed, and he couldn't put weight on his bad leg.

A hot wind lifted and ruffled his hair. He smelled the dust and the scorched rock.

Follow the wind, Jack thought. He lurched forward.

He picked his way through the street, stumbling over timbers and piles of rubble. His right foot kicked a can. He swallowed and heard his ears pop, saliva gurgling down his throat.

A mouse scuttled from its home inside a fallen eave and inspected the kicked can. Jack heard its claws scraping against the thin metal. He imagined Curtis and his friend sitting on the curb, sharpening their knives.

"I heard you," Jack said. "You come near me and I'll rip out your heart."

"Jack."

He spun and lost his balance. Reverend Fowler rushed to his side.

"*Be careful*," Jack said. "I heard someone across the street."

"There's no one there."

"Are you sure?"

"I'm sure. Where were you going?"

"Humble."

"You can't. It isn't safe."

"I have to call Sarah."

"Is Sarah your sister? Do you have any family you can call?"

Jack laughed. Once he started he couldn't stop, and he laughed so hard he howled. "Owen was it," he said. Tears cut the dirt on his cheeks. "He's all I had."

"Curtis beat him to death. In the middle of Main Street."

"I know."

"Lord forgive—"

"Did you watch?"

Reverend Fowler nodded.

"Is that a yes?"

"Yes," the reverend said.

"And you did nothing?"

Silence.

"Who else."

Reverend Fowler sniffled. "Who else what?"

"Who else *watched*."

"Roy and his eldest. Eli stood on the sidewalk. Other folks, too. I don't know how many."

"Sheriff? Harley?"

"Not Harley. He ran away. Sheriff wasn't there. I found him passed out in a pew the next morning, stinking drunk."

"Go get Foxhall," Jack said. "Tell him to bring his oar, and the sharpest knife he can find."

"Forgive me," the reverend said.

"You're asking the wrong man."

Reverend Fowler laid his hands on Jack's forehead but Jack grabbed the reverend's face, locked his hand around his jaw, and pushed him to the ground. He pulled himself close to the reverend so he could hear his breathing and the drips of sweat sliding off the reverend's temple, blotting into the dust.

"I've figured some things out," Jack said. "This town's got fags, murderers, drug dealers, whores—all the sorts of people you'd expect to find in hell. The terrible shit I've done, it's all brought me to this. I think I died in Honduras. I think this town has been waiting for me since then. You and everyone else. You've all been waiting."

He slid his hand off the reverend's face. His fingers were wet with tears. He listened to the reverend walk away. Soon the wind swallowed his footsteps. Jack crawled across the street until his hands touched charred timber, then a wall, then glass. He nestled himself among the ruins, and waited.

Pepper ran to her front door. Someone had been banging on the screen.

"Hey, Pep."

It was Curtis. He was shirtless and shoeless. Pepper saw dried blood on his hands.

"What's going on?" Pepper said.

He shrugged. "What's going on with you?"

"I'm doing summer reading."

"Your pops home?"

"He's sleeping."

"In the middle of the day?"

"Yeah. You have blood on you, you know."

Curtis rubbed his head and looked over his shoulder. "Can I come in?"

"What happened?"

"Got into a fight with Ike."

"I'm sorry."

"I'm not."

"Hey, have you seen Jack?"

"No. Let me in. I gotta use the toilet."

"Eliza's home," Pepper said. "Ask her."

"Eliza's a mean old bitch."

Pepper frowned. "Yeah, well, I have to finish my reading. Sorry."

"Yeah, well, so am I."

Curtis kicked in the screen door and it smacked Pepper in the face. The wire cut her nose. She stumbled back, dazed, and fell over the side table near the couch. Curtis was on her like a cat. He covered her mouth with his hand. His skin was warm and rough. He pulled her up, one hand over her mouth and the other on the back of her head. He dragged her into the kitchen. Marty slept in the next room. His television applauded. Curtis hauled Pepper down onto the warm linoleum. Her half-eaten bowl of cereal sat on the table, next to a stack of books. A clock in the shape of a dog hung on the wall, eyes shifting back and forth in time with the second hand. Pepper stared past Curtis, at the white of her Prada sneakers. He grabbed her sweatpants and yanked them down. He fumbled for her underwear, ripping the cotton, his hand still clamped over her mouth.

"Keep your mouth shut," Curtis said. "It might be a little rough at first, but you'll get to liking it. Are you gonna keep quiet?"

Pepper nodded.

Curtis moved atop her. He reached down to his pants and she brought up her knee into his crotch. He grunted and she clawed at his face, kneed him again, and bucked him off, scrambling to the bedroom door. She ran into her dad's room and screamed his name. Curtis ran in behind her. She leapt over the bed, bolted into the bathroom, and locked the door.

Curtis rammed his shoulder against the frame. Pepper screamed for her dad.

"*Marty!*" Curtis yelled, laughing. "Wake up, Marty. I'm about to pop your daughter's cherry." He laughed again. "Pep, he's drunk as fuck. Now unlock the door."

"*No*," Pepper cried.

"Unlock the door."

Pepper tried to hold in her tears. She grabbed a pair of scissors from the medicine cabinet.

"It doesn't have to be this way." Curtis rested his forehead against the door. "I can make it feel good. You'll see."

Silence.

The doorknob rattled. "*Open the fucking door!*"

"No."

"Then it's your fault."

Pepper closed her eyes, scissors clutched tightly, tears streaming. The television turned louder, and once Pepper realized what was happening, she screamed.

"Maybe I should call the sheriff in Coldspring and see what he thinks of all this."

Sheriff Wade sat at his desk with his boots up and his hat pulled low. Fox stood on the other side of the desk, an oar propped over his shoulder.

"Sheriff Connor would tell you the same thing as me," Wade said. "Stick to your business and let me do my job."

"If you did your job, Owen would still be alive."

Wade sighed and brushed dust off his boots. "What do you want me to do? Arrest Curtis and Ike?"

"That's exactly what I want you to do."

"For what?"

"Murder. I'll be your first witness."

Wade set down his bottle. "Now we've gone over this before. Curtis was acting in self-defense. It was a terrible tragedy but there's no need to complicate—"

"That's bullshit and you know it. Owen wouldn't swat a mosquito."

"I have three witnesses say otherwise."

"Then let's bring it to court and see what happens."

"Fox—"

"If you wait any longer to help Jack, there might be two bodies buried atop that hill."

Wade thought for a moment. He stared out the window, at Main Street. "Esteban hates the attention. It's bad for business. Which makes it bad for us."

Fox stared. "Whose town is this?"

Wade stood up, dropped his hat onto the desk, and pushed his hair behind his ears. "All right."

"All right?"

"That's what I said." Wade flicked open the chamber of his gun and snapped it shut. "You follow me and I'll arrest you for obstruction. Understand?"

Fox nodded.

"Bob's unplugging Eliza's toilet," Wade said. "He comes back before I do, tell him where I am and tell him to stay put."

"I'm going to Two Tree," Fox said.

Wade eyed Fox's oar. "I thought you were going fishing."

Wade found Roy on his tractor behind his house. Ike trailed behind, picking out large rocks from the tilled soil and throwing them into a wheelbarrow.

Roy cut the engine. "Afternoon, Sheriff."

"Afternoon. I'm arresting Ike here for suspicion of murder."

Ike dropped his handful of rocks. Roy jumped down from his tractor.

"This doesn't concern you," Wade said to Roy.

"Course it does," Roy said.

Wade stared at Roy. "Then you can make your statement at the station." He turned to Ike. "Come along, son. I don't want to cuff you."

Roy took off his baseball cap and wiped his forehead. "Suspicion of murder?"

"Owen Cahill," Wade said.

Roy folded his arms. "Wonder what Esteban would think of all this."

"Esteban doesn't run this town," Wade said, and he took Ike by the arm and led him back across the field.

Wade walked down Main Street, still holding onto Ike's skinny arm, just as Curtis left Pepper's. He hopped down the front steps.

"*Curtis!*" Wade shouted.

Curtis stopped and turned.

Wade dropped his right hand to his gun. "I need you to come to the station."

"What for?"

"He arrested me," Ike said.

Wade turned to Ike. "Keep your mouth shut." He turned back to Curtis. "Now I don't want to cuff you, son, but I will."

Curtis didn't move. "What's the charge?"

"Come on, now. Don't make this any harder than it is."

Wade saw the trail of blood on his thigh. The fresh scratch marks on his neck. He looked at his brother's house. The front door was open.

"You and Pep have an argument?"

Curtis shrugged. "We were just fooling around."

"So you're an item now."

He grinned. "You could say that."

Wade called out Pepper's name.

"She's in the shower," Curtis said.

"Where's Marty?"

"Sleeping."

Wade grabbed Ike's wrist. He handcuffed Ike to Curtis and ordered them both into Pepper's house.

"I told you she's in the shower," Curtis said.

They stepped into the house. Wade heard the blaring television. The screen door was lying against the side table near the couch, its screen caved in.

He walked into the kitchen. A bowl of soggy cereal sat on the table. White women's underwear lay on the floor. The dog-shaped clock ticked. He clomped across the kitchen and opened the door to Marty's bedroom.

Marty lay on the bed, arms and legs spread out. A pillow covered his face. A half-empty bottle of whiskey sat on the nightstand. The TV applauded. Wade lifted the pillow and saw his brother's staring eyes. He stalked back into the living room, gun drawn, and as soon as his face came into view, Ike shot it.

Fox ran past the willow oak on the edge of town. Halfway to Two Tree, he heard the gunshot, and he stopped and looked back at Humble, the end of his oar rising and dipping with each breath. Then he ran some more, and scrambled up Two Tree Hill and dropped the oar, resting his hands on his knees as he sucked air. When he looked up he saw Reverend Fowler kneeling at the base of the stunted oak. At first Fox thought the black strips coiled around Reverend Fowler's feet were snakes, but then he saw the sun gleaming off the buckles and he realized they were belts, lying in the dust.

"Reverend?"

Reverend Fowler looked at the sky. His mouth moved in silent prayer.

"Reverend, where's Jack?"

"Fuller," the reverend said. "It's never easy for the sacrificial lamb but in time they accept their charge. I've asked to share Jack's burden, but I've yet to receive an answer." He closed his eyes.

Fox saw the scabbed lash marks on the reverend's back. A kettle of vultures circled overhead.

"Going fishing?" Reverend Fowler asked.

"The oar's for Jack."

Reverend Fowler smiled sadly. " '*Behold!*' " He spread his arms to the sky. " '*I will send for many fishers, saith the Lord, and they shall fish them; and after will I send for many hunters, and they shall hunt them from every mountain, and from every hill, and out of the holes of the rocks.*' "

Fox saw Curtis' knife lying in the dust. He snatched it and

ran. More gunshots from Humble, their echoes ripping through the dry air. He ran through Fuller, to the church, where he found a knot of bloodied bandages lying under the shadow of the remaining wall.

They buried him on Two Tree, Fox thought. He dropped the oar. Reverend said last rites, just like last time.

Fox heard something picking through the rubble on the other side of the church wall. A growl. Suddenly he was yanked to the ground and a piece of jagged glass pressed against his throat.

It was Jack, his face swollen, eyes covered in bandages. Harley's dog scampered around the wall.

"Jack," Fox said. When he spoke he felt his throat scrape against the glass' edge. "I swear I didn't know—"

"*Shhhh…*" Jack pressed his finger to Fox's lips. He took away the glass. "Did you hear those gunshots?"

Fox nodded.

"Is that a yes?"

"I heard them," Fox said. "Sheriff arrested Curtis and Ike. Your eyes…what—"

Jack lifted the bandages and Fox screamed. The dog howled.

"Where's the reverend?" Jack asked.

Fox couldn't speak. Jack heard his stuttered breathing.

"Take a deep breath. Where's the reverend?"

"Two Tree," Fox said.

"Did you bring my oar?"

"Yes."

"A knife?"

"Yes."

"Did you watch Curtis kill my brother?"

Fox squeezed his eyes shut but the tears came anyway. "I wasn't there. But I helped bury him."

"Can you get me food and water?"

"Anything you need."

Jack felt on the ground and grabbed the oar. Fox handed him the knife, then wiped his eyes. He watched Jack feel along the oar's edge.

"I would've done anything to stop them," Fox said. "Owen was my friend."

"He wasn't mine." Jack snapped open the knife and went to work. "That's what got us into this mess."

TEXAS MUD

Fox returned to Fuller with food, water, and a bleeding ear, and as Jack finished carving the oar into a makeshift sword Fox smoked a joint and told him what happened. They both heard the distant thunder and felt its rumble in the ground, a storm blowing in from the north with black bloated clouds.

"I got to my diner and Eli was sitting in a booth eating pecan pie he'd swiped from my cooler, and I asked him, 'What the hell are you doing?' and he said, 'It's come round.' I asked him what he was talking about but that's all he kept saying: 'It's come round, it's come round.' Then I got outside and Curtis was sitting under the Yellow Goose sign drinking beers with Ike, and Curtis chucked a bottle at me and I told him he better watch what he does. Ike laughed and I saw Curtis had Sheriff's belt around his jeans, and he drew Sheriff's gun and fired. I didn't know he'd clipped my ear until I got to Willie's. He looked at my ear and said, 'You been shot,' and then he just shook his head and shut his garage door. I stayed off Main Street and ran to Sheriff's, and I found Bob locked in the back room. He pointed his shotgun at me. There were bullet holes in the walls and Bob had this look… I've seen the same look, the day Reverend Fowler told me my folks died in that fire. I remember seeing myself in the bathroom mirror. I remember what I looked like. Christ, the whole town looks like that."

Jack felt along the edge of the oar. He hefted it, then grabbed a handful of dust from the ground and rubbed the handle.

"What about Pepper?" Jack asked.

"I didn't go to her house."

"Roy?"

Fox sucked the joint to its end. "I saw his truck, driving around the lake to Tejon. Once Esteban hears how things have gone to hell, he'll get his whole—"

"Someone's coming." Jack lifted his head to the wind.

"That's thunder," Fox said.

Jack stuck the tip of the oar into the ground and stood. Fox took his hand but he waved him away.

"That's not thunder," Jack said. "Go see."

Fox picked his way through the rubble and looked down the street, past the plains behind Two Tree Hill. He saw the edge of a dark sky—a thin grey line slowly closing like a curtain over the blue—and a trail of dust behind a white car.

"It's a car," Fox said.

"Sheriff?"

"No…it's not coming from Humble."

"There's two men," Jack said. "And a dog in the backseat."

"How the hell—"

"I'm just fucking with you. Get me somewhere safe."

Fox led Jack across the street and kicked open the door to a small abandoned building. Broken tables and chairs had been piled in the middle of the room, and some of the floorboards were ripped up. Jack sat on the floor against the wall, laying the oar across his lap. Harley's dog sat next to him.

"Smells like old beer," Jack said.

"This used to be a bar," Fox said.

Fox stepped behind the bar and ran his fingers along the wood. He remembered the last time he sat there. His folks had been in the ground for a year.

"Tonight I'll sneak back into Humble," Fox said. "I'll get us a car, and we'll drive to Coldspring and tell the police everything that happened. Then we can just *go*. Back to Detroit or—"

"We'll need to take Pepper. And her dad."

"Marty will come for sure. He's been wanting to leave longer than me."

"Eli. Willie. Reverend Fowler."

"No problem. We'll take them all."

"Owen."

Fox paused.

"Can't leave without Owen," Jack said. "Wouldn't be right. Do you want to tell him, or should I?"

"You don't know Humble. You don't know what—"

"I know that my brother was murdered and you dug his grave."

"You don't know *shit*." Fox kicked a broken chair, kicked it again until it split apart. "Every day I stand in my yard, stare at that hill and dream of doing *something*. But a dead man doesn't know the difference between a hero and a coward, and if you stay—"

"No one leaves this place," Jack said. "Those are the rules."

Cool wind blew through the punched-out windows. Jack sat with his hand atop the dog's head. The wait was finally over, he realized. He'd been searching for it since that night in San Benedicto. They all knew their mistakes before they made them. A nun in Santa Cecilia; a car bomb in Delgado; a boy in a living room.

Fox stormed outside. He swung at the air and cursed. He looked at Two Tree Hill and ran.

Jack leaned back against the wall and waited.

Sol stopped the car in front of the ruined church. She sat with her hands gripping the steering wheel. "Are you sure this is Fuller?"

"Was Fuller." Earl inspected the bandages wrapped around his thigh. "Looks like bones, now."

"Paloma and I were born here," Sol said. She took her katana from the seat. The storm moved slowly, but it was huge, filling the horizon. Its dark curtain of rain looked like someone had erased the world they'd come from. Everything outside of Fuller was gone. El Ray. Curacon. Coldspring. Lackawanna. Her mother's grave. Her father's head, now probably placed in the back room of a police station.

Earl walked into the ruined church and stood under the shadow of its remaining wall. A bloody strip of gauze sat in the dust at his feet.

"We should find a place in Humble," he said. "Wait out the storm."

"Here is fine." Sol lifted the gauze with the tip of her sword.

"*Here*," Earl mumbled to himself. "If I'm about to make my last stand, I'd like a hot bath and some decent whiskey, neither of which we'll find in this shithole. So if you don't mind—"

"I mind," Sol said. She stood by a heap of burnt timbers and gazed at Humble. Nice folk probably lived there, she thought. Old men living out their days in quiet living rooms with shag carpeting, thick drapes, and the murmur of TV. Microwave dinners served on plastic trays; slippers dusted with baby powder. What if Esteban was one of them? What if he was just an old, harmless man, toothless and shrunken? Would she still cut him down? Or would she send Earl?

Mincho wandered across the street. He poked his head into a building and saw a pile of broken chairs and tables in the middle of the floor. A dog trotted out from behind the bar. He knelt and rubbed the dog's muzzle, then stopped when the tip of a wooden sword touched his throat.

A tall man with bandages around his eyes held the other end. Who are you?"

"Mincho."

Sol walked in. Earl walked behind her. She unsheathed her katana and Earl unholstered his Schofield, and Jack shuffled back, oar raised. Sol looked at his carved stick, his bloodied

T-shirt, his battered, bandaged face.

"Reverend?" Jack said. "Fox?"

Sol spoke slowly because she thought he might be insane. "Do you live here?"

"Who's asking?"

"Travelers," Sol said. "Waiting out the storm."

"And you just happened to stop in Fuller."

"We just happened," Earl said.

"You see a dwarf anywhere?"

"Excuse me?" Sol said.

"A dwarf. About yea tall. Custom cowboy boots."

"Nope," Sol said.

Jack lowered his oar. "I'm Jack."

"I'm Soledad. This is Earl."

"Where are you headed, Soledad and Earl?"

"Tejon," she said.

"What are you doing in Fuller?" Earl said.

"Waiting out the storm," Jack said. "Same as you."

The dog raised its ears. Jack felt along the wall, to the window. "Someone's coming."

"That's thunder," Sol said.

"That's not thunder," Jack said. "Go see."

Beyond the ruined church, near the willow oak on the edge of Humble, Sol saw a pickup speeding toward Fuller with two men sitting in its flatbed.

"There's a pickup coming this way," she said.

"What color?" Jack asked.

"Black."

Jack pointed to his face. "The men in that pickup did this."

Earl sniffed. "Maybe you had it coming."

"Maybe I did. But not from them."

"Earl—" Sol began, but he waved her off.

"I'm on it."

He limped back to the wagon and got the Winchester. It began to drizzle, pattering on the roof. The dog ran into the ruined church and squirreled itself under a fallen beam. Sol stood by the side of the punched-out window. Jack leaned against the far wall. Earl stood near the door, double-fisted with the Schofield and Henry's Winchester. Sol told Mincho to stay behind the bar.

Roy's pickup tore down Main Street and skidded to a stop near Sol's wagon. Octavio, silver-plated .45 tucked into his belt, jumped off the back. His cousin, Pedro, followed. Roy got out of the truck and propped his shotgun over his shoulder. He wore a gray poncho. Rain dripped off the front of his hat.

"Busque los edificios," Roy said. "Si usted ve a hombre, matalo."

Roy walked across the street, shotgun held at his waist. He stopped at the bar door. He tried the knob, met resistance, then stepped back and kicked.

Jack stood in the middle of the room.

Roy grinned. "Door number one."

He brought the shotgun butt to his shoulder. A blast from the corner; Roy collapsed, clutching his knee, screaming. Earl stepped out from the shadows, Schofield smoking.

Sol slipped through the window. Octavio yelled from across the street. Pedro squeezed off a shot and ran into the ruined church.

Earl stepped into the rain, both guns leveled. He fired the Schofield. Pedro stumbled, blood spraying. Earl fired again. Pedro spun and slumped against the church wall. His hands clenched and unclenched. He shivered a moment, then stopped.

Octavio aimed at Earl. Sol stepped behind him; before he could turn she brained him with the hilt.

Earl and Sol dragged Octavio into the bar. Roy lay on the floor, knee blasted and bleeding.

"Get the rope out of my trunk," Sol said to Mincho. Then she looked up at Jack. "I hope you're the good guy."

"I am compared to them," Jack said.

When she finished tying Earl and Octavio back-to-back, she sat on the floor and wiped her face with the bottom of her shirt. Earl caught a glimpse of her smooth, brown stomach. He smiled, rolling a cigarette.

Thunder rumbled and lashed. Rain dripped from the ceiling. Mincho sat atop the bar, legs dangling over the side. They'd tied a tourniquet around Roy's leg, but it was already soaked through.

Sol saw a sheriff star pinned to his shirt: *Humble-Fuller Police Department*. She pulled his wallet from his pocket and leafed through it—photos of his son, a crinkly ten-dollar bill, a condom, and his license.

"Roy Beasley," she said.

Jack stood near the window. "He's from Humble."

"He's wearing a sheriff star," Sol said.

"He's not the sheriff," Jack said. "He's an accomplice to murder."

"Sonofabitch is lying," Roy said. "I had a warrant for his arrest." He looked around the room. "Untie me now."

Octavio jerked and twisted his hands. Sol said: "Usted de Tejon?"

He nodded.

"Por qué usted quiere matar a ese hombre?"

"Un favor," Octavio said.

"Un favor para quién?"

Octavio looked at Roy, then back at Sol.

"Conoce usted a Esteban Gallegos?" she said.

Octavio said nothing. She snatched her katana from the floor and held the point at his eye. He spit on the blade.

"I think that's bad guy talk for *yes*," Earl said.

Jack shuffled forward and knelt by Octavio, who shouted and tried to squirm away, but Jack moved his hand up to his belt. He felt the tiger head buckle.

"I met this man," Jack said. "In Esteban's bar."

"Was Esteban there?" Sol asked.

Jack nodded. "We drank together."

She closed her eyes. Earl mashed his cigarette on the floor.

"You can stay or we can drop you off anywhere between here and Tejon," she said to Jack. "I know that's not much of a choice, but it's my best offer."

"Take me to Humble," Jack said.

"Is Humble friendly?"

"It'll do."

Mincho helped Jack to the wagon. Earl lingered behind, and when Sol honked the horn, he stuck the business end of his shotgun into Octavio's cheek. Octavio closed his eyes.

"You work for Esteban?"

Octavio squeezed his lips together, blood drying on his forehead from where Sol had struck him.

"Come on, son. Be easy for me to pull this trigger. Don't make it easy."

He kept his eyes shut. "Esteban is my father."

"I'd end you if I thought it'd make a difference to him. But I don't think it would." Earl lowered his shotgun. "Sometimes I think what my life would be like, on account of not having a traumatic childhood." He squatted down. "Maybe I would have been an accountant. Or an insurance salesman. You ever think about that? About what your life could be, if your father wasn't such an evil man?"

"I'm bleeding to death," Roy said. "Untie us."

"Can't do that. Sol's calling the shots."

"We're not the bad guys here."

"But I am." Earl slipped a stiletto from his boot and left it near Octavio. "You know where to find me. I'll be wiping your dad's blood off my heel."

He mussed Octavio's hair, and walked out, whistling.

Jack leaned his head against the window and listened to the rhythm of the windshield wipers. He imagined a swirling black sky, Two Tree Hill framed by lightning, the screen door to Harley's trailer banging in the wind. He reached into his pocket and felt the watch: the cracked glass, the notched handle.

"You can drop me off at the police station," Jack said. "There should be a denim store on your right. Chayban. Next to the Laundromat."

"I see it," Sol said. Puddles grew. She saw a lake at the end of the street, an outcropping of buildings on its other side.

"Tejon," Earl said.

She let Jack out and waited by the curb, engine idling.

"That blind man's got his own troubles," Earl said. "Leave him be."

Sol closed her eyes. *I will die on a mission of revenge, or waiting in my car at a traffic light. I will die in the midst of a great battle, or in my bathtub.*

"Wait here," she said, and she got out.

She followed Jack into Chayban Denim. Cowboy boots had toppled from a shelf in the front of the store. She saw a door in the back with the words HUMBLE POLICE SHERIFF WADE GARRETT DEPUTY BOB GARRETT stenciled across.

Jack stood near one of the empty shelves. He cocked his head.

"Sol?"

"Yes?"

"What are you doing here?"

"Shopping."

Jack smiled. "Do me a favor. Look in the sheriff's office."

"What's in there?"

"I don't know. I can't see."

She unsheathed her sword. Jack limped behind. She pushed the door open. Bob lay on the floor, near the desk. Papers were scattered and the telephone had been shot, its guts dangling from the splintered plastic case. A trench ran through his skull, from behind his ear to the crown. His hair was matted red.

"Someone's dead," Sol said.

"Buzz cut or gray hair?"

"Buzz cut."

A gunshot rang from the street. They ran back outside, where Earl knelt by the side of the car, Schofield propped on the hood.

"Someone took a potshot," Earl said. "I got Mincho lying in the backseat."

Jack limped down the sidewalk. He lifted his head, hearing rain, wind, and something else: whispers, feet splashing through puddles. The squawk of a TV in a house across the street. Then he heard a shout.

Eli walked down the middle of Main Street, Bible in one hand, umbrella in the other. The umbrella's thin fabric had long ago disintegrated. Its spines were bent and the handle was wrapped in masking tape. Rain dripped from the tip of his nose.

Eli walked toward the car. Earl yelled for him to stop.

"*Don't shoot!*" Jack shouted. He ran and stumbled over the curb, falling into the mud.

A triple flash of lightning. Eli walked over the spot where he'd watched Owen die. This is where it began, he thought. He'd asked for a sign and God was silent but he'd had a dream where he died and nothing waited for him. Not heaven or hell or reincarnation. Just a grave where he could hear the shifting of dirt and worms, roots burrowing into his skin.

Earl yelled at Eli again. Behind Eli, Sol saw two young men standing at an intersection, under a sign that read Yellow Goose. One raised his arm, gun in hand. Eli raised his arm, gripping the Bible in his shaking fist. A bullet punched into the wagon's grill, and Earl fired. Eli dropped. Another gunshot and the windshield shattered. Jack scrambled to his feet and zigzagged down the street, oar held low.

Jack knew from the shots that it was Sheriff Wade's Smith & Wesson. He also knew it wasn't Sheriff Wade who'd shot it, because Sheriff Wade wouldn't have missed.

Shoot again, Jack thought. Tell me where you are.

Another crack. Earl's monogrammed bullet punched between Ike's eyes, and he fell face-first into a puddle. Curtis steadied his arm.

Jack ran closer. He waited, listening, as Curtis leveled the gun. The hammer clicked; Jack pounced.

He struck Curtis across the chest with the oar. Curtis stumbled back, dropping Sheriff's gun. He took the rebar from off his back and swung. Jack stepped aside and the rebar whistled past, then Jack brought his makeshift sword down onto Curtis' collarbone. He swung again, feeling the wooden blade bounce off Curtis' forearm, and Curtis bulled into him. They rolled, kicking and clawing. Jack scrambled atop Curtis and locked his hands around his throat. Curtis tore at Jack's face, ripped off the bandages, and sunk his thumbs into Jack's hollow eyes. Jack bore down with all his weight. He knew it was Curtis—he recognized his breath. Curtis bucked and kicked. The blood vessels in his eyes burst. He punched and scratched and gouged the skin on Jack's neck. He spit mud and rain, and soon the mud wasn't as cold, and the rain was soft, the thunder just a sleepy rumble.

Curtis' body slackened. Then there was nothing except the wind. Jack rolled off Curtis and lay on his back, feeling the rain drip into his raw sockets. He heard someone running toward him, and he wondered if it was Ike, and he realized even if it was, he wasn't moving.

Earl stood over Eli. The umbrella lay in the mud. Earl saw the Bible still clutched in Eli's hand.

"Nothing personal," Earl said. "Wrong place at the wrong time is all it was."

Sol knelt at Jack's side. She watched the rain run down his forehead, pooling in his empty sockets.

Mincho and Jack searched. They went to the diner, then to the church, where they found a thick leather strop lying on the blood-spotted floor in Reverend Fowler's office. They went to the Laundromat and the Yellow Goose, where the doors were locked and the lights were off, and Mincho saw people staring at them from their homes as he led Jack across the parking lot. Fox's house was dark and empty. Jack shouted Pepper's name but nobody answered.

They went into Pepper's house, into the bedroom where Marty lay on the bed, staring at the ceiling, tongue peeking out from the corner of his mouth. The television chattered and laughed. Jack switched it off. He heard crying from the bathroom. Soft whimpers. He walked to the door and felt along the surface—dents and splinters—but the door was still locked.

"Pepper?"

Hitched breathing.

"It's me," Jack said. "Pep—"

The door flung open and she ran out. Jack stumbled as she rushed past, scissors still in hand, cuts on her face from the screen door. Pepper saw her father lying on the bed, and she dropped the scissors.

Earl sat on Pepper's porch, on Marty's rocking chair, shotgun lying across his lap. He smoked and watched the rain drip. His leg throbbed with infection. He felt a fever coming on.

END COME ROUND

The streets of Tejon were empty, storefronts shuttered and windows closed. The whores played cards and drank, lit by candles and lamps with fringed shades. They all agreed this was the worst rainstorm they'd ever seen, all their years in Tejon. They used empty glasses to catch the water plinking from patches in the ceiling, and they got Mariana to empty the glasses into a bucket and carry it outside.

Esteban Gallegos sat at his table in the last bar at the end of Avenue de Quere. He sipped his rum and read his book, anticipating every word, every fleck of wood in the pulpy paper, every note in the margin, the handwriting of a man he'd long ago forgotten, marked only by his scrawled name on the last page:

De la Biblioteca de Rafael Santanillo

To Esteban the notes were as much a part of the story as the story itself, for Don Quixote was enigmatic to him: this man who'd built his heroism and cause on illusion.

Esteban's father's sword waited at his side, propped against the wall. The Pistolero Tequila sign flickered with every flash of lightning.

Esteban continued to read, even as Octavio and Roy walked into the bar. Roy's arm was hooked over Octavio's shoulder. Rain dripped from their hair and blood dripped from Roy's knee, a belt cinched around his thigh to staunch the bleeding. Esteban continued to read even as they walked to his table, boots clomping.

"Señor Gallegos," Octavio said.

Esteban held up one finger, glasses low on his nose. His mouth moved as he read. He licked his lips and finished with a long sigh, then set the book down and looked up.

"Jack se escapó," Octavio said.

Esteban frowned.

"He had a bitch with a sword," Roy said. "And an old man who did this—" He motioned to his knee.

"A sword?" Esteban said.

"Yeah," Roy said. "A sword. It was fucking ridiculous."

"Where is Pedro?" Esteban said.

Octavio shook his head. Esteban took off his glasses and folded them slowly.

"The woman with the sword asked about you," Octavio said. "She knew your name."

Esteban raised an eyebrow. "What did she want to know?"

"If you were here."

"Policia?"

"No se."

"Ella utilizó la espada?"

"Si. Ella era muy buena."

Esteban nodded. "What did you tell her about me?"

"Nothing."

"*Well*," Esteban mumbled to himself. He sipped his rum and sat back, resting a hand on the pommel of his father's sword. "*Well, well, well.*"

"They went to Humble," Roy said. "And if Curtis hasn't shown up yet—"

"Curtis?" Esteban said.

"The skinny boy," Roy said. "Shaved head, tattoos—"

"Ah, yes. The idiot. I have not seen him."

Roy tried to flex his knee. He winced. "I need more men. Whoever you can spare. Two would be fine, but three—"

"Why not twenty? Or thirty?"

Roy paused. Esteban drummed his fingers on the pommel.

A crack of thunder and the lights flickered.

"If Jack is as dangerous as you claim," Esteban continued, "you should be extra careful."

"He's been tearing up the entire town," Roy said. "Looking for his brother."

Esteban pursed his lips as if Roy was boring him.

"Take as many as you need," Esteban said. "And bring me the woman with the sword."

Roy tightened the belt around his thigh. "As many as I need? Hell—I'll take them all."

The rain beat like hail. Earl poked his head out from under the porch. A small boat banged against a dock on the lake. The church doors swung in the wind. A line of headlights spilled from Tejon. Earl watched them snake through the hills, rising and falling.

Sol stepped onto the porch. Her eyes were red and swollen. She'd heard Pepper scream and ran into the house to find her sobbing and clutching her father's body. Mincho stood in the kitchen, looking helpless and uncomfortable. Jack sat at the kitchen table, stone-faced, rain-soaked bandages dark with blood.

Earl flicked his cigarette and sat back in Marty's rocking chair. "How's the girl?"

"In shock," Sol said.

"She's young. She'll get over it."

"This isn't how I envisioned things."

"You thought your little mission of revenge'd be nice and tidy."

"Mariko warned me. She said it would be messy. But this—"

"Is what you've wanted all along." Earl shifted his leg. "If things end okay, maybe you can get lost in Mexico. Find a job somewhere, selling shell necklaces. That thing Judge said? About nothing much changing? He was right. Blood washes off easier than you think."

"I don't want it to be easy."

Earl grinned. "Too late, missy."

Jack limped onto the porch and knocked his oar against Earl's rocking chair.

"How's Pepper?" Sol asked.

"Safe," Jack said. "You've done more than enough, so if you need to get on to Tejon—"

"Tejon's coming to us," Earl said. "Hills east of here got a line of cars headed our way."

"How many?"

"At least a dozen," Earl said. "I checked the station in back of that denim store. The shotgun racks were cleaned out. Does any other place in town stock guns?"

"I don't know," Jack said. "I've only been here for two days."

"You made a hell of an impression," Earl said.

Sol peered through the rain. "Jack?"

"Yes?"

"You were looking for a dwarf. Yea tall, custom cowboy boots—"

Jack shouted Fox's name. Fox splashed across the street, holding his father's old hunting rifle. Water dripped from the brim of his baseball cap. He slung the rifle over his shoulder.

Earl sniffed. "Look at that. The rifle's taller than him."

Fox stepped onto the porch.

"Marty's dead," Jack said. "Curtis killed him."

Fox hefted his rifle. "And where's Curtis?"

"I took care of Curtis," Jack said.

Sol slipped Octavio's gun from the waist of her jeans. She worked the slide, just like Mariko had showed her.

"That a .45?" Jack said.

"It is."

Jack held out his hand. She gently laid the gun in his palm.

He popped the clip and felt the top round with his thumb. Then he jerked the slide and a bullet sprung up; he opened his hand and the bullet landed in his palm. He replaced the clip, twirled the gun expertly, and held it out for Sol.

"Fifteen in the clip, one in the pipe," Jack said. "Just aim and shoot."

"Maybe you should keep it," Sol said. "I'm partial to my sword."

"So am I." He brought the gun to his cheek and worked the hammer. "Anyone can shoot a gun. Even a blind man." He turned and fired. The bullet punched a hole in the Laundromat's front window. "Door?"

"Window," Sol said.

Jack smiled. "The sight must be off."

Earl looked toward the lake, at the line of cars speeding through the mud.

"Five minutes." Earl touched his throbbing leg, the skin hot, even through his jeans. "If we need to get ready, then let's get ready."

"Fox, you hole up in my room above the Bee," Jack said. "Earl said something about a rifle—"

"It's old but it works," Fox said.

"Then keep yourself low. Space your shots thirty seconds apart. Any faster and they'll mark your spot."

Fox ran. He felt he'd never run so fast, cowboy boots splashing through mud. He passed Eli, lying on the street with a sodden umbrella at his side, and he passed Curtis lying in a puddle, rain pelting off his face. He skidded to a stop and walked back. He stood over Curtis, remembering the clang of his shovel on hardpan and rock. It had taken hours to dig the grave; Curtis watched the whole time, drinking beers and cracking jokes.

Fox snorted and spit, then kept on running.

The cars and trucks rumbled onto the end of Main Street, across from the cemetery. Sol saw men swarm from their vehicles, dozens of them, scattering like ants. They shouted to one another in Spanish. Roy—crutch under one arm, shotgun in the other—limped through the mud, barking orders while rain poured off the front of his hat.

Earl stood. He lit his last cigarette, checked the cylinder of his Schofield, and aimed it down Main Street, his face flush with fever. He stared at the muddy street, at Curtis' body, at Ike lying face down with his arms spread out like he'd died doing the breast stroke, and he thought as far as last looks go, you could do much worse.

Yeah, thought Earl. It's about goddamn time.

Sol and Jack hurried into the living room, and Sol called for the boy. She'd been ready to tell him to hide, to run out the back door and find somewhere safe. But Mincho grabbed Jack's hand, his mouth set in a hard line, and she realized he wasn't going anywhere.

"Pepper's in the crawlspace," Jack said. "I told her to sit tight until it's quiet."

"Might be a while," Sol said.

"If we're lucky," Jack said.

Sol unsheathed her katana. She thought of those days in Mariko's basement. How she'd cut the air with a thousand strokes, arms trembling as Mariko sat on the bottom stair, spouting her fortune cookie wisdom:

Only the end of things is important. The last cup of wine, the last bloom of a rose, the farewell to a dear friend. One's whole life should be like this.

Sol touched Mincho's face and he stared up at her. Then she left through a window in the living room, her footsteps fading into the wind and rain.

Mincho led Jack to the window, where Jack knelt and propped his arm on the sill, .45 in hand.

"My hand is noon," Jack said. "Understand?"

"Yes."

"Where's your car?"

"One. Well, maybe one ten."

"Good."

Earl loaded the Winchester. He heard them splashing behind the houses and shimmying up to the roofs. Another minute, he figured, before someone saw him, or before the dwarf took a potshot and pissed them off. He waited until a man jogged past, shotgun in hand, then he stepped out from under the shadows of the porch and hit his man with two blasts from the Schofield. The man collapsed. Shouts in Spanish. Earl saw movement on the roof of the house next door; he raised the Winchester and pulled both triggers. The young man on the roof's knees exploded in a red spray, and he fell, screaming, while Earl popped the breech and reloaded.

Earl walked out onto the street and jerked the Winchester shut. He found one man kneeling by the Yellow Goose sign. He unloaded the Winchester at point blank. Two more shots from the Schofield for a man running atop the Yellow Goose roof. The first made him stumble, the second sheared off his jaw.

Thunder cracked. Earl raised his Schofield and fired. He loaded the Winchester, walking calmly down Main Street while bullets screamed past and zipped into puddles. A young man crept around the side of the Laundromat and fired his rifle. The bullet struck Earl in the side, tumbling into his kidney. Earl fired back. The young man yelled for his friends and suddenly he tasted metal, the tip of a katana sticking from his mouth. He clawed at the blade inserted into the back of his neck; Sol withdrew it, metal singing, and the young man slumped to the ground.

Sol found three men stalking Earl, who now walked slowly as his kidney leaked and blood streamed down his bandaged leg. She caught the first by surprise. The second man fired and missed. Sol's blade severed his arm at the shoulder. She leapt and slashed. When she landed, the third man looked at her, raised his gun, then his head toppled from his shoulders.

Roy stood behind his pickup, shotgun propped on the rear fenders. He fired at the old man who fired back. Roy shouted for his men to advance:

"Mueva adelante! A viejo hombre se atrapa!"

A knot of young men ran ahead, firing wildly. Esteban ducked around the corner of a house. Bullets tore into the siding, ripping off chunks of wood. He dropped the Winchester. Now he felt his age, breathing heavy, the world starting to dim. He reloaded the Schofield.

A bullet grazed Earl's shoulder, and he realized he'd been flanked. He turned and shot down the man who hit him. He stumbled forward. He didn't feel his legs buckle; he only felt the ground smack his knees, and he steadied himself with one hand, firing at another young man running toward him. His bullet zipped past. The young man raised his pistol; a loud crack and blood burst from the young man's forehead, and he fell stiff and straight like a mannequin pushed off its pole.

Fox worked the bolt and dropped back down under the windowsill. He tried counting to thirty but knew they had the old man surrounded, so at fifteen he popped up, found a mark, and fired. He worked the bolt and fired again, shell casings bouncing off the floor. The window nearby shattered. A picture on the wall fell. Roy yelled at one of his men to get the bottles from the front seat.

A man wearing an old New York Yankees T-shirt ran onto Marty's porch. He held a sawed-off shotgun.

"Ten," Mincho said. Jack fired. The man fell.

"Eight.

Three."

A pause. Jack heard the back door burst open. He shoved Mincho to the ground and emptied the clip. His bullets punched through through the dog clock in the kitchen, through the headboard in the bedroom where Marty Garrett lay. He scrambled to his feet and fell over the couch. He heard footsteps on the carpet. A man breathed. Water dripped onto the floor.

Jack dove at the man and tackled him. Hands clasped onto Jack's face. He took two fingers into his mouth and bit down as hard as he could, tasting hot iron and salt as the man screamed and struck with his knife. The blade sliced through Jack's cheek and clanged off his teeth. Jack picked up the oar and stood.

"Two," Mincho said.

"*Hush.*" Jack waited. He heard gunshots and screams. Rain pattering on the porch roof. The crack of a hunting rifle.

The man struck. Jack turned aside and the knife cut his arm, then he stepped back and chopped down with the oar. A yelp and a thud.

"You got him," Mincho said.

Roy's men lit the bottles and chucked them through the front windows of The Bee. They pinned Fox to the floor with a barrage of gunfire, and he shimmied to the door, fleeing into the hall as flames licked the stairwell. He ran to the stairs, then back to the second floor window overlooking the graveyard. He kicked out the glass, took a deep breath, and jumped, smacking the ground so hard he thought he'd broken his back.

Sol cut. She cut until her muscles leaked acid and the blood flowed faster than the rain could wash it away, and when she finished, she collapsed onto the sidewalk. The Bee burned, wood crackling as plumes of smoke curled into the sky. Jack sat in the mud in front of Pepper's house. Dying men moaned. The white station wagon was riddled with holes, its hood scorched, windows shattered.

Earl lay in the middle of the street, at the intersection of Sage and Main. The rain slackened. From the corner of his eye he saw Octavio, walking toward him, machete in hand. Earl got to his knees, slowly. His Schofield was long empty and he'd gone blind in one eye.

Octavio raised the machete and ran at Earl.

The blade thudded into the meat of Earl's neck. Earl grabbed Octavio's leg, pulling him down; he twisted off the tiger head belt buckle and punched the blade into Octavio's chest, holding him close while the young man kicked and bled, hiccupped and gasped.

"*Be over soon*," Earl whispered, blood bubbling in his throat. "*I just saved you a lifetime of trouble.*" Arterial red pulsed down his neck. His whisper turned into a long breath, his eyes widened, and he sunk back.

Roy stood in the middle of the street, shotgun in hand. Sol sat up, slowly.

"We just want to be left alone," Roy said. "But they come anyway, looking for cheap houses and simple folk and ten-dollar dinners they can smirk at. Do they get it?" He fumbled in his pocket and brought out a single shell. "They do not. So they stay, thinking they can bring what they had to where they are now. Does it work? It does not. But they keep trying." He fed the shell into the side and racked it. "Towns like Humble are immune to trying. We do what the town wants, you understand? If it wants to keep us all here until the sun bleaches our bones, then we stay. Nobody leaves without permission. Nobody gets out. Not you.

Not me."

He raised the shotgun at Sol. A blast; Roy's head tilted. Stiff-legged, mouth open, he dropped the crutch. Then he fell.

Jack stood, arm straight, .45 at the end.

"Door?" he asked.

"Window," Sol said.

Jack smiled. "The sight must be off."

"The sight must be off."

SOMETHING OF VENGEANCE

The shops on Avenue de Quere opened again and water dripped from their bright blue canvas awnings, while the owners set out their signs and scrubbed the mud from their doors. A woman in a red dress stood in a doorway. She watched Soledad walk past.

Sol walked into the last bar on the street. The Pistolero Tequila sign flickered, and a young woman sat at the bar with a plate of chorizo. The young woman looked up. Red onion dangled from her mouth. A long scar ran down the middle of her forehead.

"Is Esteban Gallegos here?"

The young woman nodded, wide-eyed, and pointed to the back of the room.

Esteban sat at his table. A glass of rum sat nearby, next to his father's sword. His cigarette rested on its ashtray.

"Esteban Gallegos?"

He took off his reading glasses and looked up.

Sol dropped a photo on the table. "Forty-two years ago you murdered my father, Rafael Santanillo." Her voice trembled as she dropped another photo onto his table. "You raped my mother, Luisa." She dropped the photo of her sister. "And when you finished, you took my sister, Paloma."

Esteban sifted through the photos. "Paloma is the one with the blue shorts and pigtails?"

Sol nodded.

"You came here to find her?"

She nodded again.

He sipped his rum. "Maybe I knew someone named Paloma, long ago. So many women have passed through my memory that their faces all seem the same. Beautiful, wretched, young, old—what do I care anymore? I cannot help you."

Esteban sighed.

"Let me tell you something I learned when I was your age," he said. "Revenge does not change the way things were. This is one of the saddest things in life. You will find no satisfaction in cutting me down."

"You mean I'd still have to shop for groceries and go to the dentist."

Esteban smiled. "Exactamente."

"Revenge and satisfaction are two different things," Sol said.

He sipped his rum again. Then he put his reading glasses back on and opened his book. She didn't notice his hand had slipped under the table.

Sol raised her katana. She heard a gunshot and thought something bit her stomach. She looked down. Her shirt bloomed blood.

"I would like to read you something," Esteban said.

Sol stumbled back.

" *'I should be as much a king of my own dominions as any he that wears a head. And being so I would do what I pleased; and doing what I pleased I should have my will; and having my will, I should be contented.'* "

She dropped her sword and grabbed the back of a chair. Its legs chirped across the floor.

" *'And when contented, there is no more to be desired; and when there is no more to be desired, there's an end of it.'* "

Esteban took off his glasses. Sol collapsed. She reached for her sword, lost behind a tangle of chair legs and cigarette butts. Her stomach burned and she found her legs useless.

Esteban tossed his gun aside. "If I was younger I would have challenged you to a duel. Pitted your skills against mine, your sword against my father's. How wonderful that would have been? But I am too old. And swords…they have become ridiculous."

She looked down at her stomach. Red blossoms spread,

soaking her shirt. The pain stayed far away. Her heart pounded in her ears.

"I am only interested in comfort," Esteban continued. "Some fine rum, a good book—simple things. I hope you understand. I will read to you now. This is an excellent book. Lie there and listen."

Sol imagined she walked out of the bar and into the street, and knocked on an apartment door. Inside she heard a radio playing, a woman singing quietly, the shuffle of footsteps, the creak of a doorknob. She looked down and saw her blood trickling across the dusty sill. Rain dripped from the tattered blue awning. Somewhere, far off, she heard Esteban's voice.

Paloma stood in the doorway. She was older, of course, but still the little girl in the photo. She brushed a strand of hair off Sol's forehead.

Hello, little sister, Paloma said. *You must be tired. Your journey was difficult.*

It was difficult and I am tired, Sol said. *Can I come in?*

Of course. We can sit and talk. But you will have to stay here.

For how long?

A very long time.

Sol saw a living room that looked a lot like the living room she remembered as a child. She would not have been surprised if her mother sat on the couch, or if her father walked by on his way to the kitchen, holding an open book, his head down. When she stepped over the sill, the carpet was soft beneath her feet. Paloma took her arm. It's the end of things that are important, Sol thought. Mariko was right.

Jack slept on Pepper's couch. He awoke the next morning to find Mincho cooking breakfast. They ate in silence, Pepper picking at her eggs and taking a few bites of toast while Mincho devoured his breakfast and the rest of hers. When they finished, Jack took them both outside, to Main Street, where Willie's school bus rumbled past the husk of Soledad's station wagon. Mincho saw an old black man at the wheel and the blurred faces of the townspeople staring out, their hands pressed to the plastic bag windows. Jeremiah Beasley sat in the back, near the suitcases and duffel bags, gazing at the ruins of Fox's diner. Willie cranked open the door.

"You seen Fox?" Jack asked.

"No."

"How about a woman with a sword?"

Willie just stared. The three of them stepped onto the bus.

Willie left them at Two Tree Hill. The bus rumbled away. Jack felt the sun on his face. He heard Harley's dog panting as Mincho rubbed its muzzle.

Mincho and Pepper scrambled up the hill. Harley's dog ran past them, and Mincho laughed, grabbing Pepper's hand as they sprinted to the single tree, where he dared her to climb. She said her sneakers were Prada and not meant for climbing but the boy called her chicken and she grabbed the first limb and hauled herself up.

Jack sat on the ground. He thought about Sarah. Whether she'd take care of a blind man, playing the forgetting game one last time. Then he heard the rumble of a truck and the crackle of dirt underneath its tires. Footsteps; a familiar voice:

"Hey, Jack."

"Fox. You made it."

"I did."

"How's the Bee?"

"Burned to the ground."

"Sorry."

"Don't be. I'm leaving."
"Coldspring?"
"San Antonio."
Jack smiled.
Fox sat near Jack. They listened to the wind, faces tipped to the sun.
"What happened to your cheek?" Fox said.
"I had an accident."
"What kind of accident?"
"A bad one."
"Oh," said Fox. "That's the worst kind."
Pepper and Mincho climbed the scraggly oak. Jack thought maybe he'd climb with them, and pretend as they did. He'd bury the watch beneath the tree, stand atop its magnificent branches, and gaze across the sunlit plains, at the cloud-speckled sky.

ACKNOWLEDGMENTS

Leslie Epstein and Ha Jin provided criticisms and suggestions, all of them brilliant even when the source material wasn't. Thanks to the artists Michael Allred, Tradd Moore, Russ Nicholson, and Phil Noto. The late, great Donald Westlake read the near-final draft of *Jack the Bastard* and generously supplied a blurb, which wouldn't have been possible without the help of my dear cousin Lawrence Block.

Additional thanks: Erin Canning (you made it easy), Jud Laghi (a mensch among menschen), Matthew Johnson and the folks at Fat Possum, Danny Ginsburg, Brian Jenkins, Steve Smith, and my sis.

If my influences aren't obvious by the end of this book—hell, by the end of the first story—I haven't done my job. Film buffs might catch more than a whiff of *Bad Day at Black Rock*. Bookish types might search for a unifying theme; any such thing is unintentional.